He was after her soul.

"I would very much like to know how you can consume so much wine without becoming unconscious."

"Well, you're not going to," Samara retorted, again failing to meet his eyes.

"Ah, but I expect I've had more experience than you," Reese drawled.

"It's a god-given talent," Samara answered loftily with sudden inspiration. She was totally disconcerted when he leaned back and laughed. It was, she thought grudgingly, a very lusty, attractive laugh.

"More like the devil," he finally managed, his sexy chuckle sending goose bumps down her spine.

"*You* should know," she retaliated, her confusion becoming outrage. Would he never take her seriously?

And then he saw it. A little trickle of wine running from his abandoned boot. The little minx! She was obviously far more complex than he had first thought. But what had she planned?

There was only one way to find out.

Dear Reader:

Harlequin offers you historical romances with a difference—novels with all the passion and excitement of a 500 page historical in 300 pages. Your letters indicate that many of you are pleased with this shorter length. Another difference is that the main focus of our stories is on people—a hero and heroine you really care about.

We have some terrific books scheduled this month and in the coming months: Cassie Edwards fans should look for *A Gentle Passion*; the second book in Heather Graham Pozzessere's trilogy, *Rides a Hero*, tells Shannon's story; *Samara* by Patricia Potter is the sequel to her award-winning *Swampfire*; Nora Roberts's *Lawless* is an unforgettable Western. You won't want to miss these and any of the other exciting selections coming from Harlequin Historicals.

Please keep your letters coming. You can write to us at the address below.

Karen Solem
Editorial Director
Harlequin Historicals
P.O. Box 7372
Grand Central Station
New York, New York 10017

Samara

Patricia Potter

Harlequin Books

TORONTO • NEW YORK • LONDON
AMSTERDAM • PARIS • SYDNEY • HAMBURG
STOCKHOLM • ATHENS • TOKYO • MILAN

Harlequin Historical first edition April 1989

ISBN 0-373-28620-1

Books by Patricia Potter

Harlequin Historical

Swampfire #6
Between the Thunder #15
Samara #20

PATRICIA POTTER

is a former award-winning journalist with a passion for history and books. As a reporter with the *Atlanta Journal*, she met and reported on three presidents and covered Southern news stories as varied as the space launches and the civil rights movement.

This resident of Atlanta, Georgia, has her own public relations and advertising agency. Her interests in animals and travel are not especially compatible, but she does manage to fit them both into her busy schedule. Her reading runs the gamut from biographies to espionage, and she is currently the president of the Georgia Romance Writers of America.

To my mother and father,
whose love story,
like Sam's and Connor's,
continues

Chapter One

South Carolina, 1812

Dull. Dull. Dull. The refrain sang in Samara O'Neill's mind as she jabbed the needle in and out of the sampler. Dull. Dull. Dull. The words followed each stitch as her frustration grew. Her life was just too dull. Nothing exciting ever happened to her. *Oh, I wish I were a man.*

She looked at the sampler with loathing. She was much too old for such things, but her mother had talked her into it, and her mother was one of the few people she really tried to please. So here she was...on a beautiful day...sitting inside. Her fingers, eager to finish the tiresome task, mistook skin for cloth and red blood spurted over her painstaking work. *Damn.* The oath escaped her mouth involuntarily, and she waited breathlessly for lightning to strike. She had been told often enough that no young man would look kindly upon a lady who took such liberties with her tongue. Not, of course, that she was overly concerned with the young men of her acquaintance. *Namby-pambies, all of them,* she thought with disgust.

"The devil take it," she uttered with defiance as she looked at the damaged cloth, then glanced guiltily around, sighing with relief that no one had witnessed this latest transgression. Samara wished, not for the first time, that tenaciousness was not one of the few qualities about her that could be termed a virtue. She *would* finish the dratted thing. She had a compulsion to finish whatever she started. It was her least favorite virtue because it often meant enduring a lifeless book or seeing through to the finish a task completed only with dogged perseverance.

A noise from the doorway caused her to look up. Conn, the brother closest to her own age, stood there, watching her industry with amusement. She wanted to throw the sampler at his irritating smirk.

"You look wonderfully domesticated, little sister," he commented, as the smirk developed into a full grin. "And just when I was going to ask you to go for a ride to look for Bren. But I wouldn't dream of taking you from such fruitful pursuits."

Samara's chin thrust out and she said in her most dignified tone, "*I* finish what I start . . . not like other members of this family I can name."

Conn blushed. Samara's tenacity was legendary while his own left much to be desired. Of all the O'Neill sons, he alone had not found a purpose. Bren, the oldest, ran the family shipping line; Marion had just completed medical school in Edinburgh, and Jere was in firm—and maddeningly competent—control of the family's second plantation. But Conn, like Samara, sought adventure and, with the recent declaration of war against England, had enlisted in the militia and was awaiting orders.

He eyed his pretty younger sister. Having grown up the only sister of four older brothers, she had more skill at masculine activities than feminine ones. Samara was competent with a rifle and pistol, as well as being a fine horsewoman. And she possessed a streak of stubbornness a mile wide.

"At least *I* know when to quit," he retorted. She giggled and his quick grin returned as they both recalled what was now known as Samara's "groomsman period."

At age ten, Samara had desperately wanted a horse of her own. She had, she was quite sure, outgrown her beloved but elderly pony and had embarked on a campaign that ranged from tears to tantrums. For once, neither had much impact. She was quietly informed by her mother that she could have a horse only when she was thoroughly equipped to see to its care.

With her head held high and her mouth unwisely open, she had taken up the challenge and announced to one and all that she could take care of not only one single horse but the entire stable. It had, after all, looked very simple when she watched the groom. All he did was shovel a bit, here and there.

Unfortunately, her father had taken up the offer, and Samara, dressed in her brothers' old cast-off clothes and carrying a shovel much larger than herself, had set upon the task. Her small hands grew blistered and her clothes were a horror to anyone who drew near, but she refused to cry for quarter. To her parents' amazement, she stayed with the stable all day long. She had won her horse, and had learned early not to commit quite so easily to tasks of which she knew little.

"You're sure you don't want to go with me?" Conn questioned. "I salute your diligence," he said with a mock bow, recognizing defeat as he saw the stubborn set of her jaw. "I'll tell Bren you prefer a sampler to him." He ducked as Samara threw a cushion at him and looked longingly at the door as it slammed behind her brother. Reluctantly, she returned to her work.

Dull. Dull. Dull. Samara's hands played with the threads of colored silks as she contemplated the intended verse.

You will mend your life tomorrow still you cry
In what far Country does tomorrow lie?
It stays so long, is fetch'd so far, I fear
T'will prove both very old and very dear.

It was to be a gift for her godmother in the city of Washington and one, Samara's mother promised with more than the usual laughter in her eyes, that Annabelle McLaughlin would appreciate.

Since Samara dearly loved her unorthodox godmother, she had consented easily enough, forgetting how much she hated sewing. Particularly samplers. Such memories had been lost amid her enthusiasm and, once started, no task was too odious to be left undone. Her mother knew her all too well, Samara thought bitterly.

Dull. Dull. Dull. Her fingers fairly flew now. Anything to be done, and outside, awaiting Brendan's arrival. Brendan. Her beloved oldest brother who was to sail for France in two days.

Her eyes caught the verse again. "In what far country…" Oh, how she wished she could go with Brendan and see the wonders of France, taste the adventure of outwitting the British, spend wonderful days at sea. If only she weren't a girl…

She had begged and begged to go with him, but her parents said it was far too dangerous. Indeed, she couldn't miss the concern in their eyes when they spoke of Bren's upcoming voyage. The British had effectively locked up the American ports with their navy. Just as dangerous now were the British privateers, who had expanded their hunting from French to American vessels. *Pirates*, her father called them with no little bitterness. The O'Neill shipping line had lost several ships to the private adventurers who sailed and fought for gold, not for patriotism.

But Samara knew with all her heart that Bren would outwit and outfight any Englishman. He was her god, bright and shining and heroic. Fourteen years her senior, Bren had always taken special care of her; had, in fact, spoiled her shamelessly, according to their mother and father. She loved all four of her brothers, but Bren was special. The room lit up when he walked into it.

Now he commanded his own blockade runner, the *Samara*, which he had named for her, calling her "the only lass pretty enough to give her name to the loveliest ship afloat." And the *Samara* was beautiful. Built in Baltimore, the schooner could outrun any British frigate.

Although told in no uncertain terms that she would not be allowed a voyage, Samara was hoping at least to travel to Charleston with Brendan and visit friends there. She had a standing invitation to visit the Demerest family, and, if nothing else, she could see Bren off and watch the lovely sails of the *Samara* unfurl and send it off to a new adventure. As her needle continued its path, Samara began to plot her strategy with all the skill of a general.

Dinner, as usual, was a gay affair, especially with all four O'Neill brothers home for a change. Bren had finally arrived in late afternoon; Marion was staying home for several weeks before starting a medical practice in Charleston; Jere, who lived at nearby Chatham Oaks, had come with his wife, Judith; and lighthearted Conn completed the foursome.

As always, when Samara was at home with her father and brothers, she compared them to her suitors. The suitors always emerged very poorly indeed. No one could compare with the O'Neill men. She was beginning to think she would never find anyone as wise as her father, as strong and funny as Bren, as sweet and gentle as Marion, as clever as Jere or as much fun as Connor. Everyone paled by comparison.

And then there was the special relationship between her mother and father. She would never settle for anything less after seeing them together. She knew it was very rare. None of the other adult couples she knew acted this way. Their eyes didn't continually linger on each other, nor did they use any excuse to touch each other or laugh and tease one another constantly.

Samara thought her mother beautiful, and often wished she had inherited her blue eyes as well as her lustrous black hair with its peculiar red glow. She disliked her own eyes, never realizing their dark smoky gray sparkled with the hues of the colors around her. She was the only one of the five children with such eyes, and she constantly envied the others, thinking it most unfair that Bren should have golden hair and blue eyes while she remained so colorless.

"Samara."

Her eyes jerked across the dining room table toward Bren. She had been daydreaming and her face held a question as she looked his way.

"How many lovesick swains do you have now? Have any won your heart?" His teasing voice held a slight hint of seriousness.

Samara blushed as she always did when someone mentioned her suitors. They were usually a matter of embarrassment to her... too young, too old, too short, too thin, too dull.

Her mother saved her. "Give her time, Brendan. She's only eighteen."

"And has already broken half the hearts in the parish," he said. "Perhaps I should give her a chance to do the same in Charleston."

Samara couldn't believe her ears. Was it really going to be so easy? Her eyes opened wide. "Charleston?"

"Mother told me how much you wanted to visit Melanie," he said. "And I cannot think of a better good luck charm than your farewell."

Samara's eyes were glowing. "May I, Mother? May I, really?" It would be the first time she had ever been permitted to take a trip on her own.

"I don't know about letting her loose in Charleston," her father said slowly, but a twinkle in his eye told her he was merely teasing.

Samara flew up from her chair and kissed both her parents, then Brendan, in unabashed joy.

"What about us?" clamored Marion, and Samara made the rounds, taking a playful slap here and a sly warning there. Oh, how she loved them all!

She couldn't eat anything else, not the rich pecan pie nor even an apple tart. She was going to Charleston! She would have adventure at last!

It was sometime later during the night that the thought first surfaced. As much as she pushed the unworthy notion down, it would immediately surface someplace else...like a cork bobbing in water.

I can't, she chastened herself.

But Mama did. Mama ran away and rode and fought with General Francis Marion and found Papa, the little demon inside her argued.

But it will hurt them, Samara fought back.

Ah, but you will be with Bren and they know he'll keep you safe. They'll understand; they had their adventures, the sly part of her countered.

Go away, her conscience demanded.

You know you want to go, said her devil. *It would be so easy. You can slip on board just before sailing and hide in the hold.*

Samantha knew she was fighting a losing battle. Her good side always lost to her wayward one. Her father always said an idea planted in her head never needed nourishment. It flourished on its own.

And so it was doing. Like Jack's beanstalk it grew throughout the night, gaining in strength and intensity and complexity.

She was going to France!

As Samara was determining her future, her mother and father were puzzling over it in their own bedroom.

"She needs another girl's influence," Samantha O'Neill reasoned. "She's surrounded by masculine company here."

Connor smiled as his hand played with one of his wife's black curls. "She has you, my love."

Samantha arched an eyebrow at her beloved husband. "I fear I leave much to be desired as a guide for a young woman today."

Connor laughed. He had never been able to cure his wife of donning breeches and flying over the plantation on one of her prize horses or staying up all night with a foaling mare. Nor had he wanted to. He loved her exactly the way she was—unpredictable, untamable. He pulled her to him now, delighting in the feel of her body next to his. He would never lose his enchantment with it, his enchantment with her. His only hope was that his children would find a love as fine, as totally complete as his. She had made every moment of their life together a joy although, he thought wryly, at times provoking. She loved to tease him out of his serious thoughts and lull him from worry.

She was doing that now, her fingers trailing down his furred chest, exciting him just as she had done thirty years earlier.

"Don't worry about Samara," she said. "She'll find someone in her own time, in her own way."

A frown came into Connor's eyes. "She sends everyone away. I think she compares them all to her brothers. She's with them entirely too much." A quick, proud smile erased the worry on his face. "Although I have to admit, they are all rather extraordinary."

Samantha snuggled further into his arms. "Not as extraordinary as their father..."

"Hmm," he said, feeling her hand going lower and lower, feeling the familiar surge of desire. God, would it always be this strong?

"Maybe Charleston is what she needs... a chance to meet new young people..."

"Hmm," was all he could reply as the embers blazed into fire.

"Charleston... that's it," she whispered before losing herself in the beautiful all-consuming union of their bodies.

Samara packed very carefully and was still the first person down to breakfast. The sideboard was already overflowing with bacon, ham, eggs, warm bread and jams. She took more than usual, wondering when her next meal would come. She had invaded the kitchen before anyone was up, stealing two loaves of bread, some cheese and a bottle of wine which she had hidden carefully in her sewing basket.

She gave everyone a sunny smile as they joined her, disregarding their surprised looks at her early appearance and unusually large plateful of food.

Her mother gave her a kiss and a swift embrace. "I'll miss you, Samara, even for a week."

Samara felt a sudden pang of guilt, but her course was set and her mother, more than anyone, would understand. She would worry and perhaps grieve but she would understand Samara's need. Her father... that was another matter. She knew that next to her mother she was her father's heart. He showed it in everything he did, even in his rare, mostly unsuccessful attempts at discipline. Samara went to him now and kissed him lightly on the cheek. "I love you, Papa," she said softly.

"And I love you, little one. Mind you, behave in Charleston and enjoy yourself. We'll see you in a week."

There was no more time for conscience. Brendan was ready to leave.

Leaving only the trunk for Bren to carry, Samara took her own packages out. She didn't want to have to explain any of them. There was a neatly wrapped package that contained one of her dresses but which was disguised as a present for Bren. There was her sewing kit, with the food and Annabelle's sampler. And there was the carefully written note to her parents.

It was a wonderful day as she and Bren, his horse tied behind the carriage, moved swiftly through the countryside towards Charleston. It was fall—still warm—and the air seemed alive with the aromatic smoke-tinged pungency of the season.

Bren had brought Caesar along as a driver and to accompany Samara to the Demerests after leaving him at his ship. He would be late enough as it was . . . he wanted to leave at dusk, the best time for his dyed gray sails to blend into the sky and sea. His mind was preoccupied with the task ahead of him, and he paid little heed to Samara's behavior.

But he couldn't help notice her unusual silence as they picnicked along the Pee Dee River. He looked at her thoughtfully.

"What mischief are you planning now, little sister?" he asked, his finger on her chin as he stared intently into smoky eyes.

She cast them downward before replying. "I'm just thinking how much I would like to go with you."

"You would be bored very quickly, I think. There's damn little to do on a ship . . . unless you're hauling sails or scrubbing decks, and I don't think you would like either."

Her chin went up. "Try me," she said impishly.

"Maybe sometime, after this war, I will," he said, remembering the stable episode. He had always respected his little sister's determination.

When they reached Charleston late in the afternoon, the harbor was crowded with small craft and one other blockade runner. The two would both be making the run tonight, hoping if one was sighted, the other could distract it. It was a dangerous game of tag, but one the captains knew well. Their ships were both faster than the British frigates, and the principal danger lay in too early a detection.

Samara had made her plans carefully. She took her sewing basket aboard, saying she would catch a few stitches while her brother saw to some last-minute details, and deposited it in an inconspicuous place. Then, just before sailing, she would tell Bren she'd forgotten his present and run down to fetch it, telling Caesar that one of Bren's crew would take her to the De-merests. Once back aboard, she would slip into the hold, knowing Bren would be fairly distracted. The only part that really worried her was the hold. She would have to spend enough time down there that Bren would never consider returning to port. They would have to be well past the British threat, and that meant maybe two days. She hated the hold. Bren had taken her there once and, even with his presence and a lantern, it had been terrifying—dark beyond imagining and haunted by strange creaking noises. She had put a small candle in the sewing basket, but she knew the danger of fire and hoped she would have the courage not to use it.

She straightened her shoulders in determination as she told Bren she was returning for her package. The distraction in his eyes and quick, almost indifferent, nod told her everything was proceeding to plan. Now to convince Caesar.

Chapter Two

Aboard the British privateer, the Unicorn

Reese Hampton stood at the helm of the *Unicorn*, his bare feet hugging the deck as his lean, graceful body rolled with the same gentle rhythm as his ship.

His loose, flowing white shirt whipped around him and his tawny hair, bleached gold by the sun, tumbled over a face darkened a rich oak color by the same force.

Taking one hand from the wheel, he raked it through the mussed hair, pushing the wayward strands back from his forehead. He kept it shorter than fashion, not wanting the distraction of errant hair during a battle. He cared little for current fashion or the conventions of society. Long ago he had left such trappings to his twin brother, Avery, who had, by right of birth seven minutes earlier than Reese, inherited the Hampton estates and title in England. A fortunate twist of fate, Reese often thought, for Avery had a love of the land while Reese longed only for a life at sea.

It was a day to make the heavens sing. Against a backdrop of pillowy clouds, a bright sun plowed trails of gold against the sparkling emerald and cerulean blue of an ever-changing ocean. Dolphins raced the ship, their playful antics seeming to dare the *Unicorn* to even greater speed. Reese rested his hands on the wheel, feeling the ship's quick response to his every demand. He often thought of her as a woman, sleek and beautiful and sensitive to his every caress. But much more loyal, he thought, as a wry smile curved his sensuous lips. He always knew what to expect from the *Unicorn*.

He had ordered the ship built to his exact specifications. Although British-built, she was tailored from an American design which he had admired, and he knew every inch of her. A large schooner with a sleek hull and high, raking masts, she carried two long guns as well as twenty quick-firing carronades whose grapeshot could tear rigging to shreds.

He had, with his usual sardonic wit, named the ship the *Unicorn*. It had amused him to give such a gentle name to a deadly predator.

And predator she was! Captain Reese Hampton had been a privateer for five years and had made, and spent, several fortunes off his French prizes. His choice of targets had expanded with the Declaration of War by America in June of this year, 1812. He had already taken two American vessels and sold both ships and cargo in Bermuda.

He enjoyed pitting his skill against the Americans. They were excellent sailors, unlike the French who often sat like fat sheep ready for the slaughter. And their ships brought excellent prices. For that reason, he preyed on the waters stretching along America's eastern coastline, close to the ready markets of Bermuda and the Caribbean.

His watchful eyes swept the horizon. They seemed woven by the brightest colors of the sea itself, a mesh of startling blues and greens, sometimes clashing, sometimes melding, but always reflecting the restlessness and mystery and depths of the water around him.

Reese saw nothing now but the gentle swells of the sea and the shimmer of gold across the waves. He felt the gentle caress of the sun and breeze against his body, and he spread his legs and threw back his head and roared in a shout of pure joy at being alive. His outcry expanded into booming laughter which raked the decks and startled the busy sailors.

Several looked at him and one crossed himself in supplication. It seemed at that moment that their captain, his face lifted to the heavens and his hair glinting with flecks of fire from the sun, was challenging the gods of nature.

The hold was beyond Samara's worst imaginings. She had barely settled herself when it started to close in on her. Only that streak of iron stubbornness kept her there.

It was black beyond anything in her experience. Nothing in her life had prepared her for this total void, where time was distorted and reality disappeared. The first few minutes seemed like hours and the only way she knew they weren't was the movement of the ship. She could tell from its gentle sway that it was still anchored, although she fancied she could feel its eager anticipation to be free of its tether.

How long must she stay here in this black hole? She had originally thought two days. Two days would put them so far out at sea that Brendan would never consider going back. But now, in the reality of the hideous place, she was rapidly reconsidering. Perhaps once they had cleared the English blockade, Bren would be sufficiently committed to complete his voyage to France. That should be a day...or even less. But how would she know? How could you know anything down here?

Until now Samara's plans had gone exceedingly well. Caesar had readily believed her, knowing the O'Neills' almost fanatical concern for their horses. It seemed most reasonable to him that Master Brendan would wish the tired carriage horses to have care and food as soon as possible, and equally as plausible that he would send one of his officers to accompany his sister. He had handed the package to Samara, never seeing her quick hand planting a letter in the corner of the carriage seat. It wouldn't be noticed, she knew, unless the carriage was searched or another passenger used it. When she turned up missing, she knew everything would be turned upside down for a clue.

After watching Caesar turn the horses, she had run back up the gangplank to the ship. No one had paid any attention; everyone had been at work preparing the ship for departure. The corridor to the hold was empty and she had slipped inside, praising the Lord that it was unlocked. It was filled to almost overflowing, but she had found a little cubbyhole near the door before closing it and extinguishing all light. The upper hatch on the deck had already been closed and locked. Samara very carefully placed her sewing basket, full of food, and her package, containing one dress and a change of underclothing, nearby. They were her security.

In the succeeding long, dark minutes and hours, she finally had time to consider her actions. She tried not to let doubts assault her waning optimism. Her father would be very, very angry. And very hurt. But she had made her decision and once a decision was made...

Bren would understand. He always understood her. He often said they were much alike, with a common love for nature and mischief. He sympathized when she had had to switch to a sidesaddle, and groaned with her as she was forced into stays and petticoats when all she wanted was her brothers' breeches. He would, she thought, appreciate her adventure, perhaps even admire her for it. She did crave his approval. She wouldn't let herself think that he might frown upon her action.

Oh, how dark and warm and frightening it was. She could hear little rustling noises and worried that it might be rats. She gathered her skirts tightly around her legs, hugging them close to her body, making herself as small a tidbit as possible as the rats grew, in her mind, to horrendous sizes.

Samara finally heard the creaking sounds of the ship slipping from its bonds. The movement quickened, dipping and rolling as the wind caught the sails and pushed the *Samara* out to sea.

How long has it been now? It seemed like days to Samara who, in her fear of the tiny furred things that had already touched her legs, remained steadfastly awake. She had found a quick movement chased the animals—mice or rats or whatever—away. Temporarily anyway. The first time she felt the invasion she had almost screamed, then caught her lips with her hand. Not yet. It was not yet time, she knew. How awful to go through all this, then be sent back. Instead, she steeled herself and remained alert to the tiniest little noise.

It was hot, so very miserably hot. She could feel sweat running down the stays in the back of her dress and dampening the cloth under her arms. Think of something else, she scolded herself. Think of Father.

He had spent months and months in chains in a hold like this during the previous war. For the first time, Samara understood why his eyes narrowed and his mouth grew tight when something reminded him of those terrible months. He would not talk of it, not even when she had begged him after seeing the scars on an ankle. For one of the few times in her life, he had been curt with her, saying it was better forgotten. Later, seeing Samara's hurt, her mother had sat down with her and explained how terrible it had been, how the experience had left more scars than those on his ankle. It was, her mother added, one reason why he disliked the English so much and why he was so vehemently in support of this war. He had raged at the continued impressment of Americans by the English as well as England's arrogant restraint of American trade with France.

Samara could now well understand his fury. At least *she* knew she could leave at any time. How terrible to be locked in a place like this, without sun or stars or a cool breeze to refresh you. It was like a tomb, a grave in which you were buried alive...

Only a little while now! The knowledge that she had the ability to leave helped her to stay. Had it been six hours or twelve or twenty? Hunger clawed at her, and she searched blindly in her sewing basket. There was one piece of bread left; the wine bottle felt very light, and as she put it to her lips, she greedily lapped up the last few drops.

A new scurry of feet startled her. Her companions were growing bolder, particularly when they caught the smell of food. It was time, she determined, to take her leave of this place. She started to rise, then sat again, wondering if she was yet ready to encounter Bren's wrath. A nip on her leg decided her. She stood unsteadily, stiff from her cramped position. Now where was the door? She bumped into one crate after another, completely losing her sense of direction. She looked for her sewing box containing the candle, but that too was gone.

Disoriented and frightened, she did the only thing she could think of. She screamed.

Brendan O'Neill was taking his first rest of the voyage. He had not dared leave the helm for even a few moments during the first two days out. Cloudy skies and the accompanying fog had blessedly hid the *Samara*'s gray-painted hull and dyed sails, and the ship had skimmed by the English frigates with ease, her presence no more noted than the numerous seabirds. There was still the danger of encountering a British naval ship or privateer and the ticklish business of defying British ships along the French coastline. But the first major obstacle had been easily overcome, and Bren saw it as a good omen.

He wearily took off his boots and lay his head to the pillow, hoping to catch several hours of sleep. As always, it came easily. He had trained himself on voyages over the past ten years to take rest whenever he could. Even before the war, there had been long storms to fight and the ever-present danger of pirates, and he had often gone for days without sleep.

The motion of the ship aided his intent. The sky had cleared and the ocean was calm. He relished the feel of the *Samara* moving swiftly through the water ahead of the brisk wind. He

loved his ship; it was the culmination of everything he had
worked for over the past years, the first of a new design of fast
merchant ships. Even as a boy he had watched with envy the
ships which visited Charleston and he could often be found lis-
tening to tales of their sailors. His father had sensed that Glen
Woods and Chatham Oaks held no interest for him, and urged
his son to follow his heart. Bren had taken the fledgling O'Neill
line, formed mainly to transport the plantations' indigo, and
had built it into a major shipping fleet. He rarely captained
vessels anymore, seldom finding the time away from supervis-
ing the building of new ships, negotiating contracts, finding
competent crews and managing a major business. But the
British blockade had become deadly, and he was reluctant to
send inexperienced crews against it. He would be damned if he
would ask others to do something he was not willing to do.
And, he privately admitted, he hungered for the feel of the sea
again. And for the chance of outwitting the British.

Barely had such thoughts been lost to sleep when a pounding on his door awakened him. He slipped quickly from the
bed, instantly alert and jerked the door open, his mouth set in
a scowl. It deepened when he saw Scotty, his second mate, and
someone in the shadows behind him.

"Beggin' yer pardon, sir," Scotty said. "But we seem to 'ave
an unexpected passenger." He moved aside, and Bren saw Samara, her gaze uncustomarily downward, her dress soiled beyond redemption.

Bren closed his eyes against the image before him. When he
opened them, hoping it had been a nightmare, she was still
there—standing just a little more defiantly.

With narrowed eyes and clenched lips, he stared at her in total dismay. "Where was she?" he finally demanded.

"The 'old, sir. She must have 'id there the last day and a 'alf.
I guess she got scared. She started screaming as I went by and I
found 'er."

Bren couldn't take his eyes from her, nor could he hide the
fury growing in them. What an altogether stupid and dangerous thing to do.

"Thank you, Scotty," he said, the glint in his blue eyes belying the calm in his voice. "You may go back to your duties.
Samara, come in here."

Samara met his eyes but couldn't comprehend the anger she
saw there. She slithered in, trying to make herself as small as
possible. She had never felt his rage before, indeed had never

realized he possessed such a thing. Bren was the most even-tempered person she had ever known, always laughing, always teasing, always understanding. Until now. *That* she knew instantly.

A muscle throbbed in Bren's jaw as he sought to control himself. "What," he finally asked, "in the hell did you think you were doing?"

"Going to France," she answered evenly, a slight quiver of her lips the only betrayal of her growing apprehension.

"What about Mother and Father? Didn't you stop to think for a moment what this might do to them?"

Her head went up. "I wrote them . . . they know you'll take care of me."

"And what about the British . . . do you think they'll appreciate that fact? Damn it, Samara, don't you know how dangerous this is?"

"You're better than all of them . . . they can never catch you." The words were said with such utter confidence that Bren had trouble keeping his face bent in such censure.

He shook his head. "The fact is, my dear sister, that if anyone sights us we are in a great deal of trouble. The *Samara* is a merchant ship. We don't have the guns to defend her against a warship. We are depending on speed . . . and luck."

"I don't care," she said stubbornly. "No one can touch you."

"Such faith," he replied wryly.

He held her at arm's length, taking in her tired, smudged face and thoroughly stained dress. "How long have you been planning this?"

"Just since the night before we left Glen Woods," she replied honestly.

"And I played right into your hands by inviting you to Charleston."

Only her eyes admitted the truth.

"Ah, Samara, I have spoiled you much too much. We all have. If I had thought it safe, I would have been delighted to have your company. Now it's just too damned dangerous. We're going back."

"You can't," Samara said, desperation crowding her voice. "You can't go back through the blockade again."

"We won't go into port. I'll slip close to land and have several of my men accompany you back. There's nothing else to do," Bren said gently. "Dangerous as it might be, it's less than what we'll find on the rest of this voyage."

Samara's dream crumbled. Not only had she failed, but she had unnecessarily put her beloved brother in needless danger.

"I'll do anything," she said in a low, pleading voice. "I'll scrub your decks, I'll cook."

"I don't need an extra hand," Bren said. "I should like to keep my sister in one piece. We'll talk about it no more." He looked down again at the dress. "Do you have anything else to wear?"

She looked miserable. "One dress."

"I'll see you get a bath and you can get some sleep. You look like you could use it." His mouth crooked up in a half smile. "Did you really stay in the hold all this time?"

Her gray eyes grew large as she contemplated the horror of her time there, and nodded slowly.

Bren's finger touched her cheek. "Oh, Samara . . . whatever are we going to do with you?"

He turned to go, the new course change already turning over in his mind, when both of them heard the loud cry from above.

"Sail, ho."

Bren fought back a string of curses. What miserable luck! So much for that first euphoric feeling of good omen. "Stay here, keep the door locked unless you hear my voice," he ordered Samara curtly and bounded out the door and up onto the deck.

Brendan strode to the lookout. "What flag?"

"She's not flying any."

Picking up his glass, he looked out across the distance and cursed again. The ship was a schooner, much like his own but larger and heavily armed. He knew a sudden unfamiliar apprehension.

He turned to Briggs, his first mate. "Let's make a run for it."

The ship turned to the wind and Bren ordered his men aloft to loosen the topsails. The ship picked up speed, but Bren saw that the other ship followed suit, closing some of the distance between them.

In less than an hour, the ship was within firing range and Bren saw the British flag go up, accompanied by signal flags ordering him to turn about.

In those minutes, he had a torturous decision to make, one made more difficult by Samara's presence. Many of his crew were British-born and, under British law, subject to impressment, imprisonment or even hanging if found to be deserters from the British navy—as some were. He would be condemning each and every one of them if he surrendered the ship. And only God knew what would happen to Samara. Since it was not a naval ship, it was obviously a privateer, and none of that breed was much better than a common pirate. He had heard more than one story of their mistreatment and ransoming of prisoners.

Brendan made his decision quickly. They did not have the Englishman's firepower but perhaps a lucky shot would disable their opponent's rigging enough to give them a chance to escape.

"Run up our flag," he told a helmsman. "Prepare to fire."

The next hour was what Samara imagined hell must be like. She could hear the smashing of cannonball and shot into the ship, feel the boom of the *Samara*'s returning fire, smell the smoke of gunpowder. Worst of all were the agonized screams and cries of the wounded which competed with the noise of cracking and splintering wood. Frightened beyond anything in her experience, she did as she was told and stayed in the cabin. She was thrown from her feet when the two ships met and grappling hooks from the privateer locked them together, but she kept her fear contained by convincing herself that Bren was the best. Bren would win. He would never let anything happen to her. Never.

Brendan never saw the shot that felled him. He had continued to direct the firing from the quarterdeck and had taken the wheel when his helmsman fell. The decks were now slippery with blood and the air acrid with smoke. He knew the smell of defeat, but something in him refused to acknowledge it. Just as he took the wheel, seeking to turn the ship and slip from the privateer's reach, a cannonball hit one of the yards above him, splintering it into hundreds of sharp missiles which rained down on top of him. One piece hit his head while another went into his arm and pinned him to the deck. As blood splurted from his wound, he lost consciousness.

With its captain downed, the ship easily capitulated. The crew, badly outnumbered, were mostly peacetime sailors, untrained in the close-in fighting now required of them. They threw down their arms, one by one, and stared in apprehension as a golden-haired blood-splattered giant jumped lightly aboard and took control of the ship.

Reese Hampton's eyes quickly scanned the deck for the captain. He had not expected the kind of opposition he had received and he wanted no more surprises. Only one man seemed to have any authority.

"Captain?" he queried, his voice harsh and demanding.

"No," Briggs growled. "First mate. The captain's near the wheel, badly wounded. He needs medical attention."

Reese strode over to the fallen man. "His name?"

"Captain O'Neill."

Reese leaned over and pulled the piece of wood from Brendan's arm. Ripping a piece of cloth from the man's shirt, he wrapped it tightly around the bleeding wound and gestured to several of his men.

"Take him to the *Unicorn*; tell Yancy to do what he can for him," he said before turning back to Briggs and ordering in a terse voice. "Separate your wounded from the others. We have a surgeon aboard."

He ordered three of his men to search the rest of the ship for any survivors and sent his boatswain to the captain's cabin for his papers. Reese wanted to know exactly what the ship was carrying and whether it had been worth the damage to the *Unicorn*. He then surveyed the damage to the *Samara*, as he wondered briefly about its strange, exotic-sounding name. The ship was salvageable, but it would take a great deal of work. What a little beauty it was! He damned the stubborn American for not yielding sooner.

He was continuing his careful perusal of his latest prize, when his boatswain interrupted him. "Cap'n, the door's locked."

Reese looked at the man with impatience. "Then break it open, Evans."

"Well, sir, it seems to be latched from the inside...someone's in there...I thought you might want to know."

A frown darkened Reese's face. It didn't make sense. Why would anyone be hiding now? Surely it was known the ship was taken. Perhaps to destroy some papers?

"Let's go, Evans," he said, fairly leaping for the hatchway.

Once there, he regarded the door with interest. He briefly thought about ordering the offender to open it but discarded the notion. It would only give him warning and perhaps a chance to shoot. Instead, he whispered to Evans to keep his pistol ready and rammed his shoulder against the door, feeling the wood splinter. Another lunge swung the door open and he heard it bang against the wall as he stared in utter amazement.

Standing against the wall, holding a wine bottle as one would hold a sword, eyes blazing with a mixture of fear and defiance, was one of the loveliest women he had ever seen.

Chapter Three

Samara had known something was dreadfully wrong minutes before the handle of the cabin door rattled. The sound of battle had quieted, but there had been no sign of Brendan. As minutes wore on, fear and apprehension swirled inside her, growing with each second's passing. It turned to terror when she heard footsteps in the corridor and the cabin door being tried. Then there was quiet, as footsteps receded.

Oh, God, where is Bren? He wouldn't abandon her, not unless he was wounded . . . or dead. The last thought was incomprehensible, but she couldn't drive it from her head. She sank to the floor in total despair. This couldn't be happening. She heard boots tramping above her, heard orders being shouted by strange voices and then a noise at the door again.

She looked frantically around for a weapon . . . anything. Then the door rumbled and splintered and the only thing she saw was a wine bottle apparently brought for Bren's dinner. Grabbing it, she backed up against the far wall.

She was prepared for anything but what suddenly confronted her.

For a moment, Samara thought she was seeing the devil himself. He seemed a giant, taller than her father, than any of her brothers who usually towered above all others. Even in the darkening cabin, his tawny rumpled hair flickered with streaks of gold and copper. Dressed only in a white flowing shirt and cutoff white breeches, he was splattered with blood . . . from his two bare feet to his wide shoulders. But even as her mind somehow registered all of this, she felt pinioned to the wall by his eyes. She had never seen any like them. They were a deep, restless greenish-blue which seemed to glitter like a multifaceted gem, quickly changing from anger to amusement to something more complicated. She didn't know exactly what it was, but it sent shivers through her. She tried to back up further, but there was no place to go and, instead, she raised the bottle in bravado.

"I knew I had a rich prize; I just didn't know how rich," the giant said in a deep, lazy voice, and Samara's shivers grew. He leaned against the doorjamb, all strength and grace like a jungle cat, as his strangely brilliant eyes first scoured, then mentally undressed her.

For the first time in her life, Samara wished she could faint at will...anything to get away from those eyes. No one had ever looked at her like this, no one had ever dared. She felt naked before him, not only her body but her mind and soul, as well. She knew he could read her fear and was amused by it, and that shamed her even more than the obvious lust in his eyes.

"Do you really intend to do battle with that bottle?" The question was part interest, part mockery, and she hated him at that moment. She instinctively held it higher. As poor as it was, it was the only thing between them.

His voice softened to the purr of a tiger. "Come now...there are much better things to do with a bottle of wine."

There was something hypnotizing about the invitation in his voice. She sought desperately to break the spell he was spinning. She finally managed a few words. "Captain . . . Captain O'Neill . . . is he . . . ?"

The giant continued to lean indolently against the wall, studying her, and Samara felt herself flush under his intense gaze.

Reese was intrigued. She was filthy, her face smudged and dress stained, but it didn't detract from the interesting promise of her willowy figure. The violet color of her dress was reflected in the huge uncertain gray eyes that flickered between fear and an almost touching defiance. Black hair, streaked with a red glow like flame, tumbled down her back and framed a truly lovely face. Who could she be? Not a wife. No captain would take a wife on such a dangerous journey. Nor, he thought ruefully, would they wish to. Most men he knew went to sea to escape such bonds. Mistress? Likely, he concluded. The thought excited him. If she were the captain's mistress, she

would, perhaps, not object to becoming his. He was seldom
denied any woman's favors.

Already, his blood was warming and, unconsciously, his half
smile turned into a full leer.

Samara didn't miss the change in his eyes nor the tightening
power of his body. Almost desperately, the bottle went higher.
"The captain . . . where is the captain?"

"He's on my ship," Reese said slowly, wondering how much
it really mattered to her. "He was wounded but I think not
badly. My surgeon's looking after him."

"I want to see him," she demanded, with a boldness she
didn't feel. She bit her lip to keep it from trembling.

His eyes softened slightly and some of the leer left his face as
he heard her concern. There was no doubt she cared for
O'Neill. But how much?

"What is he to you?" he asked softly, his eyes changing
again, puzzling her. The small half smile, which told her nothing, was back.

With her fear for Bren somewhat allayed, she turned her full
attention to her captor. He was the most striking man she had
ever seen. His face seemed chiseled from stone, each feature
strong and clearly defined . . . from his deep-set eyes to the determined chin. It was nearly bronze from the sun, making his
gold hair and glittering aqua eyes startling by contrast. Arrogance and power radiated from him, and she almost gasped at
the shaming shivers of her body. She had never been so affected by a man.

He was an Englishman.

And a pirate.

And a thief. He was stealing her ship.

And possibly, her brother's murderer.

Reese Hampton read the confusion in her face, saw the flush
as her eyes examined him as carefully as he had her, smiled as
she bit her lip in embarrassment at being caught at it.

She looked impossibly innocent . . . and vulnerable. Reese felt
a fleeting moment of compassion but quickly shrugged it aside.
She couldn't be as innocent as she looked, not a woman alone
on a ship full of men.

She hadn't answered his question about O'Neill. He tried
again, bowing slightly. "I'm Captain Reese Hampton. Whom
do I have the honor of addressing?"

The bottle came down several inches. Samara's hand was
becoming tired and she was beginning to feel very silly. As if the

bottle would do any harm to the warrior across from her. But as he stepped toward her, her arm raised protectively once more.

"The bottle." The words were spoken softly, but with a confidence that once more stirred her to a confusing mixture of anger and desire. She flinched as he continued to move, cat-like, toward her, his hand held out.

Samara tried to inch along the wall in a vain attempt to place distance between them, but she was suddenly trapped between two long arms, and the bottle was being pulled gently from her fingers and set firmly on a nearby table. She sought to duck under his arm, but one hand caught her chin, cradling it as he forced it upward until her eyes were staring straight into his. A finger from his other hand traced her cheekbone with feathery lightness, and she felt unfamiliar flickers of flame race through her.

"Please..." Her voice was very low, very uncertain.

"Please what, my sweet?" he replied, the warmth in his tone nearly mesmerizing her. "Please continue... or please stop?" He felt confident of her answer. Her body was trembling under his hands as it unconsciously strained towards him.

"S-s-stop."

In answer, his lips met hers, and Samara felt herself whirling as if swept up by a tornado. She had never been kissed like this, had never been touched like this, had never known feelings like this. His touch ranged from a gentle sweetness to fevered want, carrying her progressively from note to note, arousing depths she hadn't known existed until now. In sudden terror at what was happening, she jerked away, her hand instinctively going back and swinging at his face with a force created of desperation. The impact stunned them both, the sound of the slap magnified by the closeness of the room.

Samara looked at the bright red color left by the blow and stood paralyzed, waiting for the retaliation she was sure would come. Her eyes now dominated her face, looking like those of a trapped dove as a hawk attacks.

Reese's first surge of anger quieted under her obvious fright. He had never mistreated a woman, nor taken an unwilling one. He forced himself to relax, but his body did not want to cooperate.

"Why didn't you just tell me no?" he asked finally.

"I...I...I...tried..."

"Not very hard," he said with the former mockery, and she flinched at his words. He was right.

He put his hand to his cheek ruefully. "Your captain should have put you up on deck. Maybe he would have won."

His words brought Samara painfully back to reality. "I have to see him."

"Please," he said tauntingly. "Say please."

For a moment, she felt a surge of satisfaction that she had slapped him. She only wished it had been harder. "Please..."

"Please, Captain Hampton..." he urged, continuing to bait her.

"Please, Captain Hampton," Samara replied sullenly, ready to do anything to leave the cabin...and him...and her shameful, inexplicable reaction to him.

"And who is asking?" He questioned with a mocking insolence that masked his real interest.

Pleading eyes lifted to his glittering ones. "Samara," she said finally, almost hopelessly. "Samara O'Neill."

Reese felt as if he had been kicked. So she *was* O'Neill's wife. That accounted for the ship's name. His disappointment startled him. He had a very limited number of rules for himself, but he had vowed long ago that married women were taboo. It was a decision made after a friend had died in a duel with an irate husband. No woman was worth dying for, or killing for, particularly one who betrayed her husband. There were altogether too many fish in the ocean to fight over one already netted.

"Captain O'Neill is your husband?" He couldn't resist the question, even knowing the answer.

Samara looked at him, startled. She had never thought he would assume that. But she didn't miss the new restraint in his voice, nor the almost imperceptible withdrawal. It was difficult to believe that this...this pirate would respect marriage, but perhaps he did. Perhaps that would save her from him, and she from herself. Even now, she felt strange new urges tugging at her senses, and she had to restrain her hand from reaching out to touch him. *He's a pirate*, she kept telling herself, *and an Englishman*. She didn't know which was worse. But together...

She closed her eyes for a moment, then opened them and stared him straight in the face. "Yes," she said. "And I would like to see him...if that's not too much to ask from a pirate."

Reese's eyes narrowed. "I am a privateer, Mrs. O'Neill, and our countries are at war."

"That's just an excuse for murder and thievery," Samara said, suddenly brave as she echoed her father's words. Her terror was gone; she had lost her fear of any physical harm from the man opposite her. *Don't think about the other. Don't think about the way he makes you feel.* To protect herself from him, she planted a seed of anger and willed it to grow. This man, this "pirate," had attacked the ship named for her and was responsible for her brother's wounding. He was everything she had been taught to despise, and she loathed herself for feeling even the tiniest bit of warmth or attraction for him. The result of all this emotional turmoil was a baleful glare sent in the general direction of the Englishman.

To her everlasting mortification, it seemed only to amuse him. The sides of his mouth twitched, and his eyes gleamed with humor. He moved to the table where he had deposited the wine bottle.

"I think I will take your deadly weapon with us," he said, grabbing it with a strong brown hand. "I might need it," he added, deliberately.

She looked up. He was laughing at her. His eyes fairly danced with merriment at her discomfort, and Samara clenched her hands in frustration. She wanted to hit him again but she didn't quite dare. She knew he would be ready this time.

Reese's grin grew wider. He couldn't mistake at least part of her thoughts; he had had much too much experience with women for that. Perhaps rules were made to be broken, he thought with a start. Perhaps she was not so very married. In any event, it should prove to be a very interesting voyage.

With a small mocking bow, he took her arm, completely disregarding her attempt to free it, and steered her out the door and up on deck. This time, she didn't have to force her anger. She could have joyfully murdered him.

The full horror of the previous several hours did not dawn on Samara until she reached the upper deck. Her stomach lurched as she viewed the cluttered wreck that had once been Brendan's well-tended ship. Torn pieces of sail floated like kites over the carnage. Splintered wood and jagged pieces of iron littered the usually immaculate deck. Bright crimson stains looked like a madman's painting, the thick globs forming obscene patterns on a wooden canvas.

Samara couldn't take her eyes from the mayhem, where each sight was worse than the last. She saw some of Brendan's crew, their clothes black with gunpowder, working under armed guards. Others, obviously wounded, were huddled in a corner, awaiting some disposition. The fear in their faces told her they didn't know what it would be—death or salvation.

In still another corner were several bodies. She saw a familiar striped shirt and jerked loose from the Englishman, running to the still form.

She knelt beside him. "Scotty," she whispered, her hand reaching for his and finding it covered in blood. She had known Scotty for years and he had been unfailingly kind to her. She remembered now how glad she was to see him...just hours ago when he rescued her from the hold.

"Oh, Scotty," she repeated, unaware of the warm tears that had formed in her eyes and started down her cheeks. She had never seen violent death before, never been exposed to anything more than the usually quiet leave-taking of aged animals. Even that had created tears for days; even when she knew death had come gently after a long life.

"Mrs. O'Neill." The pressure on her arm was gentle...but commanding. "Mrs. O'Neill," the voice came again as through a fog, "this is no place for you."

She stood up then, staring at him as her rage grew from a tiny bubble to a boiling cauldron. Samara whirled and faced her captor. "You," she said with cold hatred. "You did this. Damn you. Damn you to hell." Her hand went back, just as it had earlier, but this time Reese was prepared.

His hand whipped out and caught it in midair. His other hand caught her left wrist, and he pinned both of them behind her. "One," he said tightly, "is all you're allowed."

She stood there shaking, tears streaming down her face as he pulled her closer. Then the wetness traveled to his shirt, and she could smell a pungent mixture of musk and blood and sweat. Something wild and primitive inside her responded, and she trembled as her heart beat so loudly she knew everyone could hear. *What was happening to her?* She couldn't seem to move, to breathe, to think. Think about Scotty, she told herself.

With sudden determination she pushed away, surprised to feel his arms fall from her. She forced herself to look at him, prepared to meet his hatefully amused eyes with her own disdainful ones. But his weren't amused, and the warmth and unexpected gentleness she found there almost undid her again. She quickly dropped her own, thinking, knowing she had been mistaken about his sympathy. He was a pirate. He had created all this destruction.

When she looked up again, she knew she was right. His eyes were penetrating. Cold.

"This is no place for you," he repeated. "I'll take you to your husband."

Without waiting for an answer, he steered her to where the two ships remained locked together. A plank made easy commerce between the two, and Reese easily swung her up and leaped up behind her with the same catlike grace she had noticed before. He placed his two hands firmly around her waist.

The feel of his hands sent new fire through her, and she sought to throw them off, losing her balance on the narrow plank in the process. To her humiliation, she started to fall until two arms scooped her up and held her tightly against a rock-hard chest. She knew the touch of his breath, the feel of his heat and the sound of his heart. He held her as easily as she would a feather, and she wondered at his strength. Then they were across, and still he was holding her, his face staring down at her with some strange expression she couldn't decipher.

"You seem determined," he finally said, in the same amused drawl that had angered her earlier, "to wreak even more damage."

Samara glared at him with renewed fury. "Put me down," she demanded haughtily.

"Only if you promise to behave," he said. He raised a questioning eyebrow, and Samara thought he looked more than ever like her mental portrait of a blond Lucifer.

He sounded as if he were speaking to a child, and Samara's outrage continued to flame. How dare he? She wriggled to free herself, only to find her body even more enmeshed in his arms.

She could feel the laughter rise in his chest as he drew her tighter to him, making it nearly impossible for her to move. She steadfastly avoided looking at him, sensing that he would read what his closeness was doing to her. His very touch burned her like a brand, and she couldn't understand it. She should hate him. She *did* hate him! *Bren. Keep your mind on Bren.* Why, oh why, hadn't anyone warned her she could feel like this?

His arms relaxed, and she was settled, ever so gently, in a corridor before an open door. Too stunned by events to move, she could merely stand there, trying to restore some measure of control.

He was taking her arm again, leading her inside, and somehow her eyes focused on those within. Bren was on a table, silent and still, his usually sun-darkened face pale and set. A man was leaning over him, pulling a needle through her brother's skin, oblivious to his patient's quick withdrawals of breath as the pain ebbed and flowed with each stitch.

Samara forced herself to watch silently, afraid that to disturb them would increase the torment. Unexpectedly, she felt the Englishman's hand on her shoulder, not cruelly or even possessively as before but, once more, almost with gentleness. She looked up quickly, again catching that fleeting glance of something vulnerable. She instantly dismissed it as whimsy and turned back to Bren.

As the doctor tied his final knot, she ran over to her brother. Bren's eyes widened at the sight of her. Everything had happened so quickly, he had almost forgotten Samara. There had been the attack, the thunder of guns, then pain and, finally, blackness. He had regained consciousness just minutes earlier, his head reeling with pain and his arm a fiery furnace of agony.

"My husband...my dear, wonderful husband," Samara said as she rushed to him, leaned down and kissed him.

Bewilderment...total bewilderment...clashed with his pain, as fogged eyes questioned her.

"I was so worried about you," she rattled on, ignoring his incredulous expression. "This...this...pirate," she looked back at Reese, "said I could see you."

All of a sudden, Bren comprehended. For some reason, Samara thought it wise to masquerade as his wife. He didn't question her reason. His eyes told her he understood and his left hand lifted and squeezed hers. He tried to rise slightly, but nausea forced him back down. He could only look helplessly around him.

In addition to the doctor, there were two seamen, apparently standing by as guards. As if he could move, much less fight back. A bitter smile formed on his lips.

Behind them was a tall figure, lounging against the wall in apparent disinterest. But despite the careless pose, Bren sensed something intense and dangerous about him. It was in the narrowed eyes, a certain recognizable tautness that was quietly menacing.

The man approached him now, and Bren feared for his sister. This was no man to play for a fool.

"Captain O'Neill," the voice was low and pleasing, carrying little of the precise English inflection Bren had expected. "I'm Reese Hampton, captain of the *Unicorn*. You and your crew are my prisoners."

"My ship?"

"Afloat. Just barely. We're trying to salvage it."

"And Samara...my wife?"

"She will be safe enough...hostage, as you will, to your own good behavior. Not that she sets a very good example." Bren heard the laughter in his voice, and his fear for Samara quickened.

"If you touch—"

Reese's mouth tightened. "You are in no position to make threats, Captain. But I'll tell you, just once, that I don't make war on women."

Bren had to be satisfied with that. He knew from his captor's face he would get no more. "My crew?"

"Seven were killed. The injured are being cared for. The others will work for their keep."

"On a British ship?" Bren snarled.

"If they want to eat, yes," Reese replied mildly.

"And then?" The words came with difficulty. Brendan O'Neill had no experience as a supplicant, but his concern for his English-born crew members overrode everything else.

Reese's stern expression relaxed only slightly. "If you cause me no trouble, I'll put you and your crew ashore at a neutral place."

"All my crew?"

Reese had little difficulty in recognizing the question's meaning. One of the causes of the war had been Britain's unyielding insistence that anyone born in England, Scotland or Ireland remained subjects of the king and liable to impressment or worse.

"All," he agreed. "I have no particular desire to fill the navy's ranks. I'm more concerned with getting these two ships to Bermuda."

"An English port," Brendan sneered. "Is that what you call neutral?"

A muscle throbbed in Reese's cheek, the only sign of his growing anger. "I'm not accustomed to having my word—or my honor—questioned," he said.

"Honor?" Bren's voice was tinged with contempt. "A privateer? Why should I believe you?"

Reese's voice was silky now. "Because you really have no choice, Captain." He turned to the two seamen. "Take him to the hold with the other officers." He had considered allowing the enemy crew run of the ship, but O'Neill's hostility changed his mind. O'Neill, he knew through years of experience, could be a great deal of trouble. He had also learned long ago to separate the crew from their officers; without leadership, there was usually little rebellion.

"No!" Samara's voice interrupted the silent duel between the two men.

Reese turned to her, both eyebrows raised in mock surprise. "No?" he repeated softly.

Even Brendan's eyes were disapproving now.

"I...I..." she couldn't continue. She only remembered her own frightening hours in the dark hold. She couldn't stand the thought of Brendan, with his wounds, imprisoned there.

Reese ignored her plea and turned his attention back to O'Neill. "Why, under all God's mercy, did you bring your wife with you?"

Bren closed his eyes in frustration. The censure in the Englishman's voice was clear.

"He didn't bring me," Samara broke in, unable to let Bren assume the blame for her misdeed. "I stowed away. He found me just before you attacked."

Reese couldn't hide his astonishment. So that's why she had all those smudges. They were at least two days from any port. Bemused, he considered the words. It was completely outside his comprehension that a woman would go to all that trouble and discomfort to be with her husband. There must be more between these two than he'd first thought. His eyes continued to dart between the two, sensing a deep affection, yet finding something amiss. He hadn't, he knew, mistaken the girl's reluctant awareness of him, nor the sparks that snapped between them. There was none of that between the two standing before him.

From the beginning, he had noticed she was not wearing a wedding ring. Yet there was no denying the familiarity between his two unwilling passengers, nor the fact that the ship bore her name. One didn't usually name ships after mistresses; it was much too public.

He shook his head to clear it. He had time to solve this particular mystery and solve it he would.

He placed a restraining hand on Samara and repeated his instructions to the two crewmen.

Bren shot Samara a warning look and struggled to sit up. "What about my wife?"

"She'll have my first mate's cabin. Nothing will happen to her, nothing she doesn't want to happen." Reese eyed O'Neill as he made the last suggestive comment. He wanted to take more of a measure of the man. He wasn't disappointed.

"Damn you," Bren raged as he lunged towards Reese, only to find his legs wouldn't hold him. Only the intervention of Reese's two crewmen kept him from falling. "I'll kill you if you harm her."

Reese's steel-like grip on Samara kept her from reaching for Bren. The Englishman, with Samara firmly in tow, stepped back to allow the two guards and their prisoner to leave. Samara could only watch helplessly as Bren, his eyes a mixture of rage and fear for her, was half dragged, half carried away.

Chapter Four

The first mate's cabin was tiny, holding little but a narrow bunk built into the cabin wall, a table bolted to the floor, a chair and a trunk tucked into a corner. It was as spartan as a nun's cell.

Captain Hampton had opened the door and ushered her in, studying her with insolent interest. He bowed slightly. "I beg forgiveness for the quarters but we had not expected so lovely a guest," he said.

"I would prefer to be with my...husband," Samara said, still defiant.

"I'm afraid that's not possible," Reese said, with the grin she was beginning to hate. "He is not the only one there, and I think propriety, if not modesty, would prevent you from sharing their quarters."

She could only glare at him.

"Do you have some other clothes aboard your ship?" he asked as he regarded her critically.

Samara suddenly realized how she must look. Her worst fears were confirmed by the twinkle in those ridiculously blue-green eyes. She jutted out her chin, not realizing that any dignity was compromised by the childlike smudges on her cheek and chin.

"I had a dress...in a package...in the captain's cabin."

"I'll send for it," her tormentor said, "as well as a bath." He said the last as his eyes glided up and down her with what Samara catalogued as a wickedly lecherous look. The tingles started inside her again even as she fought to subdue them.

"There is no need," she said, trying to put indifference into her voice. "I'm perfectly fine as I am."

"Ah, but there is a need," the Englishman drawled. "I wish your company for dinner and I think I would like to see what you look like after the hold washes away." His hand reached out and touched one of the deeper smudges on her cheek.

"I would rather starve," Samara spat, "than share dinner with a pirate."

"Privateer," he corrected again, then added, "Ah, but would your husband and his fellow officers?" The gleam in his eye belied his mild tone.

Samara looked at him with horror. "You wouldn't?"

The side of his mouth twisted up. "No?"

"I detest you," she said, trying to think of the worst possible way to insult him. "You are no gentleman."

He threw back his head and roared. "There are many who would agree with you on that point. Besides, what else would you expect of a pirate?" He was mocking her again, using her own words against her.

She looked around, hoping for a weapon of some sort. Impotent fury filled her eyes as she found none.

"I'm afraid," he said, reading her thoughts exactly and more than a little intrigued with her seemingly unconquerable spirit, "I dropped your wine bottle on the other ship. Now be a good girl and take a bath." With that, he slipped from the cabin, and she heard the door lock.

Despite her brave words, the bath felt wonderful. A cabin boy and deckhand appeared almost immediately after Hampton's departure, one armed with a bathtub which barely fit inside the cabin and the other with buckets of hot water. The boy, his eyes wide with interest over the new passenger, also carried her package and some towels.

"'ere ye are, mistress," he said. "''ope ye enjoy yer bath."

Samara eyed them both with suspicion until they retreated under her baleful stare. Despite everything, the bath did look inviting. For one used to bathing daily and changing clothes often, she felt horribly miserable under the layers of dirt and dried perspiration.

She tried the door, finding no lock on her side and, instead, propped the chair against it. Eyeing the bath with the intensity of a starving man approaching food, Samara quickly slipped from her dress and into the water.

The warm liquid felt like velvet against her sticky flesh and she slid down further, letting it encompass her like a cocoon. Instantly, she felt guilty at the comfort. How was Bren being treated? She saw Scotty's body again, and the wounded. How were they? Rage flowed through her like hot lava. That she was attracted to the man responsible shamed her to the core. What was she to do now? Captain Hampton had told Bren he would not hurt her, but what guarantee did she have? He had demonstrated his ruthlessness over and over again—in his treatment of her brother, in his threats to starve the *Samara*'s crew. It was obvious he did not take easily to being thwarted in his wishes. And there was no hiding his interest in her. She had never seen such an openly lecherous leer.

If only he weren't... But Samara wouldn't let herself think "if only." It was altogether too dangerous, and only kindled those new, tormenting feelings. The English captain was so arrogantly handsome, so compelling. She had never seen a person completely dominate everyone and everything as easily. A warmth crept through her as she remembered the flashes of heat where he touched her, those strange unfamiliar cravings that surfaced when he had pressed her to him.

"No," she whispered. "He is our enemy. Bren's and mine. He's a rogue and a pirate and he's stealing the *Samara*." And no one, no one could do anything about it.

Or could they? The little voice which had urged her to stow away returned. Her gray eyes lighted as it continued to prick at her consciousness. Only too aware of the consequences of its latest mischief, she tried to shoo the voice away. But, as always, the imp refused to obey.

He's attracted to you, it said. *Use it to help Bren escape.*

But how?

The wine. Get him drunk tonight and steal his keys.

Samara's fertile brain took the idea from there. She sat up abruptly in the bath, splashing water on the floor, her eyes wide with possibilities. She had seen her brothers drunk, much to her parents' dismay, and knew exactly how debilitating it could be.

After living in a family with so many men and eavesdropping on numerous forbidden conversations, Samara knew exactly what to do. *Laugh at my wine bottle, did he,* she giggled to herself. He'll find out how dangerous it could be. She would get him drunk, bang him on the head with a bottle or whatever was handy, steal a weapon—hopefully a pistol; she knew how to use that—and free Brendan and the others. With her usual optimism and customary disregard for realities, she smiled confidently to herself and once more sank down in the cooling water.

Reese felt a curious uncertainty as he discarded his clothes, throwing the blood-stained shirt and breeches in a pile on the floor. He washed quickly and shaved just a little more carefully, rubbing the back of his hand over the now smooth cheek.

What was it about the little she-cat that provoked more than his usual superficial interest? Especially if she was, as she claimed, married. Cat? She was more like a half-grown kitten, spitting one minute, warm and cuddly the next. He hadn't missed that startled response to him, the leap of fire between them which she tried so futilely to quench. He shook his head in frustration. There was an appealing innocence about her that just didn't fit a married woman. Unless, of course, it was all an act. He was plagued with the thought that something was not quite what it seemed.

He burrowed in his sea chest in his usual careless way, finally finding a pair of bucksin breeches and a clean linen shirt. He slipped into a pair of boots, eyed them with disfavor and exchanged them for another, this time a brushed soft leather reaching to his knees. Reese laughed at himself. It was odd that he cared so much about his appearance! He seldom did aboard ship. His smile changed to a scowl. No kitten, he vowed, was going to put her claws into him. Especially not an upstart American. And a married one at that. That was another puzzle that nagged at him. But he would solve the mystery of Samara O'Neill. And wine, he thought as his face lightened, was exactly the way to do it.

Samara had just finished brushing her hair to a fine luster when a knock came at her door. She quickly smoothed out her dress, wishing it were not the plain, sensible day dress she had deemed most suitable for an ocean voyage. The best thing about the dress was its color—a rich blue that reached to her eyes. She tensed at the sound of the knock, preparing herself to face *him* again. Strangely enough, she felt a stab of disappointment to find, instead, an attractive dark-haired man who introduced himself as Michael Simmons, the first officer. He bowed, while eyeing her with no little appreciation. He had been busy when Reese brought her aboard and was just told minutes ago that he had lost his cabin. His first irritation fled as he studied her.

"Captain Hampton asked me to escort you to his cabin," he said finally. "And I need to get a few things from the cabin."

Samara almost apologized for dislodging him before realizing she didn't want to be here in the first place. She was certainly not going to thank her captor for her prison. To Simmons's disappointment, he received only a smoldering glare as she stiffly accompanied him down the corridor, steadfastly refusing his arm.

But her bloodthirsty inclinations receded into stammering confusion when the door to the captain's cabin opened, and *he* stood there in all of his glorious splendor. And, by any standards, he was glorious. Samara's knees swayed under her as her heart seem to pound as loud as any drumbeat.

With the blood removed, he seemed almost civilized. And yet there was something primitive about him. Perhaps, she thought, it was the restless fierceness of those glittering eyes. Or perhaps it was in the chiseled perfection of his face. It reminded her of paintings of the capricious Greek gods she had seen in books. Capricious and treacherous, arbitrary and dangerous—mythical figures who thought of little but their own pleasure.

As if reading her very thoughts, Reese bowed, a sardonic smile on his lips.

"I was right," he said. "There was a beautiful woman under all that grime," his lips twitching at her discomfort.

It was that expression which restoked Samara's faltering furor. Handsome is as handsome does, she silently repeated her mother's favorite homily, and Captain Hampton was as ugly as a wallowing pig. Thus mentally fortified, she looked back up at him, only briefly remembering that her favorite pet was once a pig she had saved from slaughter. She would show no such mercy this time.

The thoughts restored her humor and a quick, delighted smile flashed across her face, catching Reese off balance. She was bewitchingly lovely in that moment, her thickly lashed smoky eyes alive with her own private joke, her lips curved in a slight, enticing smile.

He caught his breath as a raw ache started to grow within him. He looked up and saw his first officer staring at both of them, eyes traveling from one to another in puzzlement.

"Thank you, Michael," he said firmly. "Please tell Davey to serve when the food is ready." He grinned at Michael's baffled expression as his friend left, closing the door gently behind him.

Samara glanced around the cabin with real interest. Surroundings told a lot about a person, and she needed to know as much as she could about Captain Reese Hampton. It was large and comfortably, though simply, furnished. The bed was much larger than her own, and seemed to dominate the room. When she could force her eyes away from it, she surveyed the rest. There were two tables, one apparently a small working desk, the other a dining table large enough for six or more people. An intricately carved chest was pushed into a corner, and numerous maps had been shoved against the wall.

There was a strange, exotic, half-dead plant in one corner and a pair of discarded boots near the table. Whatever else he was, Captain Hampton, Samara decided, was not a tidy man. The room was clean but cluttered. He seemed to treat it with the same careless indifference that she suspected ruled all but his most important passions. And war, she sensed, was one of those passions. There had been no carelessness there, nothing left to chance. Her eyes then found the books, almost hidden by a wooden bar which held them in place. She walked over to them, her eyes opening in astonishment as she studied the titles. There were the expected military and nautical books, as well as several volumes of history along with Shakespeare and Milton and Donne. But what completely shocked her were Homer's *Illiad* and *Odyssey* in Greek.

Her startled expression stirred him to comment. "Pirates do read, you know," he said with a wry smile. He spoke in the slow, relaxed deep voice that so unnerved her.

"In Greek?" she said skeptically.

Now his eyebrows furrowed together. "You can read Greek?"

"Of course," she said airily, not bothering to mention it was quite her worst subject and that her knowledge extended little beyond ciphering the name of the books. Her parents both had a passion for knowledge and, if nothing more, had wanted their children at least exposed to both Latin and Greek. But Samara, seeing no need for such skill, had nearly driven her tutor to madness by her inadequacy in that particular area. She wouldn't admit to a certain awe, however, that someone other than a tutor could, or would even want to, read such a bewildering language.

"A glass of wine, Mrs. O'Neill?"

Her eyes went quickly to him, noticing the shirt stretched across his wide shoulders and the form-fitting breeches which displayed every muscle of his strong legs. She swallowed. Remember...handsome is as...Remember Bren.

"Yes, thank you, Captain," she said finally, her hands trembling slightly as she took a silver goblet.

"Reese," he said. "Please call me Reese." His voice was mesmerizing.

Samara struggled for control, hiding behind a sip of the wine. It was, she discovered, quite good. She had never had very much, only a glass on special occasions. She hadn't remembered it being quite so delicious. She took another sip, a larger one, and found it easier to smile brightly.

A wave of something akin to tenderness swept over Reese at her smile. There was something so vulnerable about her, something that stirred in him a mixture of protectiveness and desire. Desire won. He took one step towards her, placing his goblet on the table, then taking hers from trembling hands. He lifted her chin with his fingers, searching her eyes and finding an answering flame. His face moved down, his lips craving the touch of her. Almost in a trance, Samara stretched to meet his tall height, all her reason drowning in a tide of bewildering but undeniable need.

A knock came at the door, and Samara backed away like a terrified animal, horrified at what she had nearly done. Reese swore long and hard under his breath.

When he threw the door open in frustration, the cabin boy entered, his hands holding a heavily laden tray of aromatic dishes. The boy's face flushed when he saw Reese's frown.

"Mister Simmons said now," he stuttered nervously.

Reese's face softened. "It's all right, Davey." He turned to Samara. "This is Davey. If you need anything, you have merely to ask him."

The boy nodded eagerly to Samara who could barely manage a slight turn of her lips. She had come so close to disaster. It was the wine, she thought, disregarding the fact that she had felt similar urges without assistance. Both Davey and the captain were looking elsewhere, and Samara searched frantically for a repository for her wine. Her eyes settled on the discarded pair of Reese's boots near the table. One foot pushed them a little closer. In went the wine.

And then he was near again, guiding her to a chair, his hand like a burning brand on her arm. He politely pushed in her chair and sat down opposite her.

The smells assaulted Samara's senses. She had had very little to eat in the past three days but until she saw the food the terror and confusion of this day had obliterated her hunger. Now it attacked her with ferocity and she greedily eyed the offerings, her tongue unconsciously licking her lips, a movement which did not go unnoticed by Reese.

But as Davey filled her plate with chicken, buttered potatoes and hot bread, she thought of Bren—wounded and hungry and locked in darkness—and she despised herself for selfishness. "I don't want any," she forced herself to say, her fingers itching to reach out and grab, but her heart preventing it.

Reese watched as the conflicting wants and loyalties flickered across her face, and was surprised at the sudden ache they created.

"Would it help," he said, almost gently, "if you knew the doctor checked on Captain O'Neill and he's doing fine?" He couldn't bring himself to say husband. "And," he added wryly, "he's been fed very adequately."

Samara brightened. She didn't know why, but she believed him. Even if he was a rogue. She hesitated no longer but plunged into his offerings, only barely noticing that he refilled her goblet...and his own. At the moment, she cared little about her manners or even her plan. She had never known one could be so hungry.

Reese watched her quick fingers and mouth with amused fascination. Once relieved of guilt, she attacked the food with the single-mindedness of a starving wolf. He had never seen a lady eat with such complete abandon. For some strange reason, it made her even more attractive. She had been ready, albeit reluctantly, to forego the food despite her obvious hunger. For love? For duty?

Another knock came at the door, and Reese bade entry. It was Davey with fresh fruit. Neither of them saw Samara lean over and transfer more of her wine into the boot.

After Reese excused Davey for the night, he leaned back and eyed Samara, who was returning his steady gaze with wide, wondering eyes. He wished like hell he knew what she was thinking.

What, she pondered, is *he* thinking? She was trying to fathom something of this contradictory man, trying, after some of his kindnesses, to renew her conviction of purpose.

He refilled both of their wineglasses, thinking that she must be feeling some effects of the wine. Unfortunately, she appeared perfectly sober. He took a long swallow. "How long have you been married, Mrs. O'Neill?" he asked finally, his eyes searching her face for clues.

Samara gulped. She hadn't really thought about the details. "Two...two months."

He leaned back in his chair. "You must love him very much to stay in the hold for...what was it...two days?"

"I...I...do."

His eyes narrowed. "It gets very dark down there."

Her eyes widened as she remembered. Reese saw the horror flit across her face and didn't doubt that much of her tale.

"Some more wine, Mrs. O'Neill, or may I call you Samara?"

"No...no."

"No what? No more wine, or may I not call you Samara?" The former mockery restored her senses. Remember. Remember the plan. Her eyes saw the wine bottle. It was empty. He would have to rise, and turn, to get some more.

"It would not," she said with as much dignity as she could muster, "be proper for you to call me by my given name. And, yes, I would like some more wine."

As he rose and turned, more to hide laughter than anything else, more wine went into the boot. This time, she could hear it slosh. The fool boot was rapidly filling.

When he turned back to her, a fresh bottle in hand, he re-filled both goblets, wondering at her capacity. Even he, who had been known to outdrink the best, was beginning to feel the effects. Perhaps she just didn't show it. He probed again.

"Tell me about your home. Where do you live?"

"South Carolina," she said cautiously.

"And your family...what would they think of this?"

Her family. She had forgotten her family in the past hours. For the first time, she considered their anguish. A sudden pain struck her heart. She had thought of no one but herself, and now she knew not what would happen. Her mother and father would suffer dreadfully if they lost both Bren and herself. Struck anew by guilt, she could only stare at Captain Hampton and take a hasty draft of wine. It warmed her and filled her full of new false confidence. She would save them both. She took another sip of wine.

Reese watched, thoroughly absorbed by the changes in her face. He wondered if she had any idea how enchantingly transparent she was. It was obvious that she had some mischief in mind. He looked at his goblet. Perhaps she was not the innocent she seemed. Perhaps she was trying to get him drunk. And then? It might be interesting.

He refilled both their goblets, then directed her attention to the chest in the corner. "I found it in India," he told her as he poured his wine in the nearby half-dead plant. "You might like to take a look at it." Samara turned wide eyes toward the chest while her left hand tipped her wine into the boot. She wondered momentarily exactly how much a boot held. Her eyes, all innocence and wonder, turned back to Reese as she lifted the empty goblet to her lips and pretended to drink.

No sooner did she place it on the table than Reese refilled it. Damn the woman, he thought. She must have a cast-iron system.

"You didn't tell me," he reminded her softly. "I asked about your family."

"Oh, I'm an orphan," she said, crossing her fingers and asking forgiveness of . . . whomever.

A raised eyebrow questioned her. He had met orphans, and none of them had Samara's well-loved look. There was none of that terrible hunger in her—hunger for love, hunger for belonging. Despite all her confusion and earlier terror, she had the confidence of one who had never known real want or hurt.

Samara read her mistake in his eyes. "My uncle raised me..." With a burst of inventiveness, she added, "Bren is my cousin. No one thought we should get married; that's why I ran away to be with him." It was partly true, she justified to herself. That was what happened to her friend Melanie's parents. She had heard the story often and thought how romantic it was. Now she took it as her own.

Reese accepted the story. It would explain much, including the easily familiarity and lack of grand passion between the two. They had probably been good friends and family opposition made marriage attractive. It wouldn't be the first time. Somehow, the thoughts assuaged his conscience.

"What about you?" Samara's direct question startled him. There was real interest in her eyes. "Do you have a family?"

"A brother," he said, a slight smile on his lips. "A twin brother. In England."

There was no mistaking the affection on his face, and it startled Samara. He seemed like a man alone . . . with few attachments or roots.

"Is he a pir . . . ?

"A pirate, too?" Reese interrupted, undecided as whether to laugh or be irritated. "You do persist in thinking the worst of me. But no, he is not a privateer." Now he did laugh. The very thought of his dignified, responsible brother being a pirate sent ripples of laughter coursing through him.

Although offended by his continued amusement with her, Samara was fascinated. There was no guile, only interest, when she leaned forward. "Tell me about him."

"He's the Earl of Beddingfield, by grace of being seven minutes older," Reese said, the wine making him more loquacious than usual.

Recalling her first sight of him with bare feet and bloody shirt, Samara was stunned. "*You* are the son of an earl?"

Reese chuckled. "It does seem unlikely, doesn't it?"

Samara tried to remember everything she knew about British nobility. "Does that make you 'my lord,'" she said, with a hint of American disdain.

"Only 'Honorable,' I'm afraid," he admitted, with a raffish grin that was altogether too charming.

The expectant expression and tease in his voice started a rumbling volcano of giggles inside Samara that bubbled and boiled until they burst freely from her mouth. It was, she knew, a humiliating loss of composure, a condition aggravated not a little by the wine. Despite her best diversionary tactics, she had imbibed more than she had intended. As she struggled to control the little explosions, she caught the suddenly boyish expression on his face as he shared her amusement. It was the first time, she thought, that he had laughed with her rather than at her, and she was startled by how entirely pleasant it was. More than pleasant, really. Something magical was happening between the two of them and their eyes met with surprised awareness, hers mixed with dismay, his with a sort of shocked astonishment.

Samara forced her gaze away. She tried to subdue the growing realization that she might actually *like* him. She suppressed the notion quickly. It was bad enough to fight the seemingly unquenchable little blazes that darted from her toes to some mysterious place deep inside. He was an Englishman which, according to her father, was the next thing to a devil, and he was after her soul. And, Samara was mortally afraid, he was not being entirely unsuccessful.

Concentrate, Samara lectured herself. Concentrate on freeing Bren. Concentrate on the plan. Concentrate on the goblet.

Concentrate on anything but the vitally alive, magnetic man across from her.

"May I have some more wine?" Samara asked finally, her voice trembling slightly, cringing at the knowledge that he was hearing it, that he must know all the extraordinary things going on inside her.

His crooked smile and teasingly arched eyebrow told her only too well that he did. She had no doubts that he was very aware of the effect he had on women, and her in particular, and that made her angry enough to stiffen her weakening heart. She pretended to drop a fork and reached over, draining the wine in the almost saturated boot. Why, oh why, doesn't he get sleepy, or unconscious, or whatever it is that men do when they drink? She felt tired and giddy and excited and frustrated all at the same time. She put on her brightest and most ingenious smile. "Tell me more about your brother," she said. "Did you resent him becoming the earl?"

"Good God, no," Reese said, and Samara couldn't doubt his sincerity. "This was one time fate did things right. I bless the stars every night that I was the second son . . . that I am free of the responsibility of so much land, so many people. I was restless from the day I was born. The prodigal son, so to speak."

"And your brother . . . did he also want to be free?"

"Not as I did. He was always the steady one, the responsible one. Although," he said, warming to the subject, "not dull. Avery is never dull. He's interested in everything—books, politics, new ways of improving the land." Reese didn't know why he was babbling on like this. He had never done it before, particularly with a woman. Perhaps it was the real interest in her face, perhaps the challenge in her eyes. Damn her. Would she never succumb to the wine and say more about herself? She was like a clam, yet she was slowly invading what he had always considered private territory.

"But there's responsibility in running a ship."

Her observation startled him. At first he thought her a very pretty, but very young, piece of fluff. Spoiled. Reckless. Trouble for a husband. Even more trouble for anyone else. He had insisted that she join him for dinner because he had been without feminine company for a very long time, and she intrigued and amused him. He was used to simple prostitutes, experienced courtesans and confident ladies who were only too aware of their beauty and lineage. He had wearied of all three. Samara O'Neill was an entirely new experience and there was something extremely appealing about her little rebellions and the confused awareness in her huge eyes which kept changing color. She stirred something new in him, and he wasn't quite sure whether he liked it.

"Responsibility..." she was saying again, not really wanting an answer.

"Even for a pirate?" he resorted back to his old mockery. "Hasn't anyone ever told you pirates have no responsibility?"

He didn't miss the sudden disappointment in her eyes, something close to hurt. His heart clutched just for a moment, then he willed it released. He owed her nothing, particularly not a piece of himself. He would never let her know how much the *Unicorn* meant to him, how much each and every man in his crew stood in his regard, how much his brother and even the estates were a part of him, or how most of his prizes now went to their upkeep. Best let her think him a pirate, the vilest of the vile. For that, he could tell in her all-too-artless eyes, was what she was, indeed, thinking.

"And you, Mrs. O'Neill," he said, his face sardonic, "would you favor me with more about yourself?"

She looked at him uncertainly. How quickly his moods seemed to change. Like quicksilver. She ducked her head, not wanting to confront those probing eyes with her own guilty ones. "There's nothing to tell," she said sullenly, as he leaned over, inspected her empty goblet and refilled it.

"Well," he said with the old laughter, "I would very much like to know how you can consume so much wine without becoming unconscious."

"Well, you're not," she retorted, again failing to meet his eyes.

"Ah, but I expect I've had more experience than you," he drawled, not wanting to admit that his plant would probably be quite debilitated itself tomorrow.

"It's a god-given talent," Samara answered loftily, with sudden inspiration. She was totally disconcerted when he leaned back and laughed. It was, she thought grudgingly, a very lusty, attractive laugh.

"More like the devil," he finally managed, his sexy chuckle sending goose bumps down her spine.

"*You* should know," she retaliated, her confusion becoming outrage. Would he never take her seriously?

"If you won't tell me that," he continued as if he hadn't heard her, "tell me where your name came from. I've never heard it before."

Samara gulped. "It's a family name."

"And you're an orphan? No brothers or sisters?"

"No," she said defiantly. He saw the flicker in her eye and knew she was lying. He just didn't know why.

And then he saw it. A little red trickle running from his abandoned boot, going first in one direction, then another with each gentle lift of the ship.

"More wine?" he asked softly, wondering just how much of his very fine wine had been diverted this night. He coughed to hide the laughter that was threatening to erupt again. He pondered briefly, with no little humor, whether either his boots or plant would survive this night. The little minx! She was obviously far more complex than he had first thought. But what had she planned? There was only one way to find out.

In the course of the next half hour he let his mouth slacken, his eyes dull and his words slur. With each new sign of debility, her eyes brightened. Finally, he let his head drop.

He somehow kept his eyes closed as he heard her move around the cabin, opening the trunk, looking in corners. He heard a sigh of satisfaction as she found something, then listened to more exploration. A hand reached in one of his pockets, extracted what he knew were keys to the locks in the ship. It was all he could do to keep still, but he wanted to know exactly how far she would go. He could feel, rather than hear, as she hesitated above him, then felt a whisper of air as something was raised. His hand reached out and grabbed her descending wrist as a bottle went skidding across the floor.

Instantly, he was up and out of the chair, his hand still clasping hers like an iron band. He twisted it towards him, making her face him.

"H-h-h-how?" she stuttered as she looked at the anger on his face. Gone was the quiet amusement and the lazy manner. His eyes were like green flames and his mouth was curved in a tight, cruel smile. Samara shriveled, knowing very real fear.

"Tell me," he said in dulcet tones that were more menacing than a roar, "were you planning to kill me or just do substantial injury?"

Samara tried to step back, to tear her gray eyes from his glazing ones, but it was as if she were hypnotized.

"Nei-nei-nei..." she said, hating herself for showing her fear so plainly. "I...I...I just...just wanted...wanted you...you to sleep..."

"Sleep, my sweet?" came his hatefully smooth voice, "with a full bottle of wine? Do you truly not know how easy it is to crack a man's skull?" His hand tightened on her. "Because if you don't, you're a very dangerous child."

Her eyes went wide as she considered his words. She had truly never wanted to do any real harm. And then his last words registered. "Dangerous child." Her tempestuous temper rose, reducing, a degree at a time, her fear.

"I wish I had," she said nastily. "And I'm not a child."

"No...?" His tone told her she had just made a very grave error. "I think I'll find out..."

Before she could say anything more, his mouth was pressed against hers. This time there was no gentleness, only a cruel, punishing savagery. He forced her lips open, and his tongue darted in like Eve's serpent—malevolent but tempting, beguiling while traitorous. To her horror, she couldn't stop her body's response, even as she knew it was punishment, not pleasure, he intended. Every physical part of her rebelled against her mental anguish. All she knew was how much she wanted him to continue, to bring her body alive.

His mouth softened as he felt her surrender, and his body throbbed with need. His hand released her wrist and encircled her slim waist, pulling her closer. He could feel the tremors of her body, as it arched towards him, and the ache deep in his loins. And then he remembered her treachery.

"You disappoint me, Madam," he said now, with icy contempt. "First you try to murder me, apparently for the sake of your husband; then you're wont to betray *him*. Perhaps my little entertainment tomorrow will not be as effective as I'd hoped."

The cold disdain in his voice and expression cut her to the quick. From his point of view, she supposed she deserved it. He thought her married, and now she was responding to him like any courtesan. God in heaven, what was happening to her? As his words sunk in, her face went white.

"What entertainment?" she was barely able to whisper.

His voice was silky again, but his piercing, burning eyes impaled her, and his body was taut with anger and frustration. She couldn't stop the shivers that shook her.

"I shall let you wonder about it tonight," he said. "What price attempted murder? What price mutiny?"

Samara was stricken by the implications of each deliberately uspoken word. She had seen many sides of him in the past twelve hours—some of them warm, even boyish—but this cold, hard stranger staring at her with such contempt froze her to the very core.

"I will take you back to your cabin, Madam," he said now, disregarding the terror in her eyes. His sympathies, at the moment, lay not with her. Those wonderful eyes—those large, pleading, vulnerable eyes—merely covered a treacherous heart. He had been a fool to ever think otherwise. He felt a momentary regret for Captain O'Neill. It replaced the envy that had, sometime during the day, crept upon him.

His hand took Samara's arm with the same strength as earlier but with new cruelty. He didn't care overmuch if he hurt her. For the first time in his life, he really wanted to strike a woman. He knew, if he analyzed his feelings, that it was because none had ever touched him in this way before, and the disappointment at her perfidy was deep and wounding. He half pulled, half dragged her down the corridor and into her room. He did not leave her there, as she had silently pleaded, but entered, filling her full of new apprehension. But he paid no attention to her as his eyes searched the neat cabin, apparently looking for weapons. His hands released hers, but she dared not move, as he roughly searched his first mate's trunk.

When totally satisfied, he turned to her, his brilliant eyes now hooded. "You *will* replace those items in the trunk . . . neatly," he said, his voice as hard as agates and as unyielding. "You will do, from now on, exactly as you are told." Then he added meanly, as if the word were an insult, "Madam . . . do you understand me?"

Samara could merely nod her head as she tried to rein in the tears that were gathering in her eyes. She could bear almost anything but this horrible, icy mockery. She could withstand his anger, his rage, but not this complete repugnance. Why did she care? Why did she care anything about what this . . . this pirate thought of her? But deep inside, she did. Desperately. Could she explain to him that Brendan was not really her husband? That she was not just another unfaithful wife—as he apparently believed. But there was no chance for words as the door slammed closed behind him, and she heard the lock.

* * *

Reese Hampton did not go to his cabin but went up on deck, pacing restlessly as he tried to cool his rage. The extent of his anger surprised him.

It was deep night, and millions of sparkling gems made the sky a backdrop of infinite beauty...and apparent peace. But there was no peace in him. What was it about the little she-wolf that had worked its way into his self-contained world. Her fiery spirit had amused and warmed him; her apparent vulnerability had touched him, her unusual dark beauty had stirred him, and her reluctant but very real passion had aroused him to near madness. He wanted her...more than he had ever wanted a woman before. Even now. Even knowing she was not above betrayal. Even knowing that those innocent eyes hid a not-so-innocent heart.

Tomorrow. He would find out more tomorrow. He was not particularly proud of what he was planning, but Samara O'Neill needed a lesson. And he was going to give it to her.

Chapter Five

It was probably the most wretched night in Bren's life. His arm felt as if some demon were sticking red-hot needles in it, and his head ached from the blow. His physical surroundings didn't help. He shared a small room with five of his officers, and they each had just enough space to stretch out. There was no bedding, no chairs...only a slop bucket that cast a fetid odor in the enclosed space. The only light came through a grilled window where two guards stood watch. It had been closed for a time when the rest of the *Samara*'s crew had been marched to another place in the hold for the night. They were then, for those moments, encased in total darkness.

But the physical discomfort was slight compared to Bren's mental agony. He had never known failure before; it was an unacceptable word to the O'Neills. Now he had lost his ship and failed to protect Samara and his men. He had neglected to prepare his crew for what had befallen them. In his blind arrogance, he accused himself, he had thought his ship swift enough, himself clever enough, to elude the British.

At least he and his officers had been spared the additional discomfort and humiliation of chains. He had noticed, in the dim light of the cell, the rings imbedded in the walls. In some contradictory twist of his mind, he partly resented the fact they hadn't been used. Did he seem so weak, so powerless to the Englishman? The thought galled him as he recalled Hampton's insolent stance and arrogant words.

And Samara. Just the thought of his sister in Hampton's not-so-gentle clutches made his hands tighten into clenched fists. He had not missed the man's deliberately provocative words, and he grew sick with worry. Samara, spoiled and protected, was no match for a man Brendan instinctively recognized as very dangerous—and obviously used to getting his own way. The problem, he knew, was that Samara would think she could handle him—as she had so many unwanted suitors—and go blithely running into trouble. Her impulsiveness had frequently amused her family, and there had been a private conspiracy to protect her, without her knowing it, from her own follies. Now Samara was on her own, and the thought tormented him.

They had been amply fed. Brendan had been surprised at both the quantity and quality of the stew given them, but he could eat nothing, the nausea from the wounds and the worry about Samara had stolen his appetite. He had passed his own bowl to the other captives. He knew he should eat to regain his strength, but the very thought of food brought bile rising up inside him and he could not force himself. Instead, he spent the endless hours thinking of ways to even the score with Captain Hampton.

He knew of the passage of time only by the changing of the guards and the temporary closing once more of their tiny window, again, he supposed, as his crew was marched out to work. Hate—an emotion usually foreign to him—swirled inside him. His helplessness fueled its reckless course until he was consumed by it.

When the door opened, he knew no caution, only the need to release the fury inside him. Disregarding the pain in his arm, he threw himself at one of the guards and was hardly aware of the sound of the door slamming shut as he was pulled out quickly, leaving the rest of his officers pounding on the door. He threw himself at one, then another, using his head, his feet, his left arm. And then with agonizing pain, his arms were seized and his hands quickly tied in front of him. He was pushed and pulled down the passageway to a narrow stair, then partly dragged, partly carried, up to the quarterdeck.

He blinked when he reached the top, his eyes barely tolerating the harsh glare of the sun after so many hours in the darkness. He took his time to accustom them to the light, trying to regain some control. Slowly they found Hampton. His enemy's face was inscrutable, his eyes hooded. One hand was on Samara's shoulder, holding her there next to him. Brendan saw Samara's eyes widen as she saw the fresh blood on his shirt, the new bruises, the stubble on his unwashed face. He saw her try to step forward toward him, a move firmly prevented by a tightening of Hampton's hand. He saw the fear and the dis-

tress in her face, and he felt his hate expand. He tried to move
forward, but his arms were firmly held.

Hampton finally spoke, his voice cold and impersonal. "I
told you your wife was hostage to your behavior. She apparently didn't understand that you were also hostage to hers." His
hand tightened on Samara's arm as he felt her struggle, and he
knew she sensed what was coming.

"She tried, rather unsuccessfully I might add, to kill me last
night," Reese continued in the same cool, almost unconcerned tone. "Since I do not feel disposed—at the moment—to
punish her, you will take her place."

"No," Samara screamed, trying to jerk away from the Englishman.

Reese completely disregarded her protest and her frantic
movements. "Lash him to the mast," he directed the two men
holding Brendan. "I think twenty strokes will be sufficient."

Bren closed his eyes but made no struggle as he was led to the
mast. His hands were untied, his blood-stained shirt stripped
from him, and his wrists retied, this time around the mast so he
was hugging it. Neither he, nor the nearly hysterical Samara,
saw Reese's crew look at each other with bewilderment. In all
their years with him, Captain Hampton had never permitted,
much less ordered, physical punishment. Offenses were always
met with dismissal from the crew or, in less serious cases, several days in the hold. Since the *Unicorn* was both a profitable
and happy ship, threat of banishment was usually sufficient.

Reese, for his part, was ready to end the little charade. He
had made his point; he would inform Samara that the out-
come would be much different if she persisted in mischief. He
was about to order O'Neill released when she tore away from
him and ran to O'Neill, throwing her arms around him.

"No," she said, this time her voice strong and determined.
"I did it . . . not Brendan. If anyone is to be punished it should
be me. I'm only sorry," she added with defiance, "that I didn't
kill you."

The crew's eyes went from one figure to the other. The actions of their captain were incomprehensible. And they couldn't
help but admire the girl's courage and spunk.

"Get her out of here." O'Neill's words broke the long, tense
silence. "She's my wife. I am responsible. Just get her away
from here."

Samara's arms went tighter around him. There was no
childishness about her now. She looked back at Reese, her eyes

pleading. "I'll do anything," she said quietly, and Reese knew she meant it. So did Brendan.

Brendan struggled against his bonds, and blood flowed anew from his wounded arm. "No," he shouted. "Damn you, Hampton, get her out of here and get on with it."

Reese had never felt quite so small. Self-disgust swept over him in waves. He had meant to teach a lesson and instead had received one, one in honor and self-sacrifice and love. So she did love him. An unexpected pain assaulted him. He whirled around.

"Cut him down," he said curtly. "Take him to the doctor, then to my cabin."

"You," he said to the first mate, whose mouth was agape with astonishment over the proceedings, "take Mrs. O'Neill back to her cabin." Without any additional words, he disappeared, leaving his crew staring at each other in disbelief.

Leaning back in his comfortably curved chair, his legs stretched out lazily in front of him, Reese nursed his brandy as he waited for O'Neill. His indolent pose belied the turmoil inside him. He, like Samara, had drunk more than he had intended the previous night and he felt terrible. But at the moment he needed the brandy, to erase the sorry scene topside from his mind. He was disgusted to find it did little to calm his disquiet. His head sank into the palm of his right hand as every second was repeated, over and over again. He had never mistreated a prisoner before, particularly a wounded one, and he felt shame wash over him. He had made a total fool of himself, and why? Another man's wife. His pride had been wounded last night, but it was nothing compared to what he had done to himself this morning. The devil take the little she-cat.

Damn if she hadn't been glorious this morning. The contempt he had felt last night disappeared in admiration—a feeling that did nothing to ease an unusual ache in his heart. He knew now that she had not been betraying her husband by the kiss but, instead, seeking a way to help O'Neill. He must have imagined her response to him, or else she was a consummate actress. Either way, he would keep his distance.

A knock on the door broke his reverie, and without moving from his chair he bade entry. O'Neill stepped inside, flanked by two of Reese's burly crewmen. Reese's eyes quickly flickered over his prisoner. Yancy had found the man a shirt, but the sleeve couldn't hide the bulky bandage, and the arm was now held stiffly against his chest by a sling. His eyes glittered hatred, and Reese didn't blame him one bit.

"Beggin' yer pardon, sir," one of the men said. "Mister Yancy said to tell you if yer determined to kill this gent, do it all at once 'stead of pieces. Save 'im trouble."

"Tell Yancy to mind his own damn business lest he taste the cat himself," Reese said, a softening around his eyes belying the severity of the words. "Leave us alone."

"Want we should wait outside, sir?" one of the men said.

"No," Reese said softly, and watched O'Neill's body tense with anticipation.

The two men eyed each other warily as the door closed behind the crewmen. Reese had earlier poured a second glass of brandy and placed it on the large round table. Now he shoved a chair forward with his boot and nodded towards it. "Sit down, O'Neill."

It was as if Brendan had not heard him. He continued to stand, swaying a little. He had lost a lot of blood and eaten nothing in the past forty-eight hours. He only hoped he would not disgrace himself by falling. He would show no weakness before this man he now considered a hated enemy.

Reese slowly unwound himself from the chair and stood up, his eyes never leaving O'Neill's. The two men took each other's measure, neither finding a deficiency. They dueled silently several moments without words.

Reese was the first to speak and he did so quietly. An almost imperceptible flexing of a cheek muscle told Brendan how much it cost the man.

"I've never apologized to a man before in my life. I've never thought I needed to," he said slowly. "I wanted to teach your wife a lesson this morning.... I let it go much too far. I'm sorry."

Brendan was stunned. Nothing in the past hours had made this side of Hampton plausible.

His eyebrows arched in question and his hands clenched. "My . . . wife. She hasn't been harmed?"

A flash of temper crossed Hampton's face. "I told you I do not make war on women. She is unharmed. More so than she would have me!"

"You also told me you would do nothing...that she did not want," Brendan said, wanting to believe this new dimension of

Hampton but not quite ready to do so. "There was a certain...shall we say...implication in those words."

"Are you so unsure of your own wife?" Reese taunted, his anger growing.

"She's very young," Brendan answered, his eyes intent on Hampton's face, "and very vulnerable."

"Not as vulnerable, I think, as she would have you believe," Reese said ruefully.

The two men's eyes met again, this time with a new but still wary understanding.

"Samara's very headstrong," Brendan said unnecessarily.

"And very loyal," Reese said. "Recklessly so." This time, there was a warning in the quiet voice.

Bren's legs started to fold, and he put his hands on the table to steady himself.

"I don't usually give orders twice," Reese said. "Sit down."

This time, Brendan obeyed. He was forming a reluctant admiration for the man across from him.

"The brandy might help," Reese offered, noting O'Neill's clenched lips as he fought against the pain and weakness.

Bren ignored his suggestion. "What do you want from me?"

Reese shrugged at the man's renewed hostility, choosing to ignore it. "I have an offer."

Brendan's eyes framed the question.

"I'll give you and your officers free run of the ship...if you promise to give me no trouble."

"And my crew?"

"They will still work during the day...at night they can sleep where they wish."

Brendan hesitated but not for long. There was no way he and his crew could even attempt to retake the *Samara*. They were outnumbered, they had no weapons, they were, most of them, no match for Hampton's experienced warriors. And there was Samara. Free, he would be able to watch over her and protect her.

He nodded curtly.

"You understand you will also be responsible for your crew...and your wife?"

Bren nodded again, his lips clenched. God, he hated surrender. But he saw no other alternative, not with Samara aboard.

Reese threw him a key. "Your wife...she's in the next cabin. You can share it with her." He was careful that his tone was indifferent. It hid the jealousy that was battling his inherent sense of fairness.

Brendan heard the dismissal in Hampton's voice. He rose painfully and made his way to the door. He turned, searching Hampton's face for some clue as to the happenings of the past hour. Hampton remained seated, still looking relaxed with his legs stretched out, the brandy in his hand, his face void of any emotion, his green-blue eyes dark and hooded. He seemed not to notice the other man's hesitancy. Brendan opened the door, went through the opening and closed it behind him. He heard the sound of glass shattering behind him and surmised that his glass of brandy had shifted with the movement of the ship and broken. He gave it no more thought.

Reese continued to sit, the stem of the glass still between his fingers. The upper part had broken with the unconscious pressure of his fingers. Some of its splinters sprayed his hand, giving rise to little streams of blood. They went unnoticed as he stared, unseeing, at the closed door.

The door to Samara's cabin was locked. Brendan tried the key, and the door swung open. Samara was crouched in the corner of the small bed, her face wary and fearful as he entered. It relaxed only slightly as she saw him.

"It seems," he said slowly, "that we, as an old married couple, are to share this cabin." There was an unmistakable censure in his voice that Samara had not heard before.

For one of the few times in her life, Samara had no words. Everything she had done since leaving Glen Woods had ended in complete disaster. Her large eyes reflected regret too deep to utter. A simple "I'm sorry" wasn't, she knew, sufficient. She had wanted to die this morning when she thought herself the cause of Bren's torment. She had been wrong, so wrong, when she had run away, when she had hidden in Bren's ship, when she had so easily let Captain Hampton think she was Bren's wife, when she had been foolish enough to believe she could outwit the *Unicorn*'s captain. In the past few hours, she had reviewed all her actions and found them sorely lacking in both maturity and common sense. She had acted like a child and been treated like a child. It was a very bitter realization.

Even more vexing were the recurring images of Captain Hampton that continued to plague her. Eyes, which alternately went from green fire to green ice, inserted themselves into every thought—as did the searing heat each time she remembered his touch. His practiced touch, she reminded herself. He knew exactly what he was doing. She had been completely helpless under his hands; those damnable, knowing, tormenting hands. His contempt last night had been extremely painful, but his careless cruelty this morning had been worse. She had sat huddled in this spot since, locked within—wondering, fearing, hating. And something else. Something she wouldn't admit.

Now she looked at her brother with an uncertain face. "What happened?" she whispered.

"What happened?" Brendan repeated. "I'm not completely sure myself. It seems Captain Hampton has a certain reluctant honor."

"Honor? That villain! That pirate! That blackguard! That . . ." She stopped when she saw her brother's raised eyebrow.

"I think the lady doth protest too much," he said evenly, as anger clouded his eyes. Perhaps he had been wrong to trust Hampton. He strode over to his sister and took her chin in his hand, forcing her to look up at him. "Did anything happen between you and Hampton?"

"No," she said fiercely, conveniently ignoring the fiery kiss of the previous night. "I hate him."

He regarded her levelly for several minutes, seeking the truth. Her eyes seemed to blaze with new passion, but it could well have been hate, after this morning. The scene on deck had not been pleasant. Nor, he knew, would Hampton have released him if the man had intentions towards a woman he believed to be his wife. It would have been very easy to keep him locked up while he tried to seduce Samara. Another telling factor was the fact that Hampton apparently accepted the marriage. He obviously had no suspicion that Samara was a virgin.

Brendan released her chin. "You've stirred a devil's pot, my lovely sister, and now we're trapped in it. How in the hell are we both going to sleep in here?"

She looked at him miserably. "I'll sleep on the floor," she offered.

"You would, too, wouldn't you?" he said, his eyes merry again, more like the old Bren. "I really don't think that's necessary. But I will take the bed right now, if you don't mind. I've had damned little sleep in the past four days . . . and my arm hurts like Hades."

Samara scooted from the bed and took the chair. "Did he . . . did he say anything about me?"

Once more, Bren looked at her quizzically. There was more than a little interest in the question. "Only," he said slowly, "that I'm responsible for your conduct. He was, I think, rather annoyed with you. What *did* you do?"

"I tried to get him drunk," she admitted in a small voice, "and then tried to hit him over the head with a wine bottle."

Bren put a hand over his face, trying to hide the smile. He dared not give even tacit approval, for fear of what she might do next.

"And what, dear sister, do you know about getting a man drunk?"

"I listen," Samara said righteously. "Remember that time . . . ?"

"No . . . I don't think I want to," he said. "Didn't you think you might get drunk at the same time?"

"I didn't drink very much," Samara said smugly. "I hid it."

"Where?" Bren asked, now quite fearful of the answer.

"In his boot" came the self-satisfied reply.

Bren sputtered, then coughed, failing, this time, to contain his laughter. He was becoming more and more surprised that Hampton hadn't carried out his threat this morning. The man was rapidly rising in his estimation.

"Aren't you ever afraid of tweaking the tiger's nose?" he asked finally.

"I was this morning," she answered honestly, the mischief gone from her voice.

"Good," he answered quietly, "because I think Captain Hampton is not a man to play with. I want your word that you will behave. No more rescue missions, no more tempting fate. Do you promise?"

She nodded, still remembering the horror of this morning. She had seen a very cold, very ruthless side of the Englishman and even she did not wish to provoke it again. She would stay away from him. If only her thoughts, too, could stay distant from the Englishman's restless, tawny perfection.

Samara's good intentions lasted approximately three hours. Some food arrived: bread, cheese, salt beef. Bren wolfed most of it down, his hunger finally realized and his concern for

Samara somewhat quieted. He then took off his boots and, within minutes, was asleep.

Samara sat in the chair, watching him. She couldn't remember seeing a man asleep before. Privacy was a much valued quality in the O'Neill house and her brothers' rooms had been off-limits. She would sometimes sneak in, but they had always been awake. She studied Bren, amazed at how much younger he looked now that the lines of responsibility were erased from his face. His light blond hair, several shades lighter than Captain Hampton's, curled around an unguarded face, and she thought how much she loved him, how good and caring he had always been toward her. Even now when she had caused so much trouble.

She would be ever so good now. She would do whatever he said; would, in fact, be the model young wife. *Wife.* How strange a word. It made her think again of Captain Hampton.

Did he look this boyish when he slept? Did his hair curl in the same mussed way? Did sleep make him look more approachable, wiping away that half-amused, half-sardonic expression he usually wore?

I hate him, she told herself. *He's cruel and he's hateful. A reluctant honor, indeed.* The man had no honor. She couldn't understand why Bren had said such a thing, not after what happened this morning. There had even been a note of...liking? Never. Bren would never succumb to the man's insidious charm. He was their country's enemy; he had killed some of Bren's crew; he had stolen Bren's pride, the *Samara*. He had...he had taunted her, and laughed at her and taken liberties. That she might have assisted in those liberties, she refused to acknowledge.

Samara straightened in the chair, wishing the cabin were a little larger. One could stare at a sleeping brother only so long, even one as wonderful as Bren. She looked at the first mate's trunk. Perhaps he would have a book at the bottom. She had not seen one last night when she had replaced the items so roughly searched by Captain Hampton. Perhaps she had missed something. She had been shaken; shaken and terrified and perhaps even a little tipsy.

But there was nothing there. She wished momentarily for her sewing basket, but the Lord only knew where that was now. Was it only five days ago when she thought her life dull? Did she wish it returned to that stationary condition? Never to have lived through a battle? Never to have seen Captain Reese

Hampton? Never to feel the all consuming fire that rushed through her with only a glance . . . not to mention his touch?

She bit the knuckles on her hand, a most unbecoming and unladylike habit, she knew. But she had to find something to take her mind from the Englishman. Or she would go quite mad. This she knew.

A book. There were many in the captain's cabin, and he would probably be back on the top deck now. She had heard him pass earlier, and he would never miss one wee book.

Her good intentions sublimated by need, Samara crept across the cabin floor and slowly, very quietly, opened the door and peered out. There was no one in the corridor. She hesitated a moment, then taking a deep breath rushed for the captain's cabin, opening and closing the door quickly. She stood just inside for a moment, remembering Reese's almost gentle expression as he had sat there talking of his brother, remembering the sensuous twist of his mouth as he had mocked himself. She shook her head to rid it of the images. A book, she reminded herself. She went to the shelf, her eyes quickly running over the titles again before selecting Shakespeare's *Macbeth*.

So absorbed was she in her search she didn't hear the door open, nor the captain's almost soundless approach. "You *are* a bloodthirsty little thing, aren't you? I thought it was just me who spawned your violence . . . or do you like mayhem in general? Or," the low, droll voice paused, "are you looking for a different method to dispose of me? Perhaps considering giving up on wine bottles? I would be appreciative since my supply went down considerably last night."

Samara whirled at the sound of his accursed drawl, her suddenly lifeless fingers dropping the volume.

Reese Hampton was leaning against the door, making it impossible for her to flee. He looked incredibly masculine and untamed, his hair mussed from the wind, his tight-fitting fawn breeches hugging his legs, and his feet bare once more. Samara stared at them. She had never thought feet beautiful, but his were. Like everything else, damn him.

He caught her look. "You must forgive my attire, little cat, but during the night my boots were, somehow, filled with wine. Since I don't believe in miracles, I can only assume some human hand erred. I don't know which loss I regret more . . . the boots or the wine."

His voice was silky now, taunting her, challenging her.

"I'm...sorry," she said, not really sorry at all as she glanced at his icy eyes and twisted smile.

"Exactly what are you sorry about?" he asked, the sarcasm in his voice deepening. "My wine, my boots, or my failure to be your willing victim?"

She could merely stare at him as if she were a trapped mouse. "I meant you no real harm," she said slowly. "I just wanted time to..."

"Time to rescue your love," he jeered, surprised by the depth of his anger. "So now what are you doing here? Where's O'Neill? You have what you want."

"Not the *Samara*," she couldn't help blurting out.

"Not only bloodthirsty but greedy," he said. "Did your husband send you here to ply your wiles? Because if he did, it's useless. Pretty as you are, my love, I wouldn't pay that high a price for you."

Stung and humiliated beyond reason, Samara attacked him. He was ready for her hand but not for her foot which aimed recklessly forward and made contact with his shin. He winced and the pure unexpectedness of it made him drop her hand. It went straight for his face and, with no little satisfaction, she heard a resounding smack.

A long stream of oaths came tumbling from his mouth and he sought to control her again. Hands like steel bands encircled her, and she was being lifted and carried, then set down, her stomach over a heavily muscled thigh.

"It's time," he said, through gritted teeth, "that you learn you can't keep slapping people with impunity."

Samara felt her skirt being smoothed down around her, then felt the slap even through the garment. She struggled for freedom, but his hand was unyielding as the other came down soundly. Once, twice, three times. Never had anyone touched her in anger, and she felt an overwhelming humiliation that he was doing this to her. Even in her dismay, however, some part of her recognized that he was husbanding his anger. There was some hurt, but not much with the layers of clothing protecting her; it was mostly the ignominy of the situation, and she knew that was exactly what he intended. It did nothing to endear him to her.

When he was finally through, he smoothed down her dress and set her upright—almost gently. His finger traced a tear that had escaped her eye, and when she looked up at him, she saw something like wistfulness in his eyes. It was gone so quickly she thought she must have imagined it. They were cloaked again . . . and as cold as the Atlantic.

"I've never raised my hand to a woman before," he said finally. "But, damn it, you would provoke a saint."

At her incredulous look, he flashed the quicksilver smile that was so devastating. "Not, of course, that I'm claiming sainthood . . . although you may well drive me to it."

"More like Satan's apprentice," she muttered, just loud enough for him to hear.

He laughed, his eyes warming. She looked so hopelessly lovely with her eyes wide and glazed silver by the tears she was so determinedly holding back. He wanted to kiss her and tell her all was well. He wanted to hold her and protect her from everything. But she was someone else's, and he would not poach, no matter how much he wanted her . . . and he was astonished at how much that was. In some peculiar way, the situation had, this morning, become a matter of honor.

His smile disappeared. "You may take the book," he said finally. "But the next time you will ask, and Davey will fetch what you need. Is that understood?"

Again, his rapid change of mood confused her. Samara nodded, anger and hurt and wanting and hating all mixed up. She couldn't bear to see him looking at her so coldly, not realizing that he did so to protect himself. Leaning over, she picked up the book which earlier had fallen from her nerveless hands, and, clutching it as if her life depended on its safety, she fled the cabin.

Chapter Six

Time crept painfully along for Samara. Her brother's ship had apparently been patched sufficiently to sail slowly to Bermuda, and crews on both ships were preparing to get underway.

Bren had still been sleeping when she, and her sore backside, returned to the cabin. She was unreasonably resentful that he had slept so peacefully through her ordeal. But when he woke, at Hampton's summons, she couldn't bring herself to tell him of her misadventure. She was, instead, the picture of innocence, sitting where a porthole directed a stream of light, reading intently or at least appearing to read intently. He had not asked, thank the heavens, the source of the book. The O'Neills all had an uncanny ability to find books no matter where they were.

He left the cabin almost immediately to talk with his officers, who had already been freed from the hold, and discuss the terms of their parole. He was then taken to the *Samara*, where he relayed a similar message. An hour later, he returned to the *Unicorn* and watched silently as the *Samara*'s repaired sails were unleashed and his ship rode the sea under the command of another.

Reese Hampton, understanding only too well, allowed the American his privacy. His initial respect for O'Neill, which had started with the fierce and very competent battle, had grown steadily in the past two days, peaking this morning on the quarterdeck. The subsequent interview in his cabin had strengthened that opinion. O'Neill had done what he had to do, and done it with dignity... without harsh words or accusations or meaningless threats. It took courage to do so, as much as it took to fight, perhaps even more. It was a quality Hampton admired above all else, and, he supposed, the reason he had so reluctantly decided to leave Mrs. O'Neill alone. He would have to suppress that rush of blood that flowed so swiftly when he saw her, tame his fascination with her dauntless and unquenchable spirit. Much to his surprise, he found himself wondering if he would, this minute, exchange places with O'Neill. That he would even consider such a trade horrified him. A ship for a woman! His freedom for a pretty face! Yet he couldn't drive Samara's face from his thoughts, and he knew he was smiling when he recalled her various expressions—from mischief to cunning to outrage.

He finally joined O'Neill and stood silently beside him, a curious comradeship binding them.

"I'll miss her," O'Neill said quietly, without self-pity.

Reese knew he meant the ship. "She's a beauty," he acknowledged.

"I designed her," Brendan replied, with no little pride. "Next time," he added ruefully, as he looked over Hampton's *Unicorn,* "I'll add more sail."

"But then you would need more depth and you wouldn't be able to hide in those rivers and shallow waters so easily."

Brendan turned to Hampton with an appraising look. "And I suppose you'll be lurking just outside."

"Probably," Hampton said easily. "I admire your ships."

"I can see that," Brendan replied, noting the similarities between his ship and the *Unicorn.* The *Unicorn* was larger and able to handle the additional canvas and the heavy guns, but it had the same sleek hull—bare of ornaments—and the same high, raking masts. Because of its size, it would not be able to slip so easily into hidden coves, but it could still tack quickly through narrow waters. It had obviously been carefully designed with privateering as its specific purpose.

"And I suppose *you* designed this ship," Brendan said finally. The two men regarded one another with new esteem, both realizing abruptly and with some dismay, that under other circumstances, they would like each other immensely.

Reese shrugged. "As I said, I admire your ships. I'm afraid I stole many of your countrymen's ideas. You do have a unique feel for shipbuilding." He left O'Neill then, sensing the man's need to be alone.

Samara had come up on deck during the last of the conversation. Still humiliated over the scene in Captain Hampton's cabin, she watched the two men from a distance, afraid that if she approached, Hampton would reveal their latest encounter to her brother. She watched the two men carefully, saw their intent expressions as they talked, saw the camaraderie that flashed across their faces. Resentment bubbled up inside her. How could Bren talk so easily with an enemy? With his captor? With the man who had laughed at her and...beat her? Men! She silently cursed them all. With no little anger, she stomped back to their cabin, slamming the door behind her.

Her rage continued but her restlessness kept pace with it. The tiny cubicle was more than she could stand. A tear formed in her eye and she felt Bren's betrayal acutely.

She was still there, her resentment simmering when Bren entered. His eyebrow arched at her sullen expression. He knew her moods only too well.

"I thought," he said cautiously, "that you might like some fresh air...I'll take you topside if you wish."

Samara looked at him rebelliously. "I *was* up," she said. "You were too busy with that Englishman to notice." She spat out the word Englishman.

Bren regarded her interest curiously. Her reactions seemed surprisingly vehement...even for her. Samara never did, or felt, anything halfway. The morning *had* been very harrowing for her, he realized that, but Hampton had attempted, in his own way, to make amends.

"Strangely enough," he said now, "I can't help but like him."

Samara stared at him in disbelief. "He's a pirate," she insisted. "Papa says they're all pirates."

"Then we have a fair amount of pirates of our own," Bren said reasonably. "We have our own privateers, remember."

"That's different," Samara replied, trying frantically to think why. "Besides, it's the *Samara* he's stealing. How can you just talk to him as if nothing's happened?"

Regret shadowed his face. "It was the chance I took, Samara. I knew the risks. I'm sorry that he found us, that he captured her, that you were with us. But I don't hate him for it."

"Well, *I* do," Samara said furiously. "What about Scotty, what about the others?"

Brendan sat down. How could he explain? How could he tell her each had evaluated the risks and chosen to take them. He mourned Scotty's death; the sailor had been with him for sev-

eral years and had been a good friend. But the war had caused
Scotty's death, just as a storm had caused others. Personal
blame seemed as senseless against one as the other. He gave up.
Samara, particularly in her present mood, would never understand.

"Would you like to go up?" he asked again, ignoring her
question.

Part of her did. The other part flinched from seeing *him*
again. But she would go quite insane if she didn't leave this
cabin. She nodded.

He offered his arm. "We *are* married, you know," he said
with a slight smile, trying to rouse her from her unusually dour
mood. "I suppose we should act like it."

Samara looked at him banefully. She was in no mood to be
teased.

"We could," he tried again, "tell him the truth. Then you
could have the cabin all to yourself once more."

The thought was shattering. Without Bren's presence and
protection there was no telling what the Englishman would do.
Or, more to the point, what *she* might do. Her legs still turned
to melting wax when she looked at the despicable man.

"No," she answered almost frantically, causing Bren to look
at her once more with puzzlement.

It was worse when they reached the main deck. The sun was
beginning to set, and the sky was haloed with what seemed
dozens of shades of coral and pink and orange, each weaving
its own intricate pattern against pillowy clouds. The sea was
darkening with the day, its deep blue catching traces of gold
from a faltering sun. Samara turned to look for Reese Hampton and saw him at the wheel, his body at one with the ship, his
strong hands resting easily on the polished wood. His feet were
still bare and his white shirt, much like the blood-covered one
he had worn the day before, was open to the waist. Golden hair
shone against a sun-darkened chest and muscles flexed as he
easily, oh so easily, turned the giant wheel. A shadow fell across
his face but she didn't need to see his eyes to know they were
glowing, alive with that great energy only he seemed to have.
She shivered as she thought, once more, how like a mythical
creature he was. She had wondered about the name of his ship,
the *Unicorn*, but no longer. It seemed, somehow, fitting.

Just then, he turned and his eyes fastened on her. She had
been right. His eyes blazed with vitality and exuberance and
pride. This was so obviously his domain. The ship moved, un-

der his hands, as if it caressed the ocean, and he stood, braced against the wind, his back framed by a multicolored gem of a sky as her heart fluttered, swelled and became a discordant symphony of warring feelings.

His mouth curved into a smile as he watched her, and she knew he was reading her feelings. Conceited oaf, she denounced him mentally. But nothing, she knew with dismayed certainty, would ever erase that portrait from her mind. He was like the wind—free and unpredictable—and who had ever tamed the wind?

Moments later, he joined them at the railing, having given the ship to Michael Simmons.

"I wondered," he said smoothly to Brendan, "whether you would honor me with your presence at dinner, you and Mrs. O'Neill. Mr. Simmons and the ship's surgeon, Yancy, will also join us."

Samara's foot reached out to kick her brother, but he either didn't understand or decided to ignore it. He bowed slightly, and Samara wanted to hit him. "We accept," he said, disregarding her frantic attempts to gainsay him. He had not looked forward to an evening alone with Samara's foul temper.

"Mrs. O'Neill?" Captain Hampton's eyes were full of humor. Her reluctance was very evident.

"I find myself overly tired," she said, "particularly after the distress of this morning." The stilted words brought even more amusement to his face.

"I'm sorry to hear that, Mrs. O'Neill," he said. "I'll have something brought to your cabin." He turned to Bren. "You'll still join us, I hope."

Bren glanced from Samara's furious face to Hampton's amused one. Something was going on between the two, and he wished he knew what it was. He was suddenly afraid for Samara; there was an unmistakable current between his sister and the English captain. He would use tonight to search out Hampton's intentions.

Some of the cordiality in Bren's voice was gone when he answered affirmatively.

"Good, then," Hampton said. "My cabin boy, Davey, will call for you." He bowed politely to Samara. "And my sympathies for your... your distress." He was gone before Samara could think of a suitable retort.

Instead, she rounded on Bren. "How could you have dinner with that scoundrel?"

"Forgive me," he said gently, "but I thought that's exactly what you did last night."

Samara turned an unbecoming shade of red. She really didn't want to be reminded of last night. Or this afternoon in the blackguard's cabin. She didn't want to be reminded of him at all. "I was just trying to help..."

"Perhaps," he said even more gently, "that's what I am trying to do, too."

Samara looked up at his worried blue eyes. There were new creases in his face, and his lips were uncharacteristically tight.

"I'm sorry," she said penitently. "I keep saying that, don't I. But I am. I'm sorry for worrying you...for this morning...for my terrible temper."

Brendan studied her carefully. She was no longer a child. He had seen the hunger in her eyes when she looked at Hampton, watched her flustered confusion when he neared.

"Watch yourself, little sister," he said. "I think he probably eats little girls like you for breakfast."

So great was her distress that she failed to respond to "little girl," and Bren knew it was worse than he imagined. He was beginning to understand why she had insisted they remain "married." He would make that relationship very clear to Hampton tonight.

His brother had always told Reese that he could, when he wished, charm the stars from the heavens. For some perverse reason, he wished to do so tonight.

The dinner table included four—Reese, Brendan, Yancy and Michael Simmons. The latter two could only exchange amused and intrigued looks as their captain sought to learn everything there was to know about their American prisoner-turned-guest—and his wife.

Fortunately, Samara had during the day briefed Brendan on all she had said to the Englishman, receiving a very pained look when she told him of her sad life as an orphan.

"Mother and Father will be distraught to hear of your unhappy childhood," he said with a lift of an eyebrow. "You, my dear sister, should write some of those silly novels you read."

She gave him a look of utter disdain. "They are very good," she said, "and maybe if you read some you would know what you are missing and finally take a wife."

He grinned at her. "Well, you seem to have arranged that," he said, "even if I can't have some of the more interesting advantages of matrimony..."

So now he could answer Hampton's questions with some confidence. He remained aware, however, that the man was certainly no fool, that the icy blue-green eyes probed every expression, and quick ears heard every nuance in his words. It was disconcerting to Brendan, particularly since he hated to lie and especially to someone he respected, however reluctant that emotion was.

"And where were you taking your cargo?" Reese was asking now. "I understand France is not much more welcoming than my own country."

Such, Brendan knew, was only too true. The only reason the United States declared war on England and not France was England's seizure of American seamen. Both France and England were similarly arrogant in prohibiting and blocking free trade, but the fledgling nation could not fight both at once.

There was no real reason to withhold his destination from Hampton. He had certainly guessed it by now. "There are some in France who don't like her trade policies," he merely said.

Reese's mouth twisted into a slight smile. "Smuggling?"

Brendan shrugged. "Some might call it that. We need markets for our cotton and indigo. The war between England and France has made them slim."

"And what do you bring back?"

"Guns, of course," he replied. His eyes reflecting a certain playful challenge. "Guns and ammunition and cannon."

The two men smiled at each other in perfect understanding as their quiet dinner companions merely shook their heads.

As they finished an excellent meal of freshly caught fish, buttered potatoes and apple tart, the four shared a bottle of brandy.

"I want to thank you," Bren said slowly, suddenly watchful, the brief companionship gone, "for your courtesy to my wife. She told me what she tried to do. I think you've shown great forbearance."

Remembering the scene on the deck this morning, Yancy and Simmons exchanged questioning looks. Neither had thought the Captain showed any forbearance at all and both privately condemned his action, but neither did they know what had prompted the unusual display.

"As you said," Reese replied easily, "she's very young." And very beautiful, he added to himself. "Have you been married long?"

Bren shrugged. "A few months. I'm afraid she hasn't learned obedience yet."

Nor will she ever, both men thought almost simultaneously, their expressions identically wry.

Bren couldn't miss Hampton's deep interest, despite the man's attempt to conceal it. Damn, he thought to himself. Hampton and his sister! What a match that would be! An English lord . . . nearly, according to Samara. A man who was probably as much at ease at court as at the helm of a ship. And his fiery little American sister. He couldn't stop the grin spreading over his face. It could well be a repeat of Shakespeare's *The Taming of the Shrew* with Hampton as imperious Petruchio and Samara a marvelously bedeviling Katharina.

He immediately shook the image from his mind. Samara was much too young, too innocent, too unworldly to be more than a passing fancy for Hampton. Their worlds were diametrically opposed. She was instinctively right in her fear, and he would do his best to protect her. But, by all that was holy, it would have been interesting!

Samara threw the bowl of mush against the wall with all the fury she possessed. Which was, at the moment, considerable.

The bowl had arrived with a note from Captain Hampton. She could almost see his roguish grin as he wrote it.

I am desolated that you are indisposed tonight and unable to join us. I had planned a very special meal. But since you are feeling unwell, I thought this might best serve you and your poor appetite. I wish you a speedy recovery.

Hampton

From the moment she declined his invitation, she regretted her action, but pride forbade changing her mind. Even before her sparse meal arrived, she had sat in the cabin remembering all the wonderful food of the previous night and even more devastating, the force of Reese Hampton's personality. Her mind was filled with his raw magnetism and enchanting moments of boyish charm. She shivered as she relived the angry kiss that ended an evening which had swung so erratically between pleasure and pain.

And then Davey arrived with her dinner, if it could be called that, along with the insolent note which mocked her, and anger overwhelmed desire. He was the most infuriating, condescending, overbearing, egotistical knave she had ever had the misfortune to encounter. The bowl, still full of its unappetizing contents, went against the wall, splashing gray puddles over the floor. How could her brother sup with the man? How could he exchange civil words with him? Damn men. Damn them all. Damn their peculiar sense of honor. She saw no honor in what had happened during the past several days.

Unable to bear the small cabin any longer, she opened the door and climbed the ladder to the open deck. She found a little hidden place and sat, letting the wind ruffle her hair as she stared out to sea. She could see the lights of the *Samara* at a distance, and she felt a quiet sadness at the sight. Bren had treasured the ship as little else; it was something he had created completely on his own—without any assistance from his family. It carried his pride.

Reese Hampton had taken it…and, oh, so easily. As he had taken some inner part of herself, a part that would never be wholly hers again. She knew this as surely as she knew the sun would rise in the morning. He had awakened feelings and sensations she hadn't known existed, a craving for some unknown yet irresistible wonder, an awareness of her own vulnerability. She had never thought of herself as weak, but Captain Hampton made her so. She knew she must stay away from him but realized, just as thoroughly, that she could not. Like a lost child, she looked for a star to wish upon. There were millions from which to choose, all of them brighter than any diamond against a flawless, midnight blue sky. How very lovely it was, she thought. How very lonely. And she did feel lonely in her confusion and doubt and wanting…wanting the impossible, desiring the unobtainable. For Reese Hampton was her enemy, a member of English nobility and, just as bad, a heartless rogue who obviously valued his freedom.

She finally found her star. *Let me forget him,* she whispered. *Take these feelings away.*

The star seemed to wink back at her, but somehow she had the feeling that it was not her spoken plea it heard, but another silent one.

She could feel him before she heard a sound. It was like an approaching storm, when everything seems to come to a stop; even the wind stills and you can almost taste the peril in the atmosphere as the elements prepare their assault. She had always felt helpless before such a rampage; she felt the same now as Captain Hampton approached.

Her hands clenched as she waited for him to speak, sure that he would goad her again. She stiffened, then stood, prepared to renew the battle. But he stood silently, saying nothing, and Samara felt goose bumps climbing their way up and down her arms.

When he finally spoke, after what seemed endless hours, it was done pleasantly. It was one of the few times she had heard him without laughter or anger or mockery, and she thought how warm and deep and pleasurable it was.

"It is beautiful out here tonight," he said simply. "God must smile broadly when he looks upon what he created."

Samara, who had been trying to look at anything but the Englishman, turned around and stared at him. He almost sounded awed. And sincere. But Reese Hampton . . . talking of God as if they were on a familiar basis? She suddenly had a suspicious thought. He was trying to throw her off balance. This was simply a new tactic to disarm her, to amuse himself.

He didn't give her a chance to retort. He could read the disbelief in her eyes. He merely smiled.

"You looked very wistful," he remarked in a half quizzical, half gentle tone.

"I was wishing on a star," she said defensively, not entirely sure what to make of him at the moment. She halfway thought she would like the old teasing Englishman back; at least then she would have some defenses. She had few against him at any time, and even fewer at the moment. She wanted, more than anything on earth, to lean up against him and feel his lips on hers.

Reese thought he had never seen such an exquisitely enchanting creature. Moonlight danced against her long black curls, accenting the red sparks that shone like fire in its glow. Her gray eyes, at first defiant, now puzzled, seemed to reflect the infinity of the night as tiny silver lights illuminated their depths. Her lips were slightly parted, and her tongue unconsciously had moistened them as she stood regarding him with a wondering face.

His heart thumped in a most unusual way and his hands clenched into tight knots of want and frustration. His right hand finally eased and, almost of its own accord, wandered up to touch a dark curl, and he marveled at the softness of it, at the sweet clean smell that intoxicated him. It was as if she was bewitching him...this child-woman of the night...this lovely siren who was someone else's wife. Which was she? Innocent or temptress? At the moment, he didn't care as his head bent, almost unwillingly, towards her lips, unable to break the spell that was drawing him, inescapably, inevitably to her.

Samara was caught in the same magic. The moon glow that touched her embraced Reese, seeming to caress him, showering him with glistening pieces of radiant light. More than ever, he seemed to come from a distant world, some mythical kingdom that she longed to enter. Any resistance she tried frantically to summon melted under his smoldering eyes. She forgot everything else, everything but his approaching lips as she offered hers up for the taking.

Their mouths met, melding together as if destined, his lips wanting, hers needing. Samara felt herself whirling and spinning in a fantasy beyond any commonplace dreams. Every sense was alive, singing with joy, crying for more. Her hands crept up, around his neck, and played with the tawny locks of his hair as her mouth opened and she sought an even greater taste of him. She felt his tongue tease and beguile until she knew she could stand no more of the exquisite pain, the sweet torment that was welling up inside her.

She broke away suddenly, staring at him as if he had stolen an essential part of her. And he had. At that moment, she knew she was lost, that she was his, and would always be his. But with agonizing clarity, she knew it could never be. Their worlds were too far apart, would always be too far apart. With huge, sorrowful eyes, she backed slowly away, then turned and ran.

Reese stayed at the railing, staring at the sea. He didn't know what had just happened. He had felt a moment of complete joy, of rapture, but now there was only emptiness. Heaven and hell. He had never known how close they could be.

When Brendan, fully prepared for a disgruntled Samara, arrived back in his cabin, he found only a broken bowl and splashes of some unappetizing substance all over the floor and walls. He didn't even want to guess what it might be.

A piece of parchment crunched under his boot heal, and he reached down to pick it up, reading it swiftly. He grinned.

He could well imagine Samara's outrage. Reese's impudent note would be like putting a match to tinder. He could see the evidence of the resulting explosion.

Brendan thought about going on deck and searching for his sister, but he hesitated. This day's foul mood of hers had evidently deteriorated into pure fury, and he had no desire to confront her. It would be best, he reasoned, to let her cool off on her own. He did not worry that she would encounter Hampton; he had left the man comfortably ensconced with his first mate and ship's surgeon, and it appeared they would be there for some time.

Brendan knew Samara was badly spoiled. She had come late to her parents' life, the last child, and his mother, he remembered clearly, had had a difficult time in childbirth. After four boys, only their mother believed the fifth child would be the much-wanted daughter. He would never forget that night, never forget his father's tenseness and fear, his mother's screams while he comforted his frightened younger brothers. And then there was joy as each of the boys was allowed a brief glimpse of their new sister. Brendan thought he had never seen anything so small—so small and perfect. She took his finger and squeezed it, and he puzzled over the strength of the tiny being. She had, at the same time, grabbed his heart and had never let it go.

His father and mother both doted on Samara. They loved their sons—each son knew their warmth and affection and, best of all, their recognition and appreciation of them as individuals—but Samara had always been something special to all of them. She had a vitality and mischief and inherent goodness that enchanted them all. She could be contentious and uncommonly stubborn, on occasion, but then so completely thoughtful and sweet that no one could resist her. She was particularly gentle with animals and children and would often beg forgiveness for an erring servant.

All the brothers adored her, teased her, played with her, but Brendan, who was fourteen when she was born, was most often responsible for her. He had admired her spirit, spurred her curiosity, and applauded her independence. And spoiled her. By protecting her, overmuch he now thought, he had made her unaware of the consequences of her often impulsive acts. She had now run into someone who would not tolerate her schemes and who had a will as strong as her own. And she simply did not know how to cope. There should be, he thought, some interesting days ahead! Samara had never known humility. He had the feeling she was going to learn. Perhaps even Hampton might acquire a little. He shook his head at the thought.

Just as he decided to go in search of her, the door opened with a crash, and Samara rushed in, her hair in a tangle, her face white. All his protective urges surfaced again.

"What happened?" he said tightly. "Hampton promised..."

"Nothing," she said, her voice shaking, but she went to him for comfort and he put his arms around her.

"Nothing?" he questioned softly. He could feel her shake.

"What is it like to be in love?" She asked the question fearfully.

He pulled away and stared at her. He couldn't really answer as he had never been there—not like his parents. There had been brief infatuations, but nothing more. He had hoped and waited and wanted, but that all-consuming passion for another human being seemed always to evade him.

"Do you think you're in love with Hampton?" He feared the answer. Despite his momentary fancies that the two would be an interesting match, he questioned whether Hampton could ever be held by one woman.

Her gray eyes were enormous, and tears swam in them, creating little pools of misery. "I...I...don't know...I can't...can't..."

"Did he touch you?" There was anger in Bren's voice.

"He...he...kissed me...I wanted him to...he...knew it."

He swore. Samara was so damned inexperienced.

"Do you want to tell him you're not married to me?" he asked finally.

"No!" The indecision was gone. "I know it can never be." She didn't have to explain the reasons; they hovered silently between them in the air.

Brendan's anger grew. For all Hampton knew, he was trifling with a married lady, with the wife of the man he had just entertained. He had violated his word.

"Go to bed, little sister," he said. "I'll take a walk while you undress."

She merely nodded, for once spiritless. He opened the door, looked back at her drooping shoulders, and quickly strode toward the ladder.

Reese had stayed on deck, hoping that the rising wind would blow away his troubled thoughts. For the first time in his life, he wanted something he couldn't have. And he wanted it desperately.

Samara O'Neill had bewitched him; that could be the only explanation. He had vowed to leave her alone and, in just hours, had violated that vow. He despised himself for that weakness, but he had been unable to restrain himself as she had stood there in the moonlight, an answering desire flickering in her eyes.

Her response had confused him, her flight bewildered him, and he damned himself for a fool. Was she a faithful wife or was she caught in the same inexplicable fire that was consuming him, and too inexperienced to cope? All the signals were mixed and for one of the few times in his life he was totally at a loss. He had always thought marriage a trap. In his class, marriage was usually for convenience: to bind two families, to build a fortune, to consolidate estates or titles. It had been so with his brother. The marriage to Lady Leigh Albarry had been planned when both were children. It had, apparently, turned out much better than most such matches. The most recent time Reese had been at Beddingfield, the two seemed happy enough, and they adored their two children. But Reese had decided long ago that no one would tell him whom to marry. He had doubted, in fact, whether he would marry at all. He had no desire to tie himself to property, home and a demanding wife.

But then Samara intruded into his thoughts once more and he thought how very lovely she was, how challenging. She made him laugh in a peculiarly warm way. She would never be dull, by God. She would lead anyone a merry chase.

Reese heard some steps behind him and turned, only to see a fist come directly at his face. He tried to duck, but he was too late. He went smashing down on the deck.

The blow was not that strong, and Reese knew it had been surprise, rather than strength, that had felled him. O'Neill had used his uninjured left arm.

Reese rubbed his jaw and looked at the American with a wry curve of his lips. He shook his head as several men came rushing up, prepared to seize O'Neill. They dispersed reluctantly at their captain's silent gesture.

He slowly stood up, the same fixed smile on his lips. "I don't think," he said, "I want to meet you when you have two good arms."

Brendan merely continued to glare at him. "You gave your word..."

"So I did," Reese said with a grimace. He could only assume that Samara had told her husband about the kiss, or that Brendan had suspected something from Samara's distress. He loathed himself intensely at the moment. He liked the American, had given him his word and then quite dishonorably violated it. He turned away from Brendan, for once at a loss for words. His fists found the railing and tightened around it. "Your wife will be quite safe," he said finally. "I would suggest, however, that you accompany her when she comes on deck. My men...all of us...have been too long at sea."

Brendan knew the words were another apology, and he relaxed. He felt a strange sense of guilt himself. Samara still wasn't fully aware of her own beauty or charm, and he could well imagine her impact on the Englishman. He also realized that Samara, unwittingly, had probably invited the kiss. She had created this convoluted situation which was now weaving all of them into a tapestry of lies and deceit. He didn't like it one bit and was tempted, here and now, to tell Hampton the truth. But Samara's misery-clouded face appeared in his mind, and he wondered once more if she was ready to face Hampton on different terms. He would wait and watch. He merely nodded curtly and returned to the cabin, leaving Hampton to muse alone.

Chapter Seven

The next few days formed an unhappy pattern for Samara.

Brendan laid down rules in no uncertain terms and for once in her life Samara obeyed without question. She knew she had caused no little trouble to everyone, including herself. She had never been so unhappy, so troubled, so completely unsure of herself.

Among them was that she was not to go wandering about by herself. She was to leave the cabin only in the company of Brendan or one of his officers. The only exception was Yancy.

Yancy had become one of her several friends among the English crew. She had accompanied Brendan to Yancy's small hospital to visit several of his wounded crew members and found a use for herself. Yancy was extremely busy with wounded from both ships and grateful for Samara's offer of help. Like every other plantation wife and daughter, she knew a bit of rudimentary medicine and didn't flinch at the sight of blood or wounds. After discovering this, Yancy allowed her to change bandages, feed those who could not feed themselves or just try to cheer the most critically injured. Although sorely heartsick herself, Samara was able to summon a smile and that, alone, according to Yancy, was invaluable medicine.

As for Yancy, he remained a puzzle. He apparently had no other name, at least none he would admit to, and Samara couldn't discover whether it was his first or last. He was a taciturn man who seldom smiled or gave a compliment. But Samara knew he cared about his charges; with them he was consistently gentle, while often irascible with his captain and even easygoing Michael Simmons. She had liked him instantly and sought his approval. Captain Hampton and his damnably amused gaze often made her feel a willful child; Yancy made her feel a useful person.

Working with him gave her something to do other than think of Reese Hampton. She wondered about the surgeon and tried to pry—to no avail. He would say nothing, absolutely nothing, about himself but instead turn the conversation to her. Since she also had a secret past, the conversations were limited in content. But she knew little escaped his wise eyes, and there was interested speculation when he watched her with either Brendan or Reese or both.

She wasn't entirely convinced that just her presence helped the wounded but she did her best, and with the same stubborn dedication she tackled everything. One particular sailor, a member of Hampton's crew who had lost a leg in the battle, became her particular challenge. She would often sit with him and talk about his sweetheart. She tried to convince him that the loss of his leg wouldn't matter; it wouldn't matter to *her*, not if she loved him. The boy had responded eagerly, wanting to believe but not yet quite able, not when the waves of pain assaulted him, and he could feel the agony in the limb that was no longer there. Yancy explained that such feelings were quite common and often persisted long after removal.

When it happened, Samara would hold the boy's hand and avert her eyes from the tears in his face.

She was still clutching his hand one afternoon when he fell asleep. She didn't want to risk waking him, so she remained by his side, her hand around his, compassion evident in her grieving eyes and the bowed position of her body. She felt a gentle hand on her shoulder, and turned, staring up at magnetic green-blue eyes which held no laughter.

Captain Hampton, almost tenderly, unlocked her hand from the boy's and without a word led her into the corridor and up on the top deck. Once there, he released her and stared out to sea.

When he finally spoke, the voice was soft. "Yancy said you've done much for Rob and the others. Thank you."

"What will he do? How will he live?" Samara's voice was broken, her mind still on Rob's pain.

"He'll have enough money from this trip...and others...to buy a cottage, to live comfortably for the rest of his life."

"Comfortably?"

Hampton's lips tightened. "No . . . I suppose not . . . but I'll do what I can for him."

"Give him back his leg?" she retorted, angry now. "Why do men like war? Why are they so eager to kill . . . and maim . . . and . . . ?" Her voice faltered. It wasn't just Captain Hampton, it was her brothers and her father; they had all been eager for war. She hadn't really understood before; war was something bloodless and distant, something you just talked about. But now there were Scotty and Rob and the other wounded. There was Bren who had come so close to death. She couldn't comprehend why anyone would welcome war or gladly participate in it.

Reese saw the confusion in her eyes, but he had no words. Her devotion to the wounded, particularly to the English sailors whom she claimed to hate, intrigued him. He had stayed away from her, and Yancy's rooms, but his friend had kept him apprised—and with irritating frequency. And then today, as he was passing, he had seen her bowed, unhappy figure and couldn't resist touching her. He didn't know how to comfort her, or even if he should try. That was her husband's privilege.

But she looked so sad, so unlike the vibrant, rebellious Samara that first night aboard the *Unicorn.* They both touched him in different ways. He had known many women, some even lovelier than Samara O'Neill, but none had ever so enchanted him with the spritelike magic he had found at dinner, the compassion she showed toward others and the courage the morning he had threatened to whip O'Neill. She was many different people, and he was fascinated with each one—even when she tried to do him bodily harm. Samara was entirely different from any woman he had ever met: freer in spirit, yet obviously very well educated. She was a mystery, and she had woven some charm around him, one from which he could not seem to extricate himself, no matter how hard he tried. And he *had* tried.

She looked at him now with those splendid eyes, waiting for an answer he couldn't give. How could he explain the exhilaration he felt before and during a battle or the challenge of outmaneuvering an opponent or the way the proximity of death made every moment more exciting and precious? How could he explain that this is what he did best? He belonged to this world as he never had to Beddingfield.

Beddingfield. He had never coveted Beddingfield, but he had coveted his father's attention. It had all gone to Avery, who had been groomed from his youngest years to manage the estate.

And while Avery studied and learned, Reese ran free and wild, often getting into trouble and earning his father's wrath. It was a pattern that had continued when he went to Oxford. Reese had a hunger for knowledge and an equal appetite for women and cards, and he was one of the few who could mix the three successfully. His father died shortly after he completed Oxford, and Avery inherited the title and estate while Reese received a large financial settlement. Perhaps in defiance of his father, Reese had promptly squandered the inheritance—much to Avery's dismay. He wenched and gambled and drank and earned a reputation as one of London's most reckless and charming rakes. He had nearly depleted his funds when he met Capt. Amos Kendrick at a club and the two had become friends. They gambled frequently and one day made a different kind of wager. Amos, an American who had made a fortune from smuggling, wanted to turn to the slightly more respectable profession of privateering. He needed the Hampton influence to obtain letters of marque, and he needed Reese on board ship to legitimatize the venture. So the wager was made: a thousand pounds against Reese's presence aboard the *Maryanne*. Reese lost.

At first chagrined and angry, Reese soon found his real vocation. He was challenged by the sea as by nothing else in his life. Seamanship came as easily as breathing; so, he discovered, did leadership. He had a confidence and magnetism that naturally attracted men. Slowly, other latent qualities started to emerge: among them a sense of fairness and justice that kept men loyal to him. When Amos was killed two years later, he left Reese the ship. In the next ten years, Reese Hampton was a merchant, smuggler and privateer, earning and wasting several fortunes on cards and women. He relished the freedom, and money meant little—until he discovered that Avery and Beddingfield were in financial trouble. From that time, most of his funds went to Beddingfield. When the *Maryanne* was badly damaged in a battle, he designed the *Unicorn* and watched carefully as the ship was built—personally inspecting every piece of lumber that went into her.

His lack of funds did little to discourage feminine interest nor attempts to trap him into marriage. They were traps he easily and often arrogantly avoided, and they only increased his cynicism toward the opposite sex. Still, he heartily enjoyed the company of women and their favors. His taste usually ran to blondes and to a certain sophistication; he was thoroughly

confused, therefore, by his fascination with a dark-haired
hoyden who not only poured wine in his boots but threatened
to do him bodily harm.

His hand went involuntarily to the dark hair blowing beside
him in the wind, and he touched a curl, feeling its softness in his
fingers. The lovely eyes were slightly misted as they searched his
face, the endless shades in them changing as her emotions ran
from anger to wistfulness to sadness. There was always a certain current between them, and he felt it even stronger now.

"Why?" she insisted, in the low musical voice he had grown
to hear even in the silence of his cabin. "Why do you destroy...?"

There were answers, of course, but none he could voice. It
would be like giving part of himself away, and he couldn't do
that, especially to Samara O'Neill who had already stolen
something from him.

Instead, he merely grinned, forcing a gleam into his eyes.
"Because, of course, I'm a rogue and a pirate and I enjoy living well." The words and tone were condescending. "And
now," he added, "I think it's time to take you back to your
husband. I warned him about letting you wander alone. It
seems he doesn't value you overmuch."

Samara's eyes filled with fury. It was always thus. He would
lull her into liking him, and then he would turn sarcastic, once
again making her feel like a child. She hated him.

She was much too angry to let the words go. "He thought me
safe with Yancy," she said through clenched lips. "It was you
who forced me away. Damn you." She turned and stalked
away.

Reese watched Samara go, her back stiff and unyielding. He
knew she was hurt. Why, for God's sake, did she have such a
hold on him? Why did he feel, at this moment, like such a bastard?

It was impossible for Samara to avoid the English captain.
Especially when, for some perverse reason even he didn't understand, Reese continued to invite the O'Neills to dinner with
Yancy and Simmons and, occasionally, other officers. He made
the invitation an order for Brendan, and Samara didn't want to
give him the satisfaction of her refusal. Mealtimes were all the
same—equally horrible. Captain Hampton exuded charm and
dominated the conversation, regaling the company with tales

of faraway ports. Brendan was wary and reticent, a departure from his normal ebullient nature. Yancy and Simmons usually remained silent, although Yancy occasionally raised an eyebrow. Samara picked at her food, unable to eat much at all with Hampton sitting across the table, his mouth curved into a cynical smile and his eyes always assessing her.

Reese was unfailingly courteous and polite to her. Too courteous, too polite. It was worse than his most scathing derision. When she could no longer keep her eyes from him, his gaze was carefully cool. It sent a red-hot flare of pain stabbing through her. To her complete mortification, she knew Yancy recognized—and pitied—these wayward feelings. She would catch his compassionate dark eyes intent on her, his mouth in a worried frown.

Yancy's age was indeterminable; he could be anywhere between thirty-five and fifty, Samara thought. His light brown hair was laced with gray and his face was creased with worry lines, but his step was lively and he was seemingly tireless. His almost black eyes were, by turns, wise, tolerant, impatient. But there was always a hint of pain in them.

He and Hampton seemed to have an unusual relationship, one that transcended that of captain and crew member. They challenged each other frequently, Yancy having none of the courteous respect that marked the rest of the crew. But no one could miss the affection between them. Samara wondered about the bond.

After dinner, she and Bren would take a walk on the top deck. He was often silent on these strolls, and she knew the inactivity was taking its toll on him. He would stare morosely at the *Samara* in the distance and refight, in his mind, the battle that had lost her.

It was, Samara thought often, an altogether terrible time for both of them. As hard as she tried, she couldn't still the explosive thrill when she saw Captain Hampton, nor the pounding in her heart. It did not help to realize that in a matter of days he would be gone. Forever.

It was the sixth day when the pattern broke.

Samara was helping Yancy when she heard the cry, "Sail, ho." Minutes later, Reese strode into the hospital area and curtly ordered her to follow him to his cabin. After one look at his tense face, she obeyed without a word. Simmons had located Brendan, and both men were already in Reese's cabin.

"It's a British frigate," Reese said without preamble. "They want to board."

Samara saw Brendan stiffen. All his crew were subject to imprisonment, and the British-born members to impressment or worse. He had heard that some taken from American vessels had been hanged as traitors. His eyes searched Reese's face for intent.

The Englishman saw the look and his jaw tightened. "I told you," he said, "that your crew would be safe. Despite what you may think, I *do* put some value in my word." He turned to Simmons. "Tell the crew to share their clothes with the Americans." He turned to Bren. "Any British officer worth his salt need take only one look at your crew to know you're Americans. And you," he added to Bren, "are now a deckhand. I don't want anyone approaching you as an officer. Your speech would betray you in a minute."

He turned to Samara. "And you, Mrs. O'Neill, are now Mrs. Hampton. No one other than a captain would ever be allowed to bring a wife. I rather expect our visitors will be surprised enough that *I* allowed you aboard a warship."

"How will you explain so large a crew?" Bren asked curiously.

"With difficulty," Reese answered quickly with a disarming charm. "But I suppose I can say, disallowing modesty, of course, that I expected to take a number of American ships and needed the extra men." He saw Bren flinch at the reminder.

Reese became all business, his charm gone in a barrage of orders. Brendan was told to talk to his men, tell them what was expected and see to their change of clothing. He told Samara to bring what few belongings she had to his cabin and place them conspicuously about.

"I want you to look your best," he added to Samara, "and join me topside. We will greet them together...Mrs. Hampton." With a devilish grin at her discomfort, he turned to Brendan. "I'm sure you won't mind if I borrow her for a while...considering the alternatives."

Samara looked quickly at Brendan, who nodded. She disappeared out the door toward their cabin.

Brendan stared at Reese for a moment before following her. "You're taking a chance. If they find out you're hiding Americans you could be charged with treason. And what about your crew? Will they all be silent?"

"They will do as I say," Hampton replied curtly. "And I very much doubt whether any junior officer will question my papers . . . or my loyalties. And don't you make that mistake, either."

"But why are you doing this?" Brendan persisted.

"Damn it, O'Neill. We don't have time to debate my reasons."

"Aye, sir," Brendan said with a slight smile as he turned and disappeared.

The *Unicorn*'s crew was uncommonly sloppy in returning the signals, trimming sail and finally preparing for boarders. Brendan and his crew were busy tending sail when a party of eight, led by a young lieutenant, climbed aboard Reese's ship. Suspicious eyes raked the deck, then settled on the tall commanding figure and the extraordinarily lovely woman beside him.

The lieutenant's salute was perfection. "Captain Smythe sends his compliments, captain," he said crisply. "We have heard of the *Unicorn*."

Reese felt Samara tense, and his hand cautioned her. "Please return *my* compliments to Captain Smythe," he said smoothly. "What can I do for you?"

"I must check your papers," the lieutenant said, almost apologetically now. "And Captain Smythe noticed you have taken a prize." He gestured to the *Samara* which rode the water not far from Reese's ship. "He suggests taking the prisoners off your hands."

Reese bowed slightly. "I am most grateful, but I have none. I took the American vessel near the Carolina coast and set the crew ashore. I had neither the room nor the inclination to trouble with them. Contentious lot, they were. As you see, we're already carrying extra hands for prize crews."

"You are very confident," the young officer said.

Reese merely smiled. He felt Samara wriggle again . . . in irritation, he rightly guessed. He couldn't resist the next words. "These Americans," he said disdainfully, "they're such easy prey." Only his tight grasp kept Samara at his side.

The lieutenant nodded eagerly. He had, Hampton guessed, not yet encountered an armed American vessel. Well, he would learn.

"Captain Smythe will be disappointed," the young lieutenant said. "We're shorthanded. He was hoping to impress some of your prisoners...there's usually several Irish and Scotsmen amongst American crews."

"I apologize," Reese replied with such fine-tuned sarcasm that only Samara recognized it. "I shall remember that in the future. In the meantime, perhaps I can moderate his unhappiness with a few bottles of excellent wine. It has been used for far less noble purposes." This time, even Samara had a difficult time suppressing a giggle. He was quite incorrigible.

"My wife," he continued smoothly, "will be very pleased to find you several bottles. She's quite inspired in her grasp of wines."

Samara bit her lip to keep from laughing at his impudence. She gave Reese an irrepressible smile that forgave his earlier comments. "Ah, my dear husband...you are the source of my inspiration. You always seem to spur me to new...and more creative...accomplishments."

Reese didn't miss the challenge in the words, and he too couldn't resist a smile, even as he realized they were playing a dangerous game. He was tempted to grab her, then and there, and set his lips on her teasing ones. "Go then," he said with difficulty. "Davey will help you."

She knew the reason for his last comment. She had no idea where he kept the wine, much less the quality of the different bottles. Her use had been entirely indifferent to that aspect.

Afraid to say anything more least she give away her brother, she merely nodded and went in search of Davey, leaving an admiring lieutenant.

"You have a very lovely wife," he said, envy thick in his voice. "But I'm surprised you would bring her on such a voyage."

"My wife has a mind of her own," Reese said wryly. "And we were just married. You can see how difficult it is to say no to her."

The lieutenant swallowed, and nodded.

"If you will just follow me," Reese said, "I'll show you my papers. I would like to get under way while the wind is still so favorable."

The lieutenant nodded. Once in Reese's cabin, his eyes couldn't miss the feminine articles, particularly an undergarment. He gulped, quickly accepted a glass of wine and downed it in one swallow. He barely glanced at Reese's letters of marque. Davey soon knocked, laden with five bottles of wine which he offered for Reese's approval.

"My wife," Reese said to the lieutenant, "did her usually outstanding job. I'm sure your captain will enjoy these." Almost without the lieutenant's awareness, he ushered the man out. "So grateful for your kindness and speed," he said. "My brother, the Earl of Beddingfield, will also be grateful. He's close to several in the Admiralty, you know."

"No...no...I didn't," the man stuttered, all thoughts of a more complete inspection gone.

"And please convey my compliments to your captain...he has a fine officer in you," Reese continued, steering the man to the ship's ladder. He watched as the wine was carefully lowered into the small boat, and the oarsman turned toward the British frigate.

"Let's get the hell out of here," he told Simmons who had come to stand next to him. "I don't want his captain to have any second thoughts."

The two crews were only too happy to comply. In minutes, they were under full sail.

A new harmony fell upon the *Unicorn*. Bren's crew, which had been silent and bitter since their capture, was now somewhat perplexed and grateful for their deliverance. Their captors had nothing to gain and much to lose by their protection of the Americans, and it was difficult to understand why they risked so much. The Americans, better than most, knew the penalty for treason. They decided not to question that which was unanswerable, but instead joined the Britons in their messes, in their games, in their music. Friendships, forged now by shared danger and common interests, flourished.

Brendan sought out Reese Hampton. The English captain was a complete enigma, as seemingly changeable as the sea itself. Hampton was constantly revealing yet another side of himself and no one side stayed long enough to brand him. He apparently acted on whim, completely unfettered by convention or traditional codes. He wished, not for the first time, that they were not on opposite sides. There was something about Hampton, as mercurial as he was, that inspired loyalty and obedience. He had seen it repeatedly in the English crew, but never so much as today.

He found Reese in the sick bay, talking in a low voice to Yancy. He heard only scraps of the conversation, including Yancy's violent oath. "Bastards...bloody arrogant bastards.'' Bren saw Reese shrug, and he backed away. It was obviously a private conversation and, after this morning, he had no desire to eavesdrop. He waited at a fair distance for Captain Hampton to finish.

When finally Reese appeared in the passageway, the man's face was tense and his eyes clouded. He curtly acknowledged Brendan's presence.

"If you want to continue the conversation we had earlier, don't," Reese said. "I told you before I had no interest in filling the navy's billets."

"Nonetheless," Brendan said with a bow, "My men and I are grateful."

"There's no need. I had my own reasons, and they had nothing to do with you." Some of the tenseness left him and Hampton's mouth stretched into a wide smile. "Your wife is very quick. I think she mesmerized that poor lieutenant. If he belonged to me, by God, I would have him court-martialed. He barely glanced at my papers, much less at the odd number of crew members. Alas. The British navy isn't what it used to be."

Bren could only stare at Hampton's colloquy. Then he saw the twinkle in Reese's eyes and recognized the game. In mocking the navy, he was mocking himself, erasing the debt which he knew Brendan felt. He obviously wanted neither thanks nor gratitude nor even an acknowledgment of what had happened. By orally reducing the risk and belittling its scope, he was attempting to reduce it to nothing.

Brendan nodded and grinned in understanding. He knew deep inside, spoken or unspoken, he would forever be in the man's debt. Not so much for himself but for those crew members whose lives had been saved this day.

Reese turned toward his cabin without additional words, and Brendan wondered whether he would ever cease to be amazed by him.

Samara was likewise mystified. Despite the danger, she had thoroughly enjoyed those few minutes of banter while the English lieutenant looked on. Her arms still tingled from Reese's touch, and she would never forget that warm teasing fire in his eyes. It had been quite glorious to be called Mrs. Hampton. A wife twice, she pondered, and a virgin still. It was unfair. Especially when all these wonderful new urges inside were demanding her attention. Her body tingled with expectation, and her nerves felt as if they had been pierced by hundreds of little pins.

The door opened and she looked at it partly with expectation, partly with apprehension. It was only Brendan, a slight smile still on his face.

"Your captain, dear sister, is a most unusual man."

"He isn't *my* captain," Samara said slowly, wishing right now that he were.

"You looked mighty convincing on deck," her brother chided. "What did he say? I could tell you were trying not to laugh."

Samara recited the conversation, and Bren threw back his head and laughed. He stopped when he saw the sudden pain in her eyes.

"Are you sure you don't want to tell him the truth, Samara?" he asked, knowing it was useless. Once his sister made up her mind, it was impossible to change. He was startled, therefore, at her brief hesitancy.

"It wouldn't matter," she said finally. "He's like a seabird. He will never live as you or I. It's better this way. Better to think of myself as married . . . better that he believes it."

Her voice was sad and wistful and more mature than he had thought possible. Even he couldn't guess at the pain behind it.

"You may be right," he said slowly. *And you might not,* a nagging voice whispered. But it was her life, her decision, and he would never forgive himself if he interfered and it turned out badly. Still, he couldn't forget how natural they seemed together earlier, or how they had smiled at each other, mischief lighting both their faces.

"Think about it," he said finally. But her closed face told him she would not change her mind. It was that damned stubbornness again, he thought. He shook his head in frustration.

Dinner was even more difficult than during previous nights. Samara agonized as she played with her well-seasoned chicken. It had been easier when she had convinced herself she hated him, that he was ruthless and cruel and dishonorable. He still was, she tried to insist to her doubting mind. There must be some nefarious purpose behind his otherwise inexplicable action today. But Brendan certainly didn't think so as he now conversed ever so easily with the man across from him. The two men chatted as if they had been friends forever, comparing notes on sails, debating the world's most treacherous waters and even finding taverns in common. It was disgusting. She caught Yancy's eyes on her, and tried to summon a smile but it was weak at best. He smiled sympathetically as if he could read her thoughts. She quickly turned her face away.

Reese was all proper courtesy and charm, turning to her just enough to be polite, asking imbecilic questions such as how she enjoyed her meal. As if he didn't know her stomach was churning and her senses reeling. Her knees probably wouldn't hold her up if she tried to stand. She could merely glare at him impotently, fuming at the amused twitch of his lips.

She would be content only when she saw the last of him. But curiously the thought brought an aching hurt. Thus inwardly embattled, Samara raised her eyes to feast upon him, and saw his smile falter as he turned to her. No one at the table could miss the current that suddenly engulfed the two of them, sweeping them along to some special place of their own. It was, for a moment, as if no one else existed, as their eyes met, sparking tiny fires then gently surrendering, leaving tides of emotion neither could fathom. The air was palpable with the runaway feelings that seemed to swell, wave by wave, as minutes passed.

Yancy looked at Brendan, expecting anger, and saw only a small cryptic smile which disappeared the second the American noticed the doctor's eyes on him. Yancy raised an eyebrow in question, receiving only a blank look in reply.

Michael Simmons was nearly hypnotized by the scene, his eyes darting from Reese to Mrs. O'Neill, bewildered by the strength of what was passing between them.

"Ahem." Yancy's interruption was forceful. It did nothing to break the spell. "Captain!"

This time the sound reached Reese's mind, but it took several seconds for it to register. He shook his head to clear it, wondering what had happened. Samara's eyes had lowered, but the magic was still there; the invisible cord still bound him as tightly as any ropes.

Reality struck and he slowly took measure of those around the table. Simmons looked both embarrassed and dumfounded; imperturbable Yancy looked interested; and O'Neill...

Brendan O'Neill returned his gaze steadily, his mouth crooked in a position which was neither smile nor frown but something indefinable. Reese had expected anger; he didn't know how to interpret the quiet, inscrutable man across from him. His eyes moved back to Samara, and pain struck him with unexpected impact when he saw tears pooling in her lovely, wistful eyes. Abruptly he pushed away from the table, sending his chair crashing to the floor.

"I have duties to attend to," he said to no one in particular, his voice harsh. Four pairs of eyes followed him as he almost staggered from the cabin.

Brendan paced the small cabin restlessly. Samara was sitting on the bed, her face pensive. He realized now the strength of the attraction between his sister and Hampton—and the fascination. Whenever the two were together the air was alive with tension, as if caught in a summer storm: all thunder and lightning. He could feel the magic between them and could well understand. Samara was a lovely woman, made even more so by her unawareness of the fact. She had humor and intelligence and an innocence that must completely perplex Hampton. And Hampton? Brendan knew he should be worried about Samara, but he couldn't ignore a persistent feeling that the two of them were right for each other. He had hated Hampton originally but in the past days had learned a healthy respect for him. He was the type of man Samara needed, one who would never be ruled by her but who would respect and encourage her spirit. But these were only assumptions, and he wished he knew more of Reese Hampton. What would he do if he knew Samara was free? Would an English aristocrat, even one who apparently had shed the trappings of that kind of life, marry an unsophisticated American, an enemy of his country? Or would he just use her?

With sudden determination, Brendan decided to talk with Yancy and find out what he could about the puzzling Captain Hampton.

His pacing stopped and he turned to Samara. "I'm going to Yancy's cabin," he said. "I want to check on the men."

It was a sign of her distress that she didn't clamor to go but merely nodded in a halfhearted away. He might have been a bothersome fly, he thought as he left.

And at the moment he was. Samara had wanted him to leave and had willed it mightily. She had thought of nothing but Captain Hampton in the hours since dinner, and she had come to a decision. She could not wonder the rest of her life whether she had made a grievous error. She would tell him, this night, the truth. At the thought, her body tensed, and seem to sing with its own anticipation. Reese. She said the name. Once.

Twice, three times . . . testing the sound on her lips. She had always avoided it before, afraid that such familiarity would only
increase the yearning of her mind and body. But now it sounded
wonderful. Reese Hampton.

Her mind raced on fancifully. When he found she was free,
he would embrace her, tell her that he loved her as she now
knew she loved him. She would feel those gloriously strong
arms around her, that hard body reaching expectantly to feel
hers next to it. His eyes would soften and . . .

She could stand it no more. She quickly reviewed herself. The
dress was hopeless. It was, of course, the same one she had
carried aboard the *Samara*, and had worn almost constantly,
only once changing long enough to wash it. Her only other
garment was the stained and soiled one she had ruined in the
hold. She had tried and tried to clean and mend it, but it was
beyond repair.

She knew her hair was presentable. She had washed it earlier, and brushed it until it fairly glowed. She wore it up at dinner, and now she released it, letting it fall in waves around her
shoulders. She pinched her cheeks, bit her lips to give them
color and hurried in search of her objective.

Reese was exactly where she expected him to be—at the
wheel. He turned, sensing her presence, and his lips tightened.

"I would like some words with you,." Samara said softly,
hesitantly. She almost lost her courage when she saw the sudden anger in his face.

"Where is your husband, Madam?" he asked, his voice cold
and impersonal. She couldn't know how much control it took
to make it that way. His body was rigid with the effort.

"He went to see the wounded, but he's not my . . ."

She didn't have a chance to finish. "Then why," he said even
more icily, "are you not with him?"

"He's not . . ."

He interrupted again. "Marriage obviously doesn't concern
you overmuch." It was a statement, not a question. But before
she could retort, he continued. "But then marriage doesn't
seem important to many women. Once they trap a man, they
apparently feel free to put horns on him." He disregarded the
growing distress in her face as he continued, as much for his
benefit as for hers. *God, how beautiful she is.* "I vowed I would
never marry," he continued in an almost conversational note,
realizing from her face that each word was a whiplash, but he
had to stop this now! He had to make her understand how im-

possible it was. He had to make *himself* understand. He *had* to put a distance between them for both their sakes. "Why should I when I can get anything and everything I want without it?" The voice was suddenly arrogant and the meaning only too clear.

Samara's teeth bit into her lip and it reddened as blood escaped the wound. He obviously had nothing but contempt for her. It was, she knew, because he thought she was married, but she no longer had a reason to disabuse him of that fact. He had made it very clear that he had little respect for marriage, or for women. He had said he would never marry. Her heart felt dead, the anticipation drained, the dream lost.

"Marriage is for fools," he concluded, but the words were lost to Samara who had turned and fled, her pinched cheeks now white with anguish.

Reese gave a sudden jerk to the wheel, wondering why he felt as if he had just tortured a kitten. She had, after all, deserved every word. She had played her games, had, after all, flirted with him while her husband looked on. Damn her. He tried to convince himself that she was not worth even one thought, but every star wore her face, and the moon was dulled by her absence. Damn her!

Yancy heard the knock as he stood bare-chested, preparing to change clothes before looking in on his charges. Believing it to be Reese, he opened it without bothering to cover the scars etched deep in the skin on his back, crisscrossing each other in ugly patterns of malicious violence. They were reminders of agony so great that he tried to hide them even from himself. He allowed only a tiny shaving mirror in his cabin, and he had permitted no one other than Reese a glimpse of the nightmare he had somehow endured. Reese was allowed, because Reese had seen it happen . . . and Reese had saved him, had patiently rubbed ointment into flesh raw to the bone despite Yancy's oaths and curses and threats. Because Reese had given him the will to live.

But as he opened the door and saw O'Neill, he was half turned, and he knew the American could see at least part of the scars. He knew it from the expression on the man's face. Surprise. Pity. Compassion. Yancy almost slammed the door, then shrugged. The American had already seen his humiliation. Besides the American looked as if he had something important on his mind, and Yancy certainly had some questions of his own. He opened the door wider, allowed O'Neill in and without saying anything pulled on a shirt. Turning back to O'Neill, he simply raised an eyebrow in question.

"Hampton," the American said. "I would like to know more about him."

"Then ask him," Yancy said with an edge to his voice. Almost unwillingly his own curiosity took over. "I don't suppose you would like to tell me why you seem so indifferent to Samara?"

"Indifferent?" Brendan said. "Never."

"You seem to have a certain . . . shall we say . . . lack of proprietorship."

"Samara is not someone you own," Bren said simply. "She usually ends up doing the right thing. There seems little reason to get angry because of one look."

Yancy merely gave him a look of disbelief which said more than words could.

"About Hampton . . . have you been with him long?"

"Almost three years," Yancy said, hoping that if he gave something he would get something in return. He didn't want his friend hurt. "I knew him several years before that."

"Is he always as changeable as he is now?"

"That depends on how well you know him," Yancy replied. "I've always thought him very consistent . . ." Until now, he added to himself.

It was Brendan's turn to look surprised.

"Reese has his own code," Yancy said suddenly. "It may not be the same as yours, but he has a strong sense of justice . . . and honor." The older man hesitated a moment before continuing. "I was a doctor near the docks five years ago. His crew brought him in, half dead from a festering wound. He survived, and I didn't see him for another two years.

"One night, I drank too much brandy and was taken by a press gang. The next years were pure hell. I complained once too often about the food and treatment of the wounded. They were complaints the captain took personally. He ordered one hundred lashes, enough to kill. More than enough. We were in Bermuda when it happened, and the captain was halfway through his bloody punishment when Reese boarded to deliver some mail for England. I was already half dead.

"I found out later that Reese literally bought me, and for a tidy sum. I had been a thorn in the captain's side for a long time and he was loath to let me go. Probably wouldn't have except he thought I would die. And I wanted to. But Reese wouldn't let me. He made me so damned angry I lived to get my hands on him.''

Yancy laughed ruefully. "And when I was well enough, I still wanted to get my hands on him. I swung. He ducked. And we've been friends since.'' He shrugged his shoulders at the obvious absurdity.

There was silence. Brendan silently weighed the words. He realized it had been a difficult story to tell.

"I've never told anyone else,'' Yancy said. "And I never will. But I want you to know I'll never allow anyone to hurt him…not if there's anything I can do to prevent it.'' There was a definite warning in his voice.

Brendan nodded.

"I asked you a question before,'' Yancy said. "You didn't really answer.''

"I gave you the best one I had,'' Bren said. "I can give you no more now.''

Yancy searched the American's eyes and liked what he saw. Why in hell, of all the women in the world, was Reese so attracted to Samara O'Neill? The whole thing was a puzzle, and he knew no more now than when O'Neill had entered his cabin. But for some strange reason, he felt better.

Chapter Eight

From a distance, Bermuda looked like a muted, multicolored gem displayed on a sea of turquoise velvet. Bathed in a pink glow from the setting sun, the island resembled a fairyland, Samara thought sadly. She wished she could appreciate its beauty, but her spirit had been tapped by days of self-reproach and heartache. Her mind registered the softly muted pastels, but they didn't touch her, not as they would have days ago. She felt a stranger to herself, an onlooker who had ceased to participate in life because it hurt too much.

She stayed in her cabin at meals and ate little. Despite Bren's entreaties, she had refused to budge from the cabin unless she knew Reese Hampton was asleep. She simply couldn't bear to see him again. Samara had told him some of the conversation with Hampton, offering only that Reese apparently had a low opinion of women and had said he would never marry. It was best, she argued, that they continue their hoax. Telling the Englishman now of their trickery might anger him to the point of turning Bren and his crew over to the British navy.

Brendan had dried Samara's tears and reluctantly agreed to keep silent. He didn't want to risk either Samara or his crew if his opinion of Hampton was wrong. But he remained deeply troubled. Her brief account of the conversation with Hampton certainly didn't sound like the same man Yancy had described. He had never seen his sister so drained of enthusiasm and curiosity. The sooner they left the *Unicorn*—and Captain Hampton—the better. He, too, refused any additional invitations from Hampton, and conversations were curt and wary. Both silently regretted the loss of something they had enjoyed, but neither could explain his private reasons for the strain.

Bren's arm went around Samara. He had almost forced her on deck, not wanting her to miss the beauty of the island. He had been there previously... before the war... and never tired of its enchantment.

But it held little charm now for Samara. She suspected Reese would be at the wheel, and she carefully averted her gaze from the area. She tried to summon some enthusiasm for Brendan, but she felt dead inside. She felt his arm tightening as he sensed her unhappiness.

"You have to let it go, Samara," he whispered.

Her only reply was to lean against him, borrowing some of his strength. He had, after all, lost more than she. She had lost only a fleeting dream. She had endowed Captain Hampton with qualities he didn't have; she had been blinded by his charm and his uncommonly handsome features, and by her own fancies. She shouldn't feel so great a loss for something so superficial, so meaningless. *Oh God, help me conquer this ache; take away this emptiness. Let me feel again.* But the yawning hurt only grew greater as the sun exploded into a profusion of golds and pinks and finally crimson. Crimson for blood. Crimson for loss. Her tears soaked Brendan's sleeve. He rested his chin on her head in sympathy, then drew her away. He had hoped the sight of Bermuda would cheer her; it had only deepened her despair.

Reese couldn't keep his eyes from the two. His heart contracted as he saw Brendan's arm go around her, as the American rested his chin intimately on her soft hair. They stood there, washed in the colors of twilight, and he knew a yearning so great that everything in his life paled by comparison. The sea lost its fascination, the sky its beauty, the ship its allure. He would gladly give it all up, this moment, if Samara O'Neill rested herself so trustfully against him. *What in the hell is happening to me? I have to get her off the ship... both of them.* But how? Bermuda wasn't safe, not for O'Neill or his crew. It would take several days to sell the *Samara* and effect repairs to his own ship. Then another week or more before dropping them off in Florida where they could easily get home. The *Samara*. He couldn't avoid a stab of guilt. He had seen O'Neill's eyes follow the ship. There was much more there than the ordinary attachment of a captain to his ship. But members of his own crew had been killed and wounded in its taking, and he could not simply give back something that was not his alone. But... after it was sold...

An idea pricked his mind. It teased and challenged him, as it expanded. By God, it would solve several problems. His head lifted, and his eyes caught the last splashes of sunlight. A crooked smile touched his lips for the first time in days.

Reese left the shipping offices of Faulk and Henner with more buoyancy than he had felt in weeks. Everything had gone as he planned, and a transfer of funds had already taken place at the island's principal banking house. He had insisted on immediate payment, and Upton Faulk had been sufficiently eager for Brendan's sleek, handsome schooner to readily agree. The ship was a bargain; the cargo alone was almost worth the price agreed upon after long haggling. Reese grinned as he remembered Upton's face. The man had tried to hide his jubilation and greed after he had told him that a family emergency required his presence in England immediately and, therefore, he must sacrifice such a fine prize. Reese had always detested the dishonest Faulk and his partner; the two had tried repeatedly to raid his crew, to overcharge him for supplies, and to delay repairs on his ship. As the largest shipping firm in Bermuda, they could often control such activities. They also were active in the slave trade, a profession Reese abhorred. All in all, they had been a thorn in Reese's side for a long time. He would take great pleasure in diddling them.

Yancy, who knew the plan, was waiting at the *Unicorn's* railing for him. The doctor had no desire to go ashore, not with the harbor overflowing with British naval ships. He quickly saw from Reese's gleeful expression that all had gone well. Perhaps now things would get back to normal, and the captain's irascible humor would be replaced by his usual good nature.

Reese nodded to Yancy as he strode up the gangplank, and the doctor was delighted to see the old puckish light back in his lively green-blue eyes.

"Three days," he said. "I heard Faulk give the yard orders that the *Samara* be ready to sail in three days. He's putting all their resources on it. I told him how profitable privateering can be, even gave him the name of a good captain." He couldn't stifle a laugh. The suggested captain was the most inept man who ever sailed. The man had somehow managed to conceal most of his mistakes from his owners, but crewmen, who spoke freely in front of Reese, were not so easily fooled. The man drank to excess, was unconscionably careless, and his reputation for cruelty kept him from obtaining a competent crew.

Yancy shook his head at Reese's elaborate scheme, but couldn't halt his own spreading grin. Damn if he wouldn't like to see Faulk's face when the *Samara* disappeared.

For the next two and a half days, Reese watched the repairs on the American vessel. He had made sure the two ships were side by side. Many of the *Samara*'s yards were replaced, and new sails took the place of the mended gray ones. Parts of the hull were reinforced. The name was painted over, replaced by *Swift Lady*. Brendan, still dressed in the rough clothes of a seaman, flinched openly as he watched this last sacrilege. Reese, who had moved next to him to watch, saw a suspicious wetness at the corner of the American's eyes and, despite all his conflicting feelings, his hand instinctively went toward him in reassurance.

Startled, Brendan turned and looked at him, all trace of emotion quickly controlled. Reese had been curt, even unpleasant, in the past days. He had ordered the Americans to stay below and posted sufficient guards to make sure they did. One had remained outside Brendan's cabin at all times, and neither O'Neill was allowed on deck without a guardian. It reminded Bren constantly of his status as a prisoner, and he was on deck now only because Yancy had accompanied him.

"You will have dinner with me tonight," Reese said unexpectedly. The abrupt tone made it an order and left no room for refusal.

"Samara?"

"No." Reese continued. "The pleasure of your company will be quite sufficient."

Brendan searched the Englishman's face. There was something different about him today, an aura of mystery, of anticipation. *What in the devil was he up to now?*

"Do I have any choice?"

"None at all," Reese replied in a courteous tone which did nothing to disguise the command. "Until eight, then."

Samara was silent when Brendan told her of Hampton's order. The silence was more unnerving than any tantrum.

"I have to go, Samara. He made that quite clear."

She just nodded, and Brendan wished for the return of the old spirit.

"We're just his puppets," she said finally. "He pulls the strings and we jump."

"I'm sorry, Samara. I have you and the crew to worry about."

"I know," she said in the same listless way. Then for his benefit, she tried to force some life into her voice. "Yancy gave me a new book today, and maybe... since *he* will be in his cabin... I'll get some air."

He suddenly thought of the new name on the *Samara*. He didn't want her to see it. "I don't think that's wise right now, Samara. Stay here tonight... for me. Don't leave the cabin without me."

She smiled at his worried frown, the first smile for several days.

"I wish you *could* be my husband. I'll never find anyone as dear and generous and forgiving. I'll stay here. I promise." She thought of the nights he had slept on the floor, half of his long frame under the table. When she had protested, he had merely replied that it was far preferable to the hold. He had stayed with her when she knew he would rather be topside, and he tolerated her moods patiently.

She contained her curiosity about the dinner, and hid her anxiety. When Davey knocked at eight, she smiled at him with some of the old warmth, and Brendan hoped she was beginning to heal. She was certainly growing up.

Brendan did not believe what he was hearing.

The dinner had been odd from the very beginning. There were only Reese, Yancy and himself, and at first he wondered why he had been summoned since he was virtually ignored as Yancy and Hampton talked, completely ignoring him except for an occasional question as to whether he was enjoying the meal.

"The *Samara* is ready to sail," Reese said to Yancy. "Faulk has taken the cargo and provisioned her for several months."

Yancy shook his head. "I can't believe Captain Hendricks didn't post more guards. Almost anyone could steal that ship.... damned careless. He deserves to lose it."

"He's a poor captain by any standard," Reese replied. "It's the night before he sails and I heard he's going to a party." Reese neglected to add it was he who arranged the party. "I plan to be there... and most of the crew. What about you, Yancy?"

"You know the way I feel about the damned navy. I'll stay and keep guard. That way you can let the others go."

Reese pondered the offer. "It's an idea. There's not one who hasn't asked for liberty. And we will be sailing soon. Do you think you can handle it? There's all the Americans ... but then there's really no place for them to go." He turned to Brendan. "Is there?"

Brendan's eyes had been fastened on his plate. Now he lifted them. For the first time since his capture, there was real animation in them. "I can't think of a place in Bermuda," he said solemnly, his eyes fairly dancing with hope.

There was no more mention of ships. With little effort, Reese turned the conversation to books and music, and Brendan was startled by the man's knowledge. It seemed he was familiar with almost everything—from ancient philosophy to the new American writers.

But before long he became restless. There was much to do this night. He had learned that Hampton did everything with a purpose, even, apparently, prolonging this evening. Yancy finally left, and Reese offered him a glass of brandy. Not knowing how to refuse it at this point, Brendan accepted.

There was a long silence. Reese stretched out leisurely, putting his booted feet on the chair Yancy had vacated. He sipped the brandy thoughtfully.

When he finally spoke, the words were quietly said, but very, very final. "No one," he said, "is to know about this dinner... or the conversation. It was private, between... friends."

Brendan could only nod. He wished there were something he could say. There was nothing. The way Reese and Yancy had voiced everything, words of gratitude would constitute a betrayal. That Reese believed Brendan would recognize the complicated reasoning was a supreme compliment.

"*No* one." Once again, Reese's soft voice emphasized the insistence behind it, and Brendan knew the Englishman meant Samara specifically.

Brendan nodded again, his eyes troubled.

"I bid you good night then, sir," Reese said as he slowly unfolded himself and stood.

The two men looked at each other steadily, then Brendan slowly bowed. "It's been an honor, Captain," he said and knew he would never forget the wry, rather sad smile that darted rapidly over Reese Hampton's face.

* * *

Brendan did not go back to the cabin immediately but stopped and talked to several of his crew members, giving explicit orders to pass on to others. His guard had disappeared, and he watched as Hampton's crew left the ship in twos and threes. Among them were Michael Simmons and Hampton. The English captain never looked back.

Brendan stopped in at the sick bay. Yancy was there, bottle in hand.

"Are Billy and Adams able to take a small stroll?" he asked. "For exercise."

"With some assistance, I imagine," Yancy answered. "But see that they don't exert themselves too much. Your wife should be able to see to their needs."

Brendan thrust out his hands. "On behalf of my crew and myself, I thank you. If there's anything I can ever..."

But Yancy had turned away, his back unyielding in its rejection. He, like Hampton, wanted no acknowledgment of their assistance. Brendan could see why the two men were such close friends; they had much in common.

Yancy made one final comment. "Davey took some of his clothes to Samara for mending. But I think they're irreparable. Reese had intended on replacing them."

For a moment, Brendan would have given his soul if Yancy would, for once, speak forthrightly rather than in riddles. But he rapidly comprehended. The clothes were meant for Samara. The Americans could not risk leaving the *Unicorn* openly, or boarding the *Swift Lady* by the dock. It would put both them and Hampton at risk. They would have to swim to the other ship. It would be difficult for Samara in a dress.

"I'll see," he said finally, "that Samara does everything possible to prolong their life."

A small surprising chuckle rose from Yancy, but he didn't turn, and Brendan sensed his dismissal.

"I'll send some men to assist Bobby and Adams," he said and left.

When he returned to the cabin, Samara was pacing up and down. A pile of torn clothes lay on the bed. "Something strange is happening," she said.

Brendan looked at her with a question in his eyes.

"The guard is gone," she said.

"I think Hampton's decided there's no place for us to go."

Reluctant to think anything good about Hampton, Samara shook her head. "I think he wants us to leave. I think it's a trap. I think maybe he has soldiers waiting in town."

"What would he gain by that?" her brother queried gently.

"He had the labor of our crew . . . he wouldn't have had it if he turned us over to the navy at sea. Now he probably just wants to get rid of us." The last was said miserably.

"Then we'll fool him," Brendan said, hating himself. He had promised Hampton, and he would not break that covenant. "We'll take the *Samara* back."

Some sparkle came back into Samara's eyes. "How?"

"I noticed there are just a couple of men aboard. Two of us will swim over and take them. The rest of you will follow." His glance took in the clothes on the bed. "What are those?"

"Davey asked me to mend them," Samara said, considerably brightened now that they might, for the first time, outwit the arrogant Reese Hampton.

"Try them on," Bren said. "You'll have to swim, too." He did not worry about that; she had always been an excellent swimmer. He had taught her himself.

Samara nodded eagerly. She would be getting away from the Englishman, twitting his nose. She laughed at the thought of reclaiming the O'Neill ship from him. She laughed to hide the sudden stab of inexplicable grief and loss inside her. *Think of home. Think of safety.*

Brendan left, and Samara changed quickly. She hurried up on deck, meeting Hugh Butler, her brother's third officer, on the way. His face was alive in a way she had never seen before; he was usually quiet and somber. Now he took her arm, hurrying her along, as they met the two wounded men, young Billy Faucette and James Adams.

Hugh warned the others to stay out of sight, as he and Samara looked down at the water between the two ships. She could see her brother's long strokes barely disturbing the water and another man keeping pace with him.

Samara looked at Hugh questioningly.

"Mick," he said, and Samara remembered the tall, loud Irishman who now swam silently beside her brother. Samara watched as the two reached the anchor chain at the rear of the ship. As facile as monkeys, they climbed the chain and disappeared out of sight. Several minutes later, Brendan appeared, signaling success. Ropes were lowered over the side of the *Uni-*

corn hidden from the docks. Samara knew other ropes were being lowered on the blind side of her brother's ship.

The night was cooperating nicely, she thought. It was cloudy, and only dim light reached the dark water. She watched as man after man climbed down the rope and swam over to the other ship. Those who couldn't swim were given a partner. The two wounded men were lowered by a makeshift sling, then assisted by two swimmers each. Samara was to be among the last to go. If an alarm was raised, Brendan wanted her safely on Hampton's ship.

Samara took a last searching look around the *Unicorn*. It had become home in the past two weeks—home and something else. It held her heart, and behind the shadows she could envision a tall, laughing Englishman who had awakened the woman inside her. *Reese Hampton*. She whispered the name, despising herself as she did so. He cared nothing for her, or for the feelings he had aroused in her. He was, even now, probably with a woman, charming her with his roguish grin and challenging eyes. Her hand caressed the rail, as she had often seen Reese do. Her eagerness to leave disappeared as she considered the reality of never seeing him again. She realized, inexplicably, that she did not want to leave. Yet how could she stay? He might even now be reporting Bren to the authorities. Forget him! He had never indicated any feeling for her...except a kiss. And he probably gave them most freely. She had been a temporary diversion. Nothing more.

When she finally slipped into the water, her tears mixed with salt water, and she looked back, watching the *Unicorn* strain at its tether, as restless as her master. Desolation swept over her as she was assisted aboard the *Samara* Almost indifferently, she watched two men cut the ropes binding the ship and felt the first gentle movements as the *Samara* inched away from the deserted dock. She half expected an outcry, but the waterfront was empty. The British navy had no idea that the Americans were among them and, unknown to Samara, friends of Reese were hosting several parties. There were few guards, and those left wanted only to enjoy the revelry of the night....

As she stood staring back toward shore, Brendan was at the wheel, guiding the ship toward the open sea. He knew if he escaped the harbor, he could outrun any ship anchored here. Except, of course, the *Unicorn*. A broad smile split his face. A flash of intuition told him he would meet Reese Hampton again. In the darkness of the night, he gave a brief salute to the flickering lights of St. George and to the baffling man who had taken—and given—with such remarkable aplomb.

Chapter Nine

Home! The carriage containing Brendan and Samara turned into the tree-lined road leading to the two-story brick house with its wide verandah and climbing roses. It was near Christmas now and the roses were gone, but Samara held them in her mind. They always seemed so much a part of Glen Woods.

The house was fairly new. It had been built in 1783, replacing one burned by the British some two years earlier. It had been built with love and, accordingly, seemed to radiate warmth and comfort and peace. And that was exactly what Samara needed at the moment. A great deal of peace.

For she had found none on the voyage from Bermuda to Charleston. Every waking moment seemed dominated by a laughing, teasing giant who was gone forever. Sleep, which had always come easily, eluded her. After several restless nights she came to fear even what little came. Because if Reese Hampton dominated her days, he haunted her dreams. She was always running toward him, but as she finally came close he faded away. She would reach out but there was nothing but air and space. And she would wake with a yearning so deep and so painful that it terrified her.

There had been no books on board to distract her and she had no clothes but Davey's torn ones. Dressed in a tattered seaman's blouse and a boy's rough breeches, she had walked the ship, bow to stern, until Bren thought she would wear a path in the polished wooden decking. She volunteered her services, but other than providing minimal nursing skills, she was more a hazard than a help. The ship's cook threatened mutiny after she spilled a giant pot of stew while attempting to season it. She had thought the *Unicorn*'s food far superior to Bren's ship, although she was careful not to mention this galling fact. Then she offered to help with the sails but when one sympathetic sailor permitted it, she ripped her hand open against the rope and Brendan exploded at both of them. She tried to clean Bren's cabin, but he roared when he couldn't find his compass or his charts, and she had forgotten where she'd placed them.

It seemed she couldn't do anything right. So she wandered listlessly, unhappily, in the cooling air as they moved west. The live chickens were killed fifty miles from the Carolina coast. Brendan would be running the blockade in the early dawn and he wanted no crowing to disturb the silence. Samara heard the squawks and shuddered. The cutting off of life. Why did it seem to signify this whole miserable adventure? Adventure? She would never long for one again. Home. That's what she wanted . . . needed.

As the carriage rolled up the driveway, doors opened and people poured out of the main house, the barns, the neat rows of cabins which housed the field workers.

"Miss Samara . . . Mr. Bren." The cry went up everywhere. Brendan had dispatched a rider to Glen Woods the moment they'd docked. He had also sent Samara to a dressmaker while he'd seen the harbormaster. She was now, if not elegantly, at least decently clad.

Samara watched as her mother and father came quickly down the wide stairs of the verandah, their faces alight with welcome, and felt a deep guilt for the worry and trouble she'd caused. Before the carriage had come to a complete stop, she jumped from the conveyance and threw herself into her father's arms, tears splashing down her face. She was so glad to see them, to have their comfort. But even clasped tightly in their warmth, she knew something was missing. She had thought she would feel whole again, but she didn't. For some reason, the loneliness that had plagued her these past weeks seemed even greater.

It was her mother who sensed all was not as it should be, and she looked quizzically at Brendan. He could only shrug, indicating he would tell them later.

"Come with me," Samantha commanded her daughter. "We'll get you a nice hot bath." Connor and Brendan exchanged grins. A "nice hot bath" was Samantha's solution to many problems. After quickly dispensing orders, Samantha accompanied Samara upstairs to her room and sat her down.

"What happened, love?" she asked gently.

Samara looked at her mother hopelessly. What to say? That she had fallen in love with a pirate. A scoundrel. An Englishman. A man who despised women and marriage. A man who had probably been ready to betray them.

"Brendan's message said the ship was captured by a privateer but that neither of you was harmed. Was he wrong? Did someone take advantage of you?" Samantha's voice was tender but insistent, and Samara's resistance crumbled.

"No one harmed me," she said softly. "No one but myself."

Her mother said nothing, waiting for her to continue, knowing she couldn't force the story.

Samara looked at her desperately. "What does it feel like to be in love?"

"It can be the greatest joy known to man or woman," Samantha said carefully. "Or the worst torment."

"You and father seem so happy...did...did you...were you...?"

With a slow sigh and a fleeting frown, Samantha reluctantly recalled the worst month in her life. She had wanted to die; oh, how she had wanted to die. And she would have had it not been for the babe she was carrying. Connor had discovered she was the daughter of the enemy he had vowed to ruin and kill. He had discovered that their marriage was a sham, that their months together had been a web of lies.

"Yes," she said softly. "There was torment. Perhaps that's why our love is so strong now...it was forged from a great deal of pain."

Samara was looking at her mother with astonishment. This was a part of her she had never known. She had known there was something about Chatham Oaks, her mother's plantation, that took the warmth and laughter from her father's eyes. But she had never known exactly what, and neither, she thought, did her brothers. It was one subject never broached in the O'Neill home.

Her mother's voice broke the spell. "Will you tell me what happened?"

"I think I'm in love with an Englishman." Samara said it with such distaste that her mother smiled.

"Not all Englishmen are bad," she said. "And you and Bren are both home, safe, so this one couldn't be too wicked." *Besides*, Samantha thought, *you wouldn't love someone who didn't have a lot of good in him. I know you too well.* She sensed, however, that Samara wouldn't welcome the thought right now.

"How can you say that?" Samara said indignantly. "Father says they're all arrogant bastards and this one certainly was."

Samantha didn't know whether to laugh or scold. She decided a scolding would accomplish nothing at this time.

"Did he take advantage of you?"

"Yes...no...I..."

Samantha's lips tightened and the amusement disappeared. "Yes? Or No?"

"He...he kissed me."

"Nothing more?"

"He...he thought I was Bren's wife."

"He what?" Samantha's stomach lurched. Lies again. Lies were what had almost destroyed any chance she and Connor had. Was history repeating itself in some obscene pattern?

The story now poured out...every last miserable detail. Several times, Samantha had great trouble in withholding a smile. Reese Hampton was either a very great scoundrel as Samara accused, or the most patient man who ever lived. He was, Samantha suspected, something between the two. Well, Connor would be talking to Brendan. It would be most interesting to see how the two tales compared.

In the meantime she soothed Samara, urged her into a hot tub of sweet-smelling water and then combed her hair as she had when Samara was a child. Samara, emotionally spent and physically exhausted from her sleepless nights, finally sank her head into her pillows and went to sleep. Samantha stood over her for several minutes, thinking how very young she was...and how lovely. Could it be that she had found the one man she would love? For Samantha firmly believed that there was one man and one man only for Samara...as there had been for her. She had waited patiently, never pushing, for Samara to find him. She wanted her daughter to know the same joy, the same exquisite happiness she had found in marriage. But had Samara found it and already destroyed it with lies?

"Damned arrogant English."

Samantha sighed with frustration as she rode beside Connor along the Pee Dee River. Her husband was furious. Brendan's story was much like Samara's, although her son apparently couldn't hide a certain admiration for the English privateer. Because of his promise, he had neglected the exact details of his retrieval of the *Samara*. He did, however, tell his parents that Hampton had kept them from being taken by the British navy. Connor, like Samara, chose to believe the worst, that the damned pirate just wanted slave labor.

But Samantha had also talked to Brendan and saw something in his eyes that Connor had not. She knew she had not received the entire truth, just as she knew Brendan had thoroughly liked and admired the man Samara labelled an unprincipled blackguard.

Now she bit her lip as she listened to Connor's diatribe. Connor was one of the kindest, most just men alive—until it came to the British. She understood it easily enough; they had burned his home, killed his father, kept him chained in a ship's hold for months. Her own father, an Englishman, had killed Connor's brother. The years had done little to dim the pain, or ease the lingering bitterness. The recent high-handed tactics of the British had only heightened his outrage. And an outraged Connor was a very dangerous one. His passionate dislike had been passed on to his children, at least to all but Brendan and, perhaps, Marion who liked nearly everyone.

Samantha smiled as she thought of her oldest son. Brendan was so much like his namesake, his uncle. Quick to smile and easygoing by nature, he had the same independence of thought, judged each man on his own merit and stubbornly went his own way. Samantha knew he usually judged well.

She tried to soothe Connor. "We have much to be grateful for. He apparently didn't touch Samara or do lasting harm to Brendan. And we have the ship back."

"He damn well did do something to Samara," Connor growled. "She hasn't been the same happy child since she returned."

"She's grown up, Connor. She's no longer a child. And that's not Captain Hampton's fault."

"Isn't it?" Connor, his gray eyes icy, said angrily. "I think it is." He said it with such finality that Samantha gave up. Temporarily.

In an effort to pacify him, she spurred her horse. "I'll race you."

Connor, hearing the laughter in her voice, knew exactly what she was doing. His anger melted as he watched her. She would always be thus, free and enchanting and very knowledgeable about him. He gave his own horse its head, and his laughter joined hers.

If Yancy had thought Reese's mood foul prior to the departure of the O'Neills, it now became close to intolerable. No one could satisfy him, and the raw vitality was replaced with angry tension. That tension exploded the morning the O'Neills left. Badly hung over, he was visited by Faulk and ended up throwing him off the ship.

The man had demanded his gold back, and virtually accused Reese of complicity in the theft.

With bleary eyes and knotted fists, Reese, rage virtually steaming from him, stared at Upton Faulk with undisguised contempt.

"Are you impugning my honor?" he said. "It seems you were more than a little careless with your property and now you seek to blame it on another. Well it is *your* property now, and not mine, and I'll be damned if I'll give you a farthing for your own stupidity."

Faulk's face grew redder with each passing second and Hampton thought hopefully he might have apoplexy.

"I'm calling the authorities," Faulk blustered.

"Do that," Reese said, "And show yourself to be the biggest fool on the island. At least be grateful you have the damned cargo."

"You bastard..."

"Not exactly," Reese replied, "and I do take offense at that remark. Unless you are prepared to give me satisfaction, I advise you to apologize."

Faulk took one look at Reese's frigid eyes and backed off. "I...I...might have spoken hastily"

"Get off my ship. Now."

Faulk almost ran down the gangplank. He didn't see the amused expressions of the crew who had arrived at various times during the early morning hours to find the ship curiously empty. They knew better than to ask questions, but they could guess. And they all approved, although they didn't know exactly what had happened. They had liked the Americans, and they disliked Faulk and his captains. Quiet chuckles and guffaws were heard frequently during the day.

But when they tried to share the joke with their captain, they received only a curt reply, and the ship set sail that evening.

They had expected to return to the American coast, but Reese, instead, charted a course toward Europe. For the moment, Reese Hampton had had his fill of America and Americans.

Two French prizes in tow, the *Unicorn* reached London five months later. Reese's dark mood still pervaded the ship; he couldn't seem to shake it.

Every corner of his ship held the spectre of Samara O'Neill. Though he knew it was impossible, he could have sworn he still smelled the fresh, feminine scent of her in the cabin. And whenever he took a glass of wine, his lips would twist into a smile as he remembered that ridiculous dinner her first night aboard.

He was completely bewildered. No woman had ever affected him like this. None had ever invaded his heart and thoughts so thoroughly. He damned himself nightly as a fool, but still the images remained. He had never known loneliness before; now it ripped into him like a whip, tearing at his insides, filling him with a vast emptiness.

It was time to go back to Beddingfield, back to his roots. And he missed Avery. They had always been close, despite certain differences in their personalities. Perhaps that's what he needed, perhaps that was what his soul was craving. Not Samara at all but home.

Once secured at the London docks, Reese made arrangements for additional repairs and released his crew for three weeks. Dressed elegantly in tight, fawn-colored trousers, a shirt of fine linen, a simply tied cravat and plainly tailored blue coat, he left the ship and joined the throngs on the docks.

He was fascinated, as always, by the sounds and colors that surrounded him, the multitude of accents and the peacock dress of so many dandies. There were small boys shifting through the crowds, looking for purses to lift; and gaudily dressed women, from twelve to fifty, reaching out with filth-covered hands to offer their personal wares. Beggars, many of them former soldiers with missing limbs, held out their hands in hopeless supplication. More than a few coins left Reese's pockets to jump and jingle in a cup or hand and earn him a "God bless ye, sir."

He almost gagged from the smell of dead fish mingled with that of unwashed bodies and human waste carelessly thrown from windows. He had forgotten, perhaps because he wanted to, the filth of the city, the pervading smell of rot and disease.

Wanting to put the turmoil of the London docks behind him, he quickly hailed a carriage to take him to the Hampton home on Grosvenor Square. He very much doubted if Avery would be in residence, but he could take one of the horses the Hamptons had stabled nearby for town use. He would leave in the morning for Beddingfield.

When the carriage reached the address, Reese paid the coachman and started up the stairs two at a time, stopping only at the sound of a familiar voice.

"Hampton...I say, Hampton, slow down."

Reese turned, and his face warmed in greeting. "Jeremy...you devil. It's been a long time."

Jeremy Clayton, Earl of Sheffield, responded with his usual wide grin. "Too long, Reese. I heard you turned pirate."

Reese groaned. "Not you, too. Privateer, my friend. Privateer."

"Whatever it is, it seems to agree with you," Jeremy said enviously, looking at his sun-bronzed, heavily muscled, yet lean, friend. His eyes danced mischievously as he continued. "I hope you're not planning to stay in London long...none of the rest of us poor bachelors will have a chance."

Reese's eyes glinted with amusement. Jeremy, with his deceptively innocent face, title and wealth, had bedded half of London ladies, available or not. What was so amazing to Reese was that he had remained friends with all of them. It was difficult if not impossible to get angry at Jeremy Clayton whose love of the world, particularly the feminine world, was so uncomplicated. He quite simply liked everyone.

"You mean there's one left that hasn't yet succumbed to you?" Reese replied now. "Now however did that happen?"

Jeremy's smile was devilish. "There is one...a widow...I'll make you a small wager."

Reese arched an eyebrow.

"There's a ball tonight...at Tallant's. She'll be there. I'll wager you can't take her home."

"And the prize?" If she had spurned Jeremy's best attempts, she must be difficult indeed.

Jeremy eyed him speculatively. They had attended Oxford together and had often competed for the same women. It had become a game. Neither had ever cared enough about one particular woman to let it ruin their friendship. But both had lost substantial sums of money. It was often Jeremy's irresistible likability and title against Reese's superb good looks.

Reese thought rapidly now. Perhaps this is what he needed. A challenge. Perhaps another woman would drive the images of a dark-haired, gray-eyed sorceress from his thoughts.

"A hundred pounds," Jeremy said now, "if you lose."

Reese's eyebrows went higher. "And if I win?"

"One of Sable's colts," Jeremy replied, watching the fire leap in Reese's eyes. Hampton had frequently spoken of purchasing one of Jeremy's prize horses, but the price had always been too high, especially when Beddingfield needed so much and he was so often at sea.

"You must be very sure of yourself," Reese said now.

"I've just missed wagering with you," Jeremy answered, his face wreathed in little boy charm and innocence. "Is it a wager?"

"It is," Reese replied against his better judgement. God, he needed a diversion. And Jeremy's taste always ran to beautiful women. Usually blond hair and blue eyes. It was a taste they both shared. He couldn't think why now. The image of dark hair and thundercloud gray eyes made everyone else colorless and tame by comparison. His fists clenched in frustration. Would his mind never let her go?

Jeremy was looking at him curiously. "Don't you even want to know what she looks like?"

Reese forced himself to grin. "Blond hair and blue eyes?"

Jeremy stared at him with astonishment. "How did you...?"

Reese just laughed, but it had a hollow sound. "I trust I will be welcome...I have no invitation."

"You are always welcome, Reese. You add spice to our poor bland stew...it's been deucedly dull without you. Until tonight, then...my carriage will pick you up." He turned and walked rapidly away before Hampton could change his mind.

Eloise Stanton was indeed a beauty, Reese thought as Jeremy introduced her. Dressed in gold satin which matched the rich color of her hair, she was slim and elegant...and surprisingly cool. Her green eyes held a note of reserve as she examined Reese.

"I have heard of you, Captain Hampton," she said in a low melodic voice. "You have an interesting reputation."

Reese, who was about to deliver a lavish compliment, abruptly closed his mouth. Her comment was as close to polite condemnation as one could get. He could almost hear Jeremy's mirth, and he silently cursed the irrepressible young lord.

He bowed low, knowing that compliments would not be the route to success with this lady. "You must tell me about it, my lady, and give me a chance to defend myself."

"And could you?" she replied tartly.

"It depends on what it is." He smiled genuinely, his eyes flashing with humor. He wondered exactly how much his reputation had been embellished in his absence. He found he liked Eloise Stanton's directness. "I can assure you I do not beat women or children."

"A relief," she answered quickly, a smile finally lighting her face.

"Now that is ascertained, may I have the honor of this dance?"

Lady Stanton tipped her head in thought, but the gesture lacked coyness. Reese knew he would have been most attracted to her months ago but now...damn.

What would Samara look like, dressed in a ballgown with her red-streaked hair set aglow by the hundreds of candles in this room? He imagined her in his arms; he felt his loins ache with the thought.

"Captain!"

He looked back down at Lady Stanton's puzzled face.

"I believe your attention is elsewhere," she said, her eyes clouded with thought.

"I was only thinking how lovely you are," Reese replied.

"I don't think that's entirely true, Captain, but I'll accept it for now. And, yes, you may have this dance."

Reese offered his arm and led her toward the other dancers, briefly glancing back at Jeremy and watching the astonishment on his friend's face. He grinned in reply.

It was a pleasant evening, more pleasant than Reese had thought possible. He monopolized Eloise's time, and she permitted it despite constant bids for her attention. His liking for her increased, along with his guilt over the wager.

As the room grew close with the heat of bodies and the cloying smell of perfume, he asked her outside. They walked in the small formal garden and finally sat on a small stone bench. In days past, he would have started his seduction...a hand on the shoulder, a touch of lips against the hair, the whispering of sweet compliments. But he could force none of them. He liked Eloise, but he wanted Samara. And he liked Eloise too much to play his old games. There was a dignity about her that he respected and had no wish to destroy.

"Your husband?" he said gently.

"Killed three years ago by the French," she said softly.

"You still miss him." It was a statement.

"Every day of my life," she replied. "We had been married less than a year, but he was my heart. I often wonder if it will ever be whole again." There was a small sigh.

"Do you have any family?" he asked, watching curiously as she stiffened.

"My...husband's brother, and a sister. It was my sister who convinced me to come tonight. I'm staying with her..."

Reese noticed the increasing tension in her voice. "She was right," he said quietly. "You're much too lovely to hide."

"And you, Captain? I see a certain preoccupation."

He laughed wryly. "You see too much, Lady Stanton."

"Including a certain wager?" She had relaxed once more, and her eyes twinkled in the moonlight.

Reese was rarely disconcerted. He was thoroughly so now. "How did you . . . ?"

"I know Jeremy," she said, "and I couldn't help but notice his expression when I consented to dance with you." She laughed now. "And I knew there had to be a reason he told me all those terrible things about you today when he called on me. Especially when you showed up together...as friends."

Reese grinned. "He must be apoplectic."

"I hope so," she replied with the first real smile of the evening. "May I ask what you wagered?"

Reese didn't know why he didn't feel uncomfortable at the question. "One of his jealously guarded colts."

"Then we will have to see that he pays it," she said with satisfaction. "What do I have to do?"

Reese raised an eyebrow. "Go home with me...but you can't do that...there's your reputation." He flinched at his newly discovered scruples.

"I know Jeremy," she said. "He won't say anything...he would hate to admit that you succeeded where he did not. And it will be a good lesson. Should we bid him good night?"

"You are an extraordinary woman, Lady Stanton."

"Eloise, Captain. If we are to go to your home together, it's Eloise."

The two reentered the ballroom. Eloise introduced Reese to her sister and said the captain would be taking her home early;

she had a headache. Her sister, who had a happy glow of her own as she looked up at her husband, merely smiled, a satisfied look on her face.

Jeremy looked stunned and was, for once in his life, speechless. He could merely nod as Reese thanked him for the introduction. The astonishment gave way to admiration, then sheepishness as he acknowledged Reese's victory with a wink.

Reese took Eloise to his home rather than hers, where servants might talk. He knew the elderly couple that cared for the Hampton town home in the family's absence would be long abed. Once settled in the sitting room, Reese and Eloise sat and talked almost as old friends. Reese discovered that Eloise knew Leigh, his sister-in-law, and had visited Beddingfield several times.

"You're different from what I imagined, from Leigh's description," she said finally. "I think she was always a little afraid of you."

"Probably because Avery and I seem so different. I think she fears my restlessness will infect my brother."

"You *are* different, unusually so for twins."

"Not as much as you think," Reese said thoughtfully. "It's just that Avery knew from the time we were very young that he had to be responsible, that he would have the title. Sometimes I think he envies me my freedom."

"And *you*, do you envy *him*?"

"No," he said frankly. "I've always been well satisfied."

Surprise flickered across her face. There was also, he noted, a touch of something like fear, leaving Reese to puzzle. He offered her another glass of sherry, which she refused, and he poured himself some brandy. He studied her.

"Why did you come here tonight?" he said finally.

"You were kind," she said. "I think I had expected something entirely different." Her eyes were wide when she looked up at him. "I wanted to teach Jeremy a lesson, and I needed...a friend. In the garden, I thought I might have found one."

Reese played with his glass. "You are entirely too trusting."

"Not usually," she said, and he knew from her tone she was speaking the truth. "I had heard much about you, not only from Leigh and Jeremy but..."

"I know," Reese said dryly. "And most of it is deserved, which is why I still don't understand..."

She looked defenseless as she peered up at him, a departure from the cool demeanor at the beginning of the evening. "I could guess your intentions. I could also see how halfheartedly you were going about it. I suspect there is a lady...?"

A rueful smile touched Reese's lips. "I didn't know it was so obvious."

She just looked at him quizzically.

"She's married," Reese said slowly, "to someone I now consider a friend."

Eloise smiled in sympathy. Her loss was still too strong for her to be interested in another man. George, her brother-in-law, wouldn't accept that. Somehow, this man—this reputed rake with few known scruples—had recognized it, had respected it. She was grateful.

"What's her name?" she said now, recognizing his need to talk. How had they become friends? So quickly?

"Samara," he said, the name rolling off his tongue like a poem. She heard the caress in his voice. She was startled at his next words. "She tried to kill me with a wine bottle."

Eloise laughed. "And is that what it takes to capture Reese Hampton's heart? Perhaps I should spread that little secret."

"Good God, no," he said in feigned horror. "It was only because of her ineptness that I am here tonight." His mouth crooked as he regarded her. "But surely she did some damage, since I am here with one of the loveliest women in London, and we are only...talking." The lift of his eyebrow conveyed his mock dismay.

"Ah, Captain," she said lightly. "I believe you are sorely maligned. And it is time to go. If Jeremy followed us, he most surely will be satisfied by now."

Reese regarded her seriously, all teasing gone. There was something troubling her. "If you need anything...anything at all, come to me," he said slowly, "and if I'm not here, go to Avery. I will talk to him."

She merely nodded. "And thank you for a very interesting evening."

After Reese saw her home, he sat brooding as the coach wound through the darkened streets. He could barely believe what had happened this night, that he had been in his own home with a beautiful woman and all he could think about was a dark-haired wildcat. And Eloise? Something was frightening her; he could sense it. He would talk to Avery, do some investigating. Perhaps it would put an end to his recurring dark thoughts.

Chapter Ten

Beddingfield looked prosperous from a distance. The well-tended fields were beginning to show the first of the summer's crop and the cattle and sheep looked fat and content. The manor house, which never failed to awe Reese with its size and majesty, appeared in remarkably good repair amidst the carefully sculptured gardens.

He had not been home in three years but had been spending the bulk of his prize money for Beddingfield's upkeep. Although he cared little about the day-to-day responsibility of the estate, he wanted the lands to remain in the family. Only reluctantly had his brother told him, on his last visit, of financial difficulties. It had taken Reese days to convince his twin to accept his financial help and then Avery would accept it only as a loan. It was money Reese considered well spent. Preferable, he thought now, to London's gambling clubs or greedy mistresses.

Struck suddenly by a flash of joy and pride, he urged his tired gray into a gallop, promising the stallion a well-earned rest. Some of the unusual melancholy that had haunted him the past month lifted; by God, it would be good to see Avery again.

He left the horse in the stables with strict instructions for its keep, knowing all the time it was probably unnecessary. Avery had always selected and trained his grooms with great care. His love of horseflesh equaled and perhaps even surpassed Reese's. His twin would be delighted with Reese's present—Jeremy's prize colt—which was to be delivered in several days by a chastened Lord Sheffield. Reese grinned as he approached the house with impatient strides.

Avery was riding the estate, but Leigh was home and after several flustered moments greeted him warmly.

"Why didn't you let us know?" she asked breathlessly. "Avery will be overjoyed."

"I just arrived in London yesterday," her brother-in-law said with his old mischievous grin. "And I wanted to surprise you." He surveyed her affectionately. Leigh was pretty in a quiet, tranquil way; she had always been shy around Reese, but he had recognized his brother's contentment and loved Leigh for providing it. Now his grin widened. "The prodigal brother returns."

"And he is gladly welcome," she said. "Come inside and meet your niece and nephew."

Even Reese's steps were different, Leigh thought as she led him up to the nursery. They had an impatience that Avery's lacked. She had once thought, fancifully, that while a room was energized with unseen currents when Reese entered, it relaxed when Avery made an appearance. She had always been a little reserved around Reese—not frightened, but not quite at ease either. It was difficult to look into a face so like her husband's and see the restless eyes, the reckless spirit. It sent a quiet shiver through her as she thought her beloved husband might be hiding a similar longing for freedom and adventure.

She shook her head at the nonsensical thought. She and Avery had been married nearly seven years now, and he seemed the most contented and devoted of husbands.

Reese was amazingly gentle with the children, accepting their hugs easily and instantly captivating them with his wide smile. He even further won their hearts by talking to them like tiny adults. Leigh regarded the scene with bemusement; little Catherine was not yet born on Reese's last visit, and young Anthony had been too small to do much but gaze wonderingly at the stranger who looked so much like his papa.

Leigh did not have time to wonder long. A groom from the stable had been sent to fetch Avery and now he stood in the nursery's doorway, his wide smile matching Reese's.

Reese's shorter hair was more golden, bleached by years in the Caribbean sun, but their eyes were the same startling blue-green and now sparkled with the same depths of emotion. Their height and build had once been very similar but Reese, Leigh noted, was now leaner and more muscular from the strenuous activities aboard ship. He looked more than ever like a dangerous jungle cat. She was glad Avery had none of that aura about him.

The brothers eyed each other fondly until Catherine pulled at Reese's hand. "He looks like Papa," she said now, her mouth and eyes like little O's.

"So he does, sweeting," Avery said, then untangled his hand and clasped his brother with both arms, receiving a similar bear hug. They stood there for several seconds, in wordless understanding.

"You're going to stay a while this time, aren't you," Avery said finally.

"Long enough for you to wish my departure," Reese replied. "You know my tendency to interfere in everything."

"Not enough, Reese, not nearly enough. You know I wish you would come back permanently and work with me."

"No estate needs two masters."

Avery's face clouded. He had always felt guilty that he'd inherited, and no disclaimer on Reese's part had relieved that guilt.

"Aren't you going to offer me a brandy?" Reese asked, seeing the familiar shadow. "I want to know how everything goes, how the tenants fare. What about Joe Farley? I didn't see him at the stables."

Thus distracted, Avery led the way down to the handsome library where he poured drinks for both of them, and they settled into two leather chairs.

"Joe," Avery said of Beddingfield's estate manager, "is looking at some new mares for me."

Reese's mouth turned up in a sly smile. "I hope your stables aren't going to be too full. I come bearing gifts. One of Sheffield's colts, out of Sable."

His brother looked at him with disbelief. "I've been trying to get one of those animals for years. Would you like to tell me how you did it? For future reference?"

"I don't think you want to know," Reese answered, an enigmatic look on his face. It became an amused grin as he considered the very unlikely possibility of Avery resorting to this particular wager. "And I don't think Leigh would want you to try it."

Avery merely looked puzzled. He suspected he wouldn't receive a more substantial answer, not when Reese had the familiar gleam in his eye.

Reese changed the subject. "The estate looks well, prosperous."

"Thanks to you," Avery said, his eyes not quite meeting those of Reese. He busied himself selecting a cheroot and lighting it. He tried to suppress his feeling of guilt. He often wondered why Reese did not suspect him. One twin could usually tell instantly when the other was lying or withholding something. But Reese was obviously preoccupied at the moment, despite his observation about Beddingfield. There was something different about him, something so subtle that Avery thought few others would see it. Partly to change the subject, partly because he was intrigued, Avery started to probe gently.

"Still no ladies . . . of a serious nature?"

The shadow that deepened the color of Reese's eyes told Avery far more than his almost forced answer.

"In the middle of an ocean? And who can compete with my lovely *Unicorn*?"

"You are missing much, brother," Avery said slowly. "There's a special happiness in sharing your life with someone you love. And Tony and Catherine are little miracles. When they reach for my hand, I feel I'm the richest man in England."

A muscle flexed in Reese's jaw, and his eyes clouded.

"There is someone," Avery said.

"She's married, and she's a fervent little American," Reese replied, knowing now that Avery wouldn't stop until he knew everything. They had always confided in each other.

Avery raised his eyebrow in a fashion amazingly like his twin's, as Reese slowly related the tale. At its end, he could only shake his head. "What now?"

Reese shrugged hopelessly. "Try to get her out of my mind. Damn if I understand what happened."

"Love," Avery said softly. "Love happened. You appear to have all the symptoms."

"And nothing I can do about it," Reese said. "Rather ironic, isn't it? After all these years of denying there's such a thing, and then an American . . . a married American at that . . ."

Avery looked at him sympathetically. He had hoped these past few years that Reese would find love—and some peace. Instead, he had finally found love—and pain. Once more he felt guilt at his good fortune. "Are you planning to go back to the American coast?"

"I thought I would trouble the French a bit more. I seem to have lost my taste for American ships." The wryness was back. "Temporarily, anyway."

"Don't you think your luck might run out one of these days?" Avery asked. "Won't you even consider giving up privateering?"

The old sardonic look came into Reese's face, the one that always frightened Leigh. "I might as well give up breathing," he said.

"That might well be the result," Avery observed thoughtfully. "Beddingfield is doing quite well now; it really doesn't need any more money."

"Even if it doesn't, I wouldn't quit. Not now. Not when England is still at war with France and now America." he grinned. "I'm not as easily tamed as you, brother."

The conversation changed then, and Reese asked about Eloise.

"Any interest there?" Avery inquired.

"I like her," Reese answered quietly. "No more. And she seems troubled. She said she was a friend of Leigh's."

Avery hesitated. He had had the same feeling about Eloise. "She's been here several times to see Leigh. Now you mention it she did seem quite…almost frightened. I thought it was grief. She obviously loved her husband very much. It was one of the real love matches at court."

"What about her family?"

"There's her husband's younger brother, George Carlton. He's now the Earl of Stanton. I don't think he and Robert got along well, but of course Eloise couldn't inherit the family estate. Robert did leave her the bulk of his own money. She has one sister who's older. That's all, I believe." He looked at Reese curiously. His brother seldom showed such interest in a woman he didn't desire. Reese, Avery knew, had not held a high opinion of the female sex. This newly revealed gallantry surprised—and delighted—him. Apparently Reese had changed more than he'd first thought.

"Why don't you ask Leigh to invite her? Maybe we can find some way to help," Reese suggested.

"You constantly amaze me, Reese. I've never thought you a Lancelot."

"I'll try anything once," Reese retorted, sipping his brandy.

Avery merely laughed and lifted his own glass.

The week before Reese's planned departure, the Hamptons and Lady Stanton arrived in London. Feverish preparations were under way for a ball planned in three days' time. Invitations had been sent a week earlier and few were declined. Everyone wanted to see the notorious Reese Hampton, who was said to have amassed a fortune in his not quite respectable profession and who had a reputation as the wildest of rakes. Young ladies' hearts fluttered, while older ones remembered, but no one refused an invitation.

George Carlton, the present Earl of Stanton, was more than a little curious at his inclusion. He didn't know the Hamptons well; Avery Hampton was seldom in London, preferring the quiet life at his estate. But he was known to have friends close to the king and for that reason Stanton planned to attend. Reese Hampton was no more than an adventurer and Stanton had little or no interest in the man.

It was one more mystery. The other was the whereabouts of his sister-in-law. Damn her, anyway. Where had she gone? He had sent out inquiries but, as yet, to no avail. He had had her guarded on the estate, but she'd slipped away. When he followed her to her sister's, she was already gone and Serena had denied any knowledge of her whereabouts. He doubted he would find out anything tonight, but there was always the possibility.

His brother had left Eloise all his money, leaving George with an empty title and entailed land with little income. His own gambling had brought the situation perilously close to disaster. In the past two years, he had courted, then bullied, Eloise, threatening her sister with financial ruin and her friends with harm. He had tried to isolate her completely. If Eloise persisted in her denial of him, he had planned a tragic accident. The inheritance would then revert to him; he had forged enough documents to ensure that eventuality. But she had slipped away before he could implement his plan.

The ball was well under way when he arrived. He felt himself well dressed, not realizing how completely his bright green waistcoat emphasized his pudgy body.

The house was glittering with hundreds of candles, and he envied the richness of the furnishings if not the conservative taste of them. His attention wandered slowly around the room, noting the quality of the guests. There were several members of the royal family, and titles abounded, many far greater than his own. Again, he wondered at his own inclusion. Then his eyes fastened on the two women and two men standing together as they greeted guests, and his heart dropped.

There, standing with the Hampton brothers was Eloise. Elegant in a gold gown, her hair crowned by flowers, she stood close to one of the Hamptons, damn if he knew which one. As he watched, the man's hand went possessively around her waist, and he struggled for control. He approached them warily.

After brief, stilted greetings, Stanton's hand, almost involuntarily, darted out for Eloise. It was stopped midway by Reese Hampton, whose hard face, glittering eyes and grimly set mouth sent shivers of fear through him.

Hampton's voice was coolly courteous as he bowed slightly. "Eloise wanted you to be the first to know we're betrothed. We plan to announce the engagement tonight," he said in a tone loud enough to capture the attention of many of their distinguished guests.

Stanton blanched. Fury flickered across his face as his overweight body stiffened. "As her closest male relative, and protector, I will not give my consent," he blustered.

Reese now looked amused. "I don't think either of us requires your consent," he said. "Eloise will be staying with my brother until the marriage. Be advised she is under our protection." His voice grew cold and was as clear as a pistol shot in the packed room. "God help anyone who tries to interfere!"

Stanton took a step backward at the open threat, one that he knew many had heard. His face crimsoned as he saw curiosity on more than one face.

"I wish only the best for Eloise," he said. He gathered his courage, and added in a firmer voice, "Your reputation does not recommend you as a husband."

"And yours," Reese shot back, "does not recommend you as a man."

Stanton was now publicly insulted. He glared helplessly from Reese to Eloise, seeing all his hopes disappear. He knew he was no match for a man of Hampton's highly touted abilities. He could only try to extricate himself. As if he hadn't heard the last remark, he bowed carefully to the two Hamptons and to Eloise. "My best wishes," he said stiffly, the words practically choking him. Perhaps, just perhaps, he could arrange a little accident for the interfering pirate. He was, after all, in a very risky business. A word about the bastard's destination to the right ears . . . the Americans would pay dearly for such information.

It would not be the first time he had sold information. Now he would do it for pleasure, as well as gold.

Despite the amused and knowing looks he had to endure during the evening, Stanton stayed, trying to look as unconcerned as possible. His humiliation was dimmed only by his secret plotting—and the knowledge he would soon repay the arrogant pirate. He had to learn everything he could about Reese Hampton: when Hampton was leaving, where he was going.

He was, then, very attentive when he overheard Reese speaking with Jeremy Clayton.

"You're a sly one," Jeremy said. "I never thought to see *you* harnessed. When is the wedding?"

"Not until after my next voyage," Reese said. "I have some unfinished business." During the past few weeks he had changed his mind about American ships. He had grown increasingly angry over Samara's hold on his thoughts. By avoiding the American coast, he was merely giving in to those feelings. Perversely, he thought the way to end them was a direct confrontation...if not with Samara, at least with what she represented.

But he told Jeremy only that he was returning to the Carolina coast...

After the last guest left, Reese and Avery shared a few minutes together.

"She should be safe enough now," Reese said. "She can break the engagement when I come back...or before if she wishes."

"She would make a good wife," Avery said slowly.

"She would indeed," Reese replied wryly, "but not for me. Nor do I have her heart, only her gratitude."

"There have been happy marriages based on less," Avery commented, still hoping that his twin would find the happiness he himself cherished. He flinched at the morose expression of his brother's face.

"But not for me," Reese answered. His voice grew firmer. "I like my freedom." He only wished that he still believed those words.

While the two Hamptons talked, Stanton, who had left shortly after hearing the conversation between Jeremy and Reese, was meeting with an agent of the American government. And several miles away on Fleet Street, a weary printer was painstakingly assembling hundreds of tiny pieces of type in preparation for the next day's newspaper. Among the stories was the betrothal announcement of Reese Hampton and Eloise Stanton. The news had spread rapidly.

Chapter Eleven

After her weeks on the British privateer, Samara took a new interest in the war. Until her ill-fated adventure the war had seemed a long way off and politics had bored her. But now her fervor was more personal. She knew how close Brendan and his crew had come to imprisonment or impressment. She had heard from members of his crew of the horrors of British ships, and the impressment issue was suddenly very real to her.

And now she had a new source fueling her patriotism. Conn had been fighting the Creeks with the Alabama Militia. He had been badly wounded in the leg by a British musket and would always have a limp. His tales of the horrors inflicted on settlers, and the role played by the British in supporting and even encouraging atrocities against women and children infuriated Samara. Similar atrocities by Americans against the women and children in the Indian villages, and the earlier wrongs against the Cherokees, were not mentioned or dismissed as aberrations.

There were similar reports from the northwest, and stories of torture and murder—all at the behest of the British—multiplied. At the same time, there were increasing news items about the terrible conditions in Dartmoor prison in England—the holding place for many American seamen and privateers. It increased the fear of the O'Neill family, for now—at the request of the navy—Brendan had outfitted his ship with heavier guns and had turned to privateering himself. He had been gone several months and they had heard nothing.

All this continued to build Samara's rage against the British and, consequently, Reese Hampton who was a ready target for her condemnation. She conveniently dismissed Yancy and

Davey and Michael Simmons. They had to follow their captain's commands. And she convinced herself more than ever that the Englishman had been planning, in some devious way, to betray them. She could not let herself think anything good of him, for then she would indeed be even more lost and miserable than she was now. She could fight the loneliness only by convincing herself he was the worst kind of blackguard.

Not long after her return home, Samara had ridden to the family's secret cave. Beset by an anguish she could not understand or quash, she sought the place where she had once dreamed so happily. The cave held a special place in each and every heart in her family. It had been where her mother had found Papa, wounded and near death, and had nursed him back to health. Each of the O'Neill children knew the story by heart. Sore-hearted at her failure to dismiss Captain Hampton from her thoughts, Samara sat in the cave, watching the weak trails of light that came through the heavy underbrush, and wished for a knight errant of her own. An American one. But the only vision that came to her was a tawny-haired, sun-kissed giant who stood at the helm of a ship, his face toward the heavens and his eyes searching . . . always searching. There was an odd feeling here . . . as though the cave were waiting for something. There seemed to be an expectancy that she had never felt before. Mystified, she allowed herself to dream briefly of Reese Hampton, remembering the magic of that night on deck when their lips had touched so hungrily, when the moon had embraced them lovingly and had made them, for precious unforgettable seconds, the only two people on earth.

Fool. She scolded herself. *He's gone, and he probably doesn't even remember you exist.*

Even worse, chimed in another inner voice, *he could be out there even now, attacking Brendan again, or some other American ship.*

Or it could be Reese himself in danger, came the first voice. Fear hit her like a physical blow. Reese Hampton in danger? "It could never be so," she whispered to the silent walls. "Not him! It would be like stilling the wind."

But even so, she could not dismiss a shiver of premonition. Suddenly cold, she left the cave.

The strange feelings of that day—the expectancy and the fear—stayed with her. Despite repeated urgings from her family, she declined most invitations, thinking them frivolous in this time of peril. She simply had no interest. The men in the district held no attraction, and it was all she could do to even remain polite when they called. Soon, most became discouraged and invitations fell off.

She spent more and more time with her father, talking about the war. Although he worried constantly about her lack of interest in suitors or other matters, he approved of her newfound interest in the war and politics. He was usually damning the Federalists for their continuing opposition to the war, and fuming about the current military leadership. Connor O'Neill was particularly incensed one night at dinner after one major disaster.

"That damned fool William Hull ran and left a column of men to be massacred," he said. "The coward should be hung."

His namesake, Conn, bitterly agreed. General Hull had been sent to Detroit with 2,200 men. Faced by a British-Canadian Army of only 250, he had dillied and dallied until one of his supply columns was massacred. He then surrendered without firing a shot, exposing the whole American northwest to the Indians, and Hull's name was being cursed throughout the country.

"It's no better in the northeast," Connor said. "The *Gazette* said a large force moved to cross the Niagara River into Canada, but part of the army refused, leaving the first troops with nothing to do but surrender. With that kind of leadership, God knows what will happen."

Samara listened intently as she ate. The only good news came from the sea. Though tiny, the American navy was as deadly as any afloat. The captains of the *Constitution* and the *United States* had reported major victories, and the smaller brigs and sloops consistently displayed speed and accuracy superior to their British counterparts. Equally damaging to the British were the American privateers which had become a major force in the conflict. Samara had read only today that insurance rates for British ships had tripled in the past months because of losses.

She usually joined in the dinner discussions but tonight she was silent. As the war grew more bitter, it seemed inevitable that disaster would strike one of the people she cared about most: Brendan, who was now at greatest risk; Conn, who planned to rejoin the militia in Alabama as soon as his leg had healed sufficiently, and gentle Marion, who was attached to the militia as a doctor. And then there was, of course, Reese Hampton. The irony of the situation did not escape her.

* * *

The *Unicorn* seemed cursed from the moment it left London. Unlike previous voyages, when luck accompanied every nautical mile, Reese now ran into one disaster after another. The bad luck started at the docks when three of his most trusted crew members, one of them his best gunner, failed to return to the ship; after several days' search, he found that two had been killed in a tavern brawl and the other had just disappeared. Restless and unwilling to spare the time to search for competent new members, Reese decided to sail shorthanded. The *Unicorn* then ran into a series of storms, each one more severe than the one before. Oilskins were useless, and there was not a dry spot on the ship nor a dry rag to wear. The cook had to douse the galley fire, and there was no warm food. Salt water often mixed with the fresh. After three weeks at sail and ten days of continuous storms, Reese was almost numb with fatigue and the ship was battered. The canvas was badly torn, and one of the cannons had torn loose from its moorings, badly injuring two more of his crew.

Usually storms exhilarated him, creating a match of his wits against the strongest and ablest of forces. But now both he and the ship were exhausted and he wished only to see an end to it.

When morning came on the twenty-first day, it was little different from the previous one. The same thick gloom made it barely possible to distinguish day from night; a blinding rain raked the ship and the wind howled like demons as it battered the rigging. Blinding flashes of lightning ran down the conductor and hissed as they leaped into the sea, each accompanied by its own distinctive roar of thunder. The waves were mountainous and played with the ship as if it were a toy, tossing it almost at will and straining every fibre of her frame.

Reese fought the wheel as he never had before; for the first time in his sailing years he was forced to consider his own mortality as the warring elements wrestled him for control.

In late afternoon, the barometer started to rise, and Reese turned the ship over to his first mate as he studied the considerable damage. They were leaking badly, and many of the yards were splintered and useless. The wind had cut through the canvas like scissors.

Reese uttered a small prayer. If he calculated correctly, the *Unicorn* was not far from the Carolina coast—and the enemy. He would have to turn away, head for Bermuda and repairs, and pray to God they didn't encounter any American ships.

Several of their guns had torn away from their moorings and were washed overboard. One of his few remaining gunners was badly injured and until extensive repairs were made he couldn't even outrun a whaleboat.

Darkness came much too slowly, and Reese blessed the cloud-filled sky. Portholes were covered and work progressed feverishly on repairs below decks: pumping water and repairing planking. Work above deck was difficult in the almost-complete darkness. No lights were allowed; much would have to wait until the first glimmers of dawn.

McDonald, whose eyes were universally recognized as the sharpest, took watch at the masthead. Reese, who had had no sleep in three days, took a short nap before returning to duty at dawn, just in time to hear McDonald's sharp warning. Both land and sails were visible. Seconds later he reported at least two ships.

Reese cursed roundly and took the wheel, ordering as much sail as possible and heading toward the coast. If he could find a deep enough river, perhaps he could disappear. If the ships were enemy frigates, they would have a difficult time following. It was their only chance.

The *Unicorn* was sluggish, and it took all of Reese's strength to turn it against the wind and toward the coast. What in God's name had happened to his fabled luck? He tried to summon it now, praying for a fog to envelop his movements as the two ships started to close the distance. He had no way of knowing that the ships had, several days before, been alerted to his destination and had been actively hunting him. He only knew that his options were rapidly disappearing.

His desperate gamble proved futile. As the ship hugged the coast, they could find no openings, and he ordered the crew to prepare for battle, knowing as he did the severe odds against him. He knew now that he faced an American frigate with twice his gun power, and a corvette, a ship slightly larger than his own and almost as maneuverable.

Reese watched as the American flag was hoisted along with signal flags ordering him to heave-to. He answered with the raising of his own flag and a salvo from one of his remaining long guns. Reese was damned if he would surrender, not as long as there was the slimmest chance he could still find an escape.

The American frigate answered with a broadside which smashed several of the *Unicorn*'s boats and shattered her spars. The *Unicorn*'s return fire tumbled the enemy's foretopmast, but the corvette had circled around and the *Unicorn* was receiving fire from two directions.

Shot was now raking Reese's ship and he could hear the cries of his crewmen. A large shell entered the *Unicorn*'s side only a few inches above the waterline and passed entirely though it. Knowing any further defiance was useless, Reese prepared to surrender, when an explosion rocked the ship. He ordered the ship abandoned, and watched as his crewmen scurried down hastily lowered rope ladders. The wounded were carried and placed in the one surviving boat. Reese watched intently until only he and Yancy were left on what was rapidly becoming a pyre of greedy flames. Boats from the Yankee ships were already picking up the survivors, and Reese ordered Yancy off.

"Not until you go," Yancy replied adamantly, carefully watching the encroaching fire.

"I'm going to swim for it," Reese said. "I might just be able to make it. They're after *me*, and if they think I'm dead, you might have a better chance for exchange. And," he added, "free I just might be able to help you escape . . . if you're not exchanged."

Yancy knew it was possible despite the distance to shore. Reese was an extremely strong swimmer, and if anyone could survive the strong currents that existed along the coast, it was the captain. He also knew he could not dissuade him, not when Reese had that bright gleam in his eyes. Nor could he go along. He would only doom them both.

"I'll tell them you're dead, that you were killed in the last explosion," Yancy said slowly. He took Reese's hand, and clasped it tightly. "Good luck."

"And to you, Yancy." Reese's grim mouth turned up in a sudden confident smile. Cocky and almost boyishly wicked, it reflected the captain's usual relish for a challenge. That particular smile had been gone for several months, and Yancy had missed it.

The doctor felt a new confidence as he heard Reese's next words. "I'll see you in Bermuda. No later than Christmas."

"Bermuda," Yancy confirmed, and hurried over the side without a look back.

Reese took one last look at the *Unicorn*. It had served him well and little deserved this fate. His hand caressed the mahogany rail as his eyes traveled from the quarterdeck, now nearly consumed by flames, to what was left of the bow. Hidden by the flames, he slipped over the railing and dove into the sea.

The news of the *Unicorn*'s destruction traveled quickly through the Carolinas. In the months prior to the capture of Brendan's ship, the English privateer had become almost legendary as he preyed on American shipping. The fact that the notorious Captain Hampton had seized one of the O'Neill ships, and that Brendan O'Neill had stolen it back spurred tales of a feud between the two captains. Brendan had tried to squelch such rumors, feeling profoundly embarrassed about the heroic image he did not deserve. Yet other than tell the truth, which he had promised not to do, there was little he could say or deny. If truth be told, he felt like a damned hypocrite, and he cursed Hampton often for forcing his silence.

He was in Charleston, back for several weeks after a long and successful voyage, when he heard the news. His own ship, the *Samara*, was tucked away in one of the rivers flowing into the sea. He immediately sought more information and discovered from the authorities that Reese Hampton was considered dead. The English captain had refused to leave the ship and was killed in an explosion; the crew had been taken to Boston where they would probably be exchanged.

Brendan was struck by a deep sense of loss although the news hadn't surprised him. Hampton, he knew, must have been aware he would not be as easily exchanged as his men; from what he knew of the Englishman, Hampton would choose death before surrender or captivity.

But what really tormented Brendan was Samara. Regardless of what she said, or how she had railed against Hampton as an "unprincipled pirate of the lowest order," her eyes always betrayed her. They softened when the man's name was mentioned, and there was a wistfulness about her that nearly broke his heart. He had hoped that one day...

But now that hope was gone, and he wondered how she would take the news. There was no use trying to keep it from her... it was discussed everywhere, including all the newspapers. And Samara now read them all avidly. The only thing he could do was tell her himself and try to soften the blow.

It had been easier than he expected, mainly because she simply wouldn't believe him. She mourned the *Unicorn*, but insisted that Hampton was "simply too wicked to die."

"And," she added for good measure, "no one actually saw his body."

"The ship blew up, Samara," he answered patiently as if to a child. "They searched for a long time, and everyone agreed that no one could swim that far."

"*He* could," Samara said stubbornly. "Not that I care. It would be what he deserves." Her chin stuck out in an obstinate gesture Brendan knew only too well.

"The currents," he added weakly, but the chin did not retreat.

"He's not dead," she pronounced and marched out of the room, leaving him speechless and his mother, who had been there for support, wondering.

For the first time in months, Samara revisited the cave. Dressed in some of Conn's old clothes, she crawled into the interior and sat there, studying the patterns created by the sun's intrusion through the vines which protected the entrance.

"I would know if he were dead," she whispered. She could feel his energy even now, could sense that incredible vitality. For some reason she couldn't explain, she felt close to him here.

For the first time since she had returned to Glen Woods, she cried. The tears started in tiny trickles . . . thin trails down her face, and grew to great spasms that racked her body and tore at her heart. She didn't believe him dead, but the news had fired her immense need and longing for him. She cried as if her heart were breaking, and it was. It was shattering into thousands of tiny pieces. She knew now how much he was a part of her, how much he would always be a part of her. And he was out there now, alone and possibly badly wounded, in an enemy land; she was struck with a sudden desperate fear for him. She knew she cried because, for the first time, she consciously admitted she loved Reese Hampton, loved him with all the passion and life within her. And although her instinct believed him alive, she also knew her love was something that could never be. He was the enemy and he came from a life she could never accept . . . even if, by some miracle, he did want her. Which was, she felt, highly unlikely. Except for that brief kiss on deck, he had mostly treated her like a naughty child.

The tears slowed only because there were no tears left in the empty vessel that was Samara. The sobs quieted, and the spasms no longer tormented the physical body, but a worse agony pierced her mind.

Where is he? Please God, keep him safe. Just keep him safe.

* * *

Several days later, she said goodbye to Brendan, who was returning to his dangerous pursuits, and wished him Godspeed.

Before he left, he took her chin in his hand and studied the pensive face. "You have to get on with your life, little sister."

"I know," she said wistfully, "but I don't know how."

"Go out," he said. "For me, if not for yourself. You can't hide forever in a dream."

"He's spoiled everyone else for me," she whispered. "I see him everywhere."

"He's dead, Samara. You *must* believe that. There are so many young men out there who would love to put a sparkle back in those eyes. Give them a chance."

She tried to smile. "Emily Fontaine is announcing her engagement next week at a ball. I thought to refuse but perhaps..."

"For me," Bren said. "Go for me."

She nodded slowly.

"A promise?"

"Yes," she said, and she watched him leave, a slight sad smile on his face.

Samara knew her melancholy was affecting everyone in the house, and she made an effort to cast it aside. Both Conn and Marion, who was home for a brief visit, planned to accompany her to the ball. The event was to celebrate the betrothal of Emily, who was one of her best friends, and she knew of no way of avoiding it, not without hurting Emily and further distressing her family. Reluctantly, she withstood the hours of standing perfectly still while being measured and fitted for a new ball gown. When it was over, Samara barely glanced at the garment so patiently planned by her mother and the dressmaker. Unlike the pastels worn by so many unmarried young ladies, this gown had a satin underskirt of midnight blue and a silver-threaded sarcenet overskirt falling from an empire waist. The low, square-cut neckline emphasized the ivory of her skin and the swell of her breasts. The color of the gown brought out a lovely blue hue in her dark gray eyes and contrasted with the clear bloom of her complexion.

But Samara cared little for the magic of the gown and was barely tolerant as one of the maids brushed her hair until it seemed touched with fire, then wove silver ribbons through it, gathering it in the back and allowing it to fall in gentle curls over her shoulders. A silver shawl completed the costume, and she waited patiently for her brothers to finish their dress. A small trunk had been packed; the three of them would stay overnight.

It was a beautiful afternoon and would be a lovelier night. The sky was a rich deep blue without a hint of clouds. Yet there was a pleasant breeze taking the sting from the usually stifling July heat. Samara blessed the current fashions which were light and cool as she tried to enjoy the long ride. They had discussed going earlier during the day, and dressing at the Fontaine home, but Samara had demurred. She knew her mother wanted to help her dress; originally the older O'Neills planned to attend, but one of Samantha's mares was near foaling, and they'd decided to stay home.

Samara enjoyed the ride with her brothers. Both could be immensely entertaining when they tried, and they were trying now. Some of Conn's bitterness, which had festered since his wounding, dissolved as he and Marion bantered back and forth, trading amusing stories they had heard and recounting some of the most mischievous moments as children. Samara felt her heavy mood lighten, and she regarded them both fondly.

Marion was so kind...kind and thoughtful and sensitive. He had started a medical practice in Charleston before the war, but now served with the militia and stopped frequently by Glen Woods. Conn was the warrior, the only one of the brothers who had really wanted war, who had been impatient to serve. They were so different, yet so alike with their blond hair, just several shades apart, and their blue eyes.

Darkness came late these summer nights, but the full moon was already high in the sky when the carriage arrived at its destination. It was like a fairyland, Samara thought. Lanterns were strung between giant oaks and cypresses, and the air was rich with the scent of jasmine, magnolia and sweet bay.

Dozens of carriages lined the road. Marion and Conn ceremoniously helped Samara from the coach, and they entered the front foyer, greeting their hosts. Samara spied Emily and the two young ladies hugged each other. They separated, and Emily looked enviously as she studied every detail of Samara's gown. But nothing could dim the sparkle in Emily's eyes. This was *her* night; and she was delighted Samara had broken her self-imposed exile to be there.

"Come with me," Emily said, "there is the most exciting man here...he's, well, he's absolutely magnificent. If it weren't for my Jonathan..."

"Who is he?"

"I don't know exactly. He's an acquaintance of Mr. Samuels, a businessman of some kind, and he is so handsome and...sort of dangerous-looking."

Emily pulled a reluctant Samara along behind her. Samara had had her fill of dangerous-looking men and she really doubted if Emily knew the difference, anyway. Emily usually thought everyone was handsome, including Jonathan, her rather plain-looking but very pleasant fiancé.

Samara tried to see above the crowd, but it was impossible. She was being led through the large dining room past tables overflowing with food and into the large room being used for the ball tonight. Emily stopped suddenly, and Samara's eyes lifted from a blue coat which barely contained the impossibly wide shoulders to glittering blue-green eyes that flared suddenly, then glowed with a fervent fire before going blank.

Emily, in her delight at presenting so great a prize, totally missed the shock that passed over her friend's face. A surge of complete inexplicable joy exploded within Samara. Reese. Alive. Here. All the months of wanting, of suppressing those hurting aches, that longing for something unknown yet irresistible. Her hand started to reach tentatively out for him, but his expression stopped it midway. It was the look one would give a stranger. Then, almost immediately, they conveyed a silent message. Warning or plea? Samara didn't know which.

Emily's next words devastated her. She hadn't known what to think as to how Reese had come to be here, but she certainly wasn't prepared for Emily's introduction nor the name given her.

"Mr. Avery, this is Miss Samara O'Neill, my very best friend. Samara, this is Mr. Thomas Avery."

Reese bowed, and for a moment, Samara couldn't see his eyes. When he straightened, one eyebrow was lifted. "*Miss* O'Neill?"

Emily bubbled on, completely unaware of the currents between the two. "Of course, it isn't for lack of suitors. Samara is the most popular girl in the district."

"I can believe that," Reese answered in his deep drawl. A touch of mischief reached his wary eyes. "It quite defies understanding how such a lovely young lady would escape matrimony.''

Samara bit her lip, wishing that she hadn't suddenly become tongue-tied. But her mind was racing ahead, and all the thoughts were damning. What *was* Reese doing here posing as a businessman? And, most worrisome of all, why?

"Mr. *Avery*," she said finally. "You have to tell me about your business and what you are doing in our humble state. I don't think I've heard your name before."

The words were said sweetly. Too sweetly for Reese's comfort. They did not belong to the Samara he knew. But, then, how well did he know her? Certainly not as well as he had thought. The little minx. *Miss.* Damn. And damn Brendan.

The orchestra struck up a reel. Reese bowed once more. "May I have the honor of this dance, *Miss* O'Neill?''

"Certainly, Mr. Avery, although I'm afraid my poor country dancing isn't quite what you're used to."

"I doubt that," he said drily. "But in any event, my boots have probably had worse punishment." A sudden smile lit his face, and Samara melted. For an instant, she didn't care why he was here. It was just enough that he was. She accepted his arm and accompanied him to the dance floor, leaving Emily beaming with the joy of a successful matchmaker.

There was no way to talk during the dance. There were too many nearby ears. Only briefly did Samara whisper, "They said you were dead."

"Did you believe them?"

"No."

Again that smile that made her heart churn. Damn him.

As the dance ended, she leaned towards him and whispered quickly, "There's a giant cypress with great twisted roots at the back of the house. In an hour."

He nodded, his eyes searching hers for intent. He had little choice. He had to trust her.

Reese watched for several minutes, then made his way outside where he lit a cheroot. It had been a damn fool thing to do, coming here tonight. He should have refused, but Samuels had insisted.

He thought back to three weeks ago when his ship had exploded and he had barely made it to shore. There had been minutes, more than a few, when he had almost submitted to the cold and fatigue. But something inside wouldn't let him quit even when he wanted to. When he'd finally made shore he'd crawled up the sandbanks and collapsed under some ancient trees twisted by time and wind. He didn't know how long he had slept. It must have been nearly half a day because the sun was setting over the sea by the time he awoke. There were no sails now, only an empty endless ocean and miles of beach. He knew he was in serious trouble. He wore only canvas sailor trousers, and a now-tattered cotton shirt. He had no footwear, no money, no prospects. He didn't even know where in the hell he was. He did have, engraved in his mind for some such emergency, a list of secret English sympathizers in the Carolinas—a gift from his brother. But how to find them? And how could he travel like this?

Still fatigued from the days of fighting the storm and the long battle through the heavy seas, he decided to get more rest. Perhaps, then, he could think more rationally. He slept through much of the night, rising at the first light of dawn. He started north, hoping to find a farmhouse. He would claim to be a shipwrecked American. Reese was sure Yancy had convinced the Americans he was dead; there shouldn't be any alarm. He didn't worry about his accent; the American navy and merchantmen were filled with Scots, Irishmen and even Englishmen who had deserted. And he had been at sea with so many nationalities that his own speech had developed a unique flavor all of its own.

He didn't know how long he had walked, but he was immensely thirsty and hungry, and even the leatherlike soles of his feet were blistered and burned from the hot sand. It was late in the day, and he had eaten nothing when he finally found what he sought: a small cluster of huts and some small boats, none of them in very good repair.

He found both food and welcome in the tiny community. The inhabitants were people who lived with the sea's tragedies and they were ready sympathizers. They gave him a place to stay that night and shared their food, and even offered clothes they obviously couldn't spare. With a deep sense of guilt and shame for his lies, he refused, thanking them quietly for their hospitality, their food and their good wishes and he renewed his journey. Following their directions to Charleston he stayed off the main roads and through theft and burglary found some rough clothes and enough food to survive. He found Samuels' home one week after the sea battle, and met yet another obstacle. He couldn't get to the house, or even close to it. Armed guards stopped him at the main road as he turned toward the

Georgian mansion. He knew he didn't present a very comforting picture. His beard had grown to a thick stubble. His hair had not been combed in days. His rough clothes were sweat-stained and filthy, and his bare feet were bleeding. The son and brother of an earl? Even he had to laugh at that.

Only his ring, a jeweled coat of arms, seemed to make any impact. He had hidden it in a tiny pocket he had made in his shirt, and he now produced it. He was told to wait, and one of the guards took the ring and rode to the house. Almost immediately he was back with a stout, well-dressed figure who studied him intently. "Hampton?" The question was unbelieving.

Reese nodded.

"The newspapers said you were dead."

"That's what I wanted them to think."

The man finally smiled. "I know your brother. You are welcome. Come, we'll get you cleaned up and into some . . . more suitable clothes."

He had spent the next two weeks quietly at the Samuels' home. The planter had been a Tory during the revolution but had decided to stay while others left for Canada or the Caribbean. In the past thirty years, most of his neighbors had forgotten his loyalties, and he made no issue of them. But he still had a deep commitment to the crown and would arrange Reese's passage on a foreign ship to a port in the Caribbean.

It was not until ten days later that Samuels had requested a favor in return. He had been asked by a Federalist friend to secure information about the sailing of American privateers and blockade runners. Samuels knew the information was destined for the English navy. There were many in this country who wanted to see the war ended quickly, and American defeats could force an early peace. Samuels had no crop ready for shipment, no reason to ask questions. He suggested that Reese pose as a merchant who was looking for shipping contracts. There was to be a ball in the next week and many of the important figures in South Carolina's shipping business would be there.

"It won't work," Reese told Samuels. "I know one of them."

"O'Neill," Samuels said. "I heard the stories. But he left several days ago and won't be back for some time."

Reese tried to refuse again, although not out of fear. He doubted whether Mrs. O'Neill would attend without her husband; perhaps she was even with him. But he didn't like the idea of being a spy.

Samuels' good nature disappeared. He had given his assistance and was risking his life to help Reese. A favor was due. And he was calling it. Reese reluctantly agreed.

Samuels was very careful in the way he arranged the invitation. He told Everette Fontaine only that he had met Thomas Avery at a hotel in Charleston, and that the man was looking for some shipping contracts. It was enough. An invitation was sent to the hotel where Reese was now temporarily quartered, and Samuels arranged for a tailor. At the last minute, Samuels decided it best that he not even attend. Reese was left on his own....

Damn. After the past seven weeks he should have realized this would just be another in one long string of bad decisions and disasters. Reese knew he should probably leave now, but he couldn't. He had to see Samara one more time, especially now that he knew she was free. He knew he couldn't let her go without a word, without knowing how she felt. He had lived with agony for nearly a year. Perhaps she would agree to come with him. He stepped back into the ballroom and searched for her, but she wasn't there. He would have to wait. And, devil take it, he didn't know what was awaiting him. The lady or the hangman.

Chapter Twelve

Dozens of lanterns spread their magic—darting little slivers of silver and gold, intermingling and dancing in the glow of a full moon. Millions of stars hung in their intricate patterns, each contributing to the enchantment of the night and its aura of fantasy. Music, just far enough distant to be haunting, contributed to Samara's fearful expectancy, the weakness in her legs, the hammering of her heart. Reese Hampton. She had thought never to see him again . . . never except in her dreams, in her thoughts where he was a constant crippling presence. She had not been whole since that voyage to Bermuda. She had thought she would never be whole again. He had left her hollow, a shape without substance.

And now he was waiting for her, and she would betray him. She trembled at the thought. She would never forget the way his glittering jewel-like eyes leaped with what could only be joy when he saw her. Or was it joy? Perhaps just fear. But no, she knew it was not. His mouth had crooked in a small rueful smile when she was introduced as Miss O'Neill, but there was also challenge in his face. She knew he had to consider the possibility she might inform on him, and he was gambling that she would not, at least not until he had had a chance to talk to her. If nothing else, Captain Hampton was as confident, as arrogant as ever. Damn him! Damn him for entering her life again this way! Damn him for making her do something she feared she would regret the rest of her life! But she had no choice. She could not allow him to spy on her country. Brendan's life, and so many others, were at stake.

She saw him then, tall and commanding, his hair like molten gold in the flickering lights of the lanterns. He was standing under the cypress; his face, with its intricately carved features, was captured in all its strength by the moonlight. His lips, wide and sensuous, smiled in warm welcome. How completely beautiful he was, Samara thought, as her traitorous body quivered and throbbed. Knowing full well what she had just done, she wanted to die.

He reached out his hands to her, his eyes bright and mischievous. "Miss O'Neill . . . Samara . . .", he said, his baritone voice caressing her as intimately as any hand. "I think you must deal in sorcery for I have not been able to dislodge you from my thoughts. And now I find you free, as I have wished so many times. If I weren't so pleased, I think I would take you over my knee again . . ."

His eyes, his voice, his words burned into her soul. She had dreamed of this so many times. She treasured the moment, riveting it in her mind, because she knew in moments it would be broken, shattered like a delicate piece of glass.

Struggling to keep some sense about her, she was finally able to meet his eyes.

"Mr. *Avery*?" she said, questions in her tone, accusation in her face.

Some of the smile left Hampton's face. A shadow of the old mockery touched his eyes. "*Miss* O'Neill?" Her question was met with his own.

The terrible irony of the situation kept Samara silent this time. What could she say? How could she explain?

Reese Hampton looked at her quizzically, not understanding her unusual reticence. He had hoped for welcome, had expected questions, had prepared himself for accusations. The smile disappeared completely.

"Brendan is your brother, of course," he said now. It had been easy to guess once Samara was introduced; he had confirmed it through a fellow guest. "May I ask why the masquerade aboard the *Unicorn*?"

But Samara found it impossible to say anything. She had seen the figures, cloaked in shadows, as they moved quietly toward the tree. Her lips trembled, and something like desperation showed in her eyes.

Reese could resist no longer. His head bent down, his lips descended, and Samara was lost in her need to meet them. All reason fled as their lips joined; months of hunger, of wanting, of aching exploded into an inferno of raw desire.

Samara forgot her brothers, forgot her trap, forgot everything but the warm delight of his touch. Hundreds of little conflagrations flared in every part of her being as his lips gently, then urgently, pressed against hers, and his tongue made a fevered entrance into her mouth, teasing her senses and fueling her need. Her body readily gravitated to his, cherishing the hard leanness, the magnificent warmth that reached out and encompassed her. So strong was the bond that she didn't realize, immediately, that his arms had stiffened, that his lips had stilled.

A voice broke the silence, her brother's voice. Conn's voice. It was rough and angry.

"You will drop your arms, English, and move away."

Samara's heart froze at the sound. She had never heard Conn's voice so harsh. He was obviously quite ready to kill Reese Hampton. Her eyes traveled up to Reese's face, and she shivered at what she saw there.

The eyes were icy with fury and naked contempt, the mouth, so tender and passionate moments earlier, was compressed in a tight grim line. She could see him struggle for control.

"Your doing, my sweet?" he said finally, his voice dripping with scorn. She felt, rather than heard, the naked pain in it, the disillusionment, and she thought dying would be too easy.

"You are quite an excellent actress, aren't you?" he continued, now almost conversationally but his eyes reduced her to the status of the lowest insect on earth. "It's really a pity we were interrupted so soon; it would have been interesting to see exactly how far you would go." His hands tightened on her arms in quiet rage as he felt the barrel of a pistol press deeper in his back.

"I won't tell you again, English," the man behind him said. "I could arouse the house, and you would probably hang right now. I don't think this company would be sympathetic to an English spy."

"And my alternative?" Reese's voice was deceptively easy. His mind was racing ahead. How many were there? Exactly what was Samara's involvement?

"You will live a little longer: I won't promise how much."

Reluctantly, Reese let his hands fall to his side. As he did, his eyes moved from Samara, and she knew he was mentally dismissing her.

"Put your hands behind your back," came the next order, and after a brief hesitation and another jolt to his back Reese complied. His wrists were seized and he felt the rough rope as it was secured around them. He tried to flex his wrists to give him some slight freedom, but they were firmly, if not cruelly, pressed tightly together. Reese felt the final tug as the knot was tied and he discovered a helplessness completely new to him. His hands clenched into tight fists as he realized Samara had planned this. What a fool he had been to be so elated when he first saw her tonight. How incredibly arrogant of him to trust her. None of his thoughts showed in his face, however. It was as emotionless as a mask as he considered his position. There were obviously two of them because the gun barrel had remained fixed in his back as his hands were tied. What in the devil did they intend?

He felt a cloak being thrown over his shoulders, and he was pushed towards the line of coaches.

"If we are met by anyone," the faceless voice said, "You will act suitably drunk. I understand you are very skilled at that."

At this further evidence of Samara's betrayal, Reese's fury increased. His body tensed with the effort to bridle the rage until it could be used effectively. And it would be, he promised himself. He could not see her now, but the light fragrant scent told him she was still with them. God, he wanted to get his hands around that lovely neck. One of his captors pushed him towards a carriage; a driver was already in place. The barrel of the gun disappeared from the small part of his back, and he watched as Samara entered the carriage followed by a well built, well dressed man who mounted the seat awkwardly. Only now was he aware of the man's stiff leg. Damn. He had been too angry at Samara's role to detect this weakness. There had to be a way to use it. Reese looked for the pistol, but it seemed to have disappeared.

The man still standing with him nodded to the carriage. "Please get in." It was a gentler voice, polite and pleasant.

Reese's face was cold as he eyed him sardonically. "Please?" His voice was full of mockery.

The man didn't take offense but smiled slightly. "Yes, please. I would highly recommend it before someone intrudes on this rather unusual little scene."

Reese put his foot on the step and started to enter the coach. He turned around and suddenly saw his chance. The softly spoken man was directly below him, a perfect target. It would take the other one several valuable seconds to react because of his leg. By then, he could be into the woods. He didn't think about what he would do then…with his hands tied behind him. He just knew an unreasoning rage that required action. He lowered his head and went pummeling into the man below, knocking him to the ground before feeling the jerk on the rope around his wrists. He was forced up, pain arching through his arms and up into his shoulders.

The man in the carriage had been faster than Reese thought possible. Reese was thrust against the side of the carriage, and the gun, held openly now, was aimed at his heart.

The man looked down at his companion on the ground. "Are you all right, Marion?"

Light from a lantern shone down on the fallen man's face, and Reese knew a certain familiarity. He then looked at his other captor, the man holding the gun, and he saw the same features. Features that had also belonged to Brendan O'Neill. They had to be O'Neill's brothers. And, therefore, Samara's. He slumped against the couch. Brendan had obviously kept his word about their joint conspiracy and the theft of the *Samara*; the hostility of the one brother was too powerful for it to be otherwise. Nor had Samara given him the benefit of an explanation. A slight laugh escaped his lips, but there was no amusement in it. He very likely would hang because of his own magnanimity, his own sense of honor. There was a certain poetry about it, he thought bitterly as he was hustled back into the coach. He saw Samara's wide eyes on him as the brother with the gun gave it to her and then very efficiently tied his ankles together and roped them to the frame of the seat, allowing him no movement at all. His brief moment of rebellion was obviously going to cost him even the smallest comfort. The other brother groaned slightly as he moved, apparently hurting from Reese's blow. At least he could take some little satisfaction in that.

Reese's glittering eyes pinned Samara to her seat. "Very neatly done, Miss O'Neill. I compliment you on your treachery." The agony in her eyes did nothing to appease him. "Do you plan to see me hang in the same expeditious manner?" His voice was almost indifferent, his bitterness too deep, too painful, to allow itself to surface. He would not give her *that* pleasure.

He watched coldly as tears welled up in her eyes, hesitating there, like a light fog on a gray morning. "Tears, Samara? How very thoughtful. A bit late, but…appreciated." Derision dripped from his voice.

"Shut up, English," the man on his right growled. Reese could feel the fist balled up next to him. He shrugged.

On the other side of him, the man he had hit stirred. "It's only because of Samara," the man said softly, "that you're not now in the hands of American authorities." Marion had observed the exchange between his sister and the Englishman with real concern. Samara was obviously shattered; there was much more between the two than he had first realized.

He was also concerned about Conn's temper. His brother's experience in Alabama had flamed his hatred of the English. He blamed them for the Indian atrocities he had witnessed, and his leg had not softened an already fierce thirst for vengeance.

A natural peacemaker, Marion disregarded his own hurts and tried to soften the explosive tension in the coach. "I'm sorry we had to take...such measures, but we had little choice...unless you preferred the military."

Reese turned to him, his eyes raking over the American. It was hard to dislike what he saw. The eyes were steady and frank, the mouth sensitive but firm. There was something inherently decent about him. But Reese was not in a mood to appreciate such a quality. He had never been so furious in his life.

The problem was, Reese realized, that the anger should be directed at himself. Christ, how could he have been such a fool? He should have left immediately after seeing Samara, but he wanted, oh how he had wanted, to touch her, to hold her in his arms. And he had been deceived by the answering spark in her eyes, the same fierce hunger that shone in her face. He had believed her. Believed what? She had said nothing but to meet her...and he had foolishly assumed..."

Reese turned his head and closed his eyes in denial. He tried to relax his long body against the seat but it was impossible. The carriage was moving fast, and it took all his concentration to keep his balance as it swayed and jolted along the rutted road. His arms hurt like hell, his wrists burned from the rough rope, and his legs were cramping from their unnatural position. But he would be damned if he would let any of them know it. His mouth tightened in an implacable line, and he opened his eyes only long enough for Samara to see their smoldering savagery. They were closed before they saw her answering despair...and plea for understanding.

Reese lost track of time. He was so damned uncomfortable every second seemed liked hours. He cursed Samuels who had lured him into this mess, then himself for further entangling himself. Behind his back, his hands fought against the ropes to no avail, but the pain gave him some distraction from his dark thoughts. His life had not been the same since his first encounter with the O'Neills nearly a year earlier. He had never been free of the dark-haired witch; she had ruined every other woman for him even when he thought her unobtainable. His cherished freedom had lost its luster, and his preoccupation with her had, most likely, cost him his ship... and now perhaps his life. Had he totally mistaken her responses on the *Unicorn*? Had he misjudged her first reaction this evening? He had thought then he saw the same rush of joy he experienced. Had it been just a thirst for revenge instead?

He opened his eyes and studied her. God, she was beautiful. In the light of the lantern hanging from the ceiling of the carriage, the midnight blue of the entrancing gown emphasized the lovely ivory of her skin and intensified the blue shadings in the large gray eyes. The cut of the bodice, even with her lace shawl, gave more than a little hint of perfect breasts straining against the soft fabric. The flame in her dark hair was alive in the flickering light, as curls, caught in the back by a pearl clasp, tumbled around the enchanting face. His eyes, made cold by sheer strength of will, saw her hands clenching and unclenching with... with what. Distress? Fear? Regret?

Reese finally spoke, but his voice was emotionless. "Would it be presumptuous to ask my destination?" He directed his question at Samara. He was not going to let her off lightly.

But it was the brother on the right who answered. "Yes," he growled. "It would."

But Reese continued to look at Samara, his eyes piercing and hard, demanding an answer. As he intended, she was defenseless against him. She could cope with his anger, or insults, indeed would welcome them, but this strangely contained Reese was another matter completely. He was more compelling than ever as his eyes bore into her, undressing her emotions as well as her body. She trembled before the merciless onslaught.

"H-home," she finally said in a small voice.

A familiar arching of a rakish eyebrow commanded her to continue.

"Samara...you don't have to." Again it was the angry young brother.

"No, Conn," she said, her voice stronger. "He has a right to know." She met Reese's eyes now, and the old spirit was back.

There was apology and unhappiness but also a firm conviction.

"I'm sorry, Captain Hampton," she said. "I did the best I could. I couldn't *not* say anything... not when you had heard so much at the ball; Emily said you were a shipper, and there was so much talk about when ships were leaving. And how." Samara's voice faltered. "And I...I...I couldn't inform on you, not to the authorities. Not even if you did plan to betray us."

Reese's arrogant features twisted with confusion. "Betray?"

"In Bermuda. You obviously intended us to walk into a trap... why else would you leave the ship unguarded?" she answered quite logically, completely misinterpreting the shock in his eyes for guilt.

A small smile curled Reese's lips. "Why indeed?" he agreed smoothly. He was not going to explain his actions or motives, even if they would be believed. Which, he knew, they would not. Without Brendan, why should they? They would just think he was trying to extricate himself from a very ticklish situation.

He looked at her with real curiosity. "Then why, *Miss* O'Neill, didn't you just expose me? Why go to all this trouble?"

Samara's face clouded. "You *did* keep Brendan from prison."

"No other reason?" he taunted now, as he disregarded the tensing body of the hostile brother. "After all, you apparently think I did that just to trap him later. Rather inconsistent of you."

Samara's eyes were full of confusion. Her hands knotted. "I don't want you to hang," she said now. Quietly, wretchedly.

"Very comforting, Miss O'Neill," Reese replied. "So may I ask what in the hell I'm doing here? And what do you have planned instead?" There was a decided edge in his voice.

"That's enough, Hampton," the brother on Reese's right said.

Reese completely disregarded him as he addressed his next question to Samara alone. "And who, pray, are your fellow kidnappers?"

"My brothers," she said in a low voice. "Conn and Marion."

"Are there any more like you at home?" Reese asked with obvious sarcasm.

Marion spoke up now, wanting to prevent another explosion from his brother. He had listened with a great deal of interest. The sparks flying between Samara and Hampton suggested something much stronger than antagonism alone.

"Only one," he said with gentle amusement. "Other than Brendan, of course."

Reese twisted in his direction, once again unaccountably drawn to the man. He reminded him of Brendan.

Marion withstood his examination with equanimity. He rarely held a grudge and certainly did not now, despite the aches and pain he still suffered from Reese's attack. He didn't blame the man one bit; he had simply reacted. He now understood Samara's unhappiness and apathy during the past year. Hampton, even trussed as he was, was a very forceful personality. Forceful and magnetic. Marion could see the effort both their prisoner and his sister made to deny the fierce attraction that so obviously passed between them. He sighed. There would be trouble at Glen Woods, no doubt about that. It had taken all of Samara's persuasion to keep Conn from unmasking the Englishman at the ball; his brother had finally agreed to this course only because he felt his father would side with him. Marion wasn't so sure. Their father despised the English, but he also was a very fair man. And he doted on Samara.

"It won't be long now," he said softly, "before we're at Glen Woods. I expect all your questions will be answered then."

Reese merely nodded and once more leaned back awkwardly against the seat, wincing at the sudden pain in his wrists.

Marion saw his expression, and with a slight touch to Reese's arm indicated he should turn slightly. Marion inspected the bonds, his supple fingers loosening the knot slightly, reducing the strain on Reese's wrists while still holding them firmly. He noted the rope burns with dismay, and knew the Englishman was experiencing real pain. He took off his neck cloth and, with the small knife he always carried, cut it into strips. He nudged the ropes on Reese's wrists upward, then wrapped a piece of cloth around the deep bloody depressions in the skin and let the rope drop back in place, around the cloth.

The Englishman said nothing as he moved back against the seat. His eyes were veiled, and only an unwilling movement of a jaw muscle and the barely leashed tension in his body indicated any emotion. They rode the rest of the way in silence.

When the coach rolled to a stop, the driver opened the door and assisted Samara in stepping down. Marion leaned down and cut the bonds around Hampton's ankles; the gun was back in Conn's hand.

Reese stretched his legs, trying to work out the cramps before attempting to stand. He had no idea of the time and could only guess that it was in the early morning hours. Refusing to heed Conn's impatient looks or the jabs in his side, he almost lazily moved his legs, feeling sensation creeping back into them. He had no intention of taking a fall from the carriage for their amusement. When he was finally ready, he stood at the door and looked out. They were at the wide steps of an imposing home. In the light of the moon, he studied the house. It was small by Beddingfield's standards but quite handsome compared to others he had seen in the Carolinas. There was a certain warmth and dignity in the pink glow of the brick and the hundreds of roses that climbed the wide porch. He carefully descended the two steps, moving awkwardly on stiff legs, his usual grace replaced by iron determination.

He was pushed, and his bottled-up anger exploded. He shoved back and Conn, caught unaware, stumbled and fell, the pistol sliding along the ground. The house had been dark, but now faint flickering lights appeared in the windows. Samara and her brothers had not been expected home tonight.

Before Reese could make any further move, several servants came out of the house, and Marion had him firmly in tow. Conn rose, dusted himself off and glared at Hampton.

"I don't like being shoved," Reese said, fury in every word. This evening had been full of indignities, and he was damned if he was going to calmly accept any more.

Conn made a move toward him, but Marion intercepted him. "Go up the stairs," he told Reese, "to the drawing room on the left."

Reese nodded. He mounted the steps with Marion behind him, walked past the astonished servants in the doorway and, with only a moment's hesitation, entered the darkened drawing room. In seconds, servants had lighted the candles, which cast a golden glow over the richly furnished room. After a nod from Marion, the servants disappeared, and the four regarded each other warily.

"What in the hell is going on?"

Reese turned towards the door. The speaker, garbed only in a dressing robe, was nonetheless imposing. He was nearly as tall as Reese, with cool appraising gray eyes that missed little. They thoroughly inspected Reese, quickly noting the arrogant set of his head, the unusually handsome features, the well-fitting clothes on his strongly muscled body. He could not see Reese's bound hands, and he stepped forward, his hand outstretched. "Sir?"

Reese bowed with no little mockery. "I regret," he said slowly, "that I seem unable, at the moment, to return your courtesy." He turned slightly, showing his bound wrists.

Connor O'Neill's eyes narrowed as they moved from Conn to Marion to Samara, all of whom wore apprehensive expressions. Now they were here, they did not quite know how to explain the situation. Conn looked at Marion. Marion looked at Samara, and Samara looked at the floor.

In the absence of explanation, Connor's humor surfaced. "I know," Connor said finally, a glint of amusement in his voice, "that I've been wanting you to bring a young man home, Samara, but I didn't mean for you to go to this extreme."

Despite the seriousness of his situation, Reese couldn't suppress a smile as Samara's face crimsoned.

"Papa!" she said in complete mortification.

Connor stared at her for a moment, then turned back to the man standing so nonchalantly in his drawing room with his hands tied behind him.

"Since my children seem reluctant to explain, perhaps you would be so kind," he said, his eyes questioning each of his three offspring.

"I seem to be kidnapped," Reese said easily, his anger momentarily lulled by the whole farcical situation.

The older O'Neill now fixed all his attention on Reese. "I rather guessed that," he said drily. "I assume there's a reason."

"He's a spy, Papa." Conn finally found his voice. "He's an English spy."

Connor turned to his guest/prisoner. "Are you?"

Reese sighed. "I'm afraid so." There was really nothing to be gained by denying it.

Bewilderment flashed in Connor's eyes at the frank admission. He turned to his sons. "Why in the devil, then, did you bring him here?"

Both Conn and Marion looked at Samara.

"Samara?" Connor questioned. "Would you like to tell me exactly why you are bringing me an English spy in the middle of the night?"

Once more, Reese had difficulty in suppressing a smile, particularly when he saw Samara's discomfort. In any other situation, he supposed he would like the elder O'Neill.

"He's Captain Hampton, father," Samara said slowly.

O'Neill turned back to Reese, and this time his examination was much more thorough. He had heard the damn man's name more times than he wished to remember. Brendan had mentioned him with respect, and even liking, despite all that had happened. And Samara...Samara hadn't been the same in the year since that ill-fated voyage. He had not missed her wistful looks nor the tears that sometimes filled her eyes without apparent reason. "What do you expect me to do with him?" he asked his daughter. "Other than, of course, what you should have done in the beginning...turn him over to the military?" He observed the sudden tension in Hampton's body.

"You can't, Papa," Samara said. "They will hang him."

"Probably," O'Neill said. "That's what they usually do to spies."

"But he's not, not really. He's a sea captain..."

O'Neill turned back to Reese and eyed him carefully. He was both intrigued and impressed with the man's composure. Except for almost imperceptible tautness in his posture, nothing about his face or manner indicated any worry. There was no appeal, no excuses. He simply stood there as if he owned the world. "Exactly what are you, Hampton?"

Reese shrugged. "My ship was wrecked near the coast. I was trying to get back to Bermuda or England."

Conn's voice cut in. "Then what were you doing at the party, posing as a shipper, asking about shipping schedules?"

Connor O'Neill's questioning eyes also demanded an explanation.

Reese remained silent. How could he explain without exposing Samuels as a traitor? And no matter how much he resented the man for getting him into this, he couldn't do that.

Realizing he would receive no answer, Connor pondered his alternatives, liking none of them. He needed time to think. "It's late," he said. "Too late to make any decisions now...or any sense out of this whole thing." He looked at Reese. "The only secure place on Glen Woods is the storehouse; I'm afraid you'll have to spend the night there." He disappeared for a moment and returned with a set of keys, which he handed to Marion. "And you, young lady," he turned to Samara, "will go to bed now. You can expect a long overdue conversation in the morning.''

Samara started to leave but stopped at the sound of Reese's voice. She turned and saw the slow mocking bow.

"It's been very...instructional seeing you again, Miss Samara," he said, "and meeting the rest of your...charming family." When he straightened, his eyes were glacial green, and she knew from his expression he would not forgive lightly.

Connor watched his daughter flinch with every sarcastic word, and he struggled to control his anger. He couldn't miss the anguish on her face as she took one backward look before slowly, reluctantly, disappearing through the door. Samara had proclaimed the man the worst kind of scoundrel in the past months, and now she was acting like a lovesick puppy. He regarded Hampton as he would a leper.

Curtly, he nodded to Hampton. "I won't insult you by bidding you good night. In fact, I hope you have every bit as poor a night as I suspect I will." He turned on his heel and left.

"Captain Hampton," Marion said in his usual quiet voice, "you will accompany us." Conn, for once, was quiet, his truculent mood quelled by his father's disapproval.

As Reese was led to the small storehouse, his searching eyes noted the thick iron grill on the one window. The door was unlocked, and Marion went inside, lighting a small candle lamp which hung on a peg in the interior. He motioned Reese inside. As Conn held his all-too-familiar gun, Marion cut the ropes around the Englishman's wrists and stepped outside. With an apologetic glance, he closed the door, leaving Reese alone.

Reese heard the grating of the key in the lock as he rubbed his sore wrists, trying to restore the circulation. He then studied the room. The flickering light from the candle showed it to be half full of barrels and boxes. He was able to open the shutters at the window, but when he tried the iron grill, he found it well anchored. Discouraged, he slid down in a corner, cursing the perfidy of women and wondered what in the hell he would do now.

Chapter Thirteen

Samantha had barely stirred when Connor left the bed. She had been up nearly the entire night with the mare which had finally given birth to a colt, and the emotional and physical strain had taken its toll. She reached for Connor, and her hand found only emptiness. In the sudden fear that sometimes strikes the half awake, she sat upright—just as the bedroom door opened and Connor entered. The candle in his hand revealed a deeply troubled face.

"Connor? What is it?"

"It's nothing, Sam. Go back to sleep."

Samantha knew from his tone and the use of her shortened name that something *was* wrong. He rarely used it any more. Now with the renewed hostilities with England, it seemed to bring back painful memories.

Her voice trembled. "Is it one of the children?"

He went over to her, putting his arm around her shoulder and holding her tightly. "The children are fine."

"They're home? I thought they were staying...there *is* something wrong!"

Connor grimaced. Samantha was now wide awake, and there was no way of avoiding an explanation. He had hoped to put it off until morning, until he had time to think. Samantha was going to be most aggrieved that she had missed the little drama downstairs, and only the Lord knew what she would do. Even after thirty-four years he sure as hell didn't.

"Samara?" Samantha was insistent.

"*Your* children, madam," he said finally, "brought home an English spy...all neatly tied in one angry package. And I'll be damned if I know what to do with him...or what they want me to do. They just dropped him in the drawing room as easily as they would bring in a neighbor." His voice rose as his outrage increased with every passing second.

Samantha looked at him as if he had lost his wits. "A spy?"

"Hampton," he said wearily, as if that explained everything.

"Hampton . . . Samara's captain?"

Now Connor returned her incredulous look. "Samara's . . . ? He's certainly not Samara's anything."

But his wife was no longer paying any attention. There was a very strange look on her face. If he didn't know better, he would almost think it glee.

"Captain Hampton," she whispered. "But how?"

"He was masquerading as a shipper or some damn thing, apparently gathering information about ship locations and cargoes. Said his ship had been sunk which, of course, we knew. He never did explain what he was doing at the Fontaine plantation."

"Where is he now?" Her question was soft, belying the intense interest in her sparkling blue eyes.

"In the storehouse . . . until I can decide what to do with him. Though there's nothing to do but give him to the military."

"What did you think of him?" Samantha held her breath while Connor searched for an answer.

"He's arrogant . . . he all but dared me to turn him over to the authorities." Connor paused. "He even seemed amused by it all, though angry." A little twinkle came into his eyes. "He said it was 'instructional' to meet Samara's 'charming' family. That after being trussed up like a turkey half the night."

Samantha was out of bed, pulling on the pair of breeches and shirt she had worn earlier in the barn. "I want to meet him."

"In the morning," he said in a soothing voice.

"Now . . . and besides, how could you put him in the storehouse with no mattress . . . or food . . . or water or anything? What will he think?"

"What will *he* think?" came Connor's outraged bellow. "He's a spy, by thunder. He stood there and admitted it. And it's a damn sight better than a prison cell, where," he added with a warning, "he'll be tomorrow."

"Perhaps," she answered obliquely. "But tonight he's going to be comfortable."

Connor uttered an exasperated oath, but he knew he might as well try to stop a cannonball with a pillow. "I'll go with you."

"No," she replied. "You'll just get angry. I'll take Caesar and Marcus. I need them anyway to carry some things."

"They're not to leave you alone with him."

"No, sir," she replied, her lips twitching with impertinence.

"I don't like it. He's dangerous."

"We owe him, Connor," she said quietly. "He could have harmed both Samara and Brendan, and he chose not to do so. In fact, according to Bren, he lied to his own navy to keep our son and his crew safe."

"He put them in that position in the beginning," Connor said angrily. "If he hadn't attacked the *Samara*, they wouldn't have been in danger."

"Nevertheless, Bren got his ship back, and I've always thought it strange that he was able to do so."

Connor glared at her. "What do you mean?"

"Did Captain Hampton strike you as a careless man?"

"He certainly seemed so tonight."

"Perhaps," she said with finality. "But I think Caesar and Marcus are protection enough."

She didn't give him any more time to reply. She was out the door, waking the servants and issuing instructions, leaving Connor fuming. Regardless of what she said, he intended to be within rescue distance. He took off his dressing gown and started pulling on clothes.

Samara reluctantly pulled on a nightdress and blew out the candle in her room. But she knew she wouldn't sleep this night. Instead, she went to the window seat and stood there, staring down at the storehouse with its lighted window. She could see shadows of a figure pacing restlessly, and she felt consumed by guilt. He had trusted her and she had betrayed him. During those first few seconds at the cypress, his eyes had been warm and admiring, his face without mockery, his mouth inviting… It was all her dreams of the past year. And they had been shattered.

She had never seen a face change so quickly, eyes move so rapidly from hot fire to frigid fury as he realized what she had done. And from his icy comments in the coach, she knew he thought she had signed his death warrant.

But she *hadn't*. She *couldn't have*. She had only wanted to stop him from revealing what he had learned that night. Her father wouldn't let him hang. Samara shivered as she remembered Connor O'Neill's words in the library. "That's what usually happens to spies." What in God's name had she done?

"*You had to,*" came the tiny whispered voice within her. "*It was your duty. Remember Bren had just left. It might have meant his life.*

"He wouldn't have..."

"*You don't know that... you don't really know him at all.*"

"I know I don't want him to die..." Tears slid down her face as complete misery swamped her. She continued to watch the pacing man below, sensing his frustration, knowing his rage. He had shown it clearly in the coach.

I have to do something. Samara closed her eyes, trying to think. If only Bren were here...he would know what do do. But he isn't. Mother. She'll understand. She won't let father turn Captain Hampton over to hang. Her mother could always make father see her side... eventually. But would it be too late?

"I'll have to do something myself." The sound of her words echoed in the room. She had been unaware she had said them aloud. But now she heard them and they gave her courage. With the same diligence she had planned the capture of Captain Reese Hampton hours ago, she now schemed to rescue him. Of course, he would have to promise that all he had learned would be forgotten.

Step one... she would have to steal the keys to the storehouse.

Unaware that he was the principal figure in so many thoughts and schemes, Reese prowled the small room, searching for a way out. The room was hot and stuffy, and he had discarded his coat and waistcoat. His white lawn shirt was open at the throat and chest, displaying bronze skin and golden hair. He had ripped off half a sleeve to staunch the flow of blood from a jagged cut in his hand. He cursed softly as he studied both his injured wrists and his newest wound. He had torn a board from one of the boxes and tried to use it to loosen the grill. It had slipped, and a splintered edge tore though his skin and muscle. How many more things could go wrong? It had all started with Samara so many months ago. Bloody little witch. Bloody damn family. This time he included Brendan. He would flinch forever more at the name O'Neill. If he lived long enough.

He heard noises at the door, the sound of a key in a lock. Locating the board he had discarded, he gripped it in his hands, unmindful now of the pain. He stepped back behind the door. Right now, he didn't care who he hit; he just felt the enormous need to strike back.

Filled with curiosity, Samantha was the first through the door, much to the dismay of Caesar who was burdened with food and a bottle of wine, and Marcus who was carrying a mattress.

She suddenly tensed, all her old instincts returning, and ducked as a board came down towards her. Just as she knew it was about to reach her, it stopped in midair and she wondered at the strength and control it took to stop such a swing. She turned and faced her would-be attacker.

The two stood there, staring at each other with equal amazement.

Just as Samara had a year ago, Samantha was stunned by the man's height and sheer magnetism. His open shirt and tight trousers displayed a lean, well-muscled body as he towered above her, his thick, tawny hair sprinkled with gold in the candlelight. Furious, shimmering aqua eyes glowered at her, and power emanated from the now stiff figure, his hand tightening around his makeshift weapon as he reluctantly lowered it. She now completely understood Samara's bewildering behavior of the past months. Captain Hampton would frighten, charm and fascinate any woman, much less one as inexperienced as Samara.

As for Reese, he found himself facing an older version of Samara except for the eyes. His unexpected visitor was truly beautiful, with lively blue eyes that now challenged him with unspoken questions. She wore her black hair in a braid, and her slender body was clothed in men's trousers and shirt. He had never seen such clothing on a woman, and now regretted it. The masculine attire showed every soft curve. He tried to estimate her age, but could not; her face was firm, but there were little laugh lines at the corners of her eyes. And there was a maturity and confidence that came only with years—and happiness. He dropped the board, and his grim mouth curved into a rueful smile.

"Another O'Neill, I presume. I'm beginning to think there is no end to them."

Her smile in the faltering candlelight brightened the dim interior with another kind of light. "I'm Samantha O'Neill, Brendan's and Samara's mother—and, I'm afraid, also of your other abductors."

It seemed impossible that this woman was old enough to be Brendan's mother. He wondered idly whether Samara would be this striking thirty years from now. His amusement at the absurdity of the moment asserted itself although there was a bitter edge to it.

"Welcome to my humble abode," he said, his lips twisting with irony. "And to what do I owe the honor of *this* particular visit?"

"I wanted to meet you," Samantha said frankly. "You seem to have turned my family upside down."

He laughed then, his cold eyes warming ever so slightly. "No less than they have done to me, I assure you," he answered. "I rue the day I spied your son's ship."

Samantha moved then, allowing the door to open. Caesar and Marcus, their dark faces creased with concern, moved protectively around Samantha, each holding their bundles.

"I brought a few items to make your...stay more comfortable. I apologize for my husband's lack of hospitality."

Feeling almost as if he were in a madhouse, Reese watched as a mattress was carefully laid on the dirty floor, and a small table placed beside it. It was quickly covered with food, a bottle of wine and silver goblets.

"Forgive me," he said "if I don't quite understand."

Samantha's eyes twinkled at his confusion. "Whether my husband admits it or not, I think we owe a great deal to you. I will see that the debt is repaid."

One of Reese's eyebrows rose in question, and Samantha was suddenly grateful that she loved Connor so thoroughly. This man could break hearts as easily as...as birds sang.

Her searching eyes found his hand, and the bloody rag around it. She held out her own to him. "Let me see it," she commanded, and Reese surprised himself by obediently giving it to her. She gently unwrapped the ragged cut, frowned, and turned to Caesar. "Get me some water, bandages and brandy."

Caesar continued to stand there. "I can't, Miz Samantha. Mr. Connor say to stay wi' you, not to let you out of my seein.'"

Samantha turned to the tall Englishman. "You aren't going to ravish or kill me, are you?"

A glint of amusement lightened his blue-green eyes. "I might be sorely tempted on the first," he said in a dry tone, "but I'll try to restrain myself."

"You see, Caesar," she said with a wide smile. "I am quite safe. Besides, you can leave Marcus if you wish. Now go."

"But Mister Connor . . ."

"I will take care of my husband."

With a frown of great disapproval, Caesar left, leaving Marcus with his hands folded, a protective look on his face.

"You look as though you need a glass of wine," Samantha said, enjoying the confusion their reluctant guest was obviously feeling.

"And Samara told me she was an orphan!" he said now, the humor returning to his face. "I still haven't quite figured out how many brothers she does have."

Samantha was enchanted once more. How quickly his moods changed, how completely engaging he could be when he lowered his guard.

"Four . . . Brendan's the oldest, then Jere, you haven't met him yet, and Conn and Marion. I'm afraid they've spoiled Samara . . . we all have." She caught just a slight tightening of his jaw and the glint in his eye. So there was some interest on his part. She wondered how much. She decided to pry, and the best way to get information, she had learned from experience, was to attack frontally.

"Why wouldn't you let Brendan tell anyone you helped him reclaim the *Samara*?" It was a guess on her part, but she knew instantly she was correct. A muscle throbbed in his cheek, and his eyes turned wary.

"I did nothing."

"By doing nothing," she probed further, "you did something. That ship meant the world to Brendan. I thank you."

"Did he—?"

"No. It was what he didn't say." She was sure now.

"You are wrong, madam," he said coldly. "I did nothing, I meant nothing. He was my enemy . . . as I am yours."

"I think not," she replied, "but I won't debate with you. I suppose you have your own reasons."

He turned away from her, his stance rigid. Even he didn't know why he denied his very small assistance. Perhaps it was pride, the refusal to say something which could be construed as begging, or even bargaining. Perhaps he didn't want to acknowledge that he had indeed helped an enemy of his country. He turned and took the bottle of wine, deftly opening it with his left hand. He looked at Samantha O'Neill in question, but she shook her head. Reese poured himself a glass and emptied the contents in one long swallow before pouring another. He knew she was watching him carefully and, quite casually, without further acknowledgement of her presence, he downed another glass. When he finished, his eyes challenged hers. "Apparently you don't have the same fondness for wine as your daughter."

Samantha laughed. Samara had, red-faced, told her something of that dinner. "I think, by now, I've found more judicious uses for it." She liked Reese Hampton more each moment. If her husband would only give him a chance, she knew they would be friends. They had much in common, including a wry sense of humor.

"What were you doing at the Fontaine party?" she said now, back on the attack. "Didn't you know Samara might be there?"

The question surprised him. Now as he considered it, he wondered if perhaps he did. Perhaps unconsciously he was even hoping she would be present. But he couldn't admit that. Not to the woman in front of him, nor himself.

"South Carolina is a big state," he said, instead. "And I knew Brendan had already sailed. Since I thought, quite erroneously it seems, that she was *Mrs.* O'Neill I doubted she would attend a party without him...if she hadn't stowed away again." Once more, a hint of humor emerged in his voice. "But then I should have expected the unexpected. Samara *is* rather unpredictable." The last words were caustic, and the humor was gone, replaced by something which could be interpreted only as raw hurt.

Samantha's heart caught. There *was* feeling there, a great deal, even if he was making a great effort to conceal it.

"Samara did what she thought she had to do," her mother said gently. "I don't think she realized there might be dire results... She always believes everything turns out for the best."

"Including my hanging," Reese said bitterly. "I trusted..." He stopped suddenly. What was it about Samantha O'Neill that made him say so much more than he intended? He turned away.

"I can promise you that won't happen," she said softly. "I won't let it."

Before he could answer, Caesar returned with the bandages, his face creased with anxiety. Quiet disapproval was evident in his every movement.

"Wait outside," Samantha said. "Both you and Marcus."

"Miz Samantha—"

"Please, Caesar."

Reese's deep voice cut in. "I think he should stay, Mrs. O'Neill . . . I'm a dangerous spy, remember." His voice was as icy as it had been earlier, and Samantha knew she had lost what small progress she had made in gaining his trust. He apparently was regretting those few unguarded moments.

She nodded, knowing she would get no further tonight. Instead she quickly cleaned his cut, pouring brandy on the open wound. He didn't even wince as the alcohol touched the skin, and she smiled at his iron control. He simply stood there stiffly, barely acknowledging her ministrations, and that only with slight tolerance. Samantha felt a sudden fear for her daughter. Reese Hampton was an extremely complex man. Complex and dangerous and very compelling. Could any woman possibly harness that strength and energy? He was like Connor in some ways—in his pride, in his indifference to pain, in his rugged independence—but did he have Connor's gentleness? And honor? She suspected it was there, lurking behind his cynicism. But what if she were wrong . . . ?

After he left, Reese poured himself another glass of wine and blew out the candle. He sat on the mattress, his back against the wall. The night was at its deepest; the time just before the first rays of a new day penetrated the blackness. He was angry, more at himself than anyone else. He had never before betrayed feelings as he had tonight, and he damned himself for it.

Connor watched as his wife and the two servants returned to the house; he was ready to slip away himself when he saw another shadowy form approach the storehouse. The outbuilding was fast becoming the most popular place in the Carolinas, Connor thought ruefully. It was a disconcerting observation.

He identified Samara almost immediately and debated with himself as she crept toward the window. He could stop her now, or wait and see what would happen next. Remembering the pain in her face earlier, his heart ached for her and Connor decided to wait. Perhaps she needed a few private words with the man. The night was lost anyway. Would his life . . . would his

family's life ever get back to normal? He leaned against a tree
and watched...

"Captain Hampton..."

Reese had just closed his eyes when he heard the soft words.
He opened them slowly, unable to see in the darkness. But he
knew the voice and he immediately felt the electricity that was
always there between them.

His anger exploded. "Get the hell away from here."

"Captain Hampton...Reese...I have the key."

He didn't move. "You're a little late. I wouldn't trust you
again...ever. God knows what awaits me this time."

Her voice shook. "Please...I'll let you go if you promise you
won't say anything about what you heard last night."

"No promises, little cat. Now leave me in peace. I don't think
your father would approve." Each word was arctic.

Samara couldn't see his eyes but she knew they were probably just as frozen. Her voice shook as she tried again. Nothing was working as it should. Nothing was happening as she
intended. "Please...you have to leave...please promise me..."

He stood lazily now, his eyes adjusting to the darkness. He
went to the grill. "Do I detect a note of concern?"

"You have to go," she whispered desperately. "You have to
promise...please..."

Reese didn't want to take her help. But he knew immediately his obstinacy was self-defeating. Regardless of what her
mother had said, he very likely *would* see the inside of a prison
if he weren't fitted with a rope halter. Neither was an attractive prospect.

"You win," he said, not trying to hide the bitterness. He
turned away from her tentative smile towards the door, waiting to hear the key in the lock. God, what a night.

But when the door opened, Samara was not alone. Walking
soundlessly behind her was her father, and the older man could
not disguise his anger.

Reese knew he should have expected it. After all that had
happened, he was the worst kind of fool to believe his fortune
had changed. He and Connor stared at each other with open
hostility as Samara, suddenly aware of another presence,
turned and saw her father.

Samara stepped back, almost into Reese's arms. She had
never seen such censure in her father's eyes. Her face crumpled. "Let him go, Father," she said. "Please."

"It's too late," O'Neill said. "You should have thought about the consequences last night. Life is not a game, Samara. I wonder if you understand that yet."

Samara bit her lip at the sharp rebuke, but her chin jutted out defiantly. She was determined that nothing would happen to Reese. "I just didn't want...he promised he wouldn't say anything..."

"Did he now? You've been telling me for the past months that he's a blackguard and a pirate. How can you trust him now?" Connor was immensely angry. He had been prepared to let Samara talk to their prisoner through the window. He had not considered the possibility that she would try to free him. It meant, he knew, that there was much more between the two than he had first understood. He completely disregarded Reese's stiffening form as father and daughter discussed him as though he weren't there.

"Damn you both," Reese snarled in a low enraged voice. "I don't care what you do...just grant me the slight courtesy of a little peace." He turned on Samara. "And I don't need, or want, your damned pity or help or anything else...except perhaps to see the last of you." His eyes blazing with green fire, he turned back into the storeroom, slamming the door behind him.

Connor stared at the door, dismayed by his own mishandling of the situation. Hampton's angry contempt, he feared, was only too justified. Sighing heavily, he knew his own prejudice had colored his judgement. He would try to find a solution tomorrow...some way.

Connor relocked the door, and put his arm around Samara's shoulder. "Let's go to bed, little one. And don't worry. No harm will come to your Englishman."

Samara looked up at him, tears swelling in her eyes. "He's not mine, and after tonight, I doubt he ever could be."

It was as close as she had come to admitting her feelings for Reese Hampton, and Connor hurt for her. He remembered the agony he and Samantha had gone through, and he had always wanted to save Samara that pain. He wondered now if it were possible.

Reese tried to sleep; he knew he needed all his wits about him. It was all but impossible. In addition to the sounds of an awakening plantation, he was besieged by a pounding anger. He finally gave up any attempt at rest, finding it hopeless. He was tired and depressed and filled with an unfamiliar dread. He wanted some cold water to wash, but all that remained of Samantha O'Neill's bounty was tepid blood-stained water. The wine was gone, the dregs consumed quickly in the aftermath of Samara's attempted rescue. The very thought of the aborted plan made him wince. Poor Samara. All her rescue efforts seemed doomed to disaster: first, her brother, then himself. Unfortunately, her talents were apparently restricted to successful kidnappings.

As he had done the night before, he paced the floor before finally stopping at the grilled window and staring at the house across the way. In frustration, his hands clenched the ornamental iron work that so completely penned him. And he wondered if his fate was being decided.

"I say we turn him over to Colonel Miller," Conn said, referring to the the local militia commander.

"No," Samantha said quietly, her eyes on Samara's pale face. Her daughter had been unusually quiet, and she wondered if it had anything to do with the long discussion between father and daughter this morning. For one of the few times in his life, Connor had expressly prohibited Samantha from the room, and from the discussion. He had said nothing afterward, but had called a meeting of the family. Caesar had gone to fetch Jere.

When Jere arrived, he studied the room in astonishment. His sister was near tears, his mother was uncommonly solemn, his father looked badly troubled, Conn was furious and Marion . . . who ever knew what he thought?

His father quickly explained all that had happened and outlined the options. Jere was included because one of the choices would endanger him. "If we keep him here, allow him to stay as a guest, we could all be charged with harboring an enemy.

"Samara?" Jere, a gentle caretaker of the land, looked at his sister. "Bren isn't here, so we have to depend on you. You know this Hampton. Will he keep his word?"

"If he gives it," she whispered, not at all sure he would.

"Mother?"

"Brendan liked him . . . admired him . . . and you know your brother is seldom wrong about people. I like him."

Conn couldn't be still. "I don't care if he's the most charming man in England, he's still a damn spy...and it's our duty to turn him over."

Only Samantha saw Samara's and her father's eyes meet, and she knew the decision had already been made. Connor was only going through the motions, trying by patient persuasion for common agreement and support, particularly from Conn. Samantha slipped out the door and told Caesar to take the Englishman some fresh water and food. When she returned, the argument was continuing. Conn rebelliously brushed aside any proposal other than his own.

It was Samara who finally settled things. Her lips trembling, her eyes glistening with tears, she finally turned towards Conn, the brother closest to her in age and in thought. "I will leave this house if he hangs. I will never speak to you again. He was...decent...and fair to Bren and me...more than I was to him last night."

From anyone but Samara, Conn would have considered the words mere bravado, but he knew Samara. And for the first time, he allowed himself to consider the depth of emotion that must have prompted them. It did not make him feel more charitable towards their troublesome prisoner.

"Samara...you yourself called him a rogue and other names I won't repeat."

"I was angry...and confused...but I knew...I always knew he wouldn't harm me. From the first I knew that. And he and Bren *were* friends. I resented that, but they were. Bren would never forgive you if you do what you propose."

Conn looked around, but his eyes admitted defeat. He finally shrugged. "Do what you want...but I won't be taken in by him...like the rest of you. I want to be almighty sure he doesn't go any place until what he knows is too old to do anyone any good."

"Are you volunteering?" his father asked with a slight smile.

"Good God, no. I'm not going to be a nursemaid to a..."

Connor interrupted before his son could say more. There had been sufficient profanity in front of Samara. "He may not even agree to our terms," he said softly. "Our Captain Hampton may settle matters all on his own." He did not look at Samara; he did not want to see misery in eyes so like his own. "It's agreed, then," he said, and one by one the others nodded.

* * *

Reese washed his face and hands in the fresh water brought to him by one of the same servants who had accompanied Samantha O'Neill the previous night. The man offered to shave him, apparently unwilling to trust the suspicious stranger with a sharp-edged instrument. Reese nodded and sat on the small table. His right hand was stiff and sore this morning, but he welcomed the pain. It seemed the only real thing in the past twenty-four hours. The rest was almost a dream. Or a nightmare.

After the servant had gone—he suspected a second stood guard outside—he tried to eat some of the food which came with the water. There were fresh eggs and ham and hot bread. He had no hunger, but ate anyway, knowing he needed his strength. He was almost finished when one of Samara's brothers appeared, the even-tempered one he had tumbled the night before. Reese had been too angry last night to determine who was who. He just remembered names. Conn, Marion, Jere. And Bren. Bren who was on his way to raid British shipping. Dear God, how did he ever get himself in this mess?

"My father wants to see you," the young man said.

Reese merely nodded. He would not be unhappy to leave this room, and he wanted to know what O'Neill had in mind. One way or another, it was better to know.

He accompanied the brother to the house, surprised that he was not bound or given a heavier guard. Marion took him to a room which was apparently the library; hundreds of books lined the walls.

Connor was already seated at the desk and quickly rose as Reese entered. The older O'Neill nodded to his son, who turned around and left, closing the door behind him.

The interview was peculiarly dispassionate, considering the heightened emotions of both men. Reese was wary, still very angry although now more at himself than anyone else. He had left his coat and waistcoat in the storehouse and wore only trousers, boots and his now very soiled and torn shirt.

It might have put other men at a disadvantage, Connor thought, but not this one. Hampton stood straight and tense, but with untouched pride and dignity. Only a slight movement of the man's jaw indicated that this meeting was anything but the most common of occurrences for him.

There was a leashed, almost animal power in his every movement, regardless of how slight; and his flickering blue-green eyes—now cold and hostile—would have daunted men less resolute than Connor O'Neill.

Resentful of the intense inspection, Reese spoke first. "I suppose I am here for a reason?"

Although softly spoken, the words carried a hard, unyielding edge, and Connor felt a surge of admiration. Hampton might be English, but, by all that was holy, he had courage—and an audacity that was surprisingly appealing. Despite his tenuous position, the man showed no sign of defeat or surrender. Connor thought back to his talk with Samara this morning. There was no question but that she was in love with Hampton, and she would never forgive any of them if he came to harm at her family's hands. His own tragic experience—the death of his brother at the hands of Samantha's father—made him realize only too well the explosiveness of the situation. He could lose his daughter forever, as Robert Chatham had lost Samantha. Even worse, his merry mischievous daughter would be dead in spirit—if not in body. He *must* obtain the cooperation of this man who now looked as if accommodation were the last thing he would consider.

Studying the glowering eyes he started slowly, searching for words that would not fuel the hostility that still hovered between them. "You have two choices," he said, "and I doubt you'll care for either one of them. But perhaps there's some comfort in the fact that I don't like them any better than you."

All of Reese's attention was now riveted on the man. Almost unconsciously, minutes earlier, he had let his eyes roam over the extensive collection of books. Books said a lot about a man, often revealing more than spoken words. He wanted to know more of Connor O'Neill.

But now he was merely silent, waiting for O'Neill to continue.

"I can turn you over to the military authorities and do what I can to mitigate the charges. I *do* have some little influence. I might, just *might*, be able to save your neck, but most certainly you would go to prison and I doubt very much if you would be included in any exchange."

Hampton's face didn't change as Connor, searching for a reaction, paused. There was none, but Connor hadn't really expected one. Even his eyes were veiled.

"Or," Connor continued, "You can accept the same offer you made to my son. Your parole for the relative freedom of Glen Woods. You will see no one other than my family; you will contact no one. When Brendan returns, your information will be useless, and he can take you where he will. In the meantime you will be treated as a guest in this house, although, for the protection of my family, a somewhat reclusive one. Servants will talk, and neighbors will probably know we have a visitor. To avoid explanations, we will say you are a distant relative in deep mourning for a deceased wife and wish to see no one. You will not leave this house without having one of us accompany you and still another knowing your whereabouts. That way, we can warn you if we have visitors." Connor turned and looked out the window, away from Reese's still impassive face, for several seconds before facing him again.

"And I want to know the name of the person helping you."

For the first time since Connor started speaking, Reese replied. "No," he said simply.

"Not even if you hang for your silence?"

Reese shrugged with the same apparent indifference he had shown the night before, but his eyes lost their curtain and glittered with restoked anger, and his lips firmed in a tight, grim line.

"I didn't think so," Connor said finally. "But now we know a traitor exists and we'll find him." He went over to his desk and poured two glasses from a bottle of brandy sitting there. He offered one to Hampton who shook his head in refusal.

"My offer was not conditional on that information," Connor said.

"Wasn't it?" Reese said. "It sounded like it."

"I had to try."

Reese relaxed slightly. He considered the offer now for the first time. He hated being pushed into a corner and, in effect, surrendering his freedom. He didn't want to be obligated to Samara or any of the O'Neills; his pride had already taken a severe beating at their hands. But hanging was very final, and prison was no more attractive. He stated his one reservation. "I told my crew I would try to help them . . . I can't buy my freedom at the continued loss of theirs."

Connor rubbed the back of his neck in frustration. "I have some friends in Washington," he said finally. "I'll see if I can't expedite their exchange. Now that the ship . . . and captain . . . are gone, it shouldn't be too great a problem."

"Is that a promise?"

"Damn you, Hampton. You're in no position to make demands."

"Is it a promise?"

"Yes," Connor said, wondering whether admiration or aggravation was his dominant feeling at the moment.

"Perhaps, then, I *will* take that brandy," Reese said slowly. He knew he was accepting the terms. He really had no choice and at least he was winning something for his crew. As much as the situation galled him, it seemed he could do more for his crew in this manner than he could dead or in prison with them.

Connor smiled for the first time during the tense meeting. Without actually saying the words, Hampton had, in effect, just accepted the terms—however reluctantly.

Minutes later, Samantha appeared at the door and at Connor's nod visibly relaxed.

"I'll take you to your room," she said to Reese, disregarding the cool hostility in his eyes. "You can use Brendan's."

She led the way up a winding staircase, down a long hall to a closed door. When she opened it, Reese scanned the comfortable interior.

"A luxurious prison, indeed, Madam. The storehouse would have served as well... the result is the same."

Samantha ignored the icy comment. "You can use any of Brendan's clothes. They will be somewhat small, I think, but Angel should be able to alter them sufficiently to serve your immediate needs. Marion will get you some new clothes in Charleston."

"You will be repaid," Reese said stiffly.

Samantha nodded, knowing no other answer would be acceptable. "Marcus will prepare a bath. Dinner is at eight. You might want to rest until then; I think, after last night, most of us will."

She smiled, and Reese wondered at her composure. Nothing seemed to startle or anger her. She was truly a most unusual woman. Before he could reply, she was gone.

Reese looked around the room slowly, taking in every detail. There were several guns, one an old musket, hanging on the wall. He reached for it, his fingers fondling the fine workmanship. Then they withdrew. He had given his word. Reese suddenly felt more a prisoner than if he were locked in a dungeon, for then, at least, he could try to escape.

He tried to decipher his feelings towards Samara. He wanted to hate her, to dismiss her from his life. But she had stolen a deep piece of him, and despite all that had happened he still wanted her with an intensity that astonished him. But he would not trust her again. Never again.

Chapter Fourteen

How could gray eyes shoot off so many sparks?

He had already seen them in so many moods—from misty wistfulness to thundercloud anger. But now she was furious, more furious than she had ever been, even during the worst of his teasing aboard the *Unicorn*.

Despite his almost feeble attempts to keep his eyes from hers, Reese could not. He was uncomfortably seated across from Samara at this very awkward dinner—his first meal with the O'Neill clan.

Reese had remained icy and withdrawn throughout much of dinner, and attempts to involve him in conversation failed miserably. Some of Samara's guilt turned to defensive indignation . . . and then outrage. She had expected him to be angry, but she thought he would come to understand that she had tried to protect everyone; that her motives, if not exactly her means, were pure and that she would never—never, ever—let him hang.

But Reese's resentment was fed by the irony of his position. That he had placed Brendan and Samara in this very situation a year ago didn't help. "Until you walk in another man's boots . . ." The words of one of his tutors, a religious man who had taught him Latin and Greek, echoed in his mind. He was walking in those boots now, and he didn't like the fit. And having the lovely little traitorous face across from him didn't improve his temper.

Even conversation among the family members was stilted—for the first time in Samara's memory. There were few safe topics. Talk of the war, which usually dominated mealtimes, was avoided, both out of caution and courtesy.

In the uneasy silences, heightened by the raw electricity that so obviously bound the English captain and Samara, any attempt at communication was quickly exhausted. No one at the table, even the least perceptive, could mistake the strength of the attraction—or the battle—between them.

They were all there, all the brothers except Brendan, as was Jere's wife. Reese had them all firmly in his mind now—from the still glowering Conn to the insouciant Marion and the earnest Jere. Jere's wife, Judith, was very pretty in a gentle way and she, more than any of the others, sought to defuse the tension, asking about English fashions and weather. Her attempts at kindness brought the first smile from Reese, and everyone at the table had a small sample of the considerable Hampton charm. He took his angry eyes from Samara, and they lightened with mischief as he discussed, most expertly, the rising of the empire waist and the lowering of necklines. Only the sudden twinkle in his eyes indicated he knew it was not altogether suitable conversation, which was exactly why he was pursuing it.

Samantha's lips twitched, and Connor's eyebrows quirked, while Samara's own temper irrationally rose at every additional indication that Reese Hampton had in the past year paid extremely close attention to women's attire and, Samara thought bitterly, more likely to their lack of it.

When Reese finished his discourse, he sat back and his eyes returned to Samara. He grinned at her outraged expression and felt the first satisfaction since his abduction. It was quickly squelched when he heard her mother's words.

"Samara will show you the plantation tomorrow," she said easily, ignoring the immediate tension in both her daughter and Hampton. "You should become familiar with the boundaries."

The muscles in Reese's jaw flexed with ire. If he was going to have a guard, by God, the last person he wanted was Samara. "I would prefer someone else," he said evenly.

"I'm sorry," Samantha said gently. "Marion is returning to Charleston, Jere is needed at Chatham Oaks, and my husband will be busy on the plantation. There is no one else, other than Conn, and I doubt he would be agreeable company. You can, of course, stay in the house if you prefer."

Reese knew he would probably go quite mad if he had to stay inside. He nodded curtly.

Marion, amused at his mother's quite obvious ploy, smiled and changed the subject. "Do you have an interest in horses, Captain Hampton?"

"My family raises them," Reese replied with a scowl.

Undaunted, Marion continued. "Then I think you'll be most interested in mother's horses. They're extraordinary. I'll take you to the stables after dinner if you like."

The opportunity to escape the house, and Samara, and most of the confounded O'Neills was appealing. He nodded his head in agreement.

"You will excuse us?" Marion said several minutes later after dessert was finished. Silence had, once more, fallen on the table. At his father's assent, he and Reese rose and made for the door.

The two men said nothing as they walked across the lawn to the stables. Once inside, Reese was indeed intrigued by Samantha's golden horses, especially Sunswept, a large, sleek, beautifully colored stallion.

"I've never seen such a color," Reese said in admiration as he reached to touch the shoulder, then the neck. The horse tolerated Reese's touch, but arched its head arrogantly as if to display its superiority.

"He usually won't let anyone touch him but Mother," Marion said.

As Reese nodded at the backhanded compliment, Marion switched abruptly to another topic. "I understand Mother visited you last night."

The Englishman nodded warily.

Marion grinned. "And Samara and Father, and I don't even want to guess about others. All after being kidnapped at a ball. You must think us a gaggle of lunatics."

Reese couldn't restrain a smile of his own. "Something like that." For the first time, there was no anger in his words. The two men looked at each other and chuckled, then laughed. Reese could feel the resentment draining away from him.

"Did Samara tell you anything about Mother?"

"Your sister told me she was an orphan," Reese complained with a wry smile, his humor somewhat restored. "It was a very tragic tale."

"The real story was tragic enough," Marion said soberly. "Mother's father was a Tory. He killed her fiancé—who was Father's brother—the day they were to be married. So Mother, who was apparently as impetuous as Samara is now, ran away and joined General Marion, taking only a golden horse with her...this fellow's ancestress. She rode with him nearly two years; it was then she fell in love with Father, who was a major with General Marion.'' He paused, then continued thoughtfully. ''It's a history we've lived with—Brendan, Conn, Jere and Samara. Perhaps Samara's been most affected by it, since she feels she must live up to Mother. And Mother—she's always been as independent as her horses. Father says he could never tame either of them, but then I don't think he really ever wanted to.''

He was quiet for a moment, then added in a low tone, ''Samara's much like Mother, but she's always been protected...perhaps too much. She believes things will always turn out for the best, because they always have. She wished no harm to you, Hampton. She fought for you last night and this morning like a little wildcat. She even said she would leave and never come back if anything happened to you. And she meant it. That's the reason Conn backed down.''

Silence settled between the two men. Reese was reluctant to let go of his anger because it was the only thing that protected him from the little enchantress and all she represented. Commitment. Bonds. Sacrifice of a life he had come to cherish. Or had he? Had he just used it to hide a loneliness he wouldn't admit?

He returned Marion's gaze, his face noncommittal, and Marion sighed. He was beginning to think no two more stubborn people existed than his sister and this stiff-necked Englishman.

Two horses were saddled when Samara, prettily attired in a dark blue riding costume, and an aloof Reese arrived at the stables. He courteously but coolly assisted her into the hated sidesaddle and easily swung up onto his own restless bay mount. The horse was fresh, eager for an outing, and Reese enjoyed the effort it took to control him.

Samara watched as he quickly established his mastery, thinking how startlingly handsome he was. He wore buff breeches and black boots, and a white lawn shirt of Brendan's. Both the breeches and shirt were stretched taut across his muscled body, despite Angel's best efforts with a needle. The shirt strained at the wide shoulders and contrasted with the deep tan of his neck and sun-bronzed face. He exuded masculinity and strength and power, and Samara felt herself turning once more to mush as heat and yearning rushed like molten lead through her. She wished she could stay angry with him, but it was impossible. Not when he looked so magnificent!

Reese turned to her, his head lowered in mocking deference. "I am your prisoner, Miss Samara, and at your direction." His eyes glinted with something she couldn't name.

Her lips tightened at his casual insolence, even as she knew she preferred this mood to the frigid indifference of yesterday.

"Follow me," she retorted shortly, urging her horse into a canter. He paced himself behind her, just enough to be tauntingly subservient, and she knew he did it to goad her. There was nothing subservient about his proud bearing or the challenging twist of his mouth.

Some of Reese's ill humor left him as he noted her shoulders straighten in irritation. She was lovely in blue; the color intensified the sheen of the dark hair which now tumbled in curls from a clasp in back. Unlike most English ladies, she wore no hat and her ivory complexion had the slight glow of sun. From his position, he also noted that she was an excellent rider, as excellent as one could be in a sidesaddle. She moved easily and gracefully with the horse, retaining firm but gentle control of a spirited mare.

Almost as if she knew what he was thinking, she nudged her horse into a gallop, and suddenly laughing eyes looked back at him and challenged. He had merely to touch his mount and they were racing along the road, Samara's musical laughter charming him with its mischief. She had made sure she had a considerable head start.

He followed her as she left the road and raced across fields and finally into a wooded area where a narrow path made it impossible for him to pass; he could only take the clumps of earth loosed by her mare's hoofs. Little devil, he cursed, while admiring her horsemanship. She knew exactly what she was doing. She stopped so suddenly that his horse almost ran into her and reared in confusion. It took all of Reese's skill to remain in the saddle, and he swore once more as he saw the provocative defiance in her face.

He calmed his horse and dismounted, striding angrily over to her. "That was a damn fool thing to do. You could have killed both of us." He looked down at his once clean shirt. It was splattered now with great blobs of dirt and mud. And from her amused look, he knew there were similar spots on his face. His dignity suffered several seconds before his sense of humor took over and his lips twitched.

"Ah, Samara," he said in a soft almost intimate tone. It had a quizzical, almost rueful note of surrender in it as he reached his hands for her, and she most willingly slid from her horse into his arms.

They stood there together, indifferent to anything except their raw need for each other, for a surcease of the painful, inexplicable torment that had bedeviled both of them for nearly a year. Samara's face looked upward, toward him, seeking reassurance, a sign that he felt the same mysterious aching, the same fierce want as she. She wasn't disappointed. His face was rigid with effort as he sought to control himself and his gem-like eyes shimmered with the same hunger that consumed her. Heat pulsated in wild spurts, starting at her core and reaching out to claim every part of her body, and some vital irresistible craving made her tremble in his arms as she felt them tighten around her.

She strained against him, feeling his growing hardness, and in that one gesture she offered everything she had.

She felt his hand touch her chin tenderly, and lift her face upward. His lips were gentle but still seared her mouth with their warmth and hunger. They wandered, grazing her cheek, caressing her eyes, whispering in her ears, stroking her throat until she thought she would die with the pleasure and joy of it. Her hands crept up his back and played with the thick golden hair as his lips returned to her mouth and his tongue reached inside, stoking little blazes that flared like freshly lighted candles.

Their two bodies clung together as much as clothes would allow, while his hands busied themselves with the top buttons to her jacket. Samara was barely aware of them, so lost was she in the discovery of so many new sensations, new emotions, new hungers.

His mouth tore away from hers, and he hoarsely uttered her name. "Samara...Samara, my love," and there was no mockery in the endearment, only a sort of wonder. He searched her eyes, her face for fear or hesitation but there was none, only the same desperate desire that racked him.

His hands opened the jacket and the top of the dress beneath it and he slid one hand inside, feeling the taut breast. He freed it from the clothing and his head leaned down, his tongue forging trails of fire before his mouth reached for the nipple. He was engulfed with passion, driven by desires stronger than he had ever felt before. He kept expecting her to cry out, to stop the madness, but her lips were buried in his golden hair, busy with their own frantic pursuit. By instinct alone, her lips moved to his ear, and her tongue tasted the tangy saltiness of his skin, touching nerves that drew a low moan from his throat. "Little witch . . . my beautiful little witch . . ."

He was reaching for the front of his breeches, now swollen with his throbbing manhood, when he heard the rustle of an approaching rider. In an almost instantaneous return to sanity, he gently pushed Samara away. Her face was flushed, her hair tangled, her riding costume in disarray. Experienced hands quickly worked the small buttons, but nothing could be done for the heightened color in her face nor for the brightness of her eyes.

He had just finished with her buttons when Conn appeared on a chestnut gelding. O'Neill's blue eyes, so much like Brendan's except for the vivid anger in them, raked over the two faces, noting Samara's discomfort and mussed appearance and Reese's now impassive expression. He glowered at both of them.

"You followed us," Samara accused furiously.

"No," her brother said evenly. "But I thought, as you were gone an inordinately long time, you might be in trouble." His expression told her he felt his expectation correct.

Reese's low drawl interrupted the exchange. There was cold anger in his tone. "And you thought I might have ravished and killed Samara and escaped."

"Why not?" Conn said bitterly. "All we have is your word, and I wouldn't accept an Englishman's word under any conditions. I'm not as gullible as my father. And," he added nastily, "it seems I was partially right." His eyes moved from Samara's tangled hair to Reese, taking in every aspect of his appearance.

"You have no right, Conn . . ." Samara said with fury.

"I have every right, little sister. I'm not going to let him take advantage of you." He turned to Reese. "Get mounted," he ordered.

Reese's lips thinned at the terse command. He saw the tears begin to form in the depths of Samara's eyes and decided to obey. An unsuspected protectiveness welled up inside him, and he didn't want to cause her any more hurt today. He had allowed himself to get out of control and had almost seduced her. If it hadn't been for Conn...

He went over to Samara, took her now cold hand and helped her into the saddle, ignoring Conn's obvious rage. He then mounted his own bay and without looking back at either of them followed the path back to the O'Neill home.

Days passed with agonizing slowness for Reese. He had decided he would not allow himself alone again with Samara. It was much too dangerous for everyone concerned, particularly himself.

During the long sleepless night after their ride, he knew that he could not allow their relationship to go any further. He had, no matter how reluctantly, accepted the hospitality of the O'Neill family, and he would not abuse it by seducing the daughter of the house.

But the magic was always there, a seemingly invincible need for each other that grew daily, even as they tried to deny it. Each accidental meeting renewed raging fires in them; and mealtimes became ordeals to survive. Reese would charm and tease, but often he would end the farce with his hands clenched in tight fists hidden beneath a napkin.

Several days after the encounter in the woods, Reese was in the library, browsing restlessly through the books when Samara entered. He started to leave, but she placed a restraining hand on his arm, and the touch, even through his shirt, was like a brand.

"Don't go, Reese," she said. "Please. I haven't had the chance to ask you about the *Unicorn*...I didn't want to do it in front of the others."

Her wistful look stopped him and he was startled at her insight. She had sensed he needed time, that he wouldn't want to discuss the *Unicorn* in the hearing of her family. That she felt his pain and respected it served only to strengthen his longing for her. She was such a captivating mixture of mischievous child and sensitive woman.

"Tell me," she pleaded, "what happened...I know the crew was taken. Papa's trying to get them released. But how did you get away? And how was the ship sunk?"

"I don't know, little cat," he said. "The *Unicorn* was hit by one storm after another and after the last she was badly wounded." Samara couldn't miss the way he spoke of the *Unicorn* as a person, a beloved person. "And then there were two American ships ... almost as if they were waiting ... "

"The crew ... Davey and Yancy and Michael ... ?"

Her face was full of concern and involuntarily his hand touched her cheek. He was reminded of that day in Yancy's small surgery when she had comforted one of the sailors. That quality and her stubbornness despite odds were the two facets of Samara that fascinated him most.

"They all made it, I think," he said. "That's something else your father is trying to find out. But I saw the American boats picking them up. I decided to swim for it and try to help them later. I knew no one else could make it; I didn't know if I could. I almost didn't." His eyes clouded as he remembered that long, exhausting swim. "You know most of the rest."

"At least all you'll tell me," she retorted.

"That's right," he said amiably.

She was afraid to say anything else, lest she ruin the brief peace between them. "I'm glad you're safe," she whispered. "I couldn't bear it if anything happened to you."

Her heart was in her eyes, and Reese's breath caught under her soft gaze. There was so much hopeful child there, so much passionate woman.

His hand, which had stayed on her cheek, fell. "Under any other circumstances, little cat ... " He turned on his heel and left before he did, or said, something he would regret.

Late summer turned to fall, and still there was no word of Brendan. Reese became an accepted member of the family, at least to all but Conn who still regarded him with suspicion and dislike. But Conn, his leg as healed as it ever would be, planned to leave in several days to join General Andrew Jackson in Alabama. Despite a bad limp he felt fit enough to return to duty, and news of a massacre in Alabama spurred his plans. The Creeks, unhappy with white incursions on the Alabama lands, had captured Fort Mims and massacred the inhabitants— five-hundred and fifty three men, women and children. Jackson had been ordered into Alabama, where he would build forts and wipe out the Indian resistance.

The other war news was better—at least for the O'Neills. Oliver Hazard Perry met and badly defeated a British fleet on Lake Erie, resulting in the British evacuation of Detroit. The

American family tried to restrain their enthusiasm out of courtesy to their guest, but the elation was difficult to hide entirely.

In light of the war news, Reese chafed at his restrictions. His natural restlessness and impatience made him edgy; and the fate of his crew was of growing concern. He knew Connor was doing all he could, but his crew was still imprisoned. He had learned that they all survived and were being held in a Boston prison, but he feared that his own reputation had hindered their chances for exchange.

Noting his increasing unease, Connor often asked him to accompany him around the plantation, and Reese always accepted. It placed him away from Samara and he was fascinated with the workings of Glen Woods. He had been astounded when Connor explained that most of the servants and field hands were free men.

On their first ride together, Connor had noted Reese's disapproval as he watched the laborers; it wasn't difficult to guess the reason. Many Englishmen abhorred the practice of slavery, and attempts were already being made in Parliament to outlaw the practice in the British possessions. It had seemed quite odd to Connor, however, that the English persisted in using bond servants and convicts, many accused only of political crimes, in much the same fashion. He was particularly sensitive to the fact that many Irish and Scots had been sentenced to long terms of servitude first in America, then in Australia, for merely defending their rights and land. It was, to Connor, another example of British hypocrisy.

Connor disliked slavery in any form, and he explained that most of the hands on both Glen Woods and Chatham Oaks had been freed. The O'Neills did occasionally purchase slaves but then gave them an opportunity to buy their freedom after proving themselves. Artisans and skilled craftsmen could work outside the plantation and keep their earnings. It was a system that worked well for the O'Neills. Their workers produced nearly double that of other plantations.

Startled, Reese reassessed Connor O'Neill, and respect started to grow. The two often rode together now, and a friendship formed and deepened just as it had with Brendan.

From the window of her bedroom, Samara watched the two men as they approached the stable, and she couldn't bury the envy—and desolation—that buffeted her heart. With his hair glinting in the sun, and his long, strong body resting easily in the saddle, Reese was as breathtaking as he was at the helm of a ship. Breathtaking and forbidden. It was as if he were thousands of miles away instead of sharing the same house. For he had made it quite clear that he did not desire her company.

She would never let him know how devastated she was. She cherished the memories of the afternoon in the woods, cherished and held them closely to herself. From the first moment she had seen him, he stirred feelings inside her she had never known existed. Even when she tried so hard to fight him, she knew that a part of her would never be free of the Honorable Reese Hampton. Honorable. An English nobleman. Why should he care about the country-bumpkin colonial?

And he didn't. He had shown that countless times. He avoided her like he might the black death, or smallpox, or any other wretched disease. Which was exactly what she was beginning to feel like. When he encountered her alone, he bolted like a chicken which instinctively knew it was destined as the main course for dinner.

Damn Conn. He had ruined everything. When he had so abruptly interfered that day in the woods, she knew she had been on the verge of discovering something truly wonderful and magical. And since then Reese's warmth had turned to ice, his passion to amused tolerance. Only rarely did she catch a flash of fire in his eyes that was gone almost instantly, lost in the controlled void that hid his thoughts.

He had been here two months now, and each day carried its own litany of misery—of hope shattered and desire spurned. Soon he would be gone. What information he had no longer mattered, but her father wanted him aboard Bren's ship, bound for a neutral port where he could do no damage to the American cause. And so she waited in torment, wanting him to go, wanting him to stay, loving and hating, hoping and dreading. Nothing was right any more. Nothing had been right since that day—it seemed years ago—when a sampler lured her from safety to a voyage that had shaken her world.

I have to know. I have to know if it's all fantasy. There had been times, both aboard the *Unicorn* and here at Glen Woods, when his guard had dropped and she sensed the same intensity of feeling that so overwhelmed her. But it usually fled so swiftly, she could only wonder if she had imagined it all. But she couldn't let him go without knowing. Once more, she started plotting.

Chapter Fifteen

Samara planned her offensive as carefully as any general prepared for battle. Everything was perfect, everything as she knew it must be for her plan to succeed. Her father had gone to Jere's plantation; Conn had taken his protective, scowling countenance to Charleston in last-minute preparations for his return to the militia. Marion had already been gone several weeks. And her mother was in the stables, enraptured with the new colt.

Samara had planned to trick Reese into accompanying her on some counterfeit errand decreed by her father, and lead him, unsuspecting, to the cave. But when she found him in the library she had neither the heart nor the deceitfulness to implement that which she had plotted.

He was standing at the window, obviously unaware of her presence, and his shoulders were uncharacteristically slumped. She saw his hands move compulsively, clenching in fists, and she sensed his frustration . . . frustration and a sense of failure. An ache started in her and grew and became a clutching, hurtful thing as she realized *she* had done this to him.

She had realized months earlier that she loved him, but she had fought it because he was the enemy. In the past weeks, he had treated her as a problem to be avoided. Only rarely did those magnetic eyes reflect the warmth she had so wonderfully, and briefly, felt in the woods. More often, she was greeted with a grim mouth and hooded eyes. It was like watching a volcano rumble and steam, never knowing when the final eruption might come. In the past few days, she had sensed the growing pressure, the need within him for release. Samara knew he worried about his crew and considered her home no more than an elegant prison. He had been forced into a powerless position and he hated it; hated his helplessness, his enforced obedience to someone else's will. To a man like Reese Hampton who loved freedom above all, his stay at Glen Woods was becoming intolerable.

Samara knew she could not lie to him, could not deceive him into doing something *she* wanted. With sudden maturity born of recently recognized if not completely accepted love, Samara knew she would not try to manipulate this very proud man.

Instead, she went over to him and stood silently next to him, trying to tell him without words that she understood his anguish.

"You shouldn't be here," he said in a low, husky voice after a long silence.

She said nothing. His voice was somehow wistful, a departure from his usual confident tone. She turned and searched his face, and watched his jaw tense with inner turmoil.

"You shouldn't be here," he said again, as if trying to convince himself.

"I want to show you something," she said.

He smiled then, an incredibly winsome smile, tinged with a trace of irony. "And what might be waiting for me this time?" His hand, almost unconsciously, went to her cheek and touched it. It was so smooth, so silky. And her eyes were like gray-blue velvet, warm and luxurious. And dangerous. He had learned that. She was dangerous in so many ways. Ways she didn't even realize.

"Please," she said now. "Please come with me for a ride."

She saw his searching gaze, his indecision. She held out her hand to him, her eyes beseeching him.

"Little cat." The words were so softly spoken she barely heard them.

"Englishman," she said, and the sound was an endearment.

His mouth crooked in a small wry smile. "I'll always be an Englishman, you know."

"I know," she whispered, "and probably a pirate and a blackguard and . . ."

"And you, my little American, are a beguiling liar. Married! God, I should have known better."

"I think," she said slowly with a small, tentative smile, "perhaps we deserve each other."

"Perhaps we do," he admitted ruefully, and despite his reluctant reply, Samara felt her heart leap with hope. He *did* care. His mouth was saying it; his eyes were saying it.

The glinting hardness was gone, lost in the swirling blue-green depths that beckoned her. They were so intriguing, these eyes of his with all their mysteries. He hid so much in them, revealing little but his great lust for life. It had seemed dimmed in the recent weeks, and that, perhaps more than anything else, touched Samara and gave her pain.

"You look pensive, little cat," he said now, the grim taut line of his mouth softening. She was lovely, standing in a ray of sun that filtered through the window. Her eyes were large and searching, her mouth pursed in an uncertain smile which affected him in a strange and tender way. He wondered now at that emotion; he had felt many things with women, but seldom this tenderness that reached so deep inside him. Or this protectiveness that was keeping him from taking her here and now and damn the consequences.

He wanted her, more than he had ever wanted anything. Her warm, fiery passion, so uninhibited once aroused, was more seductive, more irresistible than any he had ever known. She was so alive, so filled with optimism and hope and humor. But even more appealing was her indomitable spirit which had led her to stow away on Brendan's ship and fight for Brendan's freedom. God help him, Reese thought with chagrin, it had even led her to kidnap him. Samara, right or wrong, was a fighter who pursued her own ideas of honor. From Reese's somewhat jaded viewpoint, it was a unique quality in a woman, and it fascinated and charmed him.

"Please," she said once more. She felt compelled to take him to her cave, to the place where she had felt his presence so profoundly.

Reese searched for an excuse, but discovered he didn't want to find one. He told himself he wanted to go for a ride, to get out of the house, and under the rules established by Connor, Samara was at the moment his only means. He nodded, cursing himself for a damn fool.

Samara led the way... across the boundaries of the plantation, along the Pee Dee River, past the giant oaks and cypresses draped with gray shrouds of moss. This land was unbelievably lush, Reese thought, as he rode silently, so differ-

ent from the manicured fields and gardens of England. There
was a wild, untamed beauty about it, and Reese could understand how it produced such independent and unconventional
women as Samantha and Samara O'Neill. Would either survive in England with its often brittle and cruel society and restrictive conventions? He thought of Samantha that first night
when she had visited him in breeches and shirt. He had seen
Samara sneak out in the mornings in the same unusual clothing. The sight had stirred the warmth in his loins more than any
ballgown. Even now the image fired his blood. He shook his
head to rid it of the thoughts. He must keep his senses about
him. He should never have come, but the plea in Samara's
lovely eyes had shattered what few defenses he had.

It was time to settle matters. They could not go much longer
with so many questions unanswered between them. They were
in every look, every glance. He couldn't help but recognize the
love that too often shone in her face, despite her efforts to hide
it. Nor could he deny his own attraction and hunger. But that
was all it was, he tried to convince himself, a natural response
to a very lovely girl. So why was there such a painful throb in
him at the thought of leaving her?

Samara stopped near the cave, and Reese quickly dismounted and tied the reins of his horse to a tree before offering his hand to her. Remembering too well their first ride, he
quickly released her and stepped back, waiting to see what it
was she so badly wanted him to share.

She led the way, brushing aside the thick vines around the
mouth of a cave and darting inside, leaving him to follow reluctantly. Curiously, he studied the interior which widened
from the narrow entrance into a large and deep cavern. There
were several signs of use: tattered clothes, candles, a tin cup and
pail.

He watched, fascinated, in the dim light, as Samara, oblivious to the dirt and dust clinging to her riding costume, lit a
candle. Her face glowed in the light, and her gray eyes sparkled as she searched eagerly for his reaction.

And then he felt it too . . . a peculiar warmth. The day had
been cold and the cave, untouched by sun, even colder. But now
he felt touched by a kind of radiance. He immediately dismissed the odd feeling as fancy; there *must* be a very sound
reason for it, perhaps some hot spring underneath the earth.
But all such reasoning fled as Samara moved towards him—as
did all his good intentions. She was uncommonly beautiful in

the candlelight, her hair fairly dancing with fiery streaks, her face filled with love and expectancy. He could only groan with his need for her.

"No," he tried to say, but the sound disappeared as her lips reached up for his with the same single-mindedness of purpose he had witnessed before. Her eyes were open, searching for response, for an answering warmth. For she knew she would find the truth here. She had to know it.

And she found it in the sudden violent embrace of his arms, in the tender sweetness of his lips that first barely touched, then caressed, then demanded, searing both of them with a brand they would carry forever, exploding greedy wildfires that surged through their achingly ready bodies.

Reese tried to stop, but Samara's body moved against his, sending shock waves through the core of his being. His manhood throbbed and pounded with its need to become one with her, to feel the depth of the warmth she was offering.

His tongue found its way into the welcoming mouth, and teased and stroked until he felt her shudder with unaccustomed sensations. When he finally withdrew it, they were both tense with raging fires.

Her hand reached up and played with his hair, and she stared at him with wonder. He was so handsome, so completely, beautifully masculine as he stood there, emanating strength and power and animal grace. "I love you, I think" she whispered, unable to keep it to herself any longer.

He backed away, his hands on her shoulders, his steady gaze meeting hers. He watched as her desire changed to hope and hope changed to fear and fear changed to despair. His heart began to crack as her despair turned to misery, and she abruptly turned away before he could see her welling tears. His silence had said more than words could.

His arms went around her, his chest to her back, and his lips touched her hair. God, how he wanted to reassure her, to take her now, to love her. But how could he? He was a fugitive in her country, an enemy to her people. And he was a friend to her brother and father. He should not take her without marriage and marriage was impossible, at least at the moment, at least until he found some way out.

He felt her shaking, and his arms felt the warm impact of her silent tears. He swallowed. She was so completely vulnerable.

Reese Hampton could stand it no longer. He knew suddenly that he could stand anything but her quiet anguish. And in that moment, he also knew he loved her and he would sell his soul rather than hurt her.

He turned her around, and once again his hand lifted her chin to face him. His mouth lowered to touch the tear-filled eyes, and moved down to catch the warm, salty tears.

When he finished, he straightened and his brilliant eyes fastened on her tear-glazed ones. "I love you, Samara," he said slowly. He had never expected to say those words, and they came awkwardly. So awkwardly Samara had trouble comprehending them, and she could only stare at him, bewilderedly.

He smiled a flashing, radiant smile that filled her full of golden awe. How could anyone smile like that? She still could not grasp his last statement, not after the long humiliating silence that preceded it.

"You have to forgive me, little cat," he said gently. "You see, I've never said it before."

His eyes were warm, oh so warm, and Samara finally understood. He *did* love her. Her heart thought it would burst with joy, but her eyes pleaded for more reassurance. *Tell me again*, she demanded silently.

"I love you," his words were as equally silent but just as clear and made even more potent by their delivery.

He took the blanket on the ground, shook it out and placed it next to the wall. Reese then took her hand and helped her sit before reclining next to her. He put his arm around her shoulders and held her close to him, taking pleasure in the feel of her.

"The question, Samara," he finally said, "is what do we do now?"

"As long as we love each other . . ."

His voice was very gentle. "It's not that easy, Samara. If I'm caught, I could very well hang. I can't stay here, and I wonder if you'd be happy in England."

"I would be happy wherever you are," Samara said, her reason lost in the wonderful euphoria she was now feeling. She would conquer the world for him.

He smiled at the words. They were so typically Samara. She was always so certain, so confident that everything would eventually work out well. "I'll be leaving when Brendan returns," he warned.

"I'll go with you," she announced.

He chuckled now, a deep, rumbling sound that charmed her completely. "A stowaway again?"

"If I have to," she said with determination.

"I think not," he said, but his grim tone was belied by the twinkle in his eye. By God, she would...if she had the chance.

"Then..."

"The war is not going to last much longer. It's not to the benefit of my country or yours. Negotiations are going on, and there's growing pressure in England against it. Until then, you must stay here. It's too dangerous for you to travel."

"But you and Bren..."

"Are soldiers," he completed with emphasis. "I know you didn't believe it then, but when I took the *Samara*, you were damned fortunate I had a few scruples." His soft laughter now held some self-directed mockery. "Damn few that they were, and even then I had a devil of a time holding to them. You are a bewitching young lady, Miss O'Neill, and I don't want you wandering about the seas while the war continues, with or without me."

Her fingers tightened around his hand. There was strength and grace in it, as there was in all of him. She suddenly wanted to know all about him.

"Have you ever been in love before?" she asked in a whisper. She feared the answer.

"Never," he replied solemnly. "And what about you? Your friend Emily said you had masses of suitors, all eager for your hand."

"I wasn't eager for theirs," she retorted with such disgust on her face he couldn't suppress his laughter.

"You never even thought about one...as a husband?" he teased.

"No...not ever," she said. "Not until..." She was afraid to say the word, to say "you."

"I'm doubly honored then," he said gallantly.

"Have you...ever thought about marriage before?" she said. "I heard marriages in England are arranged."

"Many are," he agreed, "but there are also many love matches. And no, even my father couldn't force me into marriage—although he tried hard enough." His eyes pierced her. "I would never marry without love," he said, "and I had never thought to find it."

Samara thought she would die from joy. He wanted *her*, just her. But she couldn't let it go. "You've never been engaged?" She just couldn't believe he had gone through so many years without attachments.

"No," he said, not counting his recent bogus betrothal. "Not," he added with a curious roughness in his voice, "until now."

She stared at him, hope leaping up in her eyes.

"If, that is," he continued, "you want to marry an Englishman, and a pirate and a blackguard—isn't that what you told your father?"

Happy laughter bubbled up inside her as he tenderly mocked her words.

"All of those and more," she replied tartly, just before his mouth hushed her.

Once more, the fires started raging and this time there was no quenching them.

His hands moved gently, but the very lightness of the touch made them more erotic as they traced intricate patterns on her cheek, moving to a sensitive earlobe and following them with whisper-like kisses that sent Samara hurtling into a sensation-filled world. Every nerve tingled with expectancy, and she was filled with an aching hunger as his lips traveled with scorching thoroughness to her neck, and his hands reached for her fastenings, releasing them with stunning quickness.

She knew her breasts were bare to him, and she felt him move to stretch out alongside her. Samara felt his lips making intimate little circles on each breast, then claiming first the right nipple, then the left with his tongue, then his lips, sending shivers of ecstasy dancing through her.

She touched his chest through the opening of his shirt as she had wanted to so many times before. Her fingers caught the golden hair and twisted and played with the enticing curls. Her fingers traced little patterns on his chest as her tongue found his earlobe and fondled it until he moaned. She laughed, delighting in knowing she could reciprocate all the wonderful feelings. The laugh was a symphony to him, filled with love and caring and desire and excitement.

Their eyes met, and their hands stilled. There was so much to say to each other, and it was all being said silently. There was no need for words.

His hands trembled slightly as he started anew on her riding costume, carefully, gently peeling it from her body, then the chemise. He looked in awe at the lovely body before him, the full breasts, slender waist, curving hips. "You are beautiful," he whispered.

Her sudden shyness disappeared at his words. He loved her. He wanted her. He thought her beautiful. And *she* wanted him with all the craving and hunger of her newly awakened body.

She watched him as he undressed...first the lawn shirt, then the boots and finally the trousers. She was stunned by the raw rugged beauty of his hard compact body.

He thought she might be frightened by him, but saw immediately she wasn't. He knelt beside her and Samara held out a hand to him. After a moment's hesitation, he took it.

"You're sure," he said slowly, afraid she would say no, equally afraid she would say yes.

In answer, she merely said, "Lie here next to me." More than anything else on earth, she wanted to feel him near her, to feel his skin touching hers, his warmth mingling with her own.

He did as she asked, feeling small explosions as they touched. Her body fit into his as if designed to do so.

Reese's arms went around her, holding her tightly, allowing her to grow familiar with his body as his mouth kissed her forehead, her cheeks and finally her lips with infinite tenderness. He could feel the sensations building in her, and his body grew taut as he sought to control his own needs. Her body moved compulsively closer to his, seeking an even more intimate union. He marveled at her lack of coyness or fear or modesty. She was open and honest and he rejoiced in it.

Samara, for her part, was too lost in the wonderful feelings to care about anything except satisfying the ache that had been within her for nearly a year, from that first kiss so many months ago. She felt no fear of him, or of what was to come, only a joy at his closeness. He *loved* her. He *needed* her. He wanted *her* as his wife.

She felt his hands teasing and caressing her, and dazzling colors took control of her mind as she responded with a passion so innocent and yet so free that it seemed to Reese a miracle of contradiction, a sensual rocketing of the senses.

He turned her, very slowly, very gently, on her back and leaned over to kiss her, letting his lips linger, glorying in the way she responded to his every touch. His hand reached down between her legs, and she shyly opened them for him while his hand stroked the warm dark curly hair. Each touch of his hand inflamed her more, and he felt her need intensify along with his own.

He kneeled above her, his legs straddling her body, his eyes making love as sensually as his hands. He slowly lowered himself, letting his manhood gently touch and tease her, and he heard her soft cries as she trembled with a yearning for something she did not yet understand.

Then, gently, he entered, his warmth becoming a welcomed part of her. There was a stab of pain, and she couldn't stop the small cry from escaping her lips. She felt him hesitate, but now she arched her body towards him, wanting desperately, despite the pain, to continue this voyage of discovery, to receive all of him, to make Reese one with herself, to bring him so close to her heart he would never go away.

As he probed tentatively, carefully, the pain waned in the exquisite tremors that swept through her. She had never imagined how wondrous this could be! Spasms of pleasure exploded from the deepest core of her body and spread like stars from a Roman candle until she thought she could bear no more. But as he thrust deeper and deeper in sure, controlled strokes, each rapturous second surpassed the last until all of her whirled in an upward spiral towards some magical destination and suddenly all she had ever known was swept away in the fiery eruption that so exquisitely rocked her body.

Afterward, she explored his body with her hands, loving the hard muscular feel of him, unable to get enough. He laughed at her greediness, hiding the desolation which had descended upon him in the aftermath. He had felt a terrible sense of guilt when he saw the blood. Although he had known Samara was a virgin, the red stain vividly drove the fact home. His distaste for himself was only slightly mitigated by the knowledge that his intentions were honorable, that he would marry her as soon as possible. But that might still be months or years, and he could not bear the thought of a child. Not until he could provide for Samara's safety.

"Is it always like this?" she asked in a wondering voice, breaking into his unsettling thoughts.

He forced himself to smile. "Very seldom, love." The endearment was unconscious. He still felt little quivers of pleasure reminding him of his dishonor. But she was so serious, so awed. "In fact, I think it's very rare indeed."

"Just us, perhaps?" she said with pardonable pride and delight at his answer.

Reese smiled at her shining eyes. Lord, she was entrancing. She would tempt a saint. And a saint he certainly was not.

"Just us," he reassured her. "But," he added seriously, "it can't happen again . . . not until we're married."

"When . . . ?"

"I don't know, love. But if you wish, I'll ask your parents for permission tonight." He gave her his irresistible crooked smile. "I doubt if they'll be very happy."

"If I am, they will be," she said quite accurately. "And I am. Wonderfully, marvelously so . . . just as Mother said it would happen some day. I think Brendan will be too, though we might have to work on Conn. He doesn't like the English."

"I've noticed," Reese said ruefully.

"Will we live in England?"

"Would you like to?"

"I don't know," she said seriously. "I have never thought about living a long way from Glen Woods. And I don't . . . didn't . . . like the English either . . . unless they're like you . . ." she added desperately, as she realized what she was saying.

His eyes twinkled at her awkward admission. And then a low rumble of laughter exploded.

Samara was, at first, offended and then she thought about what she had just said. She had hated him thoroughly in the beginning, especially when he'd inspired all those wickedly delightful feelings in her, and she had told him so repeatedly. To hold him up now as her perfect model for an Englishman was inconsistent to say the least. "Well, I *love* you," she said. "I don't really have to like you." At his wounded look she hurriedly added, "But I do. Enormously, I think."

Mollified slightly, Reese reached over and picked up his shirt and pulled it over his head, then reached for his trousers. "We'd better get back, little cat, or they will be scouring the countryside for us."

"I don't want to leave. I don't ever want to leave." But she reluctantly reached for her chemise. "You know this is where my mother fell in love with Father. She stumbled on him here after he had been wounded and she saved his life."

"Is that why you brought me here?" he questioned gently.

"No, I don't think so. But when Bren said you were dead I came here and, somehow, in this cave I knew you weren't. It was almost as if you were here with me." She stopped. "You must think I'm a fanciful child."

"Not a child, never a child," he answered with tenderness. He looked around. There *was* something about this cave—something almost alive. He shook his head and reached for her hand. "Come, love. We must make you respectable."

As they left, Reese looked back into the interior of the cave. The warmth was gone, replaced by a cold chill, and he was struck by a strange foreboding. He dismissed the idea as nonsense, brought on by Samara's tale.

Nonetheless, as he mounted and rode beside the woman he intended to make his wife, he couldn't rid himself of a certain disquiet.

Chapter Sixteen

Connor O'Neill stood in stunned silence as he listened to the accursed Hampton.

True enough, Connor had come to like and admire the vexing Englishman, but that was because he had been lulled into a false sense of security. He had *believed* the reserve between his daughter and his unwilling guest, and so he had relaxed and truly enjoyed his outings with Hampton. The man was entertaining, extremely intelligent and fascinated with everything he saw. His questions were astute, his opinions knowledgeable and his wit sharp.

But married to his daughter?

Whatever else he was, Reese Hampton was his country's enemy, a man who supported himself by pirating American ships and, worst of all, a would-be husband who would carry *his* daughter off to England.

"No," he said, as he glanced around the library in frustrated anger. He looked first at his wife, Samantha, then at Hampton. Samara had been banished from the room the second he realized the direction of Hampton's request to speak with him and Samantha. "No," he repeated. "You do *not* have our consent."

Samantha sat on the settee in the library, an enigmatic smile on her face. It hid the satisfaction she felt. She did not want to lose Samara to England any more than her husband did, but since her daughter's first reference to Reese Hampton she had recognized that he and no one else was Samara's happiness. She had worried and fretted about Reese's apparent indifference to her daughter and was mollified only by the man's occasional unguarded looks when he thought no one was watching. Now she would let Connor fume, knowing he would soon calm down and accept. It helped immensely that he liked Reese. He had told her so, more than once, in the privacy of their bedroom.

"And how do you plan to support Samara?" he said now. "By robbing her country's ships?"

Reese couldn't resist a slight grin. "As your son robs English ships?" he retorted, a combative gleam in his eye.

"The devil take you," Connor said, but he couldn't completely hide a hint of a twinkle in his eye. The man invented insolence. He remembered that first night when he'd asked Hampton if he were a spy, and his eyes grew even brighter as he recalled the answer. Hampton could charm a tiger into eating tamely from his hand.

Reese thought it time to restrain himself. "I'll seek no more American ships . . . now French, that's another matter."

"There are so many eligible *local* young men," Connor muttered, half to himself.

"And I have heard from her friend Emily that they are all groveling at her feet. I sympathize with your plight, sir," Reese said solemnly without a touch of sympathy in his voice. He was too old for this nonsense. He looked over at Samantha; his mouth twitched when she winked at him and nodded. There was no question he had her approval.

Connor also saw the movement, and it didn't help his temperament. "You too, Madam? You wish to see your daughter taken to England?"

"I don't think she should go anyplace until after the war," Reese interjected. "And afterward . . . I am thinking about purchasing some property here or in Virginia. I would not ask her to share my brother's home . . ." The words were said with a quiet sincerity that completely silenced Connor for a moment. Again he looked at Samantha as he remembered the gulf that had once divided them. He was a Whig; her family was Tory. There had been so much hate between them. And yet together they had discovered a love which still grew daily.

A slow smile replaced his anger. "You're still English, but, by the saints, I like you and I couldn't say that about any of the young dandies that hung around here."

The interview was over.

* * *

Samara, wondering how anyone could possibly be this happy, sat on the riverbank, her back leaning against the hard muscular chest of her intended.

Intended. What a wonderful word! She could barely believe that she would, one day, be this magnificent man's wife. She still did not understand entirely why he wanted her, and somewhere deep inside her there remained a kernel of fear that she was living in a make-believe world that might come crashing down around her. But when she looked at Reese she would banish the nagging uneasiness.

The bright love in her face delighted Reese. She had brought something young and fresh into his life. She was unpredictable and unpretentious, and enchantingly unaware of her beauty. He never quite knew what color her eyes would be; they changed with her mood or with the shades of her dress or the sky—or even the sea. They were smoky blue this afternoon, and as expressive as a painting. A new contentment flowed through him as he saw their quiet joy.

He had not meant to say the words he had uttered in the cave. "I love you." But they had come so easily and the moment they'd escaped his lips he knew he meant them. She had not been far from his thoughts since the day he had met her, and he thought now of those first few minutes. She had been so obviously terrified, so impossibly young, yet she had raised that ridiculous bottle against him. He had, he now admitted, probably fallen in love with her at that very moment.

His right arm tightened around her while the fingers of his left hand played with her silky curls. He could feel her burrow further into his chest, seeking his warmth on this crisp, early winter day. He had been very careful not to repeat the madness of the day in the cave, and had resisted her every attempt to lure him back. Although his body ached with its need to join hers, he would wait until they could be married. He could only hope the war would end shortly, for every day was a form of agony, a supreme challenge.

Their time together was almost over, he realized. The O'Neills had received word that Brendan had anchored in one of the several rivers along the coast. He had sent word that his voyage had been most successful, and that the *Samara* had sustained only slight damage. He would see to her repairs and provisioning before stopping at Glen Woods for a brief visit.

Connor had made the announcement at breakfast, watching the mixed emotions on Samara's face. Happiness flashed at the knowledge that Brendan was safe, but it was almost immediately replaced by the sobering realization that Brendan's homecoming meant Reese's departure. She had argued and pleaded and begged in the past week to be allowed to go with Reese, but both he and her father were united on this question. Neither would put her life in danger again and she knew she would never be able to repeat her earlier escapade.

She had planned this picnic, perhaps their last time alone, with great care. Angel had supervised the packing of a special lunch, and Reese and Samara had ridden out this morning to one of her favorite spots.

She turned her head and nibbled on the golden hairs that peeked from the open neck of Reese's shirt, her tongue tasting the musky skin, her hands tracing the corded muscles in his shoulders and chest. Samara felt she could never feel or taste or love enough of him. Her gaze went upward and she etched each beloved feature in her memory. Reese's hand tightened on a curl he was caressing as his body so readily responded to her touch. There was so much tenderness in her expression, tenderness mixed with warm passion. He had never encountered such a potent mixture. God, how he loved her, how she made him tremble. He leaned down, his lips brushing hers with infinite gentleness, thinking how much he wanted her next to him, her body melding with his. *What in God's name was happening to him?* He had to stop this now.

Reese shook as he took his lips from Samara's mouth, and his body trembled with the supreme effort it took to pull away from her.

"Samara . . . my lovely little nymph . . . we can't let Angel's efforts go to waste . . ."

"Hmm," she murmured, completely indifferent to Angel's bounty.

He smiled at the sensual purr of her response, his resolve weakening once more. A small chuckle started deep in his throat as he wondered at his complete idiocy where Samara was concerned. He had never believed a little cat, *his* cat, could turn him into a powerless mass of jelly.

He tried again. "I think we should eat . . ."

"Why?" she whispered, her tongue once more setting his skin on fire.

The little witch was seducing him, and doing it very well indeed. He felt the heat surge through his blood. *Damn her.* It was his last thought before he lost himself in her sweet, fervent sorcery.

Later, they lay in the grass, their hands touching, each still shivering with the aftershocks of their union. He had, in one supreme act of control, prevented his seed from spilling into her, but the pleasure and ecstasy of their joining had been multiplied by the knowledge of their impending separation.

"I don't know if I can bear it," she said, her mouth trembling.

He rolled over, his naked body glistening. He was indifferent to the chill but had covered Samara with a blanket they had brought along.

"I know, my love. I won't fare any better...if that comforts you."

She shook her head miserably. Nothing could comfort her. He would be in Bermuda or in England with dozens of available women—attractive, nobly born, sophisticated women.

He saw the clouded expression in her eyes and correctly interpreted it.

"There has never been," he said slowly, gently, "a woman I've longed to be with day and night, to tease and love and share my life with. There never will be, Samara, except you. You *must* believe that."

Her arms went around him, and she buried her face in his chest, her body heaving with bittersweet tears.

Reese held her tightly, trying to comfort and reassure, unaware of the moisture in his own eyes.

Reese was visiting Chatham Oaks with Connor when Brendan arrived at the O'Neill plantation. The Englishman wanted to learn as much as possible about the workings of the plantation and was particularly interested in Jere's new crop—tobacco. Jere, worried about their dependence on indigo, had recently started experimenting with tobacco on part of his land. He felt the soil was well suited to tobacco-growing—fertile with good drainage. Jere was constantly experimenting with ways to improve crops or the production of crops. He was a natural born farmer who loved the land and had a particular genius for extracting the best from it.

Of the family, only Samantha and Samara were home and they were together, talking, when the first cries came to them: "Mist' Bren—Mist' Bren is home!"

Delight flashed across the faces of both mother and daughter, despite Samara's knowledge that Bren's arrival heralded Reese's departure. It had been many months since she had seen her oldest brother, and she had much to tell him. She suspected he would approve. The unlikely friendship between Bren and Reese, which had once so annoyed her, was now a source of satisfaction. Of all her brothers' approval, she craved his most of all.

The mischief that the five O'Neill children had honed to a fine art while growing up danced in Samara's eyes.

She knew Bren had thought her most fanciful when she had protested that Reese could not be dead. And now, not only was the Englishman alive, but he was living on Glen Woods and engaged to Bren's sister. She would say nothing to her brother, just enjoy his shock when Reese returned. Then she would tell him the wonderful news. She exacted her mother's vow of silence and hurried off to warn the servants, finishing the chore just in time to run, quite happily, into Bren's arms as he dismounted and thrust his reins into a servant's hands.

He hugged her tightly, then pulled back to study her, pleased that the haunted look was gone from her face. The old sparkle was in her eyes, and the piquant face radiated happiness and confidence and an intriguing devilment. It was the old Samara—and more. He had never seen her look quite so delighted with herself, even at the worst of her pranks which were always preceded by that same sly expression.

He grinned and reached for her small waist, seizing it in his two large hands, and whirling her around as she laughed with unrestrained joy.

"You look like a woman in love," he said when he finally set her down, his eyebrows arching in question.

"Yes, oh, yes," she said, and Bren was struck by the complete bliss on her face.

Thank God, he thought. *Thank God, she's over Hampton.* He had been uncertain whether to tell her about the newspaper he had found aboard a British merchantman he had taken. The newspaper had reported the betrothal of Captain Reese Hampton and a Lady Stanton, widow of a British earl. The story had emphasized the lady's loveliness, commenting that the engagement was said to be a love match as well as a most suitable alliance between two distinguished families. The match had been announced at a ball during which the couple seemed quite enamored of each other. Bren had kept the article. He had worried that Samara might still be harboring hopes that Hampton lived. The news that Hampton had been engaged prior to the sinking of his ship might quell any lingering feelings on Samara's part. Although he still felt grief at the man's death, he was relieved that Hampton was in Samara's past—gone, and apparently forgotten.

"May I ask who the lucky man is?" he questioned now, his blue eyes warm with affection.

"You will have to wait," Samara answered playfully. "He will be here for supper."

"That long? At least, tell me if I'll be pleased."

The devil was back in her eye as she grinned. "I think so, eldest brother," she said as she hugged him tightly again. "Oh Bren, I'm so happy."

He leaned over and kissed her forehead. "I can't wait to meet this paragon . . . I know I'll approve of anyone who makes you this merry."

Bren looked up and winked at his mother who also looked very self-satisfied. He bounded up the stairs to the porch where she waited and flung his arms around her. "And you approve?"

"Wholeheartedly," she said.

"And you won't tell me either?"

She laughed. "And spoil Samara's surprise? Never. You'll just have to rein in that curiosity. Come and eat. We were about to have dinner."

"With pleasure. I'm damned tired of biscuits and salt pork." He looked at Samantha apologetically. "Excuse me, Mother. I've been aboard ship too long."

"I'm just glad to have you home," Samantha said, then asked tentatively, "When do you plan to leave again?"

"Almost immediately, I'm afraid. The ship's already been reprovisioned," he said, his tone quieting. "I'm needed. There are just too few of us. Our navy is so da...infernally small, and Congress won't spend any money on ships. The sea is where the war is going to be won. If we do enough damage to British shipping, their merchant class will demand an end to the war. They won't be able to afford it." His sheepish grin broadened. "I'm sorry," he said again, "I didn't mean to lecture. Come, little sister, tell me more about this mysterious suitor of yours.

"I'm engaged," she said proudly.

Bren spun around, delight etched on every plane of his face. "I wish you so much happiness...you deserve it, Samara. I was so afraid..." He stopped, not wanting to introduce anything which would dampen her spirts, but it was too late.

"Afraid of what?" she asked, a slight smile on her lips, her eyes insistent. She suspected he meant her "infatuation" with Reese Hampton and she thought to tease him more. It would make the surprise so much more delicious.

"Just that—that..."

"I would mourn forever for Captain Hampton?"

He looked uncomfortable, his face admitting the truth.

"You see," she said lightly, "you quite wasted your worries. I'm not distraught at all."

He breathed a sigh of relief. "That's fine because..." Again he stopped himself.

Again she insisted he continue. "Because...?

"It's just that one of the ships we took...had some newspapers. There was a report of Hampton's engagement..."

A sudden perceptible change filled the air. He watched as the joy drained from Samara's face, and it turned white with shock. Puzzled, he looked to his mother and saw disbelief in her face.

Samara finally managed one choked word. "Wh-when...?

Bren looked around in confusion. Something was terribly wrong. Could his sister still care about Hampton when she was engaged to someone else?"

"Samara?" he asked quizzically.

"When, Bren...when did he get engaged? To whom?"

Bren was now thoroughly befuddled. He knew something was terribly wrong. He answered slowly, very careful with his words. "Apparently after we left Bermuda. To a Lady Stanton." He was not going to say it was a love match. Not now. Not when his sister looked as if she would faint, and his mother wore a most untypical stricken expression.

He tried to soften the impact of his news. He didn't understand why she seemed to care so very much. Hampton was, after all, dead and gone these many months. And the two of them—Reese Hampton and Samara—had been at each other's throats more often than not.

His words were soothing now. "You know English marriages—they are mostly arranged...alliances between families, for one reason or another."

But the words had no meaning to Samara. Through the haze of pain that was enveloping her, she knew differently. Reese could never be coerced into a marriage he did not want. He simply would not tolerate it. He had said as much that day in the cave. As he had said so many other things.

She stood there, trembling, as she realized the depth of his betrayal. His soft words echoed in her head. "I love you...you see, I've never said it before..." And later...later he had said he would never marry without love.

Anguish was choking her heart as his words kept repeating themselves. How well she remembered each of them. When she had asked so foolishly if he had ever been in love, ever been betrothed, he had said no. Silent tears formed in her eyes and she turned away, wanting no one to see her agony. Oh Reese, how could you? No wonder he planned to leave her here...he never intended to come back. It had all been a game to him, something to occupy his time while he was forced, against his will, to stay. Perhaps it was even his idea of revenge. What a complete fool she had been! All the doubts that had haunted her, all the fear that she had suppressed now rose and condemned him.

Bren looked at her grief-stricken face, too stunned to react. His unshakable mother was also looking as if she had seen a ghost...a very unwelcome one. He turned to her now, his eyes full of questions.

Even Samantha had difficulty speaking. There *had* to be an explanation. She could *not* have been so completely wrong about someone. She could not have so completely misunderstood the softness and love in Reese's face when he watched Samara. And yet what honorable man would offer for a lady when already engaged?

"Perhaps," she tried, "it was another Hampton."

Again, Bren didn't understand why it was so important.

"No, Mother," he said. "It said he was captain of a ship named the *Unicorn*, and he was brother to the Earl of Beddingfield." He gave her a long, searching look. "Why do you and Samara...what...?"

"Reese Hampton," his mother said slowly, "is the man you were going to meet tonight. The man Samara planned to marry."

"The devil you say!" And then—barely audibly—the curses came in a long, fluid stream. The outburst was so angry he forgot his mother's aversion to profanity.

Samantha winced, while secretly agreeing with his sentiments.

Bren stopped long enough to ask, "But how?"

"When his ship was sunk, he apparently was able to swim to shore. He ended up at the Fontaine plantation..."

Bren, whose arm had gone protectively around Samara, could feel her tense as her mother explained all that had happened. When Samantha finished, his jaw muscles were working furiously.

All the affection and respect he had had for Hampton disappeared as the story unfolded. Not only had the Englishman acted the spy, he had taken advantage of his father's hospitality and Samara's inexperience. There could be no explanation. The formal betrothal in England took place after his sister and Hampton had met, and not many weeks before the Englishman landed on American soil. Bren shuddered at the thought of his sister reading the newspaper report. Love match. Damn the man.

"The bastard. I'll kill him," he said in a tight, controlled voice.

The slow words, each as cold and hard as steel, aroused Samara from her stupor. Still partly stunned from the gaping wound in her heart, Samara knew she could not let this happen. She did not want Reese dead, and even if she harbored such a murderous thought she could not let her brother sacrifice his life. And that, she was all too aware, would most likely be the result. Even Bren would be no match for the dangerous Captain Reese Hampton.

"No," she said, and Bren was surprised by the strength in the one word. Her face, stained by tears, was suddenly determined. "No," she said again.

Through his rage, Bren felt a flash of admiration. Samara was growing up. But what a hell of a way to do it. He wanted to tear Hampton apart with his bare hands.

"Has he...has he...touched you?" Brendan forced the words through his teeth.

Samara shivered. She couldn't let him know, couldn't let anyone know. They would either kill him, or he would kill them...all of them. Or her father would force a marriage, a marriage that now would be intolerable. She gathered her strength and said, firmly enough, "No. He never...just a kiss."

Brendan looked deep into her eyes, great gray-silver mists, and Samara summoned all the control, all the determination within her to keep from revealing the truth.

"Thank God for that," Brendan said, finally satisfied. "But what now? Damn if I'm going to carry him to safety when he's been playing with my sister's heart."

Samantha shook her head. "Connor gave his word. And," she said hopefully, "there might just be an explanation."

Samara interrupted, her voice cold and lifeless. "There is no explanation. He lied about so many things." She had never felt so deathly cold, so empty. She rubbed her hand against her face, trying to brush away the memories of the cave, the river-bank, of how readily she had thrown herself at him. She had made it so easy. "Little cat...little cat..." Even now the thought of those words, spoken so softly, so seductively, sent tremors through her.

I have to get away. That thought overwhelmed everything else. *I can't see him again. I can't let him know what he's done to me.* Her despair evolved into cold, hard fury and finally into resolute purpose.

"I want to go to Charleston," Samara said with a determination strengthened by pain. If she saw him, she would falter. She simply could not face him again, not ever. She couldn't face the raw agony of him; she would do something terrible. "I can stay with Melanie. Please, Mother. Please, before he returns."

Indecision flitted over her mother's face. "I think we should give him a chance to—"

"He lied to me, Mother. Nothing can explain that. Please let me keep my pride; let him think *I'm* leaving him."

"I don't know..."

Bren interrupted. "If you don't want me to break his neck, I think that's the best thing for everyone. You two can leave immediately for Charleston with Caesar. Marion's there; ask him to ride back. We'll take Hampton to the ship tomorrow. Hog-tied, if need be. The sooner I get rid of him the happier I'll be. If Father hadn't given his word, I swear I would take great pleasure in seeing him hang."

"I don't want Father or Marion to know...to know why," Samara said. "They would call him out. Please tell them, tell *him* I've changed my mind, that I don't want to marry an Englishman, that I've gone away to avoid a scene."

Brendan hesitated. He had never lied to his father, but Samara was right. His father *would* call Hampton out. And

probably get killed. There really wasn't any other choice. Damn
Hampton. And once he had thought him a friend. Barely con-
trolling his rage and frustration, Bren tightened his arms
around Samara, then slowly helped her up. "If you're to be
gone before they get back, you'd best hurry," he said softly. His
heart nearly broke as Samara struggled to hide the hurt and
pain, walking, ever so slowly, out the door and up the stairs to
pack.

Happily oblivious of the disaster that awaited him, Reese
threw back his head and laughed at the vivid description of his
future father-in-law's marriage to Samantha.

It had been a most satisfactory day, and he had settled several problems in his own mind, the most important of which
concerned Samara. Much to Connor O'Neill's pleasure, he had
announced his intention to settle in the South after the war.
Reese had found he liked Americans very much; he liked their
independence and their spirit and their predilection for work.
He was also drawn by the fact that there were still vast, un-
worked tracts of land available, land where he could start anew.
Honor forbade him abandoning his country in time of war, but
after . . .

He and Connor discussed the possibility of marrying Samara immediately, before Reese left with Bren, but there were
so many problems. He was not, currently, a wealthy man; he
had given most of his earnings to Avery for Beddingfield and
would have to return to privateering to amass sufficient funds
to purchase the land he wanted. "French ships," he reassured
Connor with a boyish smile. "Only French." In the meantime, Samara would be safer and happier with her family than
in an enemy land with few friends.

And there was another problem in marrying her in South
Carolina: Reese's own identity. For a marriage to be valid,
Reese would have to use his name, and it was only too familiar
in the Carolinas. He was thought to be dead and his resurrec-
tion would only put everyone in danger.

In a moment of rare confidence, Connor told Reese of his
own most unusual marriage, drawing the laugh that rolled over
the fields.

"Samantha," he recounted, "didn't use her real name when
we first married. I didn't know we weren't legally married until she was just giving birth to Brendan. She was staying with a

friend who," Connor's eyes twinkled, "ran a rather famous brothel. I ran out and kidnapped a minister and dragged him unwillingly into a 'house of sin.' The words were said just before the baby came. I doubt the minister ever quite recuperated, though he did consent to stay and toast the child. Several times. You see, you aren't the first to be kidnapped by the O'Neill family. It seems my sons come by it naturally."

Reese grinned. "You seem to have a way of mollifying your victims."

It was Connor's turn to laugh. He liked Hampton more each day. If only he weren't English . . . if only this damn war were over.

They learned at the stables that Brendan had returned, and that Samantha and Samara had left in the carriage with Marcus. No one knew exactly where they were going or how long they would be gone.

Reese felt a momentary stab of disappointment. Now that Bren was here, his and Samara's time together would be short. He wanted every minute. His humor was quickly restored, however, by the thought of renewing his friendship with Brendan. There had been few men with whom Reese had felt such a ready bond. As a man who seldom sought approval for any of his actions, he was startled by how strongly he wanted Bren's friendship and approval, not only for himself but for Samara. He knew how close brother and sister were.

Brendan had been pacing the floor in the library, trying to leash his anger. He had to keep it under control in order to keep his father and Hampton from discovering the real reason Samara had left. It would be the most difficult thing he had ever done.

Much of his rage resulted, he knew, from his own personal disappointment in Hampton. He had liked and respected the man and, in truth, owed him a debt. Several of them. He had known Hampton was mercurial, complex, but never had he thought the man would take such wanton advantage of someone as innocent as Samara. That one action wiped out everything between them. He had tried to explain, in his own mind, the man's action. But there could be no explanation. A recently engaged man simply did not so readily offer marriage to another woman. The fact that Hampton had said nothing about his previous attachment condemned him. If he had, perhaps, changed his mind about the London betrothal, he should have explained the circumstances to Samara and her family. It was also damning that he planned to leave without her.

What game had Hampton been playing? Brendan knew he must have been furious about his abduction. Had he sought revenge by seducing his sister? Although she denied it, he couldn't help but fear the worst. If he knew for sure, he *would* kill Hampton. It was enough he had dealt Samara a blow from which she might never recover. For now he had to pretend a coolness he didn't feel—otherwise, Hampton could destroy the rest of his family.

Almost eagerly, Reese entered the library, his hand outstretched, a smile lighting his striking face. It quickly faded when he saw Brendan's glacial expression just before the American turned away. Reese let his arm drop, wariness creeping into his eyes. There was a restrained violence in the room. He could smell it, taste it. It was perceptible in every jerky move of Brendan O'Neill's body.

Reese had come in alone while Connor gave the grooms instructions about the horses. His hands clenched now with foreboding.

"You know," he said softly. "You know about Samara. I've asked her to marry me. I had hoped you would be pleased."

"There is no engagement, no marriage," Brendan said harshly, as he turned his icy eyes on Reese. Distaste was written all over his face. "Samara has decided she does not want to marry you. She has left Glen Woods until you sail with me. We leave tomorrow morning."

"You lie," Reese said, his voice practically snarling now.

"I think you're rather adept at that yourself," Bren said brutally. "But in this case you're wrong. She doesn't wish to marry a man of your nationality or your profession or your character."

Reese felt a coldness envelope him. What in God's name had happened? He took a step forward, "Brendan...?" He couldn't hide the pleading note in his voice.

But he could find no softening in O'Neill's face. If anything, it hardened. "Be ready to leave at dawn."

"Not until I talk to Samara." Now the entreaty was gone from Reese's voice, and there was a hard determined edge to it.

"She doesn't want to talk to you. Not now. Not ever. She knows she has made a mistake."

"I don't believe you."

"That's a matter of indifference to me, Hampton. You *will* stay here tonight and you *will* leave with me in the morning, if I have to hog-tie you. My father promised to get you to safety and I will honor that promise. But you are a spy in my country, and I could care less about your comfort."

There was a false ring to the speech, something more to Bren's hostility than Reese's own rather unfortunate and very short-lived career as a spy.

The two men were glaring at each other when Connor entered. Like Reese earlier, his smile quickly changed to a puzzled frown at the obvious tension in the room.

"Brendan . . . it's good to see you. You know about—"

"Samara has decided she does not wish to continue the engagement," Brendan interrupted. "She just doesn't think she could live in England."

"But Reese has decided to—"

"Samara," Bren interrupted, "has gone to visit some friends for a few days. Mother went with her. I must get back to my ship tomorrow, and Hampton will go with me."

Connor started, "But—"

"It's the way Samara wants it," Brendan said. He was dismayed. He had not been surprised at his mother's affection for the Englishman. He had seen the man's charm at its most potent. But his father . . . and then he remembered how easily he too had been attracted by Reese's easy friendship. Easy and treacherous.

"I don't understand," Connor said, becoming thoroughly angry. Reese Hampton was a guest in his home, a friend. He didn't care for Bren's tone, his usurpation of authority, or his arrogance. "Where is Samara? She owes Reese an explanation."

"She owes him *nothing*." The statement was explosively bitter, and it stopped the older O'Neill. This performance was totally unlike his son and, like Reese, he knew there was something he was not being told. He did not like that knowledge at all. But he obviously was not going to learn any more in front of Reese.

He turned to Reese. "I want to talk to my son alone."

Reese, whose own anger was barely held in check, merely shrugged in a gesture now becoming familiar to Connor. His seemingly indifferent attitude was belied by the rigid muscles in his jaw and the firm set of his mouth.

"I will not leave without talking to Samara," Reese said, walking to the door. He turned back to the O'Neill father and son, and his brilliant eyes, blazing with fury, challenged them. He closed the door behind him with deceptive gentleness and walked to the front entrance, letting himself out. He stood on the porch, looking towards the bare winter trees, realizing for the first time how lonely they looked without their rich green ornaments. The gray wispy moss only emphasized their bleakness. He swallowed. In less than an hour, all his plans for a future had been smashed.

Rage was slowly replaced by an aching emptiness. Reese felt hollow inside and, for one of the few times in his life, uncertain. He had been so sure Samara loved him and wanted a life together as much as he. Perhaps he had expected too much, perhaps she *had* decided there were too many differences between them. Yet she had placed herself in his hands so freely, so lovingly. There had been no reservations.

She *was* young. She *had* been thoroughly protected all her life, but she had also shown a determined independence. What had Brendan said to her? What had caused the American's bitter animosity? A year ago, they had almost been friends. He remembered Bren's last words: "It's been an honor..."

A hand went up and rubbed the back of his neck in frustration. He walked down the steps and, lost in bitter thoughts, wandered almost aimlessly, only barely aware of the two servants who shadowed him.

"I can't believe Samara would do this." Connor O'Neill's voice was louder than necessary. "I've never seen her so happy."

Brendan turned away and stared at the book-lined wall of the library. He couldn't meet his father's eyes. "I don't think," he said slowly, "that she fully grasped what it would mean to be betrothed to an enemy, to watch him go away and know he was fighting her country, possibly even her own family."

"That's nonsense," Connor sputtered, "and you know it. He has said he would no longer attack American shipping. As for the French, who cares? They've attacked and seized enough of our ships."

Brendan spun around, his face almost accusing. "So he's charmed you, too. Can't you see him for what he is? What do you think he was doing when his ship was sunk . . . after he met Samara? Has he told you the names of his accomplices? He had to have help here. What do you really know about him? He could already be married, or betrothed for all we know. Members of the English nobility don't marry commoners, nor do they marry for love. They *make* matches. Have you thought that perhaps, just perhaps, he might be using Samara? Using you all?" Brendan stopped, aghast at his own words. He had never spoken with such rudeness to his father, nor had he intended to reveal so much. His temper had simply taken over. He had gone much too far. He could see it in his father's furious face.

"I thought," his father said coldly, "he was your friend. You certainly gave me that impression months ago."

"That was before I knew he was a damn spy," Bren said, weighing his words more carefully.

"That doesn't explain Samara," his father insisted. "She knew, and she didn't care."

In a more moderate tone, Brendan tried to extricate himself. "She just wanted more time to think about it . . . and she felt she had to do it alone."

"It's not like Samara to run away from a problem. To run to one, perhaps, but not away."

Bren frowned. "This one was bigger than most." He played his trump card, "And Mother agreed."

Connor regarded him with sheer astonishment, then disbelief. Samantha had been Reese's champion from the beginning. She had always felt that Samara and Reese were meant to be together. It was one reason he had capitulated. It was only later that he had grown very fond of Reese and considered him almost a member of the family.

"There's something you are not telling me," he said now.

"There is nothing. Any engagement will only hamper Samara now. The war could last one or two or even three more years. Hampton could die, or change his mind or any of several things. It's best to wait until the end. If they both feel the same way . . . then he could return, and we'll all know he really loves her."

"He won't agree."

Brendan's voice hardened. "I don't care if he does or not. He's put this whole family in danger, not to mention his own fate if discovered. And how would Samara feel about *that*?"

Connor, at least, agreed with that observation. Spiriting Hampton out of sight every time there was a visitor had become awkward. There were also questions in the parish as to why the usually hospitable O'Neills had almost completely isolated themselves. He sighed in defeat.

"Where did your mother and Samara go?"

"Mother's accompanying Samara to Charleston. Both will stay with the Demerests for a few days. They've been invited often enough."

Connor raised an eyebrow. "You've worked all this out rather nicely, haven't you?" He was quietly outraged. As far as he was concerned, his entire family was acting abominably. Unfortunately, there was, at this point, little he could do. Hampton was in great danger here, and his presence endangered every member of Connor's family. He could only try to convince Hampton that Samara's doubts were normal, that she would get over them, and be waiting. It would probably be best if Hampton *did* leave now, he thought reluctantly. For the safety of everyone.

Reese went to the stables. He would take a ride, try to clear his head and think things out. All restrictions on his movements had been lifted weeks earlier. He was only cautioned to stay within Glen Woods for his own protection.

But when he asked for his usual mount, he was met with an apologetic smile. "Sorry, Cap'n . . . Mr. Bren's orders."

Reese stiffened in anger. So even his word was no longer given credence. He nodded curtly to the groom and walked outside, where he stopped. He leaned against a fence and closed his eyes.

When did it start? What second, what minute, what hour had he begun to lose control of his own life? The instant he decided to attack the *Samara*? When he saw a dirty, dusty bedraggled girl bravely confront him? When she was trying, so terribly ineptly, to get him drunk? It seemed everything after that had led inevitably here: his restlessness in England, his decision to return to the Carolina coast, the Fontaines' ball. One inexorable step after another.

Well, he would break the pattern. Perhaps he was well free of Samara, of her whole damned family, of the bonds that had been tightening so securely around him. He had never needed anyone. He didn't now.

He heard the sound of footsteps, but he didn't turn around.

Connor's voice was deep with regret, even pain. "I'm sorry, Reese. Perhaps after..." His words trailed off. If he had been Hampton, he wouldn't want to hear them.

"I'll be ready tomorrow," Reese said. Despite himself, the tone, the slow words, reflected a deep hurt. He had expected so much of this day. One hand clenched the rail in front of him before he turned to face Connor and added softly, "I know you risked much for me. I will do nothing to make you regret it." His brilliant green-blue eyes met Connor's gray ones, and Connor was struck by the raw pain in them.

With quiet dignity, Reese turned and walked back to the house.

Connor O'Neill watched him disappear and knew an unprecedented desire to strangle nearly every member of his family.

Chapter Seventeen

It was the most wretched Christmas Samara had ever experienced. It was made even worse since, weeks earlier, she had expected it to be the best.

When she had returned ten days earlier from Charleston, Reese was gone, and nothing seemed to matter. She had to force herself to wrap the presents she had so halfheartedly purchased in Charleston ... she who had loved Christmas better than anyone. There was one present she didn't wrap; it was buried deep in her trunk, but out of sight did not mean out of mind. She had spent many nights knitting a handsome scarf for Reese, in the hope that he would be able to remain at Glen Woods until Christmas. It had been a labor of love for Samara who so hated handwork. But she had wanted to give him something special.

Fool she chastened herself. Stop thinking of him. If only she could. Where was he now? On his way home to England—and to the woman he planned to marry. Or had he obtained another ship and gone back to attacking American vessels? Certainly not this quickly. He was probably celebrating his freedom—freedom from Glen Woods, freedom from her—in some tavern or worse.

Just thinking of his long, beautiful masculine body next to someone else filled her eyes with tears. She had never cried much before she met Reese Hampton. Her brothers thought it unmanly for themselves, and she could never be less than her brothers. She had never cried at hurts or disappointments. But now the tears wouldn't stop coming, and at the most unexpected times. She would be at dinner or reading a book or riding, and something would remind her of his aqua eyes or his easy graceful walk or the way he dominated a room.

"Samara." Her father's voice broke the trance.

Hastily rubbing the wetness from her face, she reluctantly turned to him, knowing the telltale stains remained.

His voice softened. When Samara had first returned home, he hadn't tried to hide his censure. He had been deeply disappointed with his daughter for the first time in her life. He had thought she owed it to Reese Hampton to face him. He had, in fact, been so hard on his daughter that his wife finally decided to tell him the truth. Reese was gone, after all. The danger of a duel, or any kind of retribution was gone.

To her amazement, her husband had become even angrier— at her, at Samara and, most of all, at his oldest son. She had realized then that Connor had become much closer to the Englishman than anyone had realized. And she had conveniently forgotten how very much her husband hated lies and subterfuge. Connor had always been the fairest—most honest—man she had ever known.

"He was going to buy property in Virginia—for Samara—so she wouldn't have to leave this country, so she wouldn't be so terribly far from us. Does that sound like a man planning to marry someone else?"

"Maybe he just wanted—"

Connor interrupted. "You don't ask the questions he asked, with that intensity, without being very serious. And you don't look at a woman as he looked at Samara without being in love." He paced the floor with more and more agitation. "You, Sam, you should know better than anyone how much damage silence can do."

"You should have seen her, Connor. She begged me."

"I'm seeing her now," Connor said roughly, "and it can't be any worse. For God's sake, why didn't you give him a chance to explain?"

Samantha could only shake her head miserably. "What can we do?" she asked.

"I don't know," he replied wearily. "If I were Reese I wouldn't want any more to do with this family. I'll try to write him in Bermuda and England, but God knows what words I'll use, or when and how he will receive it . . ."

Now this Christmas afternoon, he sat quietly next to his daughter, feeling her grief. He debated whether to give her the gift he held in his hand, but he had promised Reese. Prior to

Bren's arrival, Reese had designed it and asked Connor to have
it made by a silversmith. Connor had been given a promissory
note in payment. On the morning of his departure, Reese had
asked Connor to give it to Samara at Christmas.

Connor handed her the small package. "It's from Reese," he
said. "I thought you might like to open it alone." He stood and
walked away. Samara held it for several minutes, then carefully unwrapped it. She had thought she could feel no worse.
But she knew now she could.

Wrapped securely in a piece of blue velvet was a small silver
medal. Carefully crafted on one side was an intricately etched
schooner. On the other, a wine bottle.

Her right hand tightened around it. She could almost feel the
love in the exquisite small disc. In her mind's eyes, she saw the
mischievous gleam in his eye and the soft laughter on his lips.

Not for the first time, she questioned her ready condemnation of him—and her own precipitous action. Had she allowed
her own fear and uncertainty to destroy something that was so
wondrous? Why had she leaped to such terrible conclusions?

"Was I wrong?" she whispered to herself. "Was I so completely wrong?" She hugged her knees and rocked, her grief so
great she wondered if she could endure it.

It had been a nightmare of an odyssey from Glen Woods to
Bermuda, Reese thought as he took yet another long swallow
of raw rum.

Marion had arrived the morning after Bren's hostile appearance. Reese, sleepless, was at the window of his room. He had
spent much of the night pacing, trying to puzzle out what had
happened. But he had no more answers than he had the previous evening.

The three of them—a puzzled Marion, a withdrawn and un-
smiling Brendan, and an angry Reese—had left Glen Woods at
noon. Reese's only satisfaction was that Connor's farewell to
him was much warmer than his to Brendan.

Despite threats, Reese was not bound, but Brendan made
sure that he stayed between the two brothers during the long
ride. They drank and ate in the saddle and stopped only briefly
to water and rest the horses. When they finally reached the river
where the *Samara* was anchored, Marion's usual smile was
gone. He did not know what had happened to bring about
Bren's watchful and hostile attitude toward Reese, nor Reese's

tight-lipped silence. He bid Reese a good journey and disappeared, leading the other two horses.

Reese was given the second mate's cabin and told to stay there. He heard a guard being posted outside. The cabin was tiny with only a small porthole, and he felt trapped and confused. It wasn't until the *Samara* reached open sea at dawn the next morning that he was allowed the freedom of the ship. Brendan carefully avoided him, and he ate alone on deck.

At the end of the second day, the captain summoned him to his cabin for the first time.

"We're off the Florida coast," he said curtly, "not far from St. Augustine where you should be able to find a ship. My men will row you ashore." He took a small purse and tossed it to Reese. "There should be enough there for passage to Bermuda and your needs in St. Augustine. I assume you have funds in Bermuda?"

Reese nodded, his eyes searching for a clue as to what had hardened Brendan against him.

"That does it, then," Brendan said. "It ends things between us."

"Brendan . . . ?" The question was soft; puzzled.

Brendan's jaw tightened. It was difficult, if not impossible, to ignore the entreaty in Reese's face. He knew that it must be a very rare sight, indeed, but he was in no mood to be sympathetic.

"Go back to your own world, Hampton. Go back to where everyone knows the rules of the games you play."

"What in blazes are you talking about?"

"Samara," Bren said. "Samara, damn your black heart." His temper boiled over and his fist drove at Reese's stomach. Reese sidestepped and took the blow in his side as his own hands took aim at the American. He put all his fury into the one blow, and Brendan went tumbling to the floor.

Reese stood over him, hands clenching and unclenching as he tried to control himself. Fighting Brendan would solve nothing, but he wanted to strike back.

Brendan came slowly to his feet. He too was suppressing a compulsion to whip the man in front of him. It would be a close match, and he would enjoy every bit of punishment he could deliver. Yet there was danger lurking off the Florida coast, and he dared not tarry for personal satisfaction. "Some other day," he said softly.

Reese nodded. They were the last words they spoke . . .

He had been rowed to a beach and started walking, thinking of a similar journey months earlier. But this time he had money, and was not in enemy territory. Florida was a possession of Spain, and Spanish fears of American expansionism made the English welcome. He was able to buy an old but serviceable horse and food. In St. Augustine, he found a ship headed for Bermuda...

Yancy was waiting for him on the dock at St. George. Reese's friend had met every incoming ship since he and the rest of the *Unicorn*'s crew had arrived several weeks earlier. They had been unexpectedly, Yancy reported, and very suddenly exchanged after spending three months in a Boston dungeon. Yancy had heard nothing of Hampton and didn't know if he'd survived the swim or the equally dangerous countryside. They looked at each other, smiled and headed for the nearest tavern....

A day later, Reese was still drinking. He was sprawled over two chairs, his hand resting on a bottle of rum that sat on the floor.

Yancy looked at him with deep concern. For one of the few times in his life he was thankful that the rum was watered, for the captain was finishing his second bottle of the day and his thirst showed no sign of slaking.

Yancy could hear the drunken carolers outside, reminding him once more that this was Christmas day. There were few other signs in the tavern. There certainly wasn't any in the unshaven, unkempt man across from him who bore little resemblance to the usually immaculate Reese Hampton.

"What in God's name happened to you?" Yancy said, watching as Reese took another long swallow. His friend had said nothing about where he had been or how he had escaped.

"Everything that could have," Reese said with a drunken, enigmatic expression.

"And what might that be?" Yancy persisted, thinking that Reese was the only man he knew whose speech got progressively more precise as he drank.

Reese considered all that had transpired in the past months. He had briefly, ineptly, been a spy, been kidnapped at a ball, made prisoner in a plantation storehouse, fallen in love, became engaged, became unengaged, found a friend, lost a friend. Who in the hell knew what had happened? He didn't. It all seemed a crazy nightmare. "Wouldn't believe it if I told you," he said finally.

Yancy shook his head in frustration. "Try me, friend. Perhaps I could help."

Reese opened one of his half closed eyes. "Don't want any help...better this way." He wanted Yancy's companionship but not his advice, not now. He didn't want to think about Samara. Or South Carolina. "'Tis of no matter, anyway," he said very clearly. "'Tis done. Gone. Nevermore." He rolled the last word as if tasting it. "Nevermore," he said again.

Yancy winced at the bitterness in Reese's voice. It was something new, something he didn't like. "Reese," he said, trying to divert his friend's thoughts, "the whole crew's been waiting. They've passed up good berths, even not knowing—"

"If I were dead or alive?" Reese struggled with himself. Yancy's last comment made an impact where others hadn't. Responsibility and loyalty. That's what mattered. Loyalty. There was precious little of that left. Loyalty and trust . . . and responsibility.

He took another long drink as he considered responsibility. Just as he passed out, he thought of Samara. "You finally managed to get me drunk," he whispered to her...wherever she was.

The next morning Reese wanted only to die in peace. He awoke in a strange room with a head that felt like the inside of a drum. And there was more than one person beating on it.

His stomach felt equally battered and it got worse when he smelled something suspiciously like tea. He cautiously opened one eye.

Yancy was standing there with a wry smile. "It's my turn," he said, "to make *you* better by inflicting misery. Drink this!"

Reese eyed it warily.

"Come on, Captain. You have a lot to do today."

Reese closed his eyes, wishing the doctor away.

"If you don't," Yancy threatened, "I'll tie you up and force it down. And right now you look bad enough that I could do it with one hand."

"You have no respect for your captain," Reese observed, with a pained expression. One hand went up to his cheek and felt the stubble with distaste. He was suddenly filled with self-disgust. He didn't remember much about the previous two days which was, he supposed, probably fortunate. He reluctantly took Yancy's cup, tentatively tasting the bitter brew. There was much more than tea in it, but he wasn't going to question it. He grimaced as he took a long swallow.

"That's a good lad," Yancy said soothingly, barely suppressing a broad smile. Some of the old Reese was returning. Slowly, it was true, but surely. Some life was coming back into the captain's eyes.

"There are a couple of ships you might like to look at," he said, trying to stir some interest. "They're not the quality of the *Unicorn*, but they look fit enough." He was pleased to see the first signs of interest in Reese's face. Perhaps these past two days were what the man needed to get something out of his system. He knew better than to pry. Reese would tell him when he was ready.

As Reese finished the tea, Yancy discussed the men. They had lost three to other ships, but the rest had remained steadfast, waiting for "the best captain on either side of hell." He grinned as he said it, adding slyly, "They didn't see you last night."

"And you aren't going to let me forget it, are you, Yancy?"

"Probably not," Yancy agreed amiably.

Reese relaxed. The tea *had* helped. It was good to see Yancy again. There was a constancy about his irreverence. He could almost believe the past four months had been only a bad dream. Almost. He would make them that.

"About those ships?" he said, immediately turning his mind to exactly how much money he had in the Bermuda banking house. There had been two prizes before he had taken the *Samara*. He should have sufficient funds to purchase a suitable ship and arm it.

Disregarding his discomfort, he and Yancy spent the morning looking at ships and the afternoon talking to his crew. Together, they made their choice and started outfitting her.

They would sail for the French coast in a week.

One of Connor's letters finally caught up with Reese at Beddingfield. It had been waiting there for months, unopened.

The letter was the first thing mentioned by Avery when Reese, taut with weariness and strain, visited while his ship, the *Phoenix*, was undergoing repairs at the London dock. He had been at sea nearly five months and had taken six French merchant ships. He had given his crew a larger than usual share because of their imprisonment—a result, he felt, of his own foolishness. That, plus the cost of repairs, had kept his purse lean.

Avery was in his office, engrossed in the books, when Reese unexpectedly appeared. After a warm greeting, Avery pointed to a white packet. "Who," Avery said, "do you know in South Carolina?" Reese had said nothing in his rare correspondence about his adventures in America, only that the *Unicorn* had been lost and he had replaced it. Neither had he explained the origin of his ship's name, the *Phoenix*, the mythological bird which rose from the ashes.

Reese tensed at the mention of South Carolina, and his face paled under the bronze color. He glared at the offending letter.

Avery raised an eyebrow.

"You're not going to open it? Leigh has been dying of curiosity, not, of course, to mention my own brotherly interest." Reese looked at the letter as if it were a shark and he a tempting fish. "No," he said shortly, and strode back out the door, leaving Avery to stare in astonishment, first at the disappearing brother and then the letter.

Despite his long ride from London and the lateness of the day, Reese ordered a horse saddled and spurred him out of the barn. He rode as if the devil were chasing him, as he had as a young boy frustrated by his father's indifference. He rode to rid himself of the more recent demons that made his life a misery. He thought he had conquered them, and now this.

Both rider and horse were soaked with sweat when he returned. Avery's face was a study in concern. Leigh was bewildered.

"Would you please tell me what is going on?" Avery asked.

Reese looked at the two of them, and felt a twinge of guilt. His behavior had been erratic, if not lunatic. He bent over and kissed Leigh on the cheek. "I apologize."

"You don't ever have to apologize," Leigh said quietly. "Not here, not to us. You know that. Is there anything I can get you?"

Reese looked down at his dirt-splattered clothes. "I think I need a bath more than anything else."

Leigh smiled. "I'll see to it, Reese. You and Avery talk." She left, shutting the door quietly behind her.

Avery eyed Reese intently. There was something unapproachable about him. A barrier that had never been there before.

"Is there something I can do?" he asked simply.

Reese's mouth twisted in a wry smile. "No. I thought I had it worked out . . ." He looked at the letter. "When did this come?"

"Nearly four months ago."

"Ah, blissful ignorance."

"You aren't going to open it?"

"I suppose I have to," Reese said, "or I'll be haunted even more than I am now." He disregarded Avery's quizzical look at his bitter, cryptic words. He took the letter gingerly.

Avery watched his brother's drawn face. "I'll leave you alone." He left, closing the doors behind him.

Reese stared at the parchment, wondering at the strong scrawl. It obviously wasn't Samara; he had seen her handwriting. Connor? Brendan? But surely not Brendan. Reese still smarted from their last encounter.

He slowly opened it.

Anger was his first emotion as he slowly read the letter and crumpled it in his fist.

It was soon joined by a certain anguish that there had been so little trust.

He tried to understand. He was, after all, a member of a class many Americans distrusted and, as it had been pointed out many times, he was technically an enemy of their country. But he had thought, during the months at Glen Woods, that he had gained both trust and friendship. To be condemned without a hearing was extremely painful.

And Samara . . . Did she have so little faith in him? Could she really think, after that day in the cave, that he would use her so lightly?

He smoothed out the parchment and studied the words . . . this time with great care. It was from Connor, and the words were obviously very carefully chosen. He wrote that he believed Reese deserved an explanation, one that he himself had not received until after Reese had gone. In short terse words, he relayed the substance of the newspaper report of Reese's engagement and its shattering effect on Samara. In conclusion, he said:

I know there must be an explanation, and I bitterly regret that you were given neither the opportunity nor the courtesy to make one. I believe you loved my daughter and would do nothing to hurt her. I came to consider you a member of my family, and I still do.

I know it is probably presumptuous to write you, to apologize and even to hope you will understand. But Samara, I believe, loves you deeply.

Under the circumstances, I can ask no more of you. But I felt an explanation was required.

With regard,
Connor O'Neill

With a deep sigh, Reese sank into one of the leather chairs in the study. At least, one mystery was solved. He now knew the reason for Samara's defection. Her sudden flight had preyed upon him. He had thought he knew her, and cowardice seemed not in her character. He thought of her now as she had been on the riverbank, so warm and lovely and happy. Seemingly so confident in his love. Apparently, even then there were doubts. There must have been for her to believe so easily that he could be guilty of such duplicity.

He thought of the evidence against him, and with a groan he recalled their conversation in the cave when they had both declared their love. He had teasingly asked her about beaux, and she had queried him in return. He remembered saying there had never been any attachments, and then she had seen the engagement notice!

Reese suddenly understood what had happened. He had instinctively sensed she had always been a little afraid of him—of who and what he was. As much as he had tried, he had apparently never completely conquered that fear. He was everything she had been brought up to distrust, and they had met under the worst possible circumstances.

Could any relationship between them be possible now? He loved her. He had been very sure of that in South Carolina. No woman had ever roused that tenderness in him before. Samara's face stayed in his mind's eye, her passion in his thoughts, her laughter in his heart—despite all his attempts to banish them.

But was that enough? He didn't know. He had offered everything he had, and it obviously hadn't been enough. It hadn't served to quiet the doubts nor provide the trust he needed. His right hand went to his cheek, rubbing it absently.

There was nothing he could do now, anyway. His ship would be undergoing repairs for several weeks. He had arranged, months ago, for a bank draft, along with specific instructions, to be sent to Connor O'Neill for Samara's medal and his own expenses during those lost months. He thought now about writing Connor, then abruptly dismissed the idea. He was still too angry, too wounded. At the moment, he was damned if he was going to explain anything.

"That's wonderful," Samara told Angelique, and the little girl beamed with pride as she settled her primer down on the desk.

"Canty, can you continue?"

The sixteen-year-old boy started, then stumbled as he tried to decipher the next sentence in the book. Frustration and longing crossed his face as his lips moved, but no words came. He bowed his head.

Samara's heart went out to him. He wanted so badly to learn and was terrified he could not. He was being given a chance he had never thought to have, and he was anxious, too anxious.

"It's alright, Canty, you're doing very well," she said gently.

His young, bitter face relaxed, but there was no smile. Samara thought sadly that it would probably be a long time before Canty learned that particular skill.

Her father had bought Canty several months earlier at a slave auction. Samara had been startled because he seldom attended them. He had explained that he had been passing the auction block when one of the slaves caught his attention; a young boy, with pride in his bearing despite heavy chains and a lacerated back.

Connor had brought him home, and for weeks Canty had displayed only blatant hatred. It had taken time for him to believe his good fortune: a chance for freedom, a chance to learn. He had become Samara's most eager pupil, although a certain amount of distrust lingered.

As she dismissed the class, Samara regarded her small classroom thoughtfully. She had, at first, fought the idea of teaching, thinking her patience limited and her ability to communicate nonexistent. But her mother had insisted she needed help, and Samara had quickly discovered she had a natural talent in the classroom. Perhaps, she thought, it was because she, in turn, liked children so much. Or perhaps it was a burning desire to be useful. After Reese had left, she had taken stock of herself and found little reason for pride. She had been willful and heedless of the consequences. She herself had invited disaster.

The school met three times a week in an outbuilding. Although it was not mandatory, the O'Neills urged all children between five and eleven to attend along with any older hands who wished to learn. Freedom without education meant little, and the O'Neills intended all their servants and field hands to be free.

Those who attended the school—from the youngest child to the oldest man or woman—understood and appreciated the rare privilege, since education for slaves was considered almost treason in South Carolina. They were a joy to teach because they wanted, so badly, to learn. Samara always felt a certain accomplishment after a morning in the classroom. It lessened the hurt, but the loneliness never faded.

She hurried to the house, anxious to relate the day's accomplishments to her mother. They had always been close, but now there was a new dimension to the relationship: a mutual respect and understanding, and a shared passion for teaching.

As Samara entered the dining room, her mother was sitting at the table, fingering a letter, her face creased with indecision.

"Mother?"

"It's a letter from Annabelle," Samantha said. "She would like you to come for a visit."

Samantha couldn't miss the sudden glow in her daughter's eyes. Samara loved her godmother dearly and seldom had a chance to see her. Annabelle lived in Washington with her husband, Joshua McLaughlin, a retired sea captain.

The light in Samara's face, however, died quickly. "I can't leave the school," she said. "Canty's just beginning to gain some confidence . . ."

Samantha smiled. Samara had matured greatly in the past six months. There was a new sense of purpose about her, a new grace and gentleness. She had been tempered, perhaps, by sorrow. It was a feeling Samantha well recognized, and while she suffered with Samara she also knew pride. She knew now that nothing could defeat her daughter.

Perhaps a trip to Washington would cure some of the melancholy that still seemed to haunt Samara. Annabelle said it was an exciting place, and Annabelle was always in the center of things. Samantha feared Glen Woods still held too many memories.

And Samantha secretly hoped Samara might find another young man. She felt a deep guilt about Reese Hampton after her husband's explosion, and had prayed for some word from him. Connor had sent letters to both Bermuda and the Earl of Beddingfield, but there had been no reply. Either they had not reached Reese or he, quite understandably, wanted nothing more to do with them. She sighed. She had wanted things to be easier for Samara than they had been for her, and she felt at least partly responsible that they were not.

"You forget, little one," she said, "that I've been teaching a lot longer than you. I can take over the school for a month."

"But you have so many other things to do."

"I would love to get back to teaching," Samantha said truthfully. "I've missed it."

"I *would* like to see Annabelle again," Samara said slowly. "It's been two years..."

"Then it's settled. We'll have some dresses made. Your father can take you the first week in July. He can visit Marion then, too."

Expectancy filled Samara. Marion had been sent to Washington with his militia unit, and she had missed him sorely. Of her brothers, only Jere was in South Carolina. Bren was back at sea, and Conn was someplace near the Florida border with Andrew Jackson.

Connor fell in readily with the plans. He too felt it would do Samara good to get away, and Annabelle was the best tonic in the world.

The day before she was to leave, Samara dressed in some of Conn's old clothes and rode to the cave. She had been there only once since Reese had left, and that was right after Christmas. She had sat there for hours, trying to comprehend what had happened. Reese's gift had shattered her anger. The time, thought and humor that had gone into the silver medal showed he did, in some way, care. But why had he lied? Why had he not said something about the woman in England? She recalled his vivid green-blue eyes as he said he loved her. How warm they had been! She had resolutely buried the medal, trying to bury her memories with it.

Now she dug it up, as she had always known she would. She could not leave it behind. She rubbed it with her shirt until it shone, and felt a pain as sharp and new as it had been the day she ran from Reese. Would it ever dull with time? Somehow, she knew it would not.

Reese's eyes searched for the expanse of the open sea as he guided the *Phoenix* down the Thames, away from London's squalor. He needed the sea now as he had few other times in his life. He hungered for it, for the challenge that would cleanse his soul.

Already the air had changed and the sky was a clearer blue. He felt a sudden pleasure as the river widened and the brown and green earth tones of land gave way to deep blue, sparkling water. His eyes regained some of their usual brilliance and his face lifted to the sun, eager to feel its healing touch. The last weeks had tried his spirits sorely as he brooded about his future. Whatever it was, he knew it did not exist at Beddingfield. He had grown increasingly restless—day by agonizing day—as Avery tried to draw him more and more into the management of the estate. He had listened as they had ridden over every acre, though he knew it well. But Avery needed no help; he had seen that immediately. Apparently whatever shortages there had once been, they existed no longer. Seldom had he seen a better managed property. Although he had no wish to stay at Beddingfield, which was his brother's, he had become increasingly committed to the idea of purchasing property in Virginia after the war. With or without Samara O'Neill.

He had given much thought to the idea of building something of his own. His days of privateering, he knew, were nearing an end. The war with France had ended a few weeks before; he suspected the war with America would not last much longer. In any event, he would no longer attack American ships, and he had little desire to be a merchant or a real pirate—the only two choices remaining if he continued at sea.

Strangely enough, during his rides and conversations with Connor the prospect of farming had become unexpectedly appealing. He discovered that part of him yearned for the stability of a home and land of his own. He had previously mocked the idea, perhaps because he knew he would never have Beddingfield. He had gloried in his freedom, and he now wondered at his motives.

But he would have to wait until the war ended. He wanted that land to be in America. Part of the reason was financial. His limited funds would purchase a much larger tract in the young country than in Britain. But more importantly he was attracted by the energy and independence of the feisty new nation. It suited his temperament far better than England.

Part of that attraction, he realized ruefully, was Samara. After weeks of trying—quite unsuccessfully—to forget Samara and the O'Neills, he surrendered to a compulsion that would not let him go. He could not let her think he had so easily dishonored her. His own wounds were probably equaled or surpassed by those she had suffered. He knew he could write, but he rationalized that no letter could say what was in his heart. And he had feared, after all that had transpired, a letter would not even be believed. His eyes narrowed as he refought the battle within himself: his pride against his all-consuming need for her. He had to see her again!

He had finally told Avery—and Eloise—some of what had happened. Avery urged him to go, and Eloise was devastated at what their small intrigue had wrought. She had made her home at Beddingfield, despite several attempts by her late husband's brother to dislodge her. She now felt safe enough to make a public announcement that the engagement was off, though she would remain at Beddingfield under the protection of Avery and Leigh.

He had gathered Yancy and other members of the crew, warning them that there would be no prizes on this trip and, indeed, that he might well sell the *Phoenix* in Bermuda after a possibly dangerous trip to the Carolina coast.

"We'd sail with ye to hell," said one crewman, echoing the sentiments of most.

"I trust that's not our destination," Reese returned lightly, though his eyes glowed with pride and affection.

Three days later they set sail.

Unlike the *Unicorn*'s earlier storm-swept voyage, the *Phoenix* skimmed over calm seas beneath a radiantly blue sky in record time—less than three weeks. A good omen, Reese thought, as he anchored in Bermuda's St. George Harbor amidst a huge armada of British navy ships. He intended to refill his water and food stores before trying to find a certain river along the Carolina coast. He gave orders to Michael Simmons, who still served as first mate, while he and Yancy went in search of information. They found it at the White Horse Tavern.

The tavern was filled with British officers, many of them boisterously drunk. Reese searched among the faces, his eyes skimming from one to another. With a slight smile, he finally recognized an old school friend. He made his way carefully through the crowded room, apologizing several times to avoid a fight with battle-ready men.

"Longley," he said to an impeccably dressed colonel. "I thought you were with Wellington."

The scarlet-coated officer stood hastily, his hand outstretched. "My God, Hampton. It's been a long time. Join us, will you?"

Reese nodded and introduced Yancy, whose hostility was barely veiled. "Best doctor on the seas," Reese said.

"You should bring him along with us, then," Clifford Longley said. "It seems we're headed for another fight."

"Where?"

"Don't know exactly yet," Longley said. "The Admiralty's still trying to decide. Could be Washington. Could be Baltimore. My bet's on Washington. I understand that's what George Cockburn wants. One thing's for sure, there will be a fight. It's time to teach Madison a lesson." He chuckled. "Chastise, that is. The Admiralty wants him 'chastised.'" He looked at Reese carefully. "Are you still privateering? I heard you took a number of French ships."

"And several American," Reese said cheerfully.

"Why don't you tag along with us," Longley said. "I understand it's open season on the coastal areas."

"When are you sailing?"

"August the first," Longley replied. "Day after tomorrow."

Reese grinned. "We should be ready. I'll follow you at least part of the way. Now tell me about Napoléon's defeat. You were there?"

The next two hours Reese was regaled with the final hours of the war with France. "Even the French were eager to rid themselves of Napoléon," he said. "Paris surrendered, leaving Napoléon with few places to go."

It was late before Yancy and Reese got back to the ship. They stood on deck several minutes, watching the flickering lights on more than a hundred warships—frigates, schooners and transports.

"Are you quite sure about this?" Yancy asked, thinking the question foolish as he saw the determined gleam in Reese's eye. "You can get caught by either side, you know—and hung."

Reese looked around at the ships. "At least we have protection from the Americans part of the way."

"You're a damn fool, Reese."

"Quite possibly," Reese answered with equanimity, "but how do you explain your presence?"

"I'm a damn fool, too. You think you have a monopoly on it?"

"You keep telling me so," Reese retorted affectionately.

Yancy sighed, shook his head and went to his cabin, leaving Reese to his own thoughts.

Reese followed the armada for several days, then grew impatient with its pace and veered on his own toward the American coast, his sails picking up a lusty wind and bringing him closer to the Carolinas. He spent hours in his cabin pouring over charts, looking for one particular inlet and river, the one in which Brendan had anchored the *Samara*.

Although he had been locked in the cabin, he knew the river's general location by judging the number of miles they had traveled by horseback that day. And through the small porthole, he had noted several landmarks. He knew the waterway was deep enough, and isolated enough, to hide his ship for several days. He only briefly considered the possibility of encountering the *Samara*. The odds were exceedingly slim.

It took a day of searching but he finally found the mouth of the river, and he carefully guided the ship upriver far enough to hide its mast among the giant oaks. They anchored; and Reese, after leaving detailed orders with Simmons, slipped from the ship with Yancy who insisted on accompanying him. Reese simply nodded, knowing that Yancy would follow anyway—regardless of orders.

They walked for miles before spotting a small farmhouse. To Reese's delight, he spied several horses grazing in a corral. Telling Yancy to stay out of sight, he rubbed dirt on his trousers and shirt and approached the farmhouse.

He bartered with the farmer and his wife for nearly an hour, saying his horse had thrown him and galloped away. The farmer, back from the field for his meal, insisted on his visitor joining him for some cider. He was reluctant to part with any of his animals, he declared, as he eyed Reese's fine lawn shirt. Finally a bargain was struck, and Reese gained a fairly decent-looking horse for a ridiculously large number of coins. He picked up Yancy and they traveled several more miles before repeating the performance.

Reese took the road leading to Glen Woods with a rare feeling of uncertainty. He didn't know how he would be received—or by whom. If Conn or Brendan were home, there might be trouble. And Samara? What kind of reaction could he expect from her? It had been nearly eight months. His heel touched the side of his horse, and he cantered toward the barn.

"Cap'n." Reese heard Marcus' delighted greeting. "Mighty pleased to see you again, sir . . . Mist' O'Neill will be, too."

Reese's grim mouth relaxed a little. "This is my friend, Yancy," he said. "Is Mister O'Neill at home?"

"Why, yes, sir, he is. Came in just a few minutes ago. I'll tell him you're here." He called a groom to take the horses. "Come with me to the house."

"I would rather stay here," Reese said, not knowing exactly who was at home or what his welcome might—or might not—be. "Would you ask him to come out here alone?"

"Yessir, be mighty glad to, Cap'n." With a broad smile, he hurried away.

"It seems you have one friend here," Yancy said drily.

"That might well be the sum total," Reese replied with a skeptical smile. Despite what Connor had said in his letter, Reese had learned to expect the unexpected from the O'Neill family.

Reese took Yancy inside the barn and showed him Samantha's horses while they waited. He wanted to be out of sight of the main house.

The barn door opened, and Reese heard Connor's confident steps and his soft, low voice. "Reese?"

Reese stepped into the sunlight and stood there, waiting, his compelling eyes wary.

"It *is* you," Connor said, his eyes lighting, then he noticed Yancy. His mouth crinkled at the sides. "Another spy, Reese?"

"I'm neutral this time, Connor," Reese said, his mouth relaxing. "And my friend even more so. I suspect his sympathies lie with your countrymen. This is Yancy, my ship's surgeon. I think I mentioned him to you."

"You're welcome, Yancy." Connor turned back to Reese. "My God, I'm glad to see you. I had hoped . . . come up to the house."

"Samara?"

Connor's face clouded. "In Washington. With her godmother . . ."

"Washington?" Reese's response was dagger-sharp, but Connor attributed it to disappointment.

"She's been there a month, plans to stay another few weeks. Annabelle's husband is ill and Samara seems to feel she's needed. I'll write to her, of course, and let her know..."

"I can't stay, Connor," Reese said, his stomach churning. He had learned Longley's supposition was right. The British were headed towards Washington, and it was very likely they would destroy the city—or try to. He felt sick inside. There was no telling what Samara might do if confronted by British troops. And the officers he had talked to in Bermuda were of no mind to be gentle. They blamed American stubbornness for prolonging the French-English war. He and Yancy exchanged unhappy glances.

"Stay at least a few days," Connor was saying. "I...we have much to talk about."

Reese's expression was bleak as he realized the trap he was in. Even if Connor wrote Samara today, it might well be too late. The British navy was probably already near the mouth of the Chesapeake. And he couldn't betray British plans to Connor or even to Samara. He could not play the traitor. Leadenly, he followed Connor to the house, his mind searching frantically for a solution.

In the library, Connor poured them all a glass of brandy while a servant was sent for Samantha.

Connor looked at Reese closely. "You received my letter?"

Still reeling from the shock of Samara's whereabouts, Reese merely nodded.

"Is that why you're back?"

"There was...is...some unfinished business," Reese said slowly. "I wanted you to know what happened, and I didn't think I could do it by letter." Liar, he told himself. You wanted to see Samara. The muscles in his jaw tensed. "I didn't want Samara to think...I didn't care."

"Do you? Still?" Connor said gently.

Reese started pacing. "I don't know," he said, knowing it a lie as he mouthed the words. "If there's no trust, then there can be little else."

He started to speak again, but the door opened and Samantha stood there, a dawning of hope in her face. "Reese?" she said as her lovely blue eyes searched his face for an answer.

Reese bowed slightly, but his face remained grim, and Samantha's tentative smile faded.

"This is my ship's surgeon," he said only. "Yancy."

Samantha turned her charm on Yancy. "I've heard much about you from Samara. Thank you for being her friend."

Yancy was as stunned as Reese had first been on meeting Samantha. He couldn't imagine this small, energetic woman with the lively blue eyes having five children, one the age of Brendan.

"It was my pleasure, ma'am," he replied with a small smile.

Samantha turned her attention back to Reese. "I think...my husband believes...I owe you a very great apology."

Reese turned away, but it wasn't rudeness—more of a need to gather his thoughts. "Perhaps," he said slowly, "it was my fault. Perhaps I should have mentioned Eloise, but I saw no need. It held no importance to me."

He turned around and faced the couple.

"I was betrothed in name only, to protect a lady I knew and respected. It was not a true engagement, only a charade to keep someone from threatening her friends and family. I didn't mention it because it meant nothing to me. To tell the truth, I didn't even think of it." His voice turned bitter. "It could have been easily explained had I been given a chance."

His last words were like slaps to Samantha. She had given in to both Brendan and Samara against her better judgment—and she might have ruined Samara's life in doing so.

"I'm sorry," she now whispered.

Reese's face did not soften. He had suffered the agonies of hell in the past eight months, first from Samara's almost incomprehensible flight and her loss and later, after Connor's letter, from a deep biting hurt at the O'Neills' lack of trust.

Connor understood only too well. He too had suffered, probably similarly, when Samantha had refused to trust him— or their love—thirty-odd years earlier.

"You could have explained in a letter," he said now, searching Reese's intentions. "This is a long way to come—not to mention how dangerous it is—to say something which could be conveyed by letter."

"Would Samara have believed it?" Reese retorted harshly. He turned to Samantha. "Would you? It seems my words are worth little."

Connor regarded him calmly. "Not to me," he said in a deep voice. He hadn't mistaken the depth of pain in Reese's voice. "Will you stay until I send for Samara?"

Reese looked at him, his eyes bleak. He shook his head slowly. "I'm sorry. I can't. We'll leave this afternoon."

Connor's expression was puzzled. Reese Hampton had come across the Atlantic to see Samara and right things. He didn't understand the Englishman's haste in leaving. "Samara? What should we tell her?"

"That I will be back. I don't know when. I don't know how, right now. But I'll try to get back." *If I don't see her first,* he thought privately. *Damn.*

"Are you going back to England?"

Reese hesitated. He wanted no more lies, no more misunderstandings, but he could not tell Connor of his intentions to join the British invasion of Washington . . . if only to see that Samara remained safe.

Instead, the question was avoided with a brief shrug, and Reese asked about Samantha's horses. Connor noticed Reese's clever attempt to avoid an answer and a cold shiver ran through him. Reese had once said he would no longer participate in the war, but perhaps he no longer felt that obligation. After all that had transpired, he felt he could say nothing nor question him further.

After eating dinner with Samantha and Connor, Reese and Yancy took their leave. As Glen Woods disappeared from view, Yancy turned to Reese.

"I take it we're heading for Washington."

Reese merely nodded, and both men spurred their horses into a gallop.

Chapter Eighteen

Washington was in a panic. British troops, battle-hardened after years of fighting in Europe, had moved up the Chesapeake and were only a few miles away.

A messenger from Samara's brother, Marion, had ridden in the night before, advising Samara and Annabelle to leave the city. The British had defeated American troops at Bladensburg and were moving toward Washington. The American troops were in shambles and unable to stop them; they had been ordered to retreat to Georgetown, leaving Washington undefended.

But Joshua's health was failing rapidly. He was past eighty, and old wounds aggravated his heart condition. Annabelle was afraid to move him. And Samara would not leave them.

After a sleepless night, Samara and Annabelle discussed what was to be done. One of the most important issues was the stockpiling of the medicine and sleeping draughts that Joshua required. If the British did invade Washington, there was no telling what would happen to the city's medical supplies.

The streets were in chaos. Buggies filled with household goods mingled with swarms of American soldiers escaping the oncoming British. A horseman rode by, shouting warnings of redcoats and rape. Samara made her way down the road to Dr. Ewell's home, only to find the doctor gone. She decided to continue on to her friend Julien's store.

Julien had been one of her earliest friends in Washington and the two had grown closer in the recent tense days. Samara knew that Julien, the son of French emigres who now owned a mercantile store, was half in love with her, but as hard as she tried she could never consider him more than a friend. Her thoughts of Reese were too strong.

The store was closed and shuttered against looters, and Julien was standing outside watching the frightened retreat of both citizens and soldiers. As one bumped her, Julien hurried over and took her arm, guiding Samara to safety.

"You shouldn't be here," he said protectively.

"I can't just sit and wait at Annabelle's. There is too much to do. What have you heard? Has President Madison left yet? Where are our troops going? Where is General Winder?"

"Whoa," he said. "Slow down. I don't know any more than you. No one's seen President Madison—he was at Bladensburg with the army. I understand Dolly Madison is preparing to leave and I don't know what General Winder's going to do."

"Are you leaving?"

"Mother and Father are still French citizens, and they are neutrals now that Napoléon has surrendered," he replied. "They think they will be safe enough and feel they can protect the store. You can't imagine how many people are seeking out the French minister, Louis Serurier, for protection. You and Mrs. McLaughlin should go."

"We can't," Samara said. "Joshua can't be moved. Annabelle is afraid it will kill him."

"Then I'll stay with you," he said, his hand tightening on her shoulder.

She smiled her thanks, grateful for his help. She was beginning to feel the first twinges of fear as she watched the fleeing troops. "I'm trying to find Dr. Ewell," she said.

"Wait until I tell Father," Julien said. "Then I'll go with you."

They searched in vain in the confusion. Rumors were running wild, and more and more people were fleeing. They heard that General Winder was in full retreat to Georgetown, and that Mrs. Madison, clutching a portrait of George Washington, had left the White House.

Samara and Julien went back to Annabelle's to check on Joshua. Joshua was raging, furious that he could not fight, and it was taking all of Annabelle's persuasion to quiet him.

Dusk fell, and Samara and Julien decided to try once more to locate Dr. Ewell before the British actually entered the city. As they left the house, they could hear the explosions. Powder trains at the navy yard were being destroyed by retreating American troops, and they watched as the flames and smoke gushed upward, casting a red glow over the city. Samara shuddered with apprehension, imagining she could feel the heat. Terror battled with purpose, but her concern for Joshua won. The young couple started toward the Ewell home, only to meet a detachment of scarlet-clad British soldiers. An officer, eyeing Samara appreciatively, asked their destination and ordered one of his soldiers to escort them there. All civilians, he announced, were to stay in their homes.

"To be burned in our beds?" Samara asked with open rage. These were invaders!

The lieutenant looked at her more carefully, obviously admiring her courage. "We have orders not to burn any private residences," he said slowly. "Not unless we're fired upon. You will be safe enough if you stay inside."

Samara stood there, despite Julien's attempts to draw her away. "What are you going to burn, then?" she demanded, noticing the torches in some of the soldier's hands.

"'Tis none of your concern, little miss," he said. "'Tis only government buildings."

"The White House," she said tightly and, at his reluctant nod, added, "*That's* a private residence."

The stern-faced lieutenant grinned at her impertinence, but then saw a senior officer glaring at him. The smile faded.

He turned to Julien. "You'd best get her off the streets, and rein in that mouth." Detailing yet another man to accompany the two, he turned in the direction of the President's House.

Flames now danced heavenward throughout the city, as more and more government buildings were torched. Samara noted that she and Julien were the only civilians on streets filled with British troops. She eyed their unwelcome escort with scorn before turning to Julien. "Come on, Julien, we had better get back to Annabelle." With her chin up, Samara turned and led the way home as two embarrassed privates followed them.

All night, they could hear sporadic firing and small explosions. Julien volunteered to stay since there were only two elderly manservants in the house for protection. Annabelle had armed herself, as did Samara, and they sat at the windows watching the destruction, wondering if one of the many fires would reach their home.

The hours crept by and Samara thought the night would never end. By dawn's light, British soldiers prowled the streets, rifles ready. The small group in Annabelle's house ate their breakfast, wondering aloud what the day would bring.

"Julien and I will try Dr. Ewell's again," Samara said. Annabelle, growing increasingly worried about her husband, agreed. The night had not helped Joshua's agitation.

The two set out, passing British soldiers who ignored them. Samara had deliberately dressed in an unbecoming shapeless frock and hid her rich hair in a bun covered by a cap.

When they reached Dr. Ewell's home, Samara was dismayed to see the number of British soldiers around the building. She gathered her courage and went to the door, noting the broken panes in the front windows. As she reached up to knock, it swung open and a tall British colonel almost collided with her. His hand went out to keep her from falling, and his lips curved into a warm smile.

"Colonel Clifford Longley at your service, miss," he said with a courtly air. "May I help you?"

Samara's brows drew together in confusion. "Dr. Ewell. I was looking for Dr. Ewell." Her voice gathered strength as new anger flooded her. "This is Dr. Ewell's house. What have you done with him?"

Longley's eyes flickered with amusement at the angry little American. Despite her unbecoming dress, his keen eyes didn't miss her beauty. "Why nothing at all, miss. He invited General Ross and his staff to use his home as headquarters."

"I don't believe you," Samara hissed through clenched lips. "He would never willingly have *English* in his home." She might as well have said snake or something worse. The insult was all too apparent in her tone.

"You wound me, Miss...Miss...?" The question hung there.

It continued to hang. Samara had no intention of giving this man the courtesy of her name. Her chin went higher, and her gray eyes were dark thunderclouds. Her hand clenched in frustration. "Where is Dr. Ewell?" she demanded.

"I'll see if I can find out for you," the British colonel said in a clipped accent that was strangely attractive. *Perhaps he reminds you of Reese*, she thought miserably. Although Reese's speech had been softened by years at sea with men of many nations, he had, in times of anger, reverted back to his native accent. *Don't think about him. Think about Joshua.*

She followed the colonel into the house and stood uncomfortably in the drawing room as men rushed back and forth. Colonel Longley asked her to wait in the drawing room while he checked to see if anyone knew of Dr. Ewell's whereabouts. Most of the officers, including General Ross, were still asleep.

Perhaps the doctor was, also. As she and Julien waited impatiently, her eyes wandered about the room and rested, fascinated, at the open door leading into the doctor's library. From where she stood, she could see Dr. Ewell's desk, its usually neat surface cluttered with papers.

"Julien," she whispered with excitement in her voice, "watch at the door for that officer." Before he could catch her, she had run into the study and leaned over the desk, her eyes eagerly scanning the papers. There were maps of Washington with targets pinpointed, maps of the countryside with routes apparently marked. She couldn't take those; their absence would be noted too quickly. But she could try to remember them. Her eyes then spotted a thick leather case. Drawing a deep breath, she ransacked it, singling out another map. She couldn't miss the bold circle around the city of New Orleans and other strange markings around its perimeter. "Good Lord," she mumbled to herself. Her eyes studied it intently, and she realized it must be an invasion plan of some kind.

Samara stuffed the map and several other interesting-looking papers in the garter holding up her left stocking, and hurriedly put the case back where she had found it. It seemed like hours, but she knew it couldn't have been more than several minutes. At Julien's frantic gesture, she rushed from the library back into the sitting room.

She was all innocence as the colonel and Dr. Ewell walked in. Tapping her toe impatiently, she even managed to hide her breathlessness. Dr. Ewell, his eyes bloodshot and clothes mussed, had apparently been roused from bed, and Samara said a silent prayer of thanks. So that's what had taken the colonel so long. She couldn't believe that she and Julien had been left unguarded like this, but then the British hadn't expected Americans in their headquarters, and they had had a very busy night—burning the President's House, the Capital and who knew what else. The thought angered her once more, and she glared at the offending colonel. "I would like to talk to the doctor alone," she said quite haughtily.

The officer looked chagrined at her continued hostility despite his best efforts to be helpful. "As you wish," he said, retreating into the library Samara just left. She winced, hoping he would not check the case. The sooner she could leave, the better.

"Doctor," she said, "Joshua needs some more sleeping powder. Annabelle's afraid *they*," she threw a nasty look at the study door, "will steal it all."

Dr. Ewell shook his head. "It's a bad business, this. But I must say General Ross has been very courteous and has promised not to bother the surgery or confiscate any of my medicines."

"I can't believe you're letting them stay here...like guests."

The doctor sighed. "My dear, I had no choice. They chose this house and at least as long as General Ross is here I know it's safe. I don't think they plan to stay long."

"Now that they've practically destroyed Washington, why should they?" Samara asked bitterly. Then she remembered her urgency. "I must get back quickly, or Annabelle will worry."

"And we can't let that happen," the doctor said gently. He too was a friend of Annabelle's and was distressed he couldn't do more for Joshua. "I'll go fetch the medicine."

Several minutes later, he was back, his hands holding several small bottles of liquid. Samara took a handkerchief from the small reticule she had brought with her, and carefully wrapped them before settling them inside the small handbag and attaching it to her wrist.

"Thank you," she said, and she and Julien fled out the door.

They almost made it, and would have if the papers hadn't started to slip from her garter. Samara ducked behind a house, catching the papers just as they started to fall. She tucked them in, this time more firmly.

As she came out from the shadow, her eyes widened. Julien was struggling in the grip of a British soldier. When he saw her, he suddenly jerked loose and started running, apparently to distract his captor. Samara saw a rifle go up, heard the loud explosion and watched as Julien crumpled to the ground. Mindless now of the papers, of anything, she ran to the fallen body and cradled Julien's blood-soaked head in her arms. She was completely unaware that the papers had once more slipped and were lying in the street.

Reese hardly noticed the disturbance at the end of the street. His eyes caught an image of a woman bending over a man, her head close to his, but the face was hidden from his view and a cap covered her hair. He thought briefly about seeing whether he could be of assistance, but already a number of soldiers were gathering around, and there would be little he could do. Besides he had a more urgent matter.

His ship had met the main British fleet at the mouth of Chesapeake Bay and he had sailed the *Phoenix* down the Potomac River to Alexandria. His ship was allowed to go no further, so he hastily found and purchased—once more at an exorbitant price—a horse from one of the local Tories. Guilt raked him as he passed the burned-out shipyard and several other torched buildings. His sympathies, he feared, were inching toward the Americans. He was, at least, out of it now. He would fetch Samara, take her home, and try to reach an understanding between them. He only hoped that the British invasion of Washington hadn't created a further schism between them.

He stopped to ask someone the location of Joshua McLaughlin's home and was quickly given directions. His momentary spurt of optimism was stilled by the tragic scene in the street. Perhaps a wife, perhaps a lover ...

The McLaughlin house was graceful, with fine classical lines and a small yard covered with flowers of every description. Unlike the manicured gardens of England, American flower beds bloomed riotously in a profusion of colors and shapes. He smiled to himself; it reminded him of Samara.

The door was quickly answered, and Annabelle and Reese stared at each other, each caught in sudden recognition.

Reese felt as if he knew Annabelle. Samara had talked frequently of her unusual godmother who had apparently defied convention most of her life. She stood there with warmth and curiosity in her lovely green eyes.

As for Annabelle, there was no mistaking the tall Englishman. Samara had described him, but even her goddaughter's wistful words hadn't prepared her for the splendor of the man. No man should have eyes like his, eyes that looked like the sun-kissed aqua waters of the Caribbean. He was one of the most striking men she had ever seen. He grinned and she couldn't help but smile in unrestrained delight. He was everything Samantha and Samara had said. And more. Much more.

"Captain Hampton," she said, stating a fact rather than asking a question.

He looked pleased that she knew him. "And you are Annabelle. Samara has told me much about you."

"I fear to ask what," she said, her twinkling eyes taking inventory of his now slightly soiled lawn shirt, tight-fitting buff trousers and scuffed but obviously expensive black boots.

"You needn't," he laughed down at her. "If she hadn't already claimed my heart, I am afraid you might. I loved her stories." His warm eyes told her it was no extravagant compliment.

Samara, Annabelle thought, *how lucky you are. He is exceptional. Like Connor. He is so much like Connor.* The wound in her heart reopened. She had loved Connor O'Neill for fifty years; indeed, would always love him. But it had not been destined, and over the years it had been enough that he was her friend and was so completely happy with Samantha. It was all she had ever wanted: his happiness. And now Samara's.

She was *not* going to let Samara throw it away.

"Come in, Captain," she said. "Samara's gone out on an errand. She should be back any time."

"Has she . . . said anything . . . ?"

"Quite a bit," Annabelle replied with a wry smile.

"Now *I* fear to ask what," he said with a touch of rueful laughter. "Although I could guess at some of it. Pirate, blackguard, spy. Englishman. That's the worst, I think. She could tolerate almost everything else." His smile disappeared. "I'm afraid the past few days probably haven't helped."

"Samara loves you, Captain. I don't doubt that for a second."

"I have," he admitted, with a wistful little smile that touched Annabelle's heart as little else could. "She doesn't give her trust easily."

"There was nothing to the story of your betrothal?"

"No . . . and she would have known had she asked . . . had she believed."

"I think," Annabelle said slowly, "she loves you too much. It frightens her. It frightened her mother years ago . . . Samantha also kept running away."

"How do I make her stop?"

"I don't think you can. She has to do it herself. And she will. She has bitterly regretted leaving you last Christmas."

"But now . . . with this damned attack?"

"It won't make it easier, but then I suspect you don't mind a challenge," Annabelle looked at him appraisingly.

"And you . . . ? You don't object to an Englishman in your home?"

"I think it depends on the circumstances," she replied with a smile. "If you are here to rob and plunder something other than my goddaughter's heart, I might take my rifle to you. And I'm a very good shot."

"I don't doubt it for a second," Reese said, feeling very comfortable with this unusual lady.

They talked for another hour before Annabelle started to worry.

Reese, too, was becoming restless. Samara shouldn't be wandering the streets with so many British troops about. As well disciplined as most of them were, there could always be trouble, particularly with a girl as pretty as Samara and, he admitted, one as outspoken.

"I'll go look for her," he said. "I have a friend..." He stopped in mid-sentence.

"Don't worry, Captain," she said. "Of course you have friends in the British army. Use them, by all means."

He nodded, thankful for her understanding. He only wished Samara shared some of Annabelle's tolerance.

Reese finally found Cliff Longley up the road at the Ewell home. At first, an apprehensive corporal refused him entrance. "He's in a high temper, he is," the soldier explained apologetically, after Reese used his brother's title.

"He's an old friend," Reese soothed, "and I have urgent business with him."

"'Tis on yer head, not mine," the soldier said, as he opened the door to the drawing room and pointed towards the library.

Longley, Reese noted, had lost his usual air of indifference. His lips were pressed tightly together, and his face radiated anger. His eyes did not look up as Reese hesitated at the door but remained on papers lying in front of him.

"What the devil? I said I wanted no interruptions."

"Not even from an old friend?"

Longley looked up and the grimace eased. "Perhaps from an old friend," he said. "Perhaps you can give me some advice. You seem to know a lot about women."

"Not lately," Reese muttered to himself, but an eyebrow raised in question.

"It's a nasty business," Longley said. "And I could well be booted from the army for it."

Reese's eyebrow went up further.

"A young lady came looking for the doctor who lives here. I left her outside in the drawing room while I hunted for him. She apparently got into some papers I was keeping for General Ross. Some very important papers."

Reese's body tensed, his eyes becoming very alert. The moment Longley had mentioned a young lady, he knew. "Her name?" he asked softly.

"Dr. Ewell very reluctantly identified her as a Miss O'Neill."

Reese felt himself go numb, even though he had expected that answer. He struggled to keep his expression bland while he, who had never feared anyone, felt terror rip through his body. "Are you quite sure that she was actually spying?" he asked calmly.

"Caught red-handed. Had a map on her person—and some other papers."

"Where is she now?" Reese managed through clenched teeth.

"The Washington jail. Until some decisions are made." The grim look on Reese's face finally made an impact. "Why the interest?"

"We were . . . going to marry."

Now it was Cliff Longley's turn to stare. "But she was with a man . . . he was shot trying to escape."

Reese closed his eyes, suddenly remembering the scene on the street. Samara? He had wondered . . . a wife? A lover? The woman had certainly appeared devoted to the wounded man. "Just down the road?" he asked tensely.

Longley nodded.

"What happened to the man?"

"He'll live to hang. It looked worse than it was."

"And the girl?"

Longley looked sympathetic. "We can't let her go, Reese. She stole a map with one of our most important plans. We can only assume she knew what it was."

"You wouldn't . . . ?"

"That's up to officers more senior than I. But she will surely go to England . . . at the very least."

"Cliff . . ." Reese's voice was pleading. "I didn't tell you this in Bermuda, but when my ship was sunk off the coast I located a Tory, a friend of the King. He asked me to get some information for him, and I was discovered trying to do so." He noticed Longley was watching him with intense interest. "Samara O'Neill's family protected me, kept me at their home for more than four months. They risked their lives for me—despite the fact they support the war and three of the sons are fighting. I owe them a great deal.''

''I understand,'' Longley said softly, sympathetically. ''But I don't know what I can do.''

''I could marry her,'' Reese said, once more in a soft but intense voice. ''I could take her to England myself. Now. As my wife.''

Longley nervously rubbed his hands together. ''She's a little wildcat. When my soldiers tried to separate her from the man, she scratched the hell out of them.''

''That sounds like Samara,'' Reese admitted wryly. ''She tried to kill me when I first met her.''

''And you want to marry her?''

''Odd, isn't it?'' Reese admitted. ''But yes, I suppose I do.''

''Even if she doesn't want you?'' Longley eyed his friend with astonishment. He couldn't imagine the sophisticated, arrogant Hampton with the fiery American.

''She did,'' Hampton said now. ''And I think I can persuade her again.'' But his mouth tightened as he further questioned Longley about Samara's accomplice. He felt an excruciating pain as he did so. Regardless of what Annabelle had said, it apparently hadn't taken Samara long to forget him. ''The man with her . . . do you know anything about him?''

''She told my sergeant he was just accompanying her, that he had no part in it. But he attacked one of my soldiers, and I don't really believe he knew nothing of the documents. They were here together and they certainly seemed fond of each other.'' His eyes searched Hampton's face for a reaction as he added, ''They're trying to protect each other.''

''Can you do anything for him?''

''I can talk to General Ross. I suppose we could take him back to England, but he would certainly end up in Dartmoor Prison. Why your concern?''

''Because Samara would never forgive me—nor the entire British empire—if he hangs. Would you try?''

Longley shook his head in disbelief. ''I thought she was making my career a shambles. It's nothing compared to what she's doing to your life, my friend. Are you quite sure about this?''

''Will you talk to Ross?'' Reese insisted.

Longley shrugged. "All right, though I can't promise anything. General Ross is generally inclined to be lenient, however, particularly if there's a pretty woman involved."

"Thank you, Cliff."

"Don't thank me. I would be only too delighted to get her out of sight," Longley said with the first smile of the conversation. "Maybe everyone will forget about it. I can't believe it. I had a promotion due . . . but who would suspect a pretty little thing like that?"

"Who indeed?" Reese agreed with a rueful half smile.

Reese waited restlessly while Longley conferred with General Ross. His thoughts jumped from one question to another. Who was the man with Samara? How much did she care for him? A cold chill crept into him. Why had she bent over the American so tenderly? Had Annabelle been so mistaken about her feelings? And would she agree to the terms being offered? He wasn't sure he wanted a forced marriage, but he owed the O'Neills and, as much as he hated to admit it, he loved Samara and knew he always would. He despaired at the thought of her captivity in British hands—and the very real possibility of prison, if not death. A marriage, no matter how reluctant, might be the only way to save her. But what kind of marriage would that be . . . ? How different than the one he had imagined at Glen Woods! A darkness engulfed him as he considered the possible tragedy that was in the making. He had already felt so much anguish and turmoil from loving Samara. He didn't know if he wanted to open his heart again. Not yet. *I can't let her know how I feel. I can't give her that weapon.*

Thus strengthened by resolve, he watched as Longley returned, a slight, satisfied smile on his face.

"General Ross was rather fascinated by your proposal," he said. "He agrees that it is one way out of a very difficult situation. Damned if he wants to be accused of hanging a woman . . . nor does he want to take her as a prisoner aboard ship for weeks. If she agrees, you'll be married straight away by our chaplain and escorted to your ship. We require your word that you sail immediately, that she has no chance to contact anyone."

"You have it," Reese replied quickly. "And the young man? I doubt she'll agree to anything without reassurances about him. If nothing else, she's stubbornly loyal." He winced at the last words. Loyal, apparently, to everyone but him.

"He'll go to Dartmoor," Longley said. "It's the best I could do."

"Thank you, Cliff."

"Not yet. There are several conditions. I want to talk to her first. We want to know if she has any accomplices or whether..." his smile faded, "she just took advantage of an opportunity." He didn't need to add that it was an opportunity he had carelessly given her.

Reese nodded. He very much doubted whether it had been planned. He knew Samara's impulsiveness only too well.

"I would like to be there."

"I'm afraid not, Reese. I've gone as far as I can. If you're here, she might feel protected." He almost laughed at the suddenly fierce expression on Reese's face.

"Don't worry, I don't plan a thumb screw. Just a preview of her prospects, and that of her friend." He looked at Reese quizzically. "You are sure you want to go through with this?"

Reese nodded curtly. "There's nothing else, is there? You won't release her?"

"No," Longley admitted. "And *you* are to keep her silent for at least four months. Do you understand? It's essential."

"I know what's at stake," Reese said. "And I know you don't question my loyalty to England." There was an edge to his voice.

"No," Longley said. "Of course not, or I would never have agreed to this insane scheme."

"When will you bring her here?"

"In a few hours. General Ross suggested, and I agreed, a few hours in a cell might loosen her tongue."

"Damn it, Cliff. She'll be terrified."

"I hope so," Longley said grimly. "I sincerely hope so."

Samara huddled on the small bench in the nearly black cell. It was the only furniture, other than a bucket in the corner. The smell of her small space was indescribable. It reeked of sweat and dirt and fear. Her fear.

The cell was windowless except for a small grate in the door which allowed only a fraction of light to penetrate. She knew, from occasional scuffling noises, that a guard remained outside. She had asked, nay demanded, that someone contact

Annabelle. But to no avail. She had not been roughly treated, but the soldiers and, now, guards were firm in their silence.

What had she done?

She had seen the papers in Col. Longley's case and reacted instinctively. And perhaps had condemned Julien in doing so. At the moment, she was too miserable to care about her own plight. She kept seeing Julien's ashen face, the blood dripping down it and the ugly jagged wound at the side of his head. *Julien, I'm sorry. I'm so sorry.* No one would tell her anything, even whether Julien had lived or died.

She fingered her reticule. Strange how they had left that with her, although they had checked inside. She had pleaded to be allowed to keep the medicine, and a stern-faced sergeant had permitted it. She didn't know he had a daughter her own age, and that he pitied her.

The little bottles of sleeping draught were all still there, but she despaired of ever having a chance to deliver them to Joshua. Poor Joshua. Poor Annabelle who must be worried half to distraction by now.

A scurrying sound made her press closer to the stone wall. It was hot, without even the smallest stir of air. And no water. She wet her lips, feeling their dryness. From fear or thirst? She didn't know.

She forced herself to think of something wonderful. Her mouth curved in a small smile as she recalled the last time she was in such darkness. It was in the hold of Brendan's ship, but then she knew she could leave at any time. Not like now. The smile disappeared as the walls seemed to press in on her, and it took all her courage to keep from screaming.

Reese. Think of Reese. Of the warm days and tender smiles. Of him sitting so confidently on the big bay stallion or standing so free at the wheel of his ship. She could almost see the wind rustling his golden hair and hear his laughter. The bold buccaneer laughter that had both delighted and frightened her. A lump formed in her throat as she remembered their last picnic. "Where are you?" she whispered. "I need you. Oh, God, I need you."

And then she remembered. He was probably in England, perhaps already married to an English lady. She buried her head in her hands as she felt a grief too great for tears.

The hours of anguish in the dark cell did not serve to cow Samara when she was, at last, taken by closed carriage back to British headquarters. Her imprisonment, contrary to the colonel's expectation, had merely served to fuel an outrage which, in the dark hours, alternated with remorse and misery.

They were the invaders. *They* were the arsonists. *They* were the murderers and now *they* had Julien's blood on their head. *They* were bloody Englishmen.

She regarded Longley with no less distaste than she had shown in the morning. It was strangely effective considering her sorry state. Her drab dress was coated with filth and blood, her face was smudged with dirt and her hair was wild and tangled from the struggle with British soldiers as they had forced her from Julien's side.

"Miss O'Neill, sit down," the red-coated officer said coldly. Longley's face was hard, his eyes like steel, and there was none of the previous friendliness. His face was so somber, in fact, that Samara wondered if it was the same man she had encountered earlier in this very same house.

She sat, her body stiff, as her hands nervously fingered each other and the reticule she still carried, now for courage more than anything else. It was an object on which to focus, something familiar to give her hope. But though her hands transmitted fear, her eyes did not. They were like great angry thunderheads, ready to launch lightning bolts.

Longley had difficulty concealing his admiration, and for the first time stopped questioning Reese's judgment. Under the dirt and grime, she was a truly beautiful woman with both courage and spirit.

His plan to dominate the interview was quickly squashed when she angrily demanded to know about Julien Devereaux.

He leaned forward in his chair, intentionally taking his time in answering. His eyes bored into her before he said, almost nonchalantly, "He'll live to hang...as you well could." The very casualness in his voice did more to instill fear than anything else. He sounded as if it were an everyday occurrence; nothing to be bothered about, except, perhaps, by the victim. In that minute, she did not doubt that both Julien's and her lives might be forfeit.

Her chin went up defiantly. She *had* to save Julien. She had led him into this. Her stormy eyes went bleak as she remembered his ashen face.

"It was all my doing," she said, almost desperately. "He did nothing...I just happened to see those papers, and I..." She stumbled. "He's innocent. He was just trying to protect me."

His expression was glacial. "You didn't *just* happen to see anything," he said. "Those papers were packed away."

Despite herself, guilt flooded her face as she searched for an explanation. There was none.

"But it was *me*. *Only* me," she finally managed. "I saw those papers on your desk, then the case and I . . . Julien didn't have anything to do with it."

"Are you're sure you're not just trying to protect your Mr. Devereaux because you believe we won't hang a woman? If you do, you're badly mistaken. We hang spies . . . whoever they are."

"But Julien's not . . ."

"And *you* are?" the voice was unrelenting. Longley hated himself for what he was doing, but he had to find out. "You're admitting it?"

She stared at him, some of the defiance seeping away. Her hands tightened against each other. He was making it her or Julien. And she would not give him Julien.

"Yes," she said softly. "Now let Julien go. Please."

"You were alone . . . ? It will go easier if you tell me about the others."

From the shock on her face, he doubted very much if there were others. It was, as she said, an impulsive act which had had dire consequences for a number of people, including himself. He could not forget his own blame; he had almost invited it through carelessness.

Samara bit her lip at his hard stare. Did he believe her? She didn't want to die, but she could never live with herself if Julien died in her stead.

"There's also the possibility of prison," the British officer said now. "You had a small taste of it today. Believe me, British prisons are worse." He could see her shudder, and his distaste for himself rose. "You still hold yourself solely responsible?"

"Yes," she whispered, thinking what a living hell it would be. For a moment she thought death would be preferable. But only for a moment. Death was very final.

"There might still be another alternative," he said cryptically, as he nodded to a soldier in the doorway.

Her large gray eyes quickened with hope. But it faded almost immediately. What terrible thing could he offer instead? Because she was afraid to hear it, she spoke, asking the question that had been nagging her.

"How did you know about . . . that I had . . . ?"

"I didn't," Longley said. "I sent those men to accompany you home safely. Apparently your friend thought you had been discovered and attacked them. To protect you."

A familiar soft laugh came from behind her, and Samara whirled around, half rising. She remembered it well . . . as she remembered the mocking voice that followed it.

"It seems, my love, that you and I are the two most inept spies on this good earth." The corners of the inviting, sensual mouth she had dreamed of for nearly a year, were pulled up into a bitter smile and his eyes were green ice. "You see we *do* have much in common. It must be a match created in heaven. Or hell."

He was in the open doorway, leaning casually against the doorjamb, his eyes glittering. Samara recognized his mood. Whenever he spoke this quietly, there was a hard tension behind it, a taut anger barely held in check. The first bubble of joy, which had risen spontaneously on hearing his voice, burst with immediate realization.

He had been there all the time! He had listened while she was threatened, terrorized and humiliated. And he had said nothing. Not only that, his presence here in British headquarters was damning. *He* was one of *them*. Her small hands knotted compulsively and her eyes swam with a humiliating mist as part of her heart died. But she resolved not to release her tears. Not for *him*. She would not give him that satisfaction.

Instead, the words came without thought. Her quiet sincerity made them even more explosive. "You bastard!"

Longley looked shocked, then grinned. The famous rake who had won and discarded any number of hearts in England was being repaid in kind. But Reese's face did not change unless, perhaps, the eyes grew colder. Longley wondered how that was possible. His eyebrows raised as he waited for Reese's reply.

It was several seconds in coming. He had heard part of her interview with Longley and every mention of Julien Devereaux had twisted a knife deeper inside him. He suddenly wanted to hurt her as much as he had been hurt.

"It seems," Reese finally said, "that we've played this scene before." The side of his mouth turned upward slightly. "You looked like an urchin then, too."

The derisive reminder infuriated Samara. She itched to punch him, but with new insight she knew he was trying to provoke her. He was obviously furious, and she searched for the reason. She was the one who had cause for anger.

With all the willpower in her slim body, she turned to Colonel Longley. "Does he have to be here?"

"I'm afraid so," the colonel said with an amused smile. "You see, he's your third alternative."

The words gradually penetrated, and Samara looked from the colonel's obvious enjoyment of the situation to Reese's masked expression.

"I don't understand," she said nervously.

"Our good captain has offered to marry you and take you safely away... where you will have no chance to divulge the information you so inconveniently stole from us."

Samara was stunned into silence. Her eyes flooded with confusion before she understood. Or thought she understood. They were playing with her. Reese was already promised... if not married. She would not be part of their ugly game. Despair overwhelmed her because, despite all he had done, she wished nothing more than to run to him, to bury herself in those strong arms which had once held such comfort. But she couldn't. She would not surrender the only thing she had left. Her pride.

"I would rather hang," she said quite succinctly, her eyes matching the chill in his. Her stubborn chin lifted in determination.

Reese showed no emotion. "And would your friend?" He watched her closely now, looking for an indication of her feelings. He was fighting desperately to hide a raging jealousy and sense of betrayal.

The angry red in Samara's face paled. "What do you mean?"

"We're not just discussing your fate, Miss O'Neill," the colonel broke in. "Your companion is involved, as well."

"But I told you..."

"Do you really think I could let him go, knowing he might have seen those papers?" Longley said with the first sympathy he had shown during the interview.

"But he didn't," she insisted, as her face froze.

"I'm sorry. That's not quite good enough. I can't be sure... nor can I be sure you didn't tell him."

"I promise you I said nothing."

"And can I trust you, Miss O'Neill? As I did when I left you alone in this room?" Longley's calm remark told her he wouldn't change his mind.

"What are you going to do with him?" she asked fearfully, tears hovering in the gray depths of her eyes. Her hands trembled as she sought to control herself.

She didn't see Reese's face, nor the sudden intense pain that clouded his expression. She only heard his voice. It was at his sarcastic worst. "Such concern, Samara. You didn't show this kind of solicitude when you were playing with *my* neck."

Samara stood and took one step toward him, an arm outstretched in supplication. "*He* did nothing . . . except try to protect me. You can't, Reese, you can't let him hang."

"Oh, can't I?" he said, now angered almost beyond control. He had thought of nothing but Samara for a year. And now she was apparently in love with this young puppy. Why else would she offer her life in exchange for his? "Why?" he asked tightly. "Because he's your lover?"

Incensed at his perfidy, at his mocking indifference, at her own treacherous longing to be in his arms, Samara sought to even the score. "Yes," she said flatly, her gray eyes meeting his angry expression defiantly.

They were now both oblivious to Longley's presence.

"You love him?" Reese's voice was so soft she barely heard it.

"Yes," she said with reckless abandon. "He's gentle and kind and . . ."

"Everything I'm not," he finished for her, his heart filling with pain. "But, then, perhaps he had more cause to be gentle and kind."

The words bit into Samara as she stared up at him. There was a kind of wistfulness in his eyes, a hint of vulnerability she had never seen before. But then they were instantly hooded again, and she knew she had been mistaken. His voice was hard and merciless when he spoke again.

"Your answer, Samara?"

She looked bewildered. Surely they hadn't been serious.

"But you . . . are already . . ."

At this juncture, he had no wish to explain himself nor the sham engagement. This obviously would be a marriage in name only. Samara no longer loved him, if indeed, she ever had. Bitterness welled up in him as he regarded her coldly. He owed Connor this. He could never live with himself if anything happened to Samara. The marriage could be dissolved later by quiet divorce or annulment.

"It is your only alternative, Samara," he said now, "and your friend's. I have been assured that if you cooperate he'll be sent to England and imprisoned. If not," he shrugged, "he'll hang."

"But why?" she asked, through clenched teeth. "I hate you." She looked at his strong, handsome face, now creased by lines of tension, and knew the statement for a lie. She could never hate him. *Oh God, don't let him know how much I love him, how much I want to touch him.*

"Why?" she asked again, bewildered.

"I owe your father," he said curtly.

Her last hope died. He was doing it only for what he felt he owed her father. Not for her.

She thought of Julien and knew she could not condemn him to death. She bowed her head and surrendered. "Yes," she whispered. "For Julien." She would never let him think it was for any other reason.

"Very well," Reese said, in a harsh voice Samara didn't recognize. "The wedding will take place this afternoon." His eyes studied her critically. "I'll get some of your clothes from Annabelle."

"I want to see her. And Julien."

"I'm afraid that's quite impossible, Miss O'Neill," Longley said from behind them, reminding both he had heard the humiliating exchange and reluctant marriage plans.

Reese felt so painfully drained he didn't care, but Samara did. She hated the British even more for so successfully forcing her to their will.

"Why not?" she challenged Longley. She had nothing more to lose.

"Because, my dear future Mrs. Hampton," he paused, a slight smile on his lips at her infuriated expression, "we will give you no opportunity to pass on any information. You will be married here, by our chaplain, and escorted to your husband's ship." He obviously delighted in taunting her.

Samara looked from one man to the other, finding no sympathy or help in either. In all her conflicts with Reese, she had never seen his eyes colder, nor his reserve greater. Hopelessness flooded her. She was being forced to leave her country and family with a man who obviously detested her. That he was also the man she so unwisely loved did nothing to make the situation easier. Every time she looked him, she would remember his touch, the softness in his eyes, the teasing laughter as her body surrendered so wholeheartedly to his. Could she bear seeing those cold eyes and grim mouth and knowing they were bound to each other by hate, not love?

She pulled her courage together and returned Reese's glare. "You will tell her what happened?"

"I'll explain that you decided to marry me in England, that I had to leave immediately, and you send your best wishes and assurances of happiness," he said wryly. "I see no reason to worry your family."

"You are so kind," she said bitterly. "But Annabelle won't believe you . . . not without me."

"I think so," he drawled. "Annabelle and I met this afternoon and got along rather well. And you will write a note, explaining the somewhat unusual circumstances and adding that you are most happy with the arrangements."

"No," she said rebelliously. "I won't lie."

Her vehement denial of him inflamed him once more.

"Yes you will." There was steel in his voice. "Or else the marriage is off. I will not have your family thinking I dragged you off unwillingly."

"Which is exactly what you are doing," she said furiously. "I don't want to marry you."

"Think of Julien," he taunted softly.

"Damn you. Damn you to hell."

She didn't hear his words as he left, slamming the door behind him. "You have already done that, my little cat."

Her first note was rejected by Colonel Longley who could barely contain a smile as he read it. There was a pointed reference to a concern about a brother in New Orleans. The second, which was unenthusiastic at best, was rejected by Reese whose patience was wearing thin. "I will dictate, Samara, and you will very carefully copy my words."

Exhausted and numb, Samara agreed. As he started to leave, she remembered Joshua's medicine. "Wait," she said, unable to force his name. As he turned, she rummaged in her damaged reticule and took out several bottles. She held them out to him. "For Joshua."

Reese took them slowly, his brilliant eyes assessing her woeful face. His mouth twisted against the consoling words that part of him wanted to speak. The other part, the angry wounded self, kept them frozen inside. He merely nodded coldly and left.

Samara was taken upstairs to a bedroom to rest. She heard a key in the lock and when she went to the window she noted a guard beneath it. Defeated, she sank down on the bed.

Several hours later, two soldiers brought in a bathtub and steaming pails of water. Lastly, they brought in a dress—her favorite—along with her combs and brushes.

"I was told, Miss," one said with embarrassment, "that you are to be ready in an hour."

When they left, she looked at the water she once would have welcomed joyously. Now it brought nothing but dread for it meant she was one step closer to the farce of a marriage. He would hate her for taking his freedom, for keeping him from his betrothed in London. And she . . .

A tear, waiting all day to be released, trickled slowly down her cheek. So, now all the dreams would end.

Chapter Nineteen

It should have been the happiest day of her life, Samara thought, as she and Reese stood in front of the British chaplain. Instead, it was the most miserable.

As she stole a glance at Reese, he stood there stiff and unyielding, his mouth in a tight, grim line, his eyes framed by lines of strain. A muscle throbbed in his cheek, and she could feel him flinch when they were told to join hands.

Her own hand was miserably cold, she knew, and it reflected her heart. She was afraid to feel, afraid to think. A small seed of hope, which had persisted despite all reason, flickered and died when she saw Reese's face at the small gathering of British officers just prior to the horrible ceremony. He had been easy to find as she had come down the steps; he loomed above everyone else. He had turned cold, bitter eyes upon her, and the mouth, which had always smiled so easily, did not even offer a mocking twist. He had merely nodded, his eyes skimming over her appearance with neither approval nor disapproval.

Samara had tried to look her best, but she had neither assistance nor accessories. It was a matter of pride to her that she did not appear defeated to the hated enemies below. She would not admit, even to herself, that perhaps she wanted Reese to think her beautiful—as he once had said she was.

She had washed her hair, and brushed it until it glimmered with fiery red highlights. Since she had no clasps or decorations, she let it fall freely down her back.

Annabelle had sent her favorite dress—a pale blue cambric muslin which gave a blue glow to her eyes. Its low neck did little to hide the swell of her firm breasts, and the small puffed sleeves emphasized her creamy white skin. The narrow, gored skirt displayed her slender figure to perfection. But despite the admiration in the eyes of the British officers, she saw only indifference in Reese's.

She barely heard the words of the chaplain and was unaware of her own responses. It was as if someone else were speaking them. It couldn't be her, not like this, not in the midst of all these soldiers dressed in scarlet, not with this icy-eyed stranger whose cold lips touched hers in a kiss as frigid as a winter wind.

Ironically, champagne followed the ceremony. How ludicrous, Samara thought, to celebrate, but she took a glass and then a second to dull the raw pain. She felt Reese's arm around her, muttering something and then she was being guided outside to a closed carriage. Reese courteously assisted her inside and closed the door, leaving her alone. As it started in motion, Samara's best intentions shattered. She wanted to display the same indifference as Reese, but she longed for his comforting presence, to be assured that all would be all right. But he cared nothing for her, in truth he gave every sign he hated her. The tears fell silently in steady rivulets down her face.

His thoughts black, Reese settled himself in the saddle and rode in front of the coach, away from the armed escort that surrounded it. Unlike General Ross and Longley, he had no fear that Samara would try to escape, not with Julien's life at stake. The thought only deepened the emptiness inside him.

He had thought about accompanying her in the coach, but had checked himself. She obviously wanted no part of him; that much was clear at the wedding. She had not looked at him during the entire ceremony, and her lips had been cool and unresponsive when he'd touched them in a brief formal kiss. She had jerked her hand from his as soon as possible, and had spoken not a word other than the necessary responses.

It had been all he could do to keep his face impassive, to keep from touching the lovely face with tragic eyes. But they were eyes longing for another man, and he knew his touch would not be welcome. Not now. Nor, for his own sake, could he allow himself that weakness. It would be hell aboard ship. He remembered how much he had resented being captive, and it was much worse with Samara because he had used the life of her young man to bend her will.

With a raw anguish deeper than any he had thought possible, he recalled her response to his proposal, "I would rather hang." His legs tightened against the sides of his horse, and the stallion responded with a confused dance step. He absently stroked the mount's neck, realizing his hands and legs were giving conflicting instructions.

His hands loosened on the reins, and his legs once more tightened, this time giving the horse his head. Together they raced for his ship.

He had sent word ahead to Michael Simmons and Yancy, and as he approached the *Phoenix*, Reese saw the ship was ready to sail. A longboat was waiting at the shoreline to take them aboard, and Yancy, his lively eyes even more inquisitive than usual, was sitting on the riverbank when Reese, his horse lathered with sweat, arrived.

"You look like the devil's been chasing you," Yancy said.

"He has," Reese answered shortly.

"Where's the bride?"

"Behind me. I should warn you, Yancy, she's not very happy."

Yancy, who had been told nothing of the circumstances in Reese's note, arched an eyebrow.

"She was caught spying. The marriage was the only way to save her." Reese's explanation was curt, his face shuttered. It was enough to stay any additional questions.

Reese made arrangements with a British officer to sell the horse, and he and Yancy sat and waited for the carriage. Yancy could feel his friend's tension but said nothing, offering only quiet support.

When the carriage rolled up Reese reluctantly approached it, disregarding the cavalry escort. When he opened the door, he saw Samara huddled in a corner, her eyes red and swollen. It was the first time he had seen her tears and, despite every warning bell in his head, his heart ached for her. He entered and sat, his hand reaching out to her. At first she flinched, but as his hand—ever so tenderly—traced the dried tears on her face, she looked up at him and saw compassion. And something she couldn't define. When he held out his arms, she buried herself in them, new sobs shaking her body. She felt his hand soothing her hair, heard his soft whispers, telling her all would be well. And still the tears came, until she wondered how there could be any more.

When her shudders finally quieted, Samara felt his lips on her forehead. Softly. Gently. Not as a man in love, but as a comforting friend. And that hurt her more than anything.

She forced herself to draw away. "I'm sorry," she said in a small, choking voice.

His voice was warm and kind. "You need never be sorry, little cat. It's been a day to try the strongest of soldiers." Reese's hand fingered one of her curls. "You've been very brave. And everything will be all right. I promise. We'll get an annulment in England, and you can return..." He couldn't finish the sentence.

The bright flare of joy in Samara's heart faded. He was merely being kind. She forgot that she had accused him, recently, of being bare of that particular virtue. She straightened, wiping her face like a child, looking incredibly defenseless in her fruitless attempt to appear strong. "I'm all right," she said. "Truly."

He nodded, his admiration for her rising. As was his longing.

He opened the door and stepped out, turning to offer his hand. After a second's hesitation Samara took it, feeling its warmth sparking fires throughout her body. She hesitated at the edge of the seat, looking intently at Reese. He was still dressed in his wedding clothes, a somber but attractive mixture of grays. A dark gray dress coat and slightly lighter, silver-embroidered waistcoat contrasted with a snowy white lawn shirt. Light gray pants emphasized his muscular thighs, and glistening black knee-high boots encased his strong calves. Her husband. Her very reluctant husband. Once more, waves of wretchedness swept through her.

Seeing her eyes cloud again, Reese reached out his arms and took Samara in them, wondering at how light she seemed. He placed her gently in the longboat and signaled to the sailors to push off. When they reached the ship, he helped her climb the ladder and stood on the deck with her as Michael Simmons piloted the *Phoenix* slowly down the Potomac. He remained next to her as she stared at the shore, saying goodbye to all she had known.

The day passed under bright blue skies and a fair wind. Reese's anger had receded under the weight of Samara's grief. It was replaced by an enormous sense of loss and a burning, hurting ache, a bruising pain which intensified every time he looked at her. For that reason, he studiously avoided her, finding a reason to leave the top deck when she appeared.

He gave her Michael Simmons' cabin, treating her with courteous politeness. He ate alone in his cabin while Samara dined the first night with his officers.

Reese's temper with his men rose with his level of frustration, until it reached legendary peaks. Sensing the bubbling tension, Samara stayed in her cabin as much as possible until she thought she would perish with loneliness. She sought out Yancy, saying little, but the wistfulness in her eyes spoke volumes.

Yancy observed both—Samara and his irascible captain—first with bemusement, then concern. He couldn't believe they were both so idiotically blind. When one thought the other wasn't watching, his or her eyes shone brightly with need—and love. But then when the object of their gaze turned, eyes fell, hiding again in reserves that seemed unreachable. He wanted to knock their heads together, yet he knew his interference would not be welcome, and it went against his lifelong philosophy to meddle. Besides, they had weeks ahead together. If he knew anything about human nature, they would solve the problem . . . perhaps with just a *wee* bit of help.

After dinner on the second night out, Yancy took Samara up to the main deck to watch the sunset. He didn't miss the way her eyes went compulsively to Reese who stood at the wheel, barefoot once more with the wind rustling his tawny hair.

Samara had gone reluctantly. She was sick of her cabin, but even the barest sight of Reese filled her with fresh misery. His politeness was more devastating than anger. She longed to throw herself in his arms, to nestle in their warmth. But he no longer wanted her, and that knowledge kept her own feelings bound tightly. But as she and Yancy reached the upper deck, she couldn't keep her eyes from Reese, no matter how hard she tried. She could feel her heart hammer and her throat going dry. He was magnificent with the wind blowing the lawn shirt against his broad chest and the tight breeches displaying every muscle as he stood braced against the movement of the ship. Reluctantly, she turned her eyes away . . . to the sunset which seemed trivial compared to Reese Hampton. The huge sun was bright red as it almost touched the dark blue of the sea. Paths of gold and scarlet and pink trailed across the rippling water as if daring the *Phoenix* to follow them to some magical kingdom.

She heard Yancy's voice. "I have to go down for a moment. You stay here."

"I'll go with you," Samara said, a touch of panic in her voice.

"No . . . stay here. I *will* be back shortly."

Entranced by the sorcery of the setting sun, Samara agreed. For a moment she fancied being a bird, swooping in and out of the wondrous colors and climbing up into the cloudless sky. How wonderful to be so free.

"It's glorious, isn't it?" Reese's deep voice interrupted her reverie.

Lost in her thoughts, Samara had not seen Michael Simmons relieve Reese, nor the intense gaze of the *Phoenix*'s captain as he watched her lonely figure in the last golden glow of the sun.

Her hand tightened around the railing as she turned toward him, every defense gone in one bewitching moment as he too became part of the evening's radiance. All she knew was the nearness of his lips, of his eyes which were filled with warmth. Without a word, she moved toward him, unable to stop herself. She felt his hand reach for hers, and knew the soft promise of his lips, their urgency and the subsequent fires that swept her body. Her hands moved up, inch by inch, touching, loving. She was unaware of her tears as she sought that which she wanted most and had thought gone forever. She wanted his love, for she knew—beyond any doubt—that her heart was his. Yet she was afraid to say the words, afraid she would destroy this tenuous moment.

His lips traveled from her lips upward, and touched her hair before holding her tight against him, her face pressed against the golden fur of his chest. With deep pleasure, she smelled the rich aroma of musk and sea and her tongue darted out to lick his salty skin. She heard him groan and felt the swell of his manhood as he drew her even closer. "Little cat," he muttered, as if in pain.

She moved back to look straight up into his eyes and was startled by the naked pain there. Her hands entangled themselves in his hair, and her lips reached once more in a command he couldn't resist. The gentle whisper-soft meeting turned into a tempest, as both sought to quiet their doubts and questions in the nearness and warmth of each other's bodies.

Samara felt him slowly, very slowly, draw away, his lips reluctantly leaving hers. He took her hand and turned toward the sun which had now dipped below the horizon, leaving a spreading red halo in its wake.

"We have much to talk about," he said slowly. His low, warm voice made Samara's legs weak; the touch of his hand sent shudders through her now fully awakened body.

Reese looked at her expressive face. Her heart was in her eyes, and some of the emptiness left him.

"I went back to Glen Woods," he continued. "I was there several weeks ago. Your father said you were in Washington and I had heard that the capitol was to be taken. That's why I was there . . . to make sure you were safe."

"You weren't there . . . with *them*?"

"No, Samara," Reese said, a small smile on his face. "I went there to save you from yourself . . . and apparently just in time." His smile disappeared. "I was going to ask you, again, to marry me. I didn't mean it to happen as it did but circumstances, and anger, took over."

Her hand clutched his as she tried to understand. "Anger?"

"Your . . . apparent fondness for the young man . . . your lack of trust . . . your immediate assumption that I had violated my word—not once but several times."

Agony stabbed Samara's heart as the words penetrated. She *had* rushed to judgement, repeatedly. She had never once considered there might be another side. She had been too afraid of loving him. "But the announcement . . . ?"

"That's why I went to Glen Woods. When I left last Christmas, no one would tell me why you disappeared so suddenly. Apparently they didn't tell your father, either. When he found out, he wrote, knowing there must be some explanation."

Samara's voice was very small. "And was there?"

His right hand caught her chin and forced it up, until her eyes met his. "Yes. A very simple one, had you waited to ask." His voice was bitter now, and she winced at the sound.

He let go of her hand and turned toward the sea, but not before Samara saw the bleakness in his eyes. She felt the pain in the next question. "You have never trusted me, have you, Samara?"

She couldn't lie now, not when there was so much at stake. "No," she said slowly. "I suppose I didn't. You are so different from everything I know. I was afraid I loved you too much. I couldn't understand how you chose me. I knew there must be beautiful women, more sophisticated women. When Bren..."

"You little idiot," he said, thoroughly angry now. "Have you no idea how completely lovely you are? I fell in love with your spirit and your humor and your courage—misguided as it often is. And those qualities are very rare. As, I hope, is your damn stubbornness."

Samara's eyes brightened and hope filled her. "You mean...you still...you didn't marry me just because of Father? You said you wanted an annulment."

"Because I thought that's what you wanted," he said slowly. "Because you said you loved that young American." His eyes were questioning.

"Only because I thought you were in love with someone in England, and I was so angry..."

Reese's eyes glittered with humor. A chuckle started deep in his throat and spread upward as his mouth widened into a grin. He put his hand to his mouth, trying to stop it, but laughter erupted, rich and strong and lusty. Every crew member on deck, each of whom had been darting glances at the oblivious couple, stared in amazement. It was the first real laughter they had heard from their captain in months.

Even Samara looked as if he were mad, before the infectiousness caught her and she too giggled.

When he was finally finished, his eyes twinkled. "We make a fine pair," he said ruefully. "When I was speaking of stubborness, I should have included myself. I was too damn proud to tell you about that engagement, then you were too stubborn to tell me about Devereaux, and that only made me more angry..."

Her hand went up to touch his face, longingly, lovingly. "If only you knew how much I wanted to run into your arms...but you were so cold."

"And you were so angry."

"And frightened...so very frightened..."

"And beautiful and brave..."

"And I loved you so much and thought you hated me."

"We were at cross purposes, it seems," he admitted. "It's over now, Samara," he said, leaning down to kiss her lightly. He chuckled again. "I think we've probably given the crew enough to talk about. I have a perfectly good cabin, and I think we've wasted enough time..."

Samara delighted in the look he gave her. "Much too much," she agreed, "particularly since we've been married two whole days." Laughter trailed them, as Reese picked her up and strode quickly to his cabin.

Finally alone, Reese and Samara stood for several seconds, their eyes feasting on each other's faces, their hands clutching together almost desperately. Then Reese lowered hungry lips, his tongue eagerly seeking the softness of her mouth. And she just as hungrily welcomed him and the wondrous sensations that started to build inside her. She felt her body tremble with anticipation, with physical and emotional need for him. Her lips played gently with his, telling him in many different ways that she loved him. Tenderly. Sweetly. Hungrily.

Reese's hands sought the fastenings on her dress and unhooked them, deftly sliding both it and her chemise off her shoulders. He looked at her as she stood before him, her eyes bright as silver and her face flushed with love. He had missed her. God, how he had missed her. He started to take off his shirt and was stopped by her hands.

"Let me," she whispered.

She led him over to the bunk and made him sit while she pulled the white shirt over his head, her hands tickling and playing with bronze skin and golden hair. She knelt at his feet and undid the lacings of his breeches. Her hand touched him with awe and she heard him groan. "Samara..."

His one hand pulled her up beside him on the bed as the other finished discarding the restrictive clothing.

She marveled once more at the raw beauty of his body, but she had little time to study it. His mouth was on her breast, his hands tracing intricate, fiery trails on her body until the whole of her was inflamed.

Samara drew Reese to her as her hands traced the strong muscular planes of his back and her lips nibbled his ear. She heard him gasp and felt his lean hips above her. Her body arched up toward him as she was swept into a rocketing world of spinning sensations. She grasped him greedily, drawing him deeper and deeper, rejoicing in each strong thrust that brought him closer and closer to the core of her being. And then everything erupted with one shattering explosion.

For minutes they lay together, their bodies trembling from the aftershock of their union. His lips brushed hers gently and he laid his cheek against hers.

"I love you, Reese," she whispered. "I've always loved you. Since, I think, the first moment you laughed at me."

She loved the rumbling in his chest that heralded his laughter. "Does that mean I should do it more often?"

"You already do it quite enough, thank you," she replied. "Besides," she added seriously, "I don't think I could love you any more."

"I wish I had known that earlier, my sweet," he said ruefully. "It would have saved us a great deal of trouble..."

"You weren't very forthcoming yourself," she retorted.

The rumble started again. "Perhaps... but I'll make up for it."

He drew her tightly to him, and she felt the embers in her flare into bright flames. Her body eagerly reached for his.

Samara spent the night in his arms, rejoicing in his nearness. Several times she woke and stared at him with wonder, her fingers touching him to assure herself that he was real.

As several days passed, Samara and Reese spent an inordinate amount of time in Reese's cabin, much to the amused satisfaction of Yancy and Michael Simmons. The captain, in his rare appearances on deck, was a different man, his voice often raised in song or a merry whistle. Everyone stopped to watch when the pair came on deck together. They were so in love. For some, it revived memories, for others, hope.

Only one cloud darkened Samara's horizon, and that was the information she carried in her head; the information she had obtained at British headquarters. She tried to dismiss it, knowing there was nothing she could do. The *Phoenix* was on her way to England, but all the same it was information that could mean life and death to hundreds of Americans, possibly even Conn who was in the general area of New Orleans.

She was sharply reminded of it when she transferred her few belongings from Michael Simmons's cabin to Reese's. Her blood-stained reticule was among them, reminding her of that fatal morning when she had clung to it with a desperate compulsion. Inside, she discovered one remaining bottle of sleeping medicine that had somehow escaped her notice that tumultuous day and she tucked it in a corner of a trunk, not quite ready to dispose of it.

Some of Reese's elation faded as the ship's pace slowed to a crawl. The winds, which had been slight since their departure from Washington, were now almost still, and he felt far too close to the American coast for comfort.

His worst fears were realized on the fourth day out when he heard the lookout cry "Sail ho," and the ship galvanized into activity. He hurried to the fo'c'sle and took the spyglass.

"What flag?" asked Yancy, who had come to stand beside him.

Reese's face tensed. "American," he replied curtly, "A schooner...privateer, I imagine."

"What are you going to do?" He knew Reese had sworn off American ships, and his still-fragile relationship with Samara would not be aided by an exchange of fire.

"Run like hell," he said. "If the damn wind will freshen." But it didn't, and during the day the American ship, with its additional sails, crept closer. For one of the few times in his life, Reese prayed earnestly. As the long day wore on, the American ship continued to shorten the distance. Samara joined him on deck, her face apprehensive.

"What are you going to do?"

"Whatever I must, Samara," he said as a muscle throbbed in his cheek, betraying a tension he tried to hide.

"You won't consider surrendering?" she said in a small voice, already knowing the answer.

His hand went to her face, touching it tenderly, almost as if afraid it would be the last time.

"You know I can't do that, Samara. I made a promise to get you to England."

"You made a promise to me, too."

"That I wouldn't attack, not that I wouldn't defend." He turned back to stare at the approaching ship.

When he looked once more through the eyeglass he saw the cannons being primed, apparently for a warning shot.

"Yancy, tell Michael to ready our cannon."

Yancy looked from Reese's set, determined face to Samara's anguished one. "Aye, sir," he said with unaccustomed deference.

"Go below, Samara," Reese said quietly.

"No."

His voice was tired. "I don't want to do it, but I'll have you tied if I must. Now go!"

"Reese..." It was a cry of pain. She was going to lose, whatever happened.

An identical pain was in his eyes when he turned to her. "I'm sorry, Samara. I have no choice."

Her hand started to reach towards him, then fell in defeat. "Be careful," she whispered.

"Aye, little cat," he answered with a crooked smile before turning his attention back to the approaching ship. As he heard the first cannon boom and saw the eruption of water just short of the bow, he called Yancy. "Take Samara down."

Without further protest, she went with Yancy. She didn't doubt for a moment that Reese would have her bound if she didn't obey.

She accompanied Yancy to his cabin and helped him prepare for the wounded, setting out bandages and surgical instruments. She felt the ship rock with its first return of fire, then heard the explosion as a cannonball hit the *Phoenix*. Her hands clasped together until they were white. She wanted to flee on deck, to assure herself that Reese was all right, but she knew she would only distract him. Gone was her concern over the American ship: she only wanted Reese to survive. She couldn't bear to think of a life without him.

"He'll be all right," Yancy said, correctly interpreting her thoughts. "He's indestructible. I think that's why his ship is so popular with seamen. If he can't be touched, then they can't."

"I love him so much, Yancy."

"I know," he said softly. "And he loves you." He shook his head, remembering. "I've never seen anyone so miserable after he left South Carolina. He's been a different man the past few days."

The reminder of those terrible days, of her distrust, magnified her torment. She had never given him trust or support or even understanding. She had been so wrapped up in her own personal conflicts that she had ignored his own. Samara felt very small, very unworthy.

"Reese," Yancy said with understanding, "isn't very good at explaining his actions. Part of the fault is his."

"I should have trusted him...believed..." The words stopped as she heard another explosion on deck, and then suddenly, blood-splattered and powder-blackened, were pouring men into Yancy's small sick bay, and neither had time for more words.

Busy with the injured, Samara didn't notice as the explosions sounded further away nor the gentle movement of the ship. Not until Reese appeared at the door, a lopsided smile on his face. Approval spread over his face as he watched her with the wounded. He shook his head as her eyes widened at his blood-covered shirt. "It's nothing," he said, "just a splinter. See to the others first."

"What happened . . . ?"

"Jules's cannon found their mainmast and toppled it. They're dead in the water. And the wind, God be praised, finally blessed us. We're well out of range."

"The *Phoenix*?" Yancy lifted his eyes from the wounded man he was tending as he asked the question.'

"Battered. The rigging and spars are damaged, but overall I would say we were very lucky." Reese's tone quieted. "We'll have to go back to the American coast for lumber. We won't make England or even Bermuda with what's left, not if there's a storm."

That night, Reese held Samara tightly in his arms. The possibility of loss had made them frantic with need to possess each other completely. When Reese entered her warm welcoming core, she sought to bring him deeper and deeper as if to keep him there forever, to make him so much a part of her that he could never leave. Their passion increased in ever-growing swells, magnified by lingering fear, until they became a tidal wave of sensations. She gloried in the feel of his warm seed rushing through her, hoping that it would take root deep inside. Samara now wanted his child—desperately. The fear had not left and she was so afraid she would lose him. After, they lay together, still shuddering from the intensity of their union, unwilling to move. They stayed, wrapped in each other's arms, during the night.

The *Phoenix* made its way sluggishly toward the coast. Despite the ever-present danger, Reese and Samara enjoyed a contentment and happiness greater than they had imagined possible. They clasped each moment, treasuring it, as if it were the last.

The ship anchored in a small cove off the coast and Reese took a work party ashore. Before he left Samara in Yancy's care, he cupped her chin in his hand and studied her face. "Would it do any good to ask that you stay aboard ship?"

The misery in her face answered him.

His fingers caressed her before he turned to Yancy. "Don't let her out of your sight. Lock her in the cabin if you must." He leaned down and his lips touched hers lightly. "Stubborn," he muttered, and grinned. Then he was off.

Samara watched as the boat reached the shore and the men disappeared along the beach. She turned to Yancy. "I know," she said, "you want to get back to the wounded. I'll go with you."

"Your soft words do more doctoring than my poor efforts," he said, trying to coax a smile from her, before continuing in a lower voice. "Don't try to get away, Samara. Reese will forgive a lot of things, but I don't know if he'll forgive you making him a traitor. He gave his oath he would get you to England."

Samara looked at him in surprise. "You know?"

"Some of it. You gave each other a merry chase."

"Not so merry," she replied somberly. "Not very merry at all."

"Don't ruin what you have between you," he warned.

"My brother is in danger," Samara answered. "My country is in danger. How can I forget them? How can I choose between them and Reese?" She couldn't hide the heartache.

"He is your husband. England is your country too, now."

"No...not England," she denied.

Yancy sighed. "As he said, you're not to be out of my sight."

The afternoon passed into evening and finally the work party returned, the boat making several trips loaded down with wood. Yancy, true to his word, had made sure Samara was with him each moment. When she'd begged a few moments of privacy, he'd waited patiently outside Reese's cabin.

Reese was exhausted, but he managed to supervise repairs throughout the night. When he was finally satisfied, he told Samara there would be one more trip to shore in the morning and then they would leave.

He took her down to the cabin and allowed her to undress him and bathe the sweat from his body. He groaned with pleasure at her pampering as he gratefully took a glass of brandy. When he felt clean again, he drew her down to the bed and held her close, too exhausted to answer the invitation in her eyes. He closed his eyes, then opened them again, fixing them on Samara. "I sleep very lightly, my pretty little cat, and you will sleep on the inside tonight."

He did not miss the shiny brightness in her eyes, but in his growing drowsiness he attributed it to the sparks that always flew between him. He would ignite them, he thought dreamily, later.

Samara waited until she was sure he was thoroughly asleep. She knew that once Joshua took several drops of the sleeping draught nothing would wake him. She only hoped that the same would be true of Reese and his officers. She had doctored the crew's coffee earlier, and had given Reese a small amount in the brandy. Between the draught and wine and exhaustion, he should sleep for hours. She sat up, watching him. A lock of golden hair had fallen over his forehead and a small smile curved his mouth as if he were dreaming of something quite wonderful. He looked so vulnerable, so handsome. And she loved him so much. How could she leave? She remembered Yancy's warning. "He will forgive much, but . . ."

She could not live with herself, if she did not at least try to get her information to the authorities. What if Conn died? Or if Britain won a decisive victory, enough to seize American lands? Her hand stroked her husband's cheek and buried itself in his hair, wanting him to wake and stop her from doing what she knew she must. "I love you," she whispered. "Please never doubt that I love you." The words caught in her throat. She gently climbed over him and covered herself in one of his shirts. She had already written the note in her head, now with the light of a small candle, she put it to parchment.

Samara took a few gold pieces, knowing she would need them, and slipped out the door. After the ship had been damaged, she had ransacked the ship's locker and found some sailor togs that fit. She had been afraid to put them in Reese's cabin for fear he might find them. Now she gathered them from their hiding place and quickly drew on the trousers, lacing them tightly.

There would be two lookouts, she imagined, both looking seaward. She crept up on deck and made her way to a railing that was protected from sight. Quietly lowering one of the many ropes, she slid over the side and swam for shore.

Chapter Twenty

Not for the first time during the long, wet, miserable journey through southern England, Reese Hampton wondered exactly why he was subjecting himself to it.

Like so many other times during the past two years, he had been seized by a compulsion he didn't understand.

He needn't go to the grim fortress that housed American prisoners of war. Yancy had already been there several times on his behalf, and had reported that Julien Devereaux, if not very comfortable, should at least survive the war.

After hearing tales of the deplorable conditions at Dartmoor, Reese had sent Yancy to check on the man. Devereaux's imprisonment was partially due to the fact he had tried to protect Samara, and Reese hadn't saved the man from a hangman's noose to see him die in squalor in an English prison.

At least, that was what he told himself as he shivered in the cold February drizzle. Even his heavy cloak could not protect him from the pervading chill, and he wondered how the American prisoners were faring. Yancy had reported they had few blankets, little heat and less food. The doctor had done what he could, supplying Devereaux with heavy clothes and blankets and bribing the guards to supply more food, but it was always questionable whether their promises were carried out. Only Yancy's use of the formidable Hampton name might have produced compliance.

Reese shifted his position against the leather seat of the coach. He would have preferred riding, but he knew, from Yancy's description, that Devereaux would probably be too weak to travel on horseback. In the opposite seat lay a package of clean, warm clothing, a basket of food and a leather case containing the American's release papers.

The war had tentatively been over for more than a month, but the peace treaty, signed Christmas Eve, had not yet been ratified. Prisoner exchanges were also delayed, and Reese had to use every ounce of the Hampton influence to win Devereaux's early freedom, especially after the news of the British disaster at New Orleans reached London. Ironically, the battle had taken place on the eighth of January, two weeks after the signing of the peace treaty. England was stunned by the magnitude of the defeat: three British regiments decimated, with more than two thousand dead—including the commanding general. There were very few American losses.

Reese had heard the news and wondered just how much his own blindness had contributed to the debacle. He doubted that American authorities would have acted on the word of one young woman, but it would have given strength to other intelligence. In any event, Andrew Jackson had been waiting for the British....

The memory brought back, with all its pain, the September morning when he had awoken, groggy and alone, in the cabin. As comprehension dawned, he had the ship searched and then sent a boat to look for tracks along the beach. They had apparently been washed away by the tide, which meant Samara had been gone for hours. He knew immediately it would do no good to search. She had the advantage of nearly a night's head start.

Reese had almost gone after her, anyway. Until Yancy and Simmons finally convinced him that he would only endanger his ship and crew, and that he could not do. They had been too loyal to die or risk imprisonment once more for his own folly.

He did not read the note Samara left him. He did not think he could endure it. It wouldn't make any difference—in any event. She knew he had given his word, his oath, that he would see her to England. She was his wife, yet she had sacrificed his honor for her own. She had made her choice.

No words could repair the damage this time. He placed the letter over the flickering flame of a candle and watched it burn, unaware as the heat scorched his fingers. His heart turned to ashes with the parchment....

Reese looked out the window as the grim stone fortress of Dartmoor Prison took shape. Even at a distance, it seemed desolate and menacing.

It was worse inside. He nearly gagged at the odor as he looked with pity on the ragged scarecrows confined within. The guards were little more than ruffians who carried clubs and used them freely. After seeing the captain in charge, he was led reluctantly down a stone corridor to a cluster of iron doors, each with a small grated window.

"These are special pris'ners...troublemakers, spies and such scum," the burly guard said, as he stopped at one door. He gave his lantern to Reese while he took out his keys. "I don't know why a gent such as yerself concerns hisself."

"You don't have to," Reese answered, in his most intimidating voice. His contempt was obvious. "Open the door."

The door creaked open, and Reese stepped into the dark space, lifting the lantern to throw its full light on the man who was rising before him. The cell contained nothing but filthy straw and a noxious bucket. The man, dressed in rags, placed his hand over his eyes to shield them from the sudden brightness.

As the guard approached him, he shied away as if to avoid a blow, and Reese stepped between them. "Get out!"

The guard hesitated, taking a look at Reese's face, and touched his forelock in resentful obedience. "I'll be outside."

Reese's mouth hardened into a deep frown as he regarded the American. His skin above the beard was very pale, making his blue eyes appear unusually large and bright. His hair was a dull brown with dirt. His clothes were little more than rags, yet his bearing was proud.

"I thought Yancy brought some clothes?"

Julien stared. His visitor was impeccably dressed and one of the most imposing figures he had ever encountered. "You must be Reese Hampton," he said finally.

Reese nodded. He had not seen Julien in Washington, had not wanted to.

"I think I have you to thank for being alive...you and Dr. Yancy. He told me you sent him."

"Yancy always talks too much. He was to provide you with some clothes."

"Others needed them more."

"And the food?"

Julien gave him a wry look. "Don't think it wasn't appreciated. I'm afraid your countrymen do not share your generous nature. It was...spread around."

Reese stood for a moment, finding it difficult to speak. "I've obtained your release," he said abruptly. He shifted the package he had been carrying. "Some clothes. You might like to change."

"I don't understand," Julien said with a slight tremor in his voice.

"The war is over. It's only a matter of a few formalities. I've managed to expedite your release. There's a carriage waiting outside. I'll take you to London, and see to your passage home."

"Why?" came the blunt question.

"Ah, American directness," Reese said without amusement. "Perhaps I feel a little responsible for you being here." His half-smile faded. "Or perhaps it's the fact that we are bound by a young lady who led us both into disaster," he shrugged.

"What about the rest of the Americans?" Julien asked.

"They should be released in a matter of weeks. You were all I could manage."

Julien looked at him curiously. "And I imagine that took some persuasion. I've been made to understand I'm considered somewhat special." He flinched as he said the last words.

"It's over now," Reese said in an oddly gentle tone. "I'll wait outside while you change clothes."

"I'm so damned filthy."

"We'll stop at an inn, and you can bathe for hours if you wish."

He started out, but Julien stopped him. "I still don't quite understand all your trouble..."

"I don't, either," Reese answered with a slight smile. "Let's both just accept it as some sort of aberration. I would suggest you hurry before someone changes his mind."

Julien grinned for the first time. "A matter of seconds, Captain."

It wasn't much longer than that before they were hurrying out the stone walls, Reese's strong arm lending support to the weakened man. When they reached the carriage and Reese opened the door, Julien peered in at the rich exterior and drew back, his face red with embarrassment.

"I'll ride on top...I don't want..."

Reese understood immediately. Despite the clean clothes, the American must be infested with vermin as well as the prison odor that clung stubbornly to him.

"I didn't get you out to have you die of pneumonia," he said shortly. "The carriage can be cleaned easily enough."

As the American continued to hesitate, Reese's mouth curved into an easy smile. "Besides there's wine and food inside, and I would be most unhappy to see it go to waste.

Though his face still conveyed humiliation at his condition, Julien needed no more urging.

Once both men were inside, the carriage moved off quickly. Reese leaned over and opened the basket sitting beside his guest. He took a bottle of wine, motioning Julien to help himself to the contents of the basket.

Julien looked at it in amazement. It had been six months since he had seen so much food. The very sight and smell made him dizzy. He looked at Hampton, wondering if it were all a dream, or a nightmare from which he would wake just as the food reached his mouth.

"It's real," Reese said with a slight smile. "No one will take it away."

Julien forced himself to eat slowly, carefully, savoring every bite. As he sipped the wine offered by Hampton he turned his attention back to his benefactor.

"Yancy told me a little about what happened," he said. "That you married Samara . . ."

Reese's smile turned bitter. "An event which will hopefully be remedied by divorce," he said softly. "You can tell her when you return."

Julien's face questioned. "She loves you, you know. I realized that in Washington. I knew there was someone she couldn't forget . . . or let go."

Reese's face hardened, his eyes growing as cold as a distant arctic sea. "I would debate that point . . . if I cared enough," he said shortly, "which I no longer do."

"Then why are you here?" Julien said quietly. "I don't think it's entirely me."

"A debt," Reese said frigidly. "Nothing more."

"All right," Julien said. "I'm too grateful to argue. But I remember reading one of your poets, something like 'I could not love thee half so much, loved I not honor more.' I think that might pertain to women, too. At least to Samara."

Reese looked at him with sudden interest. "Lovelace," he said. "Richard Lovelace. He also wrote 'Stone walls do not a prison make, nor iron bars a cage.' I wonder if you would agree with *that?*"

Julien laughed for the first time. "I must beware of fencing with you. I'm afraid I come off poorly." With that observation, he relaxed with the soothing effect of the wine, settling against the comfortable leather cushions of the carriage.

They stopped several hours later at an inn and Reese engaged two rooms, ordering a bath and pails of steaming water for one. He also asked one of the maids to take Julien's clothes and boil them, leaving a set of his own for the American's temporary use.

Reese went to the taproom and ordered a brandy and set himself down in a corner, his demeanor warning off intrusion. He sipped his brandy slowly as he pondered Devereaux's words. Honor. What a curious word. Particularly when it meant so many different things to so many different people. He had never thought much about it. He had, quite simply, been compelled to do certain things: some to his liking, some not. And if it were the former, then why could he not accept Samara's actions? Because his pride had suffered? Because he had not realized how strong her loyalties? Because he could not bear the thought of how much that mistake had cost him? If the situation had been reversed, would he not have done much the same as Samara?

She, after all, had not given her oath not to escape . . . as he had to the O'Neills months earlier. And he knew her knowledge was far more crucial than anything he had gathered. Escape! God, how that word hurt. Escape from him!

Reese took another careful swallow, welcoming the burning liquid which he hoped would dull his pain. He had done nothing about a divorce. He seemed unable to make a decision, a condition totally foreign to his nature. In desperation, he had spent several months in London, halfheartedly pursuing some of his former vices, but the zest was gone. So he'd returned to Beddingfield, full of discontent.

He had even thought about courting Eloise once his marriage was dissolved, but there was no spark between them, only friendship. He would not destroy her life in some fruitless attempt to rid himself of personal demons.

When the war had ended, he had found himself consumed with curiosity over the young man who sought to protect Samara and nearly lost his life in doing so. Perhaps by finishing the whole sorry business, he could obtain some peace of mind. He no longer believed, as Samara had declared in Longley's presence, that she loved the American, but he couldn't shake the strange bond he felt with the man.

And he had found, during the carriage ride, that he liked Devereaux. Despite his youthfulness, there was a maturity and dignity about him. He had been quietly grateful without being obsequious. It had been difficult to tell much about his appearance with his long, ragged hair and beard, but the blue eyes were bright—even after months of deprivation.

At a sudden noise, he looked up and found the object of his thoughts standing at the table. The beard was gone, leaving a pale but pleasant face. Devereaux looked smaller than before, his thin body nearly dwarfed by Reese's clothes. A slightly abashed expression acknowledged the misfit.

"I never thought to be clean again, nor to have a full belly," Devereaux said with a faint smile.

Reese nodded for him to sit and called a barmaid, ordering wine and food for his companion.

As in the carriage, Julien Devereaux was careful to eat and drink slowly as his eyes studied Hampton. When he had completed his meal, he asked quietly, "What now?"

"We'll go to London while I secure passage for you. I assume you would prefer a non-British ship."

"You're very perceptive," Julien said, again with a wry smile.

"You have a family waiting?" Reese asked.

"A mother and father," Julien said, his face finally relaxing. "And a young sister. I will be very glad to get home. And I will repay you." Julien's eyes found the wine goblet, and his hand moved it around absently. "Come with me," he said suddenly. "Talk to Samara."

Reese smiled inquisitively. "An American peacemaker?"

Julien's grin was infectious. "I hope so."

Reese was unexpectedly moved by the generosity inherent in the man. He knew from the expression in Devereaux's eyes when Samara's name was mentioned that the American had been in love with her. Despite his efforts in the past few months, Julien Devereaux had no reason to like him nor any Britisher after the hell he had obviously suffered. Over the past two years, Reese had learned a healthy respect for Americans—for their independence and tolerance and seemingly unquenchable spirit. But it was too soon, the hurt still too deep.

He shook his head. "Not now," he said. "I have business matters to attend to."

Julien merely nodded, not willing to intrude further.

Three days later, Reese took him by carriage to a Danish ship and saw him comfortably aboard.

Feeling somehow cleansed, he left London in the afternoon for Beddingfield, resting at night in an inn and reaching the Hampton estate at midday. He immediately went in search of Avery.

"I'm going to America," he announced when he found his brother overseeing the preparation of the fields.

Avery's eyes twinkled. "I wondered how long it would take that stubborn pride to bend to good judgment. Then what?"

"I would like to buy some land in Virginia . . . It might take some time. I'll sell the *Phoenix*. That will give me a start."

Avery's mouth twitched. He knew how much the ship meant to Reese. If he would sacrifice the last vestige of his vaunted freedom, he was indeed serious about settling down. "Perhaps," he said slowly, "that won't be necessary."

Reese darted a confused look at him, but Avery only laughed. "I'll race you to the stables," he said, and any questions were lost in their frantic maneuvering for position.

A triumphant Reese claimed victory...and a drink. After the glasses were poured, Avery went to his desk, hesitated a moment, then pulled out several packets. Uncommonly somber, he studied his brother's face. It was more relaxed than he had seen it in months. Knowing the next few moments might well test their close relationship, he chose his words carefully.

"Your Samara wrote me several months ago. She sent you a letter in my care and she asked me to wait before giving it to you. She said I would know when the time was right." He handed the letter to Reese, who could only stare at his brother. Both anger and bafflement showed brightly in his eyes. "You shouldn't have held it," he said, raw fury starting to cloud his eyes.

"There's something else," Avery continued, pretending not to notice. "The money you've been sending for Beddingfield. I found I didn't need it. I've been investing it for you . . . in something other than gambling. You have a small fortune, enough to buy as much land as you wish . . . and still keep your ship." His steady eyes didn't flinch as he saw Reese's rage mount and his hands clench as if itching to hit him. Avery prepared himself for the blow. He had, he knew, unforgivably interfered in his brother's life.

The blow didn't come, but neither was there a change in Reese's angry look. Reese held up the letter from Samara. "And do you also know what is in here? Since you apparently know more about my life than I do?"

"No," Avery said softly, "though I can guess. She's a very unhappy young lady... and very much in love with you."

Reese glared at his twin. "May I now have the unique courtesy of a little privacy." Avery merely nodded and left the room.

Reese's hands held the white parchment for a moment. His eyes found Samara's small, neat handwriting, and his fingers shook as he broke the seal and opened it. He could barely restrain a smile at the greeting.

Beloved Englishman:

I asked your brother to give this to you when, perhaps, your anger had faded and, very hopefully, you had come to miss your wife.

For I consider myself such... and always will. Although if you wish it, I will agree to a dissolution. I would agree to anything to compensate for all you have suffered through me. But for once, there must be no misunderstandings.

I love you. I have always loved you and always will. You are my heart, and I feel empty with its loss. You have given me so much, so many times, and in return I have given you only pain. That knowledge haunts me day and night.

Please understand why I left the ship that night. It was the hardest thing I have ever done. But I would not have been able to live with the knowledge that I could have saved my brother... and helped my country... had I chosen to do nothing. I did not betray you, my love; I chose not to betray myself.

I will abide by your decision. But with all my heart and soul I hope and pray you will find it within you to understand. I cannot ask you to forgive. Given the same circumstances, I would make the same choice. I do not apologize for that, but grieve for the pain I know it caused—no less, I believe, to me than to you.

I will love you all my life.

Samara

"Avery," Reese roared as his fingers tightened around the letter. He grinned as he saw his brother's apprehensive face.

"Don't look so glum . . . I'll forgive and forget this time . . . but if ever, ever, you feel like interfering again..." He let the threat dangle as his eyes filled with laughter. "If ever...then feel quite free." A similar grin tugged at his brother's mouth, and they both fell on each other, their laughter exploding over the house.

Three days later, Reese and Avery rode together to London and visited Avery's banking house, leaving with a large draft. Avery returned to Beddingfield while Reese went to work, gathering his crew and supplying his ship. On the first of April, 1815, the *Phoenix* set sail for America.

In and out. In and out. Samara's fingers fairly flew over her newest sampler. She was sitting in the library, the early March sun casting a golden haze through the wide windows and catching the red fire in her hair.

She was intent on her work, a design she herself had fashioned. It was a guardian angel, who strangely resembled a golden-haired Englishman who was more devilish than heavenly. Nonetheless, she had been unable to tame her fingers to make it look otherwise.

One hand left the sampler and touched her swelling abdomen as she felt the child inside her move. *Oh Reese, I wish you were here. I wish you could feel him.* Her yearning for him never ceased. It tormented her at night, and kept her gazing hopefully out the window by day. The loneliness, even here with her family, was unrelenting. Her only solace was the babe. And even that carried its own torture.

She had not told Reese. She had known when she wrote his brother and included a letter. After all that had happened, she would nor force him into a marriage and fatherhood he may not want. And so she prayed daily that he would read her letter and understand, that he would come for her, out of love. She could not bear it if he came out of duty.

She took the last stitch and looked at the sampler critically, wondering how Reese would respond to the likeness of himself bearing wings. A giggle escaped her. He would probably be appalled.

"You're smiling." Brendan's voice broke the spell, and Samara looked up into his blue eyes.

She turned the sampler to show him. "I was thinking of Reese's reaction to being an angel."

"The pirate, the blackguard, the *Englishman*," he teased lightly although his eyes clouded. He had not forgiven himself for his interference or his treatment of Reese Hampton. He had been more than ashamed when he had learned the truth and offered to take Samara to England, but Samara had refused. She forbade him to write Reese about the child or say anything about her. It had to be Reese's decision alone.

"I'm going to England," he said abruptly. "To see your husband."

Samara sat up straight, feeling the baby object to the sudden movement. "You promised."

"I'll say nothing about the babe," he said. "If that's what you truly wish. But I think you're wrong. He has a right to know. By God, it's *his child*."

Tears filled Samara's eyes. "I won't use the child to bring him back."

"Then go with me, Samara. Talk to him. Don't make the same mistake you made before...that *we* made before." His voice broke. "We didn't trust him then...and we were wrong."

"What if he can't forgive me this time...?"

"You still owe it to him, more than ever, to tell him. You can't keep running away."

"I'm not running," she said softly, a tear rolling down her face. "I just don't want to do him any more injury. If he wants to marry someone else...someone he can trust..."

He took her face in one hand and wiped away the tears with the other. "Samara, you have to at least give him a chance."

"But he hasn't written, hasn't tried to contact me...he probably never wants to hear my name again. The kindest thing," she said, "is to let him forget me."

"You are married," Bren reminded her gently. "An annulment will not be easy...not with evidence that the marriage was consummated. Not even if you state the marriage was forced." He looked at her enlarged figure. "And it must be soon. Next week at the latest."

"I'll think about it," she promised.

"Do," Bren said. "Or you will always regret it."

Samara weighed Bren's words carefully over the next few days. He was right, and a letter would not suffice. Reese deserved to know about his son...and legal heir. And face to face, she would know whether he wanted her. Reese. The mere thought of seeing him filled her with joy.

* * *

Both Connor and Samantha supported their daughter's decision, Connor most vehemently. Samantha worried about childbirth, but was mollified when Brendan promised to take a doctor along on the voyage. Connor thought Reese should know prior to the child's birth. A birth, he declared, was a marvelous event and should be shared by both parents. Samantha thought about accompanying her daughter but was gently dissuaded. It was time Samara fought her own battles, and Connor shuddered at the thought of a gaggle of O'Neills descending upon unsuspecting Hampton.

Brendan easily found a competent doctor as well as several additional passengers. All had relatives in England and were eager to see how they had fared during the war. Communication had been rare. The *Samara*, proudly flying the American flag, sailed out of Charleston Harbor the last day of March.

Chapter Twenty-One

The voyage was quiet and enjoyable for Samara. It was comforting to look out over the ocean and see the sails in the distance without fearing them. For the first time in many years, the world was principally at peace.

Despite her growing bulkiness, she would stand at the railing for long periods, watching the sky and sea blend together. In those moments, she could almost feel Reese's presence beside her, hear his elated laughter in the sound of wind filling the sails and feel his gentleness in the touch of the sun against her face.

Now she had made her decision, she felt well content with it. She rejoiced with every movement of the baby, and realized she could finally offer Reese a gift of great value. Every rush of wind brought him closer. Each day, it blew strong, sending the *Samara* skimming over the waters. In the eventide, when the sun erupted into a rainbow of colors, she would turn toward the wheel and in the magic of the twilight she could see him there, bare feet set apart, head thrown back in challenge, eyes sparkling with mischief.

When the driver of the coach announced they were approaching Beddingfield, Samara leaned out the window, her eyes missing little. It was a beautifully maintained estate, and that surprised her. Reese had mentioned financial difficulties, and she had anticipated a more unkempt entrance. But everything was perfect, every hedge trimmed, every garden sculptured. And the house! If it could be called a house. It seemed more a castle to her amazed eyes. She stared in awe at its imposing beauty.

As Brendan descended, he told the coachman to hold the conveyance in readiness. Neither could anticipate their reception, after all that had transpired. He gave Samara a hand, squeezing hers tightly as he felt its chill and saw her tremble with anxiety. He carefully helped her down just as the huge manor door opened and a very dignified individual approached them. The man's face appeared expressionless, though there was a slight sparkle in his eyes.

Seeing Brendan's well-tailored clothes and Samara's quite obvious condition, his eyes held a question.

"Is Mr. Reese Hampton in residence?" Brendan asked awkwardly, not quite sure of the titles or protocol.

"No, sir," the man said, watching Samara's face fall and wondering who she was.

"Then his brother, the Earl of Beddingfield?"

"I believe he's at dinner," the man said quite formally. "May I give him your card?"

Brendan, sensing Samara's distress, became impatient. "This is Mrs. Hampton, Mrs. Reese Hampton, and I'm her brother."

The stern face was suddenly wreathed in smiles. He bowed slightly. "Mrs. Hampton . . . Mr. . . . ?"

"O'Neill."

"Mr. O'Neill, please come with me."

Samara and Brendan followed the servant through a great hall lined with paintings, and then through a large, richly decorated room hung with tapestries.

"Wait here, please," the servant asked.

Samara clung to Brendan's hand, all her optimism fleeing in the opulence that surrounded her. Never had she felt more out of place.

The feeling persisted until the door opened. For a moment she thought the servant must have been mistaken. It seemed as if Reese were standing there, a delighted and welcoming smile on his face. Then she noticed the differences. The hair was not as golden nor the eyes quite so brilliant. But the face was the same, and it was regarding her with no little interest.

"Samara," he said, as he smiled warmly at her. He strode over and took her two hands, looking at her, particularly at her enlarged middle. He grinned happily. "You didn't mention anything about a new member of the Hampton family."

"I didn't know if . . . Reese would be pleased."

"He will be delighted and awed, as am I, Samara. Welcome to Beddingfield." He turned to Bren. "And you are . . . ?"

"Brendan O'Neill."

"I've heard your name," Avery said, a quick flash of mischief in his voice. "I'm Avery Hampton, Reese's brother." His eyes went back to Samara. "Come, sit down."

"Reese...? Where is he?"

Avery fought between pity and amusement. "I'm very much afraid, my pretty sister-in-law, you probably passed each other on the ocean. He left some four weeks ago to find you."

Samara was stunned. "He...he was coming for me?"

Avery's eyes met Brendan's in ironic amusement. "He took your young friend...Devereaux was it...to London. When he came back he had decided to return for you and when I gave him your letter there was no delaying his plans."

"Julien? What did he have to do with Julien?" Samara was becoming more and more confused, her emotions running riot. Joy at the knowledge that Reese wanted her, grief at missing him and confusion at this new information about Julien.

"He apparently felt responsible for him...tried to do what he could. He obtained his release and found passage for him."

"He did?"

"Does that surprise you?" Avery asked gently.

"No..." Her smile was suddenly brilliant and Avery understood why his brother was so bewitched. She was lovely, and her smile would brighten the heavens.

Samara turned to Brendan. "We have to leave. Now. This afternoon and return to Charleston."

Avery shook his head as he took her hand. "I don't think that would be very wise." He looked at her large figure. "I doubt if you want to have your child shipboard. Besides, if I know my impatient brother, he'll also turn back immediately. You might well pass each other again." He couldn't restrain another smile. "I don't know if I could withstand his temper if that occurred. It was bad enough when he knew I had withheld your letter according to your instructions."

Samara impulsively leaned over and kissed his cheek. "Thank you," she said.

"You were right," Avery added. "He wasn't ready to read it...not until he saw Devereaux and worked some things out in his own mind. He *can* be rather obstinate...but then I suppose you have discovered that."

"I'm afraid," Samara said ruefully, "it's a quality we share. It has caused us no end of misery."

"Perhaps now you are both ready for it to end," Avery said gently. He turned at the sound of a door opening behind him and reached out his hand as a very pretty woman approached. "This is Leigh, my wife. Leigh, this is Samara Hampton, the young lady who's been driving Reese to distraction."

"And about time, too," the woman said softly, a warm welcome in her smile. "How pretty you are, but I didn't know…"

"Neither does Reese, apparently," Avery said wryly. "He has several surprises in store for him. In the meantime, Samara will stay with us." He turned to Brendan. "And you, Captain O'Neill, will you also be our guest?"

"I don't know if your brother would approve. Our last meeting was not friendly."

"Of course, he would," Avery said. "Your presence here already says much. We are grateful that you brought Samara to us safely."

"Then I accept. I have amends to make."

Avery's mouth twitched. "I look forward to hearing more about the O'Neill family. Reese was rather tight-lipped."

Brendan's rigid posture relaxed and a fine smile broke the harshness of his expression. "I can well understand why. Between the lot of us, I think we inflicted every sort of mayhem on him."

"*That* I would be eager to hear," Avery said. "He has thought himself immune too long. But first, I think your sister needs some rest. Leigh will show her to her room, and both of you… please consider this your home." When Leigh and Samara disappeared, Avery turned back to Bren. "I think we could both use a brandy."

As the *Phoenix* approached the mouth of the Thames, Reese felt as though he had ploughed a permanent trail into the Atlantic during the past three years. He had been at sea two months on this expedition, and his frustration was about to boil over.

There was a small sense of satisfaction in knowing that Samara had sought him out. But that was almost buried in his overall sense of vexation. Had any two people ever been so starcrossed? Their unique courtship had encountered one disaster after another. Now he was little more than a day away from her, and he couldn't help but wonder what new hindrance might appear. Avery most certainly would have welcomed them and insisted that Samara remain. That they might have passed each other again was more than he could endure.

He felt Yancy's presence beside him and took comfort in his quiet support.

"Will you be coming to Beddingfield with me?"

"I think it's time you and Samara had some time alone...at least as much as you can get in that palace you call a home."

"If she's even there," Reese sighed. "I'm beginning to think it is not meant to be."

"But, of course, it is," Yancy said. He grinned. "If you two have survived everything so far, it must be love."

"Brendan could still be there."

"Probably," Yancy agreed noncommittally. "How do you feel about him?"

"I don't know. He was protecting Samara. I can't really quarrel with that." But there was doubt in his voice. He still felt stung from that final meeting. It was, he knew, his damnable wounded pride.

"Well, it shouldn't be long now."

As the *Phoenix* turned into the vast London docks, his eyes swept the several hundred ships anchored there. It would be pure luck to find Brendan's ship among so many, but he searched nonetheless, seeking reassurance. He didn't find it, nor did the men he questioned on the dock know of such a vessel. There were simply too many of them. Feeling more and more uncertain, he nonetheless turned the ship over to Simmons, located a horse and spurred the sleek chestnut on to Beddingfield.

Oblivious to the young maidservant in the room, Samara sat on the window seat, gazing out over the long driveway into Beddingfield. Her breasts still tingled from feeding her son, who now gurgled happily in the nearby cradle. Her frown eased as she glanced at him; he was incredibly beautiful, she thought, with his dark hair and very blue eyes. Her hand reached out to touch him with a sort of wonder. He was so small, so perfect. And, finest of all, he was half Reese Hampton.

She looked back down at the road as she had nearly every day for two weeks...except for the day she had given birth to Reese's son and the day after, when the Hamptons had demanded she rest. It had been an easy confinement, and she resumed her vigil on the third day, despite protestations. No one could coax her from her post for long.

The gardens were just beginning to bloom and the first flowers danced in the breeze, the hundreds of bright shades glimmering in the sun. Samara watched as her niece and nephew played below her under their mother's close scrutiny, and her heart swelled with love. They had all been so kind to her. In the past month, Avery and Leigh and their two children had become almost as close as her own family.

Her eyes lifted from the children and once more met the road. There was a dot that hadn't been there before. She watched intently as it grew larger and she made out a horseman. Even without seeing the face, she knew. No one else sat so proudly, so arrogantly. And then she saw the sun glint against golden hair as the beloved face searched the windows. She waited no longer. She was running, running at last to meet her love.

Three weeks later...

The christening took place in the small chapel at Beddingfield.

Samara and Reese stood, hands clasped tightly together, as the clergyman baptized Tristan Adrian Hampton. Leigh and Brendan stood proudly as godparents, as Avery regarded the proceedings with a gleam of approval. It was by his suggestion that Brendan served as godfather. It was only fitting, Avery said, that the child have a godparent from either side of the family.

Brendan took his role very seriously. He held the infant carefully, looking on him with unabashed affection. When the ceremony was over, he flashed his quick, open grin at Samara and Reese, grateful for the honor.

It was, Samara thought as she squeezed Reese's hand possessively, the third happiest moment in her life. She couldn't rank the other two. One was the birth of Tristan. The other was that glorious moment three weeks ago when she had run, skirts and hair flying behind her, to Reese.

When he had seen her, he cantered his horse to her side, reached down and swung her up in his arms, holding her as though she were the rarest treasure in the world. Then he pressed her close, and she could feel the beat of his heart as his mouth reached down so eagerly for hers.

Her arms had wrapped around him and they had held each other with frantic need, each seeking to bind the other so tight they could never again be separated.

The horse shied under such unaccustomed movement, and Reese laughed—his lovely, lusty laugh which seemed to reach the skies. "I love you, Mrs. Hampton."

"And I adore you, Mr. Hampton."

He regained control of the horse and leaned back, his eyes feasting on each delectable feature. His lips then gifted her with the sweetest, most wondrous kiss; it was as if he were openly presenting his heart to her. And her hands, in turn, touched his face with such tenderness, such love that he knew, at last, her own heart was unquestionably his.

"I have a gift for you," she had whispered shyly.

"You are gift enough," he had answered. But his eyes sparkled with inquisitive interest at the quiet intensity of her statement.

But she was not to be coaxed into an answer. "You must come with me."

"Must I? I think I would rather hold you."

"Ah, but would the horse?" she questioned with mischief, as she looked with delight at his wicked expression.

"You have," he teased a trifle ungallantly, "gained a few pounds—very prettily so. You look radiant." He studied her face once more. There was, he thought, something different about her. Whatever it was, her face glowed with a beauty greater than he remembered.

She giggled. If only he had seen her three weeks ago! She wriggled in his arms, and he carefully set her down before joining her and tying the horse to a post. She took his hand and pulled him toward the house, ignoring the dignified Holmes who had opened the door. Giving Reese no time to return the servant's greeting, she pulled him, laughing, up the steps, hurrying him along, her face alight with anticipation.

Samara opened the door to her room and before permitting Reese inside dismissed the servant who had been watching the child. She reached once more for Reese's hand, unable to stop herself from lifting it to her mouth and touching the hard, callused skin with her soft lips. His head was cocked to one side, watching her curiously.

He heard a small cry, then a larger bellow. He saw Samara's smile widen. "Your son sounds like you."

Stunned, Reese simply stared at her, then in three large strides reached the source of the sound. From the door, Samara watched his changing expressions—from disbelief to wonder to shimmering, glowing joy. He looked back at her, his face begging confirmation.

Samara reached his side. "May I present your son, the youngest Hampton. I was waiting on you to choose the rest of his name."

His mouth trembled and a suspicious wetness filled his eyes as his arm went around Samara and he gazed at the tiny little being who, at the moment, had quieted and was looking toward his father with a kind of solemn regard . . .

The christening over, the family retired to the study for champagne, a prelude to a number of farewells that would be said in the next few days. Brendan would leave first, then Reese and Samara planned to sail the following week. Eloise would accompany them. Much to Samara's satisfaction, Brendan had found himself quite attracted to Eloise and asked her to stay with the O'Neills for a visit. When he first mentioned the possibility, Reese devilishly arched an eyebrow in warning, sending Samara into a fit of giggles. At least, she thought thankfully, he was philosophical about his rather unorthodox encounters with her family.

She was also delighted that he and Brendan had renewed their friendship. They had greeted each other warily at first, then disappeared together into the library. They had so much in common, including their deep love of little Tristan. The naming of Brendan as godfather only sealed the bond between them.

It had been decided Eloise would travel with Reese and Samara, both for convention's sake and because Eloise felt she could help with the baby. It would also give Eloise and Samara feminine company. After an initial hesitation, the two women had grown quite fond of each other.

Each day and night were a joy for Samara and Reese, who made their plans wrapped in each other's arms. Their passion flamed and their spirits soared as they rejoiced in each other's nearness. Their trust in each other had finally become absolute.

The morning they were to leave, Reese tenderly watched his son nurse, sucking hungrily as his tiny hands flailed.

"American impatience," Reese said fondly.

"British greed," Samara retorted with a smile.

"Ah, the best of both worlds," Reese said with the wickedly self-satisfied smile of an English pirate.

Samara opened her mouth to protest, only to find it completely sealed by his teasing lips. Quite contentedly, she surrendered.

*   *   *   *   *

ATTRACTIVE, SPACE SAVING BOOK RACK

Display your most prized novels on this handsome and sturdy book rack. The hand-rubbed walnut finish will blend into your library decor with quiet elegance, providing a practical organizer for your favorite hard-or soft-covered books.

Only $9.95

Approximately 16" x 8" when assembled

Assembles in seconds!

To order, rush your name, address and zip code, along with a check or money order for $10.70* ($9.95 plus 75¢ postage and handling) payable to *Reader Service*:

Reader Service
Book Rack Offer
901 Fuhrmann Blvd.
P.O. Box 1396
Buffalo, NY 14269-1396

Offer not available in Canada.

BKR-G

*New York and Iowa residents add appropriate sales tax.